BEYOND THE NEXT STAR

ALSO BY MELODY JOHNSON

Love Beyond Series

Beyond the Next Star

Sight Beyond the Sun (coming soon)

Night Blood Series

The City Beneath

Sweet Last Drop

Eternal Reign

Day Reaper

Holiday Anthology

Grave Promises (coming soon)

BEYOND THE NEXT STAR

MELODY JOHNSON

INCENDI PRESS, LLC

First paperback edition June 2020

ISBN: 978-1-7351499-0-5 (paperback)

ISBN: 978-1-7351499-1-2 (hardback)

ISBN: 978-1-7351499-2-9 (ebook)

Printed in the United States of America

Published by Incendi Press, LLC

All Incendi Press, LLC titles are available at special quantity discounts for bulk purchases for sales promotion, premiums, fund-raising, educational, or institutional use.

Special book excerpts or customized printings can also be created to fit specific needs. For details, contact authormelodyjohnson@gmail.com.

Cover design by Robin Ludwig Design Inc.

www.gobookcoverdesign.com

ACKNOWLEDGMENTS

To the many people who helped shape the success of this book, including my beta readers, Abby Sharpe, Leah Miles, and Margaret Johnston; my editors, Nicole Klungle and Linda Ingmanson; my cover designer, Robin Ludwig; my sometimes personal assistant and full-time bestie, Meredith Bause; and my fellow First Coast Romance Writers. Thank you for the invaluable support and advice. My craft and knowledge of the industry has exponentially improved in your company.

To my husband, Derek, for guiding us into the wrong nature trail in negative two degrees and refusing to admit it for five miles. Without you, or that day-long, ten-mile trek through the Appalachian Trail, the lorienok might never have been born. You're my heart and inspiration; even when we wander into unknown territory, we're never actually lost because we have each other. We blaze our own trail.

PART ONE

Rorak (noun): the bitterly cold season on the planet Lorien, lasting approximately nine Earth months.

ONE

When the lorienok abducted Delaney—after she'd finally accepted that she wasn't dreaming, in a coma, having a mental breakdown, or in hell—she'd given them a fake name: Jane Smith. Not an exceptionally creative or unique pseudonym by any stretch of the imagination, but having come to grips with the fact that she'd been literally abducted by aliens, her imagination was stretched dangerously thin. Intergalactic kidnapping wasn't a chronic illness, but for a time—a longer time than she was comfortable admitting to now—wasting away had seemed a preferable fate.

She didn't accomplish much by hiding her identity. She didn't have any blood relatives to protect, a criminal record to hide, or a trust fund to safeguard. Delaney Rose McCormick had about as much value associated with her name as did the fictional Jane Smith and left nearly as small a void on Earth. But all Delaney had in those early days directly following her abduction was her name and the hope that everything—the abduction, the tests, the training—was just a big mistake. Which, as it turned out, it was. Her abduction had been the biggest technological mistake in lorienok history, but that didn't change her circumstances. Days turned to weeks turned to months turned to the abandonment of tracking time. Hope died. She had nothing to her name, but her name, at least, was her own, and she would keep it for herself.

By the time her domestication specialist, Keil Kore'Weidnar, discovered Delaney's capacity to learn and taught her Lori, his native language, the issue of her name had become moot. He'd already renamed her *Reshna*, a spiral-shaped handheld tool used to drill into ice. He'd shown her a hologram of it, pointing to the spiral and then to the wild frizz of her unconditioned curls. They had a similar-looking tool on Earth, but they used it to open wine bottles. He'd named her "corkscrew" for her crazy hair.

She'd been called worse names in high school.

She couldn't say she'd lived in worse places, though. Most of her foster families, with the exception of the Todd household, had been decent people who'd given her clothes, a bed under a roof, and regular meals. Besides clothes, those basic necessities were still being met, so a little gratitude was probably in order. But only just a little, because she also had a cage. And a collar. And if she'd just translated the words and growls of the pet store manager correctly, she had a new owner.

Like most *lor*, her owner had thick, curved ram horns jutting from his head, and like all lorienok regardless of gender, he was covered head to toe in brown fur. Sasquatch did exist after all; he just wasn't native to Earth. He was roughly the same size and shape as a human bodybuilder, and in addition to the horns, his nose and mouth protruded slightly into a blunt muzzle, two rows of sharp predator teeth filled his overly large mouth, and pointy bearlike claws tipped each finger and likely each toe on his boot-shod feet.

Unlike most, this male wore his hair long. His locks were tied back from his face in a messy bun with a forest-green elastic band. His beard was also long and came to a point at the end, hanging a few inches below his chin. But his eyes were his most striking feature, assuming that one had already become accustomed to the ram horns, claws, abundance of muscle, and close-cropped body fur. His left eye was the same doe brown common to all lorienok—a smidge rounder and larger than human eyes, like calf eyes with those thick lashes and soul-deep stare—but his other eye was ice blue. A thick scar bisected his right brow, eyelid, and upper cheek, slicing directly over that unique, penetrating gaze.

His bearing was regal and confident, the sharp cut of his jawline proud, but his eyes betrayed him. He was sad—horribly sad—and he glowered at Delaney through the wire door of her cage like he was the Greek king Sisyphus and she his boulder, resigning himself to an eternity of labor over an impossible, futile undertaking.

Or maybe Delaney was just projecting because she couldn't imagine anything more impossible and futile than her current existence. *I am not a pet!* she wanted to yell. But after witnessing Keil's cold-blooded murder, she knew to keep her mouth firmly shut. If anyone suspected her more intelligent than a golden retriever, her death would be next.

ACCOMPLISHING IMPOSSIBLE FEATS WHILE ENDURING debilitating injury and sensory deprivation were challenges both expected and anticipated by the young cadets training to enter the combat and strategic intelligence division of the Federation. Qualifying exams were brutal. Training was rigorous. But for the few who didn't fail, drop out, or obtain an infirmary discharge, the rewards were astronomical. Torek Lore'Onik Weidnar Kenzo Lesh'Aerai Renaar had certainly reaped those rewards many times over, as evidenced by the four property titles bestowed to his name. He'd never been one to flinch when facing a challenge, but this order—the court-mandated appointment of an animal companion to "facilitate mental recovery"—was the challenge that finally made him flinch.

Torek stared at the human—at the beautiful, riotous hair that sprang like coils from its head and would obviously need continual cleaning and grooming, at its tiny stature and lean form that probably couldn't lift its own weight, at the lovely gray eyes and smooth, bare skin that would need layers upon layers of protective coverings to keep it warm—and he seriously considered the merits of simply retiring from the Federation.

No one would blame him after what had happened. He could return to his home in Aerai and resume the quiet, peaceful, unappreciated toil of plant cultivation he'd abandoned so many seasons ago along with his dreams of filling that home with a family.

The store manager hefted a bound book from the counter and plopped it into Torek's unwilling arms.

"What's this?" A tingle of cold dread crept across the back of Torek's neck.

"Why, it's your owner's manual, of course."

"Of course." The Federation's policies and procedures manual was the thickest book Torek had ever had the displeasure of memorizing, and it wasn't even half the size of this tome.

"You'll be the envy of all Lorien. The first to purchase a human, our newest species. She's the pilot for her breed, of course, but her domestication is progressing fabulously. They dispatched a harvester while she was still in transit, so until the next shipment arrives, she's the only human we'll have for a while yet, six *kair* at the least. You must be thrilled."

As Torek flipped through a few of the manual's pages and skimmed the table of contents, the tingle of dread that had started at his neck devoured the rest of his body and intensified to nausea. An entire chapter was dedicated to heating and insulating the human's living quarters. If her rooms dipped below a specific temperature— Torek brought the book closer and squinted, but no, his eyes didn't deceive him—and the human didn't have tailored, fur-lined coverings to retain heat, she would sicken and die. If he didn't provide her with private sleeping quarters, she would become lethargic and depressed, then sicken and die. If he didn't feed her three meals a day, complete with a cooked protein, vegetables, and some grain, she would sicken and die. She was even allergic to *ukok*, a simple seasoning. If consumed, her throat would swell, cutting off her air supply, and she would immediately die.

He would kill her.

Not intentionally, of course, but despite the wild popularity of owning foreign domesticated animals, he'd never even owned a *zeprak* let alone something as exotic, delicate, and temperamental as this human. She wouldn't survive a week in his care.

His throat tightened. His breath shortened. His chest ached, and suddenly, black starbursts shadowed his vision.

Not now. Not in public. Not again.

A loud *bang* echoed through the store, startling Torek back to himself. He blinked a few times, breathing past the panic and reorienting his mind. The store manager was silent now and staring.

He'd dropped the owner's manual.

Torek gathered the reserves of his iron will. He was not afraid of domesticated animals. He did not shirk his responsibilities. And he did not flounder. He straightened away from the store manager, stepped over the dropped manual as if he'd intended to discard it so carelessly, and eased his fist through the open petting window of the human's cage, offering the back of his hand for her to sniff his acquaintance. He didn't particularly want to become acquainted— acquaintance with an animal companion could all too easily flip to a desire for one—but that's what a normal, well-adjusted lor not on the brink of hyperventilating would do.

So, he did it.

The human stared at his fist, blinking. She glanced up at his face and then back at his fist before leaning in and brushing her cheek affectionately against his knuckles. Her skin was newborn-baby soft.

His chest constricted with renewed panic.

Torek cleared his throat. "She's an adult female?"

The store manager nodded. "Her name is Reshna."

"Fitting." Torek pulled one of those hair coils and watched with amusement as it bounced back into place when he released it.

Her hair left a grease spot on his finger pads.

Torek narrowed his eyes. Her hair, which he'd already noted would require daily maintenance, needed washing.

"How long has she been in store for sale?" Torek stroked the side of her jaw with the back of his knuckle, peeking under her collar as she shied away from his touch. Her neck was chafed and red.

"She's been the joy of this establishment for most of *Rorak*. Eh, about two-thirds of the season."

Torek stared at the manager, taken aback. "She's been in this cage that entire time?"

The store manager's smile was placating. "I assure you, animal companions thrive here under my care."

The skin on her arms, which had been smooth a few minutes earlier, wrinkled in tiny, raised spots. A slight tremor shook her body.

"Is she all right?" Torek's heart lurched painfully. "I think her collar may be too tight."

"Hmmm." The store manager stooped to pick up the manual, licked his thumb pad, and paged through it, frowning.

"You've had her this long, and you haven't memorized her manual?"

The store manager's face darkened. "Reshna is the newest, most exotic animal companion we currently sell. The few who considered purchasing her weren't willing to invest in her care after reading the manual. Like most exotic breeds, she isn't for just anyone. It takes time to find companions like her a home, and in that time, I assure you that I've cared for her as I do all our animal companions. As required by her manual."

Torek might have apologized for giving offense—he didn't know the first thing about caring for exotic animals—except that the few words he'd glimpsed from her manual screamed at him: *adult humans require private sleeping quarters and washrooms complete with...*

excruciatingly long bullet list of requirements... *Without these neces-sary living conditions, the human will sicken and die.*

And here she was, going on nearly all of Rorak in a wire cage so small, she couldn't rest without curling in on herself. If she remained here, she would sicken and die.

"I'll take her."

TWO

Her owner was a billionaire. Granted, her firsthand experience with lorienok architecture was extremely limited to the insides of a spaceship and a pet store, but as her owner flew them over the city in his hover vehicle—*in his hover vehicle*—Delaney couldn't imagine anyone but the wealthiest man, no matter the planet he lived on, would reside in what was essentially a high-tech medieval castle in the center of metropolitan Antarctica.

She might have mistaken his hover vehicle as an indication of his extreme wealth too, except that everyone in the city seemed to fly one.

Her owner navigated through a rush-hour sky jam—ha!—and Delaney tried to keep her eyes neutral and uninterested as Keil had advised. Pets were excited by treats, not alien architecture, but her surroundings were both extraordinary and terrifying for their very extraordinariness. The city was dense and built up, similar to Times Square if all its skyscrapers had been carved into the jagged cliff faces of the Grand Canyon during the ice age. The buildings shimmered like opal, white with the glimmering flecks of a rainbow, and what few places in the canyon weren't embedded with skyscrapers were covered in tundra. She squinted down into those snowy plains, but either the hover vehicle was too high to see its details or the plains were, well, plain. And really, what did she expect to see outside in such deadly frigid temperatures? If the hover vehicle's height obscured the view of the plains, it certainly didn't detract from the view of the metropolis: the ice-carved city spread to the west-facing horizon as far as the eye could see. To the east, however, her view was blocked by the magnificence of a veritable castle built high into the side of a jagged, ice-encrusted mountain.

Her owner exited the sky traffic and descended to the base of the mountain. Surrounding the castle on the ground below was a three-story stone wall with five towers jutting high above the parapets, one at each corner. The wall had battlements and arrow slits and flanking towers and buttresses. Surrounding the great wall was a gigantic frozen moat, and feeding that icy moat was a frozen waterfall. In the distance, high over several acres of thorn-covered foothills, the water-fall's massive icicles hung from its rocky cliff edge, the length and thickness of giant oak trees. Sleek and jagged, breathtaking in both beauty and lethality, those spear-sharp points glinted off Lorien's dual suns like winking fangs.

The hover vehicle crossed the unnecessary drawbridge over the frozen moat and entered a snow-covered courtyard.

The courtyard probably contained more than just blinding tundra, but at first glance, that was all Delaney could discern through the passenger-side window. Even the castle, looming over them from its icy mountain perch, appeared to be made of the same shimmering opaline stone as the rest of the city. With both of Lorien's suns glowing through the blanket of snow-spitting clouds, the unrelenting white of the courtyard reflected like a veil of glitter.

When her eyes adjusted, she noticed that lorienok were in the courtyard, their brown and blond fur blending into the scenery because of their waterproof white jumpsuits.

One of Keil's culture lessons sprang to mind: lorienok were comfortable in the cold, even during the dead of Rorak, unless their fur became wet. They were susceptible to fever or fur rot—something terrible—and they protected against such illness with waterproof jumpsuits. Keil had been generous with his knowledge, gentle in their hesitant friendship, caring and wonderful and—Delaney swallowed back the tears before they could spill down her cheeks.

Lorienok were socializing in the courtyard, sitting on benches, chasing miniature versions of themselves around a snow-spouting fountain, and walking leashed creatures of all shapes, sizes, and species, presumably their animal companions. One of those companions was soaring through the sky, a giant bat with a beak and a furry mane around its bearlike face, easily the size of a refrigerator. Its owner was smiling and chatting and enjoying her day as if she wasn't flying her pet like a kite in subzero temperatures.

As the hover vehicle passed, every one of the lorienok, pet flyer and all, without fail stopped what they were doing, bowed their heads at her owner, and touched their palms to their hearts.

He wasn't just a billionaire. He was their king.

The hover vehicle stopped, and the driver's door lifted. Delaney was draped in a thin, soft fabric that suspiciously resembled a bedsheet with a hole cut out for her head, and over that, swaddled in several layers of fur-lined blankets. All those layers were stuffed tight inside a hooded white waterproof jumpsuit—same as everyone else was wearing. The store manager had even given her boots. They were so enormously oversized that she suspected they were actually his; her owner had refused to leave the establishment until she'd been well and thoroughly bundled. Nothing was exposed to the elements except her eyes, but the cold was sharp and cutting, penetrating her outfit in seconds.

Her owner exited, walked around the vehicle, and opened the passenger-side door. Delaney stepped one foot onto the icy ground, led on a leash by her owner, and the blast of that arctic wind was death breathing down her spine.

She froze, overwhelmed by the brilliance of all that white and sparkling ice, the shimmering castle, and the deference the lorienok showed her owner. Everything was so new and foreign and beautiful and frigidly, deadly cold, and *Jesus Christ, this was her life now.*

Her owner tugged on her leash, the yanking on her neck as foreign as this new world. She tripped over a snow mound, slipped on the ice beneath it, twisted her ankle, and fell ungracefully, face-first into a snowbank.

The snow caught her in its softness, but the leash extended to its full length and yanked on the collar as she fell, cutting off her breath.

Delaney coughed, choking on the collar. It loosened nearly immediately, but then she inhaled and coughed some more, choking on the snow.

A firm hand gripped her under each arm and lifted her from the ground. She fought for a moment, searching for purchase before realizing that her feet were dangling midair. Her owner was holding her up at eye level, scrutinizing her struggles.

Delaney met his mismatched eyes, still coughing. She swallowed and got herself under control. And then her teeth started chattering.

Christ, it's cold!

Her owner's expression was intense: his mouth a frowning slash, his brow wrinkled deep in disapproval, his gaze piercing.

He spat something that sounded like a curse, braced an arm around her back, and carried her on his hip like a child. She should have struggled in earnest—and probably would have, had she been less cold and less dazed—but falling headfirst into a snowbank in arctic temperatures had sapped both her physical strength and ability to think, literally and figuratively freezing her. By the time she realized she should have considered fighting him—would a golden retriever welcome being manhandled by a new owner?—he'd already crossed the remaining distance through the courtyard and entered a carved passage into the mountainside.

The small room they entered had reflective walls. She watched over her owner's shoulder as three lorienok followed them inside. They packed into the room, cramped shoulder to shoulder. Her owner reached out with his free hand and pressed the pads of three fingers into a panel on the wall. A set of clear doors slid closed, and suddenly, Delaney's stomach bottomed out. The room catapulted up the side of the mountain. The snow-covered courtyard, its fountain, and all the many milling lorienok shrank to thumb-sized toys.

They were in an elevator. She was on an alien planet inhabited by Sasquatch, and in an elevator.

The air inside the elevator was just as cold as the air outside and growing colder as they ascended into the sky. Delaney's shivers became full-body tremors. Her owner tightened his arms around her, and inexplicably, she caught the scent of sandalwood and spiced vanilla. She leaned in minutely just to confirm, and yes, the scent was wafting from the fur at his neck, subtle but unmistakably his. Was he wearing cologne? *Vanilla* cologne? Did they have vanilla in this tundra?

He made a purring noise in the back of his throat. Keil had demonstrated the noise and taught her its meaning during their social sciences lessons. It was called a *viurr* and was most commonly a maternal noise, but also used with loved ones, the ill, the old, and animal companions, as well as small children. Her owner was attempting to put her at ease.

Maybe this charade wouldn't be the disaster she'd anticipated, assuming he finished reading Keil's manual. She'd had her doubts when he'd tossed the hard copy to the floor, but he'd begun listening to an audio edition during their ride from the pet store. Keil had been confident that their combined effort to write a care manual that was both believable and beneficial to her survival had been a grand success. His life's greatest achievement, he'd declared, and having written care manuals for seventy-three foreign animals—all of which he'd domesticated—that was quite a claim. As was the claim that his seventy-fourth would be his last.

"I've taken great pride in my lifetime of work for the Federation and in the legacy I leave behind." He'd stroked the side of her cheek with his knuckle. "But if the Federation no longer heeds my recommendations, what am I but a cog in a machine? Cogs don't feel. Cogs don't regret. Cogs only do, and I refuse to have anything to do with an industry that can't feel how wrong this is."

He'd been right in one regard: his seventy-fourth care manual had been his last. She could still smell the choking scent of feces as his bowels had released in death. She could still see the *lorok* who'd killed him, scrutinizing her through the wire cage. She'd wanted to scream her rage, cry out for help and justice, but retaliation in that moment wouldn't have saved Keil. It would only have damned her too, so instead, she'd done exactly as Keil had advised she do when under intense scrutiny: she'd let her eyes glaze and wander with ignorant unconcern. She'd become the pet they'd believed her to be.

Six months later now, and she still wanted to scream.

Delaney shifted, shaking away the memories. One of the lorienok behind them was gazing straight ahead, looking bored as he watched the snowflakes melt on her owner's back. The other was looking at Delaney with an exaggerated pout elongating her face. She was murmuring something about being poor and dear and getting warm. The woman talked too fast and in that singsong, high-pitched voice that most lorienok used when speaking to Delaney. Between its pitch and her own gaps in fluency, Delaney couldn't translate the lorok's baby talk into complete sentences.

The elevator slowed, stopped, and the doors opened.

Delaney faced forward and blinked.

The interior of the castle didn't mirror its exterior. Considering the stone and medieval architecture, not to mention the frigid weather, Delaney had expected to see a crackling fireplace, throw rugs, and a cushy leather couch with piles of pillows and blankets. She'd anticipated dark wood furnishings and thick, velvety drapes. If her owner really was their king, a squire should have greeted them, balancing a steaming cup of something to welcome him home.

But thinking she could anticipate what to expect on this planet was ludicrous. As if the furry, horned, muscular, alien Sasquatch holding her gently on his hip and rubbing her back wasn't reminder enough that the *un*expected was now her reality.

Everything inside the castle was white and silver and reflective. Three rows of stadium-style desks and chairs were set in a full circle, like a sports arena, overlooking a floor-to-ceiling, 360-degree view of the courtyard, moat, waterfall, snow plains, and city beyond. Each desk had a hologram monitor, and behind each monitor sat a lor or lorok. At least fifty of them filled the room, and each was dressed in a blue coat and pantsuit—shiny-buttoned, crisp, and professional. They were all touching their holograms, swiping and typing and clicking and drawing. They were all focused and intent.

They were all armed.

Her owner exited the elevator and strode past the arena of desks. The lorienok here didn't genuflect like the ones in the courtyard, but they looked up and nodded their heads respectfully as he walked by. He strode down a long hallway and past several open rooms: tables and chairs in one, couches and holograms in another. Between the stone castle and its fortifications, the functionality of the furnishings over style or comfort, and the uniformed occupants and their weapons, this place seemed more like a fortress than a home. A niggling concern pricked her thoughts: what were they fortifying against?

Near the end of the hall, her owner turned on his heel and strode into what was undeniably a bathroom, complete with a shower, sink, cabinets, and a massive, three-foot-deep tub made luxuriously for a seven-foot-tall man. Everything was carved from a polished white stone, similar in appearance to the opal material on the exterior of the castle, but combined with the sleek technology of its interior. In addition to indoor plumbing, the bathroom sported an automatic sink and toilet. Even the tub was automatic, spouting water as her owner waved his hand over its faucet.

He set Delaney on her feet. She winced, her ankle throbbing. She hadn't worried over it until now, distracted as she was by the cold and the shock of him carrying her, but as she bore her own weight, it became painfully apparent that her failed dismount from the hover vehicle had done some damage. On a planet where the veterinarians hadn't even read her care manual yet (a manual that she herself—without any medical training or education beyond a high school GED—had coauthored), they could probably treat a common cold and sprained ankle at best. She shuddered to think about the potential consequences of anything worse.

Her owner unzipped the front of his waterproof jumpsuit. She let her gaze slide blankly past him as if she didn't care, as if she didn't know the difference between being clothed and being nude. As if her heart wasn't pounding in overdrive as he faced the toilet to relieve himself.

"When in doubt," Keil had advised, "simply wander away."

Delaney peered into the bathtub, poked the sink, flinched away from the faucet as it spat ice water, and, with her contrived exploration of the bathroom complete, she opened the bathroom door and limped away.

THREE

Torek nearly lost his aim, staring at Reshna's retreating back. His human was extremely intelligent. After watching him open the washroom door only once, she'd mastered the use of the door's lever and proximity sensor. He'd have to be vigilant with her, perhaps program extra locks and safety protocols between rooms to prevent her from entering places better left unexplored. He imagined her touching a heating plate in the kitchen as innocently as she'd touched the faucet and shuddered.

His human was also injured. Within the first moment of her arrival, with nearly her first step on the Onik estate, she'd slipped and fallen. If her uneven gait was anything to judge by, her foot was still paining her.

And so the agony of attempting to care for and keep another living being alive began.

Torek washed his hands, brushed the snarls and oil from his body, and checked the temperature of the bath. It was absolutely scalding, just as the manual had indicated was her preference. He scowled at the tub in doubt—what living creature could enjoy such temperatures?—but his human had certainly seemed chilled even after they'd entered the lift. Her temperature tolerance and preference was some-what different from his.

Time to put his manual's guidance to practical use.

It took a few minutes, but he doubled back down the hallway and found Reshna inside one of the empty common rooms. She was sitting on the couch still fully bundled, watching today's broadcast as if she were truly engrossed in the newscasters and their political banter. Cute. But the sight was also annoying because his guard knew better than to waste energy by leaving a teleprojector on in an empty room.

He approached Reshna slowly. She'd already noticed his pres-ence, switching her focus from the broadcast to him, and the look in her eyes gutted his resolve. She was scared and hurt and wary of him, which was understandable. Most animal companions were wary upon entering a new home, or so he'd been told. Being uprooted from one place and planted in another, even if that original place had been negligent, must be disorienting. And she was in pain.

"It's all right," Torek murmured gently. "I won't hurt you."

She continued to eye him cautiously, but by Lorien's grace, she stayed on the couch as he approached. He eased within arm's reach and smoothed his knuckles over her cheek to distract her as he slipped his other hand under her collar.

She winced. A distressed moan escaped her throat.

"Okay, okay. You're all right." He remembered that her neck, already raw from wearing a too-tight collar, was chafed anew from her fall in the courtyard. He stopped petting her and took hold of her wrist instead, releasing the collar.

She relaxed slightly.

"Good girl. Such a pretty girl."

He unstrapped her boots one-handed, an impossible feat had she struggled. But he continued to murmur comforting nonsense; she seemed to take to it. Her eyes remained wary, but her body remained still.

"And now your coverings. Can't have you trailing mud and snow everywhere you go. No reason to make our cleaning crew work overtime on your first day."

He tugged her to her feet and pulled down her hood, releasing her rioting curls from their confinement. He grinned, petting her hair.

"Very pretty girl," he murmured.

He opened her waterproof jumpsuit, slipped her arms from the sleeves, and unwound the fur-lined blankets from around her arms, neck, and torso before dropping the suit down to her ankles. He pulled the blankets from her thighs and calves and tugged the ends from her borrowed oversized boots. Having bundled her so thoroughly, he'd nearly forgotten the skinny angles of her body beneath the puff of her outfit. He could actually see the bumps of each rib through the thin fabric of her borrowed *yenok*. She'd been dirty, mistreated, and malnourished in the pet store manager's care. Torek's anger bloomed across his cheeks, hot beneath his fur.

He gripped her waist, stepped on the empty suit pooled at her feet, and plucked her bodily out of her boots.

Her mouth dropped open, but when he set her down, her lips closed without any sound having emerged. She stood for a moment, then shifted, favoring her left leg.

Her skin was starting to pucker again, and a tremor shook her body. According to the brief chapters he'd listened to on the cleaning and physical care of his human, the tremors were a physical reaction to being cold; same with the clacking of her teeth and the puckering of her skin. And it was no wonder. She had hardly any natural insulation between her bones and skin. In addition to the outline of each rib, he could see the knobby protrusions at her wrists, elbows, and collarbone. And her skin was completely bare, save for the long, golden curls haloing her head and the darker, winged tuffs above her eyes, neither of which were capable of retaining much heat.

She needed fitted protective coverings for her body. He would be one of those owners whose animal companions wore clothes, he realized, groaning to himself, but what alternative did he have? Blankets and an ill-fitting yenok were woefully inadequate protection for her delicate constitution against Lorien's climate. Another strike against that store manager. Torek ran a hand down his face, his heartbeat accelerating. He should have bought an easier animal companion, one that didn't require a wardrobe. One less exotic. One less prone to dying.

You will not panic. Deep breaths, just like Shemara Kore'Onik always says, Torek reminded himself. *Reshna has a problem. Her care manual has a solution. She may die eventually, but not today.*

According to her care manual, a scalding bath would quickly elevate her temperature.

"Okay." Another breath. "Now, Reshna, let's get you out of those rags and warmed up in—"

She pulled her hand from his grasp and walked away.

"Oh no, you don't." He lunged for her wrist. "Come here. Be a good girl, and—"

She yanked her hand free again, forcefully this time—so forcefully that she actually cut her forearm on his claws—then ran in stilted, limping strides from the room, clutching her bleeding arm.

Torek cursed under his breath.

He let her go for the moment, not wanting to provide unnecessary entertainment for his guard by chasing her through the hallway, although Lorien knew they needed something to break the horrible tension. They didn't want a new commander, they said. They were loyal to him and him alone. They would spit in the eye of the Lore'Lorien herself if she replaced him, and they would spit in the eye of whomever she replaced him with. But the doubt in their expressions said otherwise. Sure, they still saluted him as befitting his rank. They spoke the words he wanted to hear, but their eyes spoke a different truth, and those unspoken words echoed in his own thoughts: maybe Dorai Nikiok Lore'Lorien was right. Maybe he wasn't fit to lead them anymore.

Granted, Nikiok hadn't spoken those words aloud, but he could see the uncertainty in her eyes too. If her most recent command, approving Shemara Kore'Onik's recommendation that he obtain an animal companion to facilitate his mental recovery, wasn't undeniable proof of her doubt, he didn't know what was. He combed his claws though the too-long hair under his chin. He didn't have the means to prove himself worthy of their continued loyalty yet, but by the strength and pride of his father, his grandfather, and the legacy of their many forefathers, he could prove himself fit to lead one tiny female human to warmth and cleanliness. That he could do today—this very minute, in fact.

He turned off the teleprojector and stalked calmly from the room. She was still in the hallway, jiggling the lever of a locked door. Her head jerked up sharply at his approach, and she limped farther down the hall, trying and failing to open doors as she went. Torek continued his slow stalk, allowing her to run. All the rooms in this wing south of the washroom were living quarters, the doors of which he knew were locked. Every single one of them. Hopefully, she tired and, in her injured state, lost her resolve, so when the real battle began, she wouldn't fight him as ardently as he suspected she otherwise would.

Eventually, Reshna ran out of doors and hope. She stood in front of the linen closet at the far end of the hallway, cornered and shaking. She was cradling her arm against her now blood-smeared yenok and still favoring her left leg.

"Easy, girl." He was nearly in arm's reach of her. "I know you're hurting, but I won't hurt you. Just—"

She ducked under his arm. He feinted left, she jumped to his right, and he snagged her around the waist. She released a truly pitiful, high-pitched moan, but it didn't matter how she fought or whined, he wasn't letting go. She was cold and dirty and scared, and since he couldn't fix any of the problems in his life at the moment, he was damn sure going to fix the problems in hers.

He clamped her hands to her sides, lifted her onto his hip, and carried her, wriggling and kicking, back up the hallway to the washroom. He shut the door again but locked it this time, careful to block her view, so she wouldn't see how the mechanism worked and learn to spring herself loose. Not that she was interested in him or the lock at the moment. She began bucking and flailing in earnest as he approached the bath. Her eyes round with terror, they snapped from him to the water and back to him.

Had he misread her manual? Was she allergic to water too? Or perhaps it wasn't something that her manual could cover. Perhaps her fear of water was a personal phobia from some traumatic experience.

"All right, Reshna. Here we go. Let's just remove this last layer, and then we'll—argh!"

Her arms locked around his neck in a stranglehold, and her legs bolted around his waist, much stronger than he'd thought her slender form capable of.

"Bad girl, Reshna." He pushed at her waist in an attempt to pry her loose, but she only clung tighter. "Let go."

She buried her face in his chest and trembled.

Since he no longer needed his arms to hold her, he tried removing her yenok as she hung from him midair. He'd only just lifted its hem to her waist when something wet dripped through the fur on his chest. He leaned back and forced her face up to meet his. Her eyes were leaking.

She was crying. Like a lorok.

Torek blinked, stunned.

He shook his head. No, she was crying like a frightened creature in pain.

He stopped trying to force her. "Where's my good girl? You're all right. Everything's all right."

He pursed his lips, glaring at the water, then at Reshna's clothes, and finally at his own. Whether her fear was personal or a trait of her breed, it was too large to expect her to overcome it alone.

Torek embraced her and, still fully dressed, stepped into and sat in the tub, submerging them both to their chests in steaming water.

He gritted his teeth against a bark of pain—being cooked alive hadn't been on today's agenda—but eyed Reshna critically. She'd frozen at first, stunned silent and unmoving in his arms except for the wide, rapid blinking of her eyes.

Then she relaxed back and dipped herself neck-deep.

"That feels better, does it?" Her shivering had subsided somewhat, and satisfaction swelled through his chest. "Let's make it even better, shall we?"

He picked up a bottle of liquid soap. Her eyes darted to his hands, and she stilled.

"You're going to be so clean and warm. Squeaky clean." He squirted a drop of soap onto the top of her head and massaged it through her hair, into her scalp. She closed her eyes. She remained stiff, but she didn't struggle away from him either. Progress. "That's a good girl. Good Reshna."

Maybe he'd be a better animal owner than he'd first given himself credit for.

He activated the water to rinse out her hair, and a fall of ice doused Reshna's back before it had the chance to heat. She screamed, leapt from the tub, and flooded the washroom floor with water and suds. Her injured ankle, now swollen and a rich shade of purple, slipped in the slosh of her making. He just barely caught her shoulders before she smacked her head on the tub's angled lip. As it was, her rump hit the tile floor, and she released an indelicate *oof* followed by a small whimper.

He sighed heartily. Then again, maybe not.

FOUR

Delaney stared up at the horned Sasquatch who had just saved her from smashing her head, if not her ass, on the slippery, unforgiving bathroom tile floor and reminded herself for the umpteenth time that he was not trying to hurt her. He was not Kane Todd. She was his pet, and caring, considerate owners cleaned their pets. This did not need to be an issue, but every time he moved to undress her, it didn't matter that her mind knew he wasn't a threat, her body reacted otherwise.

Her heart rate had spiked. Her stomach had cramped. Her reason had collapsed, and then he'd undermined all that healthy panic by submerging her neck-deep in that colossal, elephant-sized tub of blessedly warm water. But the bedsheet covering her body was now translucent and uncomfortably suctioned to, well, *everything*. She would have been outraged, and might even have blown her cover on the spot entirely, except for the outlandish and endearing fact that he had submerged himself fully dressed in the tub with her.

Because he was not Kane Todd, and he was not trying to hurt her. He was trying to warm and clean her. *Squeaky clean.* Jesus.

His expression remained constant whether he was coaxing her, scolding her, massaging her scalp, or gazing down at her ankle, as he was doing now. He bore an impressive frown—as did all the lorienok, with their high-boned foreheads and downturned lips at the corners of their blunt muzzles—but his eyes, once again, revealed the nuances of his feelings. He seemed concerned and frustrated and exhausted, and his hands—those massive, claw-tipped hands that looked capable of disembowelment—had thus far only held her gently on his hip, rubbed her back comfortingly, massaged shampoo into her hair, and saved her from eating bathroom tile.

Delaney took a deep breath, struggling to calm, and, giving up on that, struggling to stand. Her swollen foot slipped out from under her. Pain spiked up her leg, and suddenly, she was being gripped beneath her underarms and lifted up by two firm hands. Her owner leveraged himself to his feet and her into his arms.

"Now, let's try this again. The water has heated, see?"

He filled his palm with water and poured it on her arm. As promised, it was now much warmer than before. Hot, even. Deliciously, beautifully, miraculously hot.

He hunkered down into the water with a pained hiss, dipping her as well as himself up to their necks again. She met his gaze and steeled herself against the inevitability of being undressed. As if it even mattered at this point, but panic didn't understand logic. Her heart throbbed up to clog her throat.

"And now to wash out the soap." He filled his palm again and dumped the little water it contained over her hair. As if that method wouldn't take all night to rinse the mop on her head.

When he leaned forward for more water, she leaned back and dunked her head directly under the faucet.

The water was divine. It rushed over her, burning the tip of her numb nose like penance. She made a noise, a low, aching moan that might have been "Oh God," but she couldn't be sure, because all she knew was the desperate need for warmth. She pushed away from her owner, and he let her this time as she submerged herself under the spray. She closed her eyes, hugged her knees, and let the heat cocoon her.

A sound of suction, and suddenly, the water level dropped down to her chest. Delaney craned her head out from under the spray and wiped her eyes. Her owner had left the tub.

He lifted a hand, palm out, toward her. "Stay."

As if she would leave the water's newfound warmth. She fought against the overwhelming urge to roll her eyes.

He watched her watching him for a long moment. Eventually, he must have realized that she had no intention of following him from the tub, because his lips parted, revealing the tips of his pointed fangs.

"Good girl."

Her eyes did roll at that, but luckily, he'd already looked away, unzipping and unsnapping the layers of his own clothing. He peeled the soaked, clinging jumpsuit from his body, and Delaney held her breath, transfixed. Her owner wasn't the first lor she'd seen naked. Keil had deliberately given her anatomy lessons complete with life-size, 3D anatomical views to prepare her for this very moment, so when she did come face-to-fur with a naked lor or lorok, as he predicted she would, she could let her uncomprehending gaze slide by without reaction.

Golden retrievers didn't mind their nakedness, she thought, reminding herself of her own personal Golden Rule. In fact, golden retrievers minded being clothed, and they certainly didn't blink twice at anyone else, lorienok or otherwise, being naked. Because naked was natural.

Delaney blinked once, then twice, and then kept on blinking as she stared.

The anatomical hologram Keil had shown her hadn't depicted a lor with thick, powerful pectoral muscles. The abdomen hadn't been visibly defined and hadn't tapered down in a dramatic V from the broad expanse of his shoulders. The hologram had had smooth, silky fur, unmarred by a long keloid scar down the side of his abdomen, and it certainly hadn't boasted bulging, rippling biceps only marginally smaller than the circumference of her head.

The only thing her owner's body had in common with the nonthreatening anatomical hologram was, ironically enough, the part of his anatomy that was most threatening. The space between his legs was nothing but smooth fur, his penis still hidden inside him within its inner sheath.

She closed her gaping mouth and forced her eyes to wander away from the stunning sight of her owner's battle-hardened body before he noticed that her stare had thoughts and fears and curiosity behind it.

He dropped his clothes into a wet heap on the floor and stepped into a shower stall, but when he pressed a button, a whirlwind of freezing air, not water, swept through the chamber, fluttering and drying his fur.

Delaney huddled back down into the steaming bath, attempting to watch without staring as his fur dried. By the time he stepped out of the dryer, she was a little flushed and very pruned, and finally, mercifully, truly warm for the first time since Keil had been murdered. She'd thought nothing could be worse than living in the same house as Kane Todd, with his eyes that could penetrate her as deeply as his knife. And then she'd been abducted by aliens, witnessed the cold-blooded murder of her last friend in the whole universe, and been jailed in a kennel for six months.

She took a deep, steadying breath. Her owner knelt to dry the bathroom floor. If she was being honest instead of self-pitying, she could admit that living in the kennel had been less stressful than living with Kane. She'd been caged either way, but in the kennel, at least her body had remained her own.

Huddled half-dressed in a bathtub with her naked owner mopping up the water-slicked tile floor, she didn't even have that.

He stood, the floor apparently sufficiently dried, and draped a fresh towel over the closed toilet lid. He glanced at her, and then turned with the painfully slow, incremental movements of someone trying to coax a deer to eat from his hand. He inched closer, leaned over her, and turned off the faucet.

Before she could stifle the reaction, she lifted her eyebrows.

"All right, little Reshna. Good girl." His hands reached for her, his movements still slow and careful as he lifted her from the bath and sat her sopping wet on the towel-spread toilet lid. "Now. Let's take a look at that ankle, hmm?"

He squatted before her on his haunches and lifted the offending foot. While the hot water had soothed all her other limbs, it had only worsened her ankle. The bruise had darkened to a lovely shade of purple over the entire baseball-sized swelling where the sharp angle of her outer ankle used to be.

He pressed on the bruise with his thumb.

Pain zinged up her leg. Delaney flinched, but he kept hold of her foot in his gentle yet firm grip.

"Okay. Okay." He stroked the side of her calf with the rough padding of his paw-like palm, then sighed. "Looks like I'll be adding a veterinarian appointment to my schedule tomorrow."

It took every ounce of self-restraint that Delaney possessed not to shake her head.

"But in the meantime, let's see to that arm, shall we?"

The bright, almost manic tone of her owner's voice offset by his stern expression was so distracting that by the time Delaney had translated his words, he already had a bottle of something and an ointment of who knew what in one hand, and was approaching her with what looked like—but couldn't be—a cotton ball in the other hand. The climate was too cold on this planet to grow cotton. Nevertheless, he'd soaked the liquid from said mystery bottle into that absorbent white fluff, which was now hovering an inch from her bleeding arm.

Keil had educated her on standard household first-aid items—Lorien's equivalent to Earth's ibuprofen, antiseptic, and adhesive bandages—but Delaney couldn't read the labels in her owner's hand to reassure herself that he wasn't about to pour battery acid on her skin. Not that lorienok typically kept battery acid in their bathrooms, according to Keil, but sitting half-naked on an alien toilet on an alien planet with said alien about to treat her wound, she didn't feel particularly rational at the moment.

Based on his hitherto gentle demeanor, she didn't think her owner would melt her arm on purpose, but they were different species with different strengths and tolerances. He could accidentally kill her, thinking he was saving her. But she couldn't very well snatch the bottle out of his hand and read the label herself without revealing that she could read, and golden retrievers didn't have the intellectual capacity to read, and therefore, neither did she.

Shit!

By the time her panic had shaped into thought, the soaked cotton ball had already swiped over the cut and was stinging her arm.

Delaney yanked her arm back, but her owner, having anticipated her reaction, clamped her arm in the crook of that massive bicep. He made a few perfunctory shushing noises and continued his torture via cotton ball.

Let that be hydrogen peroxide, Delaney prayed. *Please, let that be nothing more than the equivalent of hydrogen peroxide.*

She wiggled her fingers just to prove that she could. Her arm hadn't melted off or become paralyzed or grown fur—not that the lorienok had medications that specifically induced those side effects. But the one thing Keil had unwittingly taught her during nearly five years of space travel from Earth to Lorien was that the human body was the most fragile of all the animal bodies Keil had ever encountered. He'd marveled at her body's inabilities, one of which was its inferior ability to fend off infection.

Christ, here comes the ointment.

It was probably a topical antibiotic. Considering her body's many inferiorities, Keil had emphasized the importance of cleanliness and wound care in her manual. So it made sense that her owner wanted to clean her wound, assuming he'd already read the chapter on first aid.

But she couldn't base the fate of her arm on assumptions. She continued struggling, fruitlessly at first, but she managed to knock the ointment from his hand.

"Bad girl," he muttered, but his words weren't heated. He didn't even glance at her—just bent to pick up the ointment. As he leaned over, Delaney craned her neck to read the label.

It was indeed mild topical antibiotic, the exact brand that Keil had recommended in her care manual. Her owner flipped open the cap, squeezed a dollop of ointment onto the pad of his forefinger, and smeared the ointment over her cut. She jumped at the contact, and he murmured nonsense and assurances.

Delaney stared at that ointment tube, so delicately cradled in her owner's meaty hand, and then at her owner himself, through his impressive frown to the man she didn't dare hope he'd be: someone who cared, someone who would strive to keep her healthy and safe, someone who could see her too, even if he did think she possessed a pea-sized brain. Someone like Keil.

Having dressed her wound, he set down the ointment and reached to lift her bedsheet tunic. This time, she clenched her teeth and let it happen without a struggle.

He lifted the sheet, exposing her thighs, then her privates and belly. He gathered the sopping fabric into a wad as he lifted it, and just as he was maneuvering the fabric in preparation for stretching it over her head, his knuckles grazed her nipple.

Delaney froze. Her throat constricted. Her eyes darted to his.

He didn't meet her gaze, but neither was he leering at her breast. He was examining her neck and stretching the fabric so it didn't choke her as he lifted it.

Delaney swallowed. Her throat relaxed incrementally, and by the time she could take a deep, steady breath, her owner had slipped the fabric over her head and discarded it onto the floor in a translucent, blood-soaked heap.

She was hunched on a toilet bowl, hugging her naked waist, but his eyes—the ice and power of that dichotomous gaze—still didn't stare. Well, they did, but not lasciviously. His eyes were all warmth and caring concern. Her composure, frayed thin from a lifetime of people fulfilling her low expectations, balanced on that look. All they had was five hours' and a bath's worth of trust between them, but that was more connection than she'd had with another person in an unbearably long time.

Her owner stood, walked to a closet, and returned with two furry towels. He draped one over her shoulders, chafing her upper arms warm with a brisk rub. He used the other towel to dry her hair, rubbing her head with that same rough efficiency. She braced herself against his gusto, but when he snapped the towel from her head a minute later, the half-dried coils of her crazy hair sprang over her eyes in gravity-defying quivers.

Through a curtain of frizz, Delaney watched as her owner's lips peeled away from his teeth. A low, rhythmic growl issued from his parted lips. His shoulders shook. "Oh, this hair will be the death of me."

Delaney blinked and then struggled to contain an answering chuckle. She'd shared the same sentiment for twenty-seven years.

He picked up a bone-handled, bristled tool—more toilet scrub than hairbrush—but his hands were exceedingly, nearly excruciatingly gentle as he combed her hair. Delaney sat as still as possible as he picked gently and tirelessly through the mess of knots—the majority of which he'd created with his enthusiastic towel drying—and tried valiantly to ignore the fact that his naked groin was six inches from her cheek.

She couldn't help but glance sideways at least once—she'd had anatomy lessons, but never from this intimate angle!—but oddly enough, it wasn't the Golden Rule that dampened her curiosity and stayed her gaze. Her owner hadn't stared at her nakedness. She could extend him the same courtesy, even if he was unaware of the intent and intelligence behind her eyes, which in some ways made her stares more an invasion of privacy than his.

He brushed her teeth—as squeaky clean as her hair!—draped a new sheet over her head, and swathed her body in a fresh, sweet-smelling fur blanket. Having finished her ablutions, her owner performed his and wrapped a towel around his own hips. Delaney found it curiously strange to witness modesty from a man covered head to toe in fur, especially considering his privates were hidden inside himself. What did he think he was concealing?

He scooped her up by the bum, cradled her on his hip with one arm, and carried her to a bedroom. The room was obviously a bedroom in the way that the room with a toilet, bath, and body dryer was obviously a bathroom. Although some of the furniture was different, it was mostly, eerily, the same. The room had mirrors, a closet, a bureau, a narrow window, a nightstand piled with books, a small black device—an alarm clock?—and a kitchenette, but only one piece of furniture caught and consumed her attention: the bed.

He could have bought it at Ashley Furniture had they been capable of intergalactic shipping. The head- and footboards were made of a dark grained material—wood, at first glance, although she hadn't seen any trees on Lorien yet—and the mattress looked soft, piled high with a thick, furry comforter, animal furs, and fluffy pillows. The bed was everything she'd dreamed of while shivering on the concrete floor of the pet store's cage, but at the same time, it was *his* bed and the core of the recurring nightmare she'd suffered at every new house since living with the Todds.

She balked. He must have felt her stiff resistance, because he tightened his hold when he strode into the room. But he circumvented the bed and approached a small cot on the floor. It wasn't raised, and it didn't have a headboard. Really, it was just a nest of furry blankets, nearly identical to the ones draped around her body, and a pile of pillows on a stuffed mat. Her owner crouched on his haunches, laid her down, and stacked several of the pillows under her foot, murmuring assurances about her ankle. He nodded, evidently satisfied by his pillow placement, stood, and climbed into the massive sea of his own bed.

"Lights off," he commanded.

The room plunged into thick black darkness.

Delaney held her breath.

Something clicked. A smaller light glowed from a handheld screen and then flicked off. A bracing squeak reverberated from the bed as he rolled and grunted and rolled again. Eventually he settled, seconds turned to minutes, and a rhythmic burring filled the silence.

He'd fallen asleep.

Delaney turned her face into her pillow and breathed in its softness. Her little cot next to his bed was cozy and warm, but most precious of all, it was hers. Hers alone, not to share.

She'd given up on human decency years ago, but as the minutes turned to hours filled with nothing but his loudening snores, her low expectations rose slightly, dangerously, into something she feared more than the nightmare itself: hope.

SLEEP IS A CURIOUS THING. DELANEY COULD SLEEP THROUGH babies crying, dogs barking, the hard slap of hands striking flesh, the shrieks of women enduring those slaps, the rhythmic mattress squeaks and guttural moans of sex, and those same noises mixed with the yelps and breathless wails of rape—but silence could keep her wide awake. Her owner's bearlike snores were a drug, lulling her into a peaceful if not deep sleep. But only a few short hours after having fallen asleep, well before the first sun had even risen, he woke, stretched, and left the room, abandoning Delaney to the dark and silence.

She lay faceup on her fuzzy floor cot, staring at the ceiling. When she blinked, she could feel the scrape of sand in the corners of her eyes. Her body ached. Her head throbbed. Her ankle throbbed too, which was admittedly the worse pain, but it might not have throbbed as bad if only she'd been able to sleep a few more hours. Or had some coffee. Jesus, how she missed coffee. And cigarettes. And the warmth of a bright, humid summer day.

She glanced out the narrow window, then sighed and stood to better take in the view. The courtyard was several stories and half a mountain below. If some lorienok were out and about, enjoying an early morning stroll, she couldn't see them through the cloud wisps. Yellow orbs of light illuminated the fountain, lined the walkways, and twinkled on the snow.

She had to urinate. She hadn't had to while lying in bed, but now that she was vertical, she suddenly had to, imminently, the urge made even more pressing because she desperately didn't want to leave the room.

The flat roof outside the window had a railing, so she supposed peeing off the balcony was an option. She wrinkled her nose, turned around, and crossed her arms to consider the bedroom around her warily. There was the sink. Otherwise, she could leave a nice warm wet welcome on the floor for her owner. Keil had insisted that she do so at least twice within the first week, because that was what pets did in a new home, even those who were house-trained. He'd recommended that she growl, misunderstand commands, make messes, and even bite if severely provoked. Being a pet was more than just being obedient, owned, and (hopefully) loved. Delaney had to play her part, and that part included being bathed, being groomed, and pretending not to recognize household appliances, including toilets.

Except that her owner had shown her how to use the toilet, hadn't he? She'd watched him relieve himself. The sight was permanently burned into her retinas.

Golden retrievers don't use toilets, she thought. But some cats did, and all cats used kitty litter.

Fuck it. She unlocked the door, left the bedroom, limped down the hall, and waved her hand in front of the bathroom door's sensor. It stayed closed.

"Give me a minute. I just got in," someone called out.

Delaney jumped back and limped down the hallway before she could temper her reaction. She huffed out a frustrated breath and forced herself to calm. She was only guilty of something if she looked guilty, and God help her, in a castle that housed this many people, there had to be more than one bathroom. She just had to find it.

FIVE

INGRAINED HABITS WERE DIFFICULT TO BREAK. FOR SIX KAIR, Torek had woken predawn before drill to squeeze in his own workout for the day. Now that he was on mandatory leave from the Federation and not charged with running drill for another several weeks, he could have enjoyed a day of leisure, slept in, and watched the morning report with a cool glass of *saufre*. But Torek enjoyed routine, reveled in it, in fact, which was one of the reasons why mandatory leave, in addition to the dictate of obtaining an animal companion, was so abhorrent. He refused to compromise any more of his routine than was absolutely necessary.

Despite his new responsibility of being an animal companion owner, he'd woken before anyone else on the Onik estate and enjoyed a vigorous two-hour hike through Graevlai. Surely, Reshna would remain safe, locked inside his living quarters to slumber peacefully through her morning, but when he returned, his door was no longer locked. Reshna's pallet next to his bed was empty.

He blew out a hard breath. His door locked from the inside, naturally, but he'd been careful to block her gaze while locking the washroom door yesterday. She must have been watching him leave this morning when he'd been groggy and considerably less careful. But he shouldn't have had to be careful; her breaths had been deep, even, and a little growly. She'd been asleep.

Apparently not, because wherever she was, she wasn't still locked in his living quarters.

Wasn't an animal companion supposed to be stress *relieving*? Wasn't that the point of all this, for her to aid in *his* recovery?

He'd squeezed in her veterinarian appointment today between his surgical follow-up and his weekly psychological evaluation. And then he had another deposition this afternoon. His day was going to be long, likely exhausting, and mostly pointless—especially the psychological evaluation—but he enjoyed having a schedule and sticking to that schedule.

Losing his human had not been on that schedule.

Adult humans require private sleeping quarters and washrooms...

Maybe after only one day of sharing his rooms, she'd already sickened and died somewhere.

Exhaling a deep, self-deprecating breath at the mixed horror and relief that thought provoked, Torek about-faced and walked down the hall. He bypassed his neighboring officers' living quarters—by Lorien's horn, skewer him if he actually needed to ask their help to find Reshna—peeked inside each common room—empty—and eventually, reluctantly, stepped up onto the dais overlooking the surveillance hall. His guard were hard at work at their monitors, some of them suddenly harder at work now that he was watching. He scanned them, keeping his expression stern as he searched the room for a glimpse of his human's long, golden head hair.

Nothing.

He nodded vaguely at the guard—as if he could approve of anything while standing this high over and far removed from them—stepped off the dais, and looped the long way back around to his quarters. As he walked the perimeter, exuding the confidence of a commander whose guard served him and Lorien well, his eyes darted between computer stations, under desks, and behind holograms, any nook Reshna might have tucked herself into.

Still nothing.

He imagined her roaming through the halls as he'd been pounding over running trails. She might have retraced her steps from yesterday. Being the intelligent human that she was, she might have mimicked the lift combination she'd witnessed him press, and considering the unlucky owner that he was, she might have adjusted her hand placement to descend. But she wouldn't know to stop the lift at ground level. She might ride it all the way down, deep below Onik's surface into the depths of the *deporak*.

Breathe.

Torek focused on slowing the panicking race of his heart and regrouped in reality before he had another attack. An alarm hadn't sounded. Reshna might very well be in the lift, but she hadn't ridden it down into the deporak. Not yet, anyway.

Torek rounded the corner and jogged back to his quarters. There were only so many places on the estate that one wee human could hide without either sounding an alarm or freezing. The cold would hopefully keep her indoors, but he'd check the lift and courtyard anyway. He'd log into the network and search for her room by room through the security camera feeds if need be. He'd double-check the common rooms, looking under the furniture, behind the doors, and inside closets. He tore open the door to his quarters. He'd—

Reshna was standing on the windowsill—an open window he most assuredly hadn't left open—looking as if she was attempting to climb out. The door slammed shut behind him, and she startled from her perch. His heart jumped to choke his throat, but she fell back inside, safely if not gracefully, to the floor on her rear. Her head whipped up, her wide gray eyes meeting his gaze from behind the curly curtain of her hair.

She pushed her hair aside and tucked it behind a small, round ear. The hair disobediently sprang out from behind her ear, but she didn't move to correct it. She just stared at him as if transfixed. Or terrified.

He took a deep breath so when he spoke, his voice didn't betray him. "Where were you this morning?" he asked calmly. "And what are you doing, trying to escape? It's a long, deadly fall out that window, little one."

She opened her mouth as if to respond—adorable!—and then just blinked.

Torek drew closer to her, his movements smooth and slow. "I've been looking everywhere for you." He held out the back of his hand for her to sniff. She flinched, but as he remained still, hand extended, her expression shifted slightly: her frown eased, her lips parted, and she swallowed.

"So skittish. But you came back after running away from me, didn't you?" He *shuffed*, a long-suffering snort through his muzzle. "Must count for something," he muttered.

She leaned forward, but instead of sniffing his hand like he'd expected, she grasped it with her own and used him to leverage herself to her feet.

He nearly pitched forward before bracing his footing. She was the lightest creature of her size he'd ever encountered. He could practically lift her with his little finger, but he hadn't expected her to initiate such an intimate, lorienok-like gesture. He blinked at *her* this time, their palms still linked.

The contact, as familiar as it was rare, reminded him of Zana and the daily walks they'd enjoyed when she was healthy—well, *healthier* —and then while caring for her as she'd deteriorated. He vividly recalled one such moment, having just transferred her from the bed to a chair in an attempt to coax soup down her throat, always an event. She'd been painfully aware of her helplessness; she'd raised his warm hand in her frail, cold one and rubbed his knuckles against her cheek. To comfort *him*.

He yanked away from Reshna's hand, burned by the memories, and she flailed. He realized too late that she'd been balancing on one leg, her good leg. She stepped back, catching herself by bearing weight on her swollen ankle, and let loose a low whimper. Eyes frantic, she looked like she might bolt, and then a different expression passed over her face, something intense. Her eyes closed, her face scrunched, and her lips compressed together into a thin, wrinkled line.

And then her eyes sprang open again. She looked down, her cheeks suddenly a shocking shade of red.

He followed her gaze and groaned.

She'd peed herself.

He passed a hand down his face. *Rak* the surgical follow-up. He was taking Reshna to the veterinarian immediately.

From the outside, the veterinarian's office looked like another medieval castle, but the sterile, sleek design inside reminded Delaney of a government research facility or maybe an academic medical center. Instead of humans—or rather, in addition to one—this hospital treated pets. Her fellow animal companions were different species from different planets. The one constant between them wasn't their physical appearance but their temperament: they were all exceedingly friendly.

They wagged their tails and wriggled their heads into palms for more pets. They jumped up and licked faces, and they writhed in ecstasy when scratched behind their ears. They were lovable. Some of them had scales and others had wings and fangs and a disconcerting number of eyes. Some walked on two legs, others on all fours, one on all eights. But they were *happy*. They sure as shit weren't cursing and punching and clawing their way out of their checkup, so neither could Delaney, even as she was separated from her owner and led to a private examination room. Even as a lor gently unwound her fur blankets, lifted her naked onto an exam room table, positioned her to crouch on all fours, and strapped her wrists and ankles to each corner.

Even as the exam room became not quite so private.

A dozen lorienok entered the room and promptly surrounded her, staring intently. Humiliation and dread and that old shame burned through her entire body, but she couldn't fight them. She needed to assimilate. Her life depended on it.

She tugged on the restraints, and the chains tinkled like sleigh bells.

If only she'd found an unoccupied bathroom. If only she'd been able to sneak out the window and urinate off the balcony before he'd interrupted. If only the flames of her blush could literally engulf her, but alas, she couldn't turn back and change time. She remained whole and healthy, even as her skin flushed a blotchy crimson.

"Is she sick?" one lorienok asked. "A skin condition, maybe?"

"Obviously, you didn't read her manual," another hissed.

"How could I?" the first whined. "The commander just rescheduled her appointment this morning."

They were young. The girls were still petite, under five feet, and the boys still had short, goatlike horns that hadn't yet curved. An older lor entered the room, and the youths' chatter silenced. Their backs straightened, and they faced forward expectantly.

"Who would like to begin?" The man met the gaze of each lorienok in the room.

Silence.

A girl—the lorok who'd chided the boy about reading her manual —stepped forward. "She's an adult female human named Reshna, animal companion to the commander. She had an appointment scheduled for later today, but several accidents occurred to expedite her visit: a twisted ankle, a cut on her forearm, and an inability to hold her bladder."

The girl stepped back, filling her place in line.

"Very good, Joennel. What reasons could Reshna have for wetting the floor?"

Silence.

"Come now. I've never known any of you to be shy. Yes, this

appointment is occurring earlier than expected, but it's our duty to Reshna, the commander, and all of Onik to come prepared with ideas. So let's hear them."

A shorter silence and then, *"Nikarok lukai?"*

"Rolorak osir?"

"Weak *nirarai* muscles?"

Delaney glanced back and forth at the students as each offered up what she assumed were their guess diagnoses. Her stomach curdled.

"Brinon Kore'Onik, could she just be scared?" Joennel asked.

Silence.

"Well, she is a new animal companion," the girl insisted. "They sometimes mark territory in new homes, but from the commander's statement, it sounds like maybe she was just nervous in a new place with a new owner."

The man, Brinon Kore'Onik, nodded. "Very good, Joennel. Let's find out, then, shall we? What's first on—someone other than Joennel, please."

A boy stepped forward. "Temperature. Blood pressure. Physical examination. And...and measurements?"

"Very good, Roerik."

Joennel shuffed.

"Let's begin. Same assignments as yesterday."

A chorus of groans.

"Come now, practice makes perfect." And then under his breath, Brinon murmured, "Lorien knows you need the practice."

Delaney's heart skipped a beat, and then they were on her, all two dozen hands. One opened her mouth to examine her gums and tongue. A second flashed a light in her eyes, while a third palpated her stomach. Another secured a cuff around her upper arm. It inflated uncomfortably, to the edge of pain, and then released. The boy glanced at his tablet—101/72, if she recalled Lori numerals correctly—referenced her manual, made a note, and patted her head.

"Good girl," he muttered.

Delaney blinked. An adolescent Sasquatch alien had just recorded her blood pressure.

One of the girls was taking measurements, documenting the length of her hair, the circumference of her neck, the length of her arms, the swell of her breasts, her waist, and lower still—yep, there she goes—the folds of her privates, and finally, her legs.

Someone slid something into her anus.

Delaney froze. Her heart leapt up into her throat. Their hands were suddenly prison bars—confining, punishing, suffocating. She couldn't breathe past them. Her body began to tremble, which one of them noted, and then she threw up.

The students nearest her leapt out of range and then pounced forward, one taking samples directly from the floor and another reexamining her mouth. The boy palpating her stomach, looking the most concerned, picked up a device from a tray table and scanned her belly.

The something was removed from her anus. It suctioned free with a wet *pop*.

A hot rush of tears rolled down her cheeks. She moved to wipe them, but the chains cut short her movement on a toll of sleigh bells.

Roerik held a tube to her cheek and bottled a sample.

Brinon approached her from behind with another device tucked unobtrusively at his side. "Joennel, will you distract her as I treat her ankle? Thank you."

Delaney craned her neck back, trying to get a better look at the device in Brinon's hand. *The other animals were happy*, she reminded herself, but she couldn't stop trembling.

"No, let's not use food. She's too nervous. It may upset her stomach again. And everyone else, stay where you are. Let's give Reshna some breathing room. Joennel, what else can you do?"

"*Tidokai* and *litork nulistorak*."

"Yes, that's right. Go ahead."

Delaney braced herself.

Joennel inched forward from the other students, her gaze shifting warily from Delaney to the stain on the floor and back to Delaney, as if at any moment, Delaney could aim her sick at her. Smart cookie, that Joennel. But with Brinon Kore'Onik watching, Joennel acted against her better instincts and approached. She raked her fingers through Delaney's hair, gently massaging her scalp with her fingertips and being extra careful with her claws—as per her manual's detailed instructions in the "How to Best Pet" chapter.

Delaney relaxed incrementally, not from the petting—which did admittedly feel pleasant—but from the knowledge that Brinon and all his students, or at the very least Joennel, had read her manual. Keil had said they would, that it was required of all physicians to read the care manual of an animal companion before practicing medicine on it, but Keil hadn't foreseen his murder, so really, everything he'd anticipated was suspect.

Brinon snapped something around Delaney's ankle. It hurt but only because her ankle was injured, and whatever he'd secured to it was uncomfortably tight.

"That's set for a lorok!" One of the students leaned as far forward as his body would allow while keeping his feet firmly planted.

"Yes. And why might I choose our setting for Reshna?"

Silence.

"Because her limbs are similarly shaped?" a boy guessed. "So the device is a good fit physically."

The device around her ankle, already uncomfortably tight, was growing tighter. Delaney took a deep breath. *They read my manual,* she reminded herself.

"Yes, very good. I wouldn't want to use a device that didn't fit properly. But why use our calibration?" Brinon asked.

More silence.

The device was heating. The chains connected to Delaney's wrists resumed their rattling.

Joennel started petting with both hands.

"Why do we use the same calibration to heal, let's say, injuries to both *lombowatts* and *pourpites?*"

"They both have scales," one of the students tried.

"Yes, on the right track. How about you, Roerik? What do you think?"

"Hmm." Roerik rocked back on his heels. "They both have split tongues too."

Joennel shuffed. "They share the same *mukar*," she grumbled.

Brinon glanced aside at her. "I don't hear you giving Reshna any tidokai nulistorak, Joennel."

Joennel stiffened, then resumed her smooth petting. "Such a pretty girl, Reshna," she said, her voice suddenly singsongy. "So pretty and doing so well. Your ankle will be healed soon. A pretty ankle for a pretty girl."

Delaney stifled the urge to snort. She'd never been so pretty to so many people before becoming a pet.

Brinon returned his attention to the other students. "Reshna is classified in our mukar."

Joennel sighed, but quietly this time and without breaking her singsong encouragements.

"Just as lombowatts and pourpites have similar physical features, Reshna here, a human, has similar features to us. We both have hair, skin, lungs that breathe oxygen from air, mammary glands, and, although we won't know for certain until we can breed her with another human—"

Delaney's head whipped up at that, the throbbing discomfort and burning at her ankle suddenly forgotten.

Joennel jumped back a pace at the sudden movement.

"—I can say with some certainty that Reshna here will develop a placenta to feed her offspring in embryo and likely nurse them with milk after birth, same as a lorok. Does anyone know why this is significant?"

Crickets.

"Come now! Mukar classifications were developed for breeding purposes, to aid our domestication specialists in harvesting animal companions that could produce offspring, thereby providing new breeds without the time and expenses of an exploration mission. The basics of ..."

Brinon droned on, but Delaney couldn't think let alone continue to translate. Even with the bone-deep shock of realizing she would be bred like a brood mare, she couldn't concentrate past the pain any longer. Her ankle was on fire, being incinerated from the inside out. Delaney fisted her hands and struggled against the restraints. They jingled merrily.

Stop. Please, stop!

She bit her tongue against the words, and a whimpering whine escaped instead. She couldn't beg them for mercy—what were third-degree burns compared to having her brain incinerated?—but she couldn't remain quiet for much longer. She *couldn't*, and with Brinon Kore'Onik's careless comment about breeding still grating in her mind, she wasn't sure she wanted to.

Joennel cleared her throat. "She's becoming increasingly upset."

"Should we ask the commander to join us?" Roerik asked.

"Owners only attend appointments if their companion is at risk of dying," Joennel reminded him.

"Well, look at her."

Seriously?

"She's fine," Brinon Kore'Onik assured them. "Joennel, please increase your tidokai and litork nulistorak."

"Yes, Kore'Onik." Joennel took a deep breath, stepped forward, and resumed petting. "Your ankle is nearly healed. You're such a good girl, Reshna. Just a few more seconds, and—"

The burning stopped—completely. No discomfort remained at all: not the lingering twinge of a burn held under cold water, not the original throbbing of her twisted ankle, not even a dull ache.

Delaney slumped in relief on the exam table, her limbs sprawled at awkward angles from the restraints.

In four years and ten months of preparation—language lessons, deportment lessons, history lessons, political and philosophical debates regarding an alien race, in their native alien tongue—Keil had apparently *not* prepared her for everything.

"Is she dead?"

"I told you we should've asked the commander to join us."

"You killed her!

Someone gasped.

"I most assuredly did not!" This from Joennel, who then undermined all her righteous indignation by glancing hesitantly at Brinon Kore'Onik. "Right?"

Delaney closed her eyes. Her leg no longer hurt, but her brain did. It throbbed inside her skull in sync with the pounding of her heart. The mortification of her situation hadn't killed her yet, but she could feel a heart attack or stroke coming on at any moment. Please God, let her have an aneurism and end this nightmare once and for all. She'd die naked and chained on an exam room table, surrounded by a dozen strangers, but at least it would be over. Of all the ways to go, becoming an alien's pet on an ice planet where her owner was the one with fur certainly took the cake.

The thought was amusing, and it wasn't the first time she'd entertained it, but it was the first time the thought made her laugh. Out loud. The chuckle started low but deep and burst in gut-wrenching waves until her abdomen cramped. Her hysteria ended on a pained groan.

"Was that a seizure?"

"*Now* she's dead."

"And you killed her."

Joennel stomped her foot. "I didn't, but I wouldn't mind killing you!"

"Would someone care to take Reshna's pulse?" Brinon Kore'Onik asked, his voice calm and so very patient. "To confirm time of death, of course."

Delaney slit one eye open. Brinon Kore'Onik was fighting a smirk. She closed her eye and sighed to herself. She didn't want to feel. She'd wanted that brain aneurism, damn it.

Two furry fingers tentatively pressed the pulse at the side of her neck.

Delaney opened her eyes.

The student, Roerik, jumped back with a startled squeak and then pumped the air with his fist. "She's alive!"

All the students cheered at this declaration of her resurrection—even Joennel, who might have known better. Brinon Kore'Onik let loose that indulgent smile.

Well, she supposed Lorien did have one thing that Earth most assuredly didn't: people who cared if she died.

"Now, who would like to heal the wound on her arm?"

A dozen clawed hands shot into the air.

Delaney groaned.

SIX

"WHAT DID SHE EAT THIS MORNING?" BRINON KORE'ONIK asked.

Torek forced his face into stoic immobility, one of the first lessons he'd learned while training for the Federation all those many seasons ago. The trick was to not allow one muscle to move, not to tighten, relax, or twitch, except to blink. His facial features naturally sneered even when he smiled, and his scar made him appear angry no matter his mood. He was intimidating when he wasn't trying to intimidate. When he tried, he was terrifying, so he wouldn't look terrified.

He was a strong, confident, well-qualified, and battle-tested commander of the Onik Guard. He'd led men from the safety of their estate in matters of business, and he'd led them in the midst of combat against the *zorel*. He was victorious on all battlefields. Surely, that same lor could care for one small animal companion. People had animal companions all the time. Zana, Lorien keep her soul, had had six animal companions, and even when she was at her worst, all had thrived under her care. Anything that Zana could do, Torek could undoubtedly do better.

Such a thought, even if only unspoken in his mind, was horrid.

50

Zana had been very dear, and he was an ass. He hadn't always been, but lately—

"Torek Lore'Onik Weidnar Kenzo Lesh'Aerai Renaar?"

Torek blinked back from his rambling thoughts. "I fed her this morning, in a manner according to her manual."

"Of that I have no doubt," Brinon said, smiling kindly.

Torek gritted his teeth to prevent his hackles from visibly rising.

"She may have a sensitive stomach, more so than the rest of her breed. She certainly seems extra skittish. Then again, her nerves might have contributed to her becoming ill. It's not unheard of in newly domesticated animal companions before they become accustomed to their new home and surroundings."

Torek glanced at Reshna, who was sitting next to him on the couch. She'd entered the appointment with an injured ankle. Her ankle was now healed, as was the raw scrape on her neck and the cut on her forearm, but something else was obviously paining her. She was a bit of a diva, needing constant comfort and reassurance while refusing to listen half the time, but in this instance, he didn't think her nerves were to blame for her behavior. He'd seen men return home from memorials in better spirits. Brinon Kore'Onik had come highly recommended and was well respected in his field—the best, according to some—but if Reshna could give her opinion, she looked as if she'd contest those assessments.

She met his gaze, her eyes red rimmed and bloodshot. She licked her lips, and then slowly, hesitantly, she leaned her blanket-wrapped body against his side. Her meager weight warmed his hip, and her head, with its mass of springing curls, rested against his shoulder. She immediately tensed, as if regretting the gesture, and peeked up at him shyly through her long, black lashes.

His stoic composure slipped, easing the tension in muscles he preferred to remain tense.

If she didn't die first, she was going to be the death of him.

He raised his hand, just as slowly and hesitantly as she had touched him, and slipped his fingers carefully into her hair to massage her fragile scalp.

She closed her eyes.

Torek returned his attention to Brinon Kore'Onik and forced the menace back into his voice. "Her manual is incomplete or inaccurate."

Brinon's nostrils flared with ill-concealed amusement. "Is that so?"

"Yes. She has an obvious aversion to water—a phobia, perhaps—that wasn't documented."

Brinon's lip twitched but settled wisely into a frown. "How was this phobia discovered?"

"I attempted to wash her last night. It's how she injured herself." He sighed at the ceiling. "One of the ways she injured herself."

"I see."

"She fought me so vehemently to avoid the washroom that she actually cut her arm on my claw."

Brinon nodded. "It's not uncommon for animals to have an aversion to bathing. I suggest introducing her to a pool or fountain. Her manual says that she can swim, so it may just be the prospect of bathing that she rejects, not the water itself."

Torek cleared his throat again, focusing on the softness of Reshna's hair to speak beyond the awkwardness of admitting ignorance. "And the urinating and vomiting? Could her manual be inaccurate about her diet as well? Perhaps—"

"Give her a week to adjust. Remain true to her diet according to her manual, and we'll reevaluate if necessary. But I think her stomach will settle when she does."

Brinon reached out to stroke Reshna's cheek. She didn't pull away, so at first, Torek didn't notice her complete lack of reaction. She wasn't moving at all. She wasn't even breathing.

Torek narrowed his eyes on their interaction. He wasn't certain what he seeing, but whatever it was, it made his stomach churn.

"Until next week, Reshna." Brinon pulled back, faced Torek, and pressed his hand to his heart. Torek nodded, and Brinon walked away, leaving them alone in the waiting room.

Reshna finally inhaled a shaky breath.

Torek leaned over and nuzzled the top of her hairy head. "I don't enjoy doctor visits either," he whispered, and he imagined, even if it was just wishful thinking on his part, that her breathing steadied because of him.

TOREK'S AVERSION TO SHEMARA KORE'ONIK'S OFFICE WAS ridiculous. The walls were painted a pleasant, neutral tan with warm undertones. They displayed tranquil landscapes depicting the simple beauty of Onik: the first sun beaming through ice and creating a rainbow; a *gramble* peeking out from its burrow, flakes of snow clinging to its quivering whiskers; the second sun setting behind the city skyline, bleeding clouds reflected blurrily in the ice moat. The furniture was comfortable, and Shemara Kore'Onik herself was a calm lorok with a gentle soul.

The office's atmosphere was irrelevant; Torek's hackles rose the moment Shemara opened the door to her office. She noticed, and as always, they both ignored the reaction. He was here. She knew he'd rather be anywhere on Lorien, and that, as she always said, counted for something. The fact that he'd rather be back in the *Genai* battle of 5014, facing not one but all seven zorels, than be here wasn't particularly complimentary of Shemara or her pleasantly decorated office, but nothing they talked about in this office was even remotely pleasant.

Shemara clasped her hands to her chest in delight the moment she clapped eyes on Reshna. "You got an animal companion! What a lovely creature. What's her name?" she asked, gesturing them inside.

"Are you surprised by her presence?" Torek stepped through the doorway and into the office.

Shemara didn't need to point out that his answering her question with a question was a defense tactic he used while feeling vulnerable.

They'd already had that discussion. Just because he was aware of his own bad behavior and by default, his vulnerability—gah!—didn't mean he intended to fix it.

"You were the one who recommended I get one. And now, here she is."

Shemara shot him a withering look as she closed the door. "The court needed a reason to hold out hope for your rehabilitation and full recovery."

Torek sat in his usual place. "So you gave them a reason to hope."

Shemara sat across from him. "So I gave them the truth."

"Lorien help us all if the commander of Onik's Guard actually lost his head."

"Is that how you feel? Like you lost your head?"

Torek leaned back in his chair. "We're doing this now? Just jumping in cold today?"

"How would you prefer we jump in?"

Torek cursed under his breath. Shemara would answer his questions with more questions until he actually answered appropriately.

Reshna glanced around the room in a slow circle, then inched toward the couch against the far wall. Her tether pulled taut halfway.

She glanced back, and Torek's nostrils flared. "Nowhere to hide this time, little one. If there was an escape, I'd have found it."

Reshna took in the parameters of the room a second time, exhaled rather loudly, and finally settled herself on the floor next to his chair. She crossed her legs in front of her, ankles tucked under her thighs. She hunched with her elbows on her knees and, after a second hesitant glance at him, leaned her shoulder against his calf.

Torek reached down to pat her head.

When he straightened to face Shemara, she was grinning.

His hackles rose, and he wondered when they'd lowered.

"Looks like you two hit it off."

Torek fought the instinct to move his leg away from Reshna's side. With most of her weight against him, she might topple backward. "Not really." And then grudgingly, because he didn't actually want to be an ass, he added, "Her name is Reshna."

Shemara nodded. "Fitting."

"I thought so too." There, he'd agreed with something. Was he done now?

"I heard that you filed a report against the manager where you purchased Reshna."

"I thought you were surprised by my having Reshna."

"I'd heard of the report you filed, but not of Reshna's purchase."

"You need better spies."

"I do."

Torek stared at her, coldly expressionless, but she'd received this treatment many times before. Unlike the guard under his command, she knew it for the mask it was.

He sighed. "Yes, I filed a report against him."

"Why?"

"He was mistreating an animal companion, and it needed to be reported."

Reshna glanced back at him, her wide gray eyes seeming to consume half her face.

He patted her head.

"Salvarok is the most popular, most well-respected animal companion purveyor in Onik."

"If they take my report seriously, then maybe they'll remain so."

"You are Torek Lore'Onik Weidnar Kenzo Lesh'Aerai Renaar. You know that report will be taken seriously."

Torek smiled again, with fangs this time. "Yes, it will."

Reshna's eyes shifted, bouncing back and forth along with their exchange as if she was not only listening to the cadence of their speech but actually understanding it. Her head was a little too far away for him to continue petting without leaning forward, but her shoulder was in arm's length. He stroked a finger down her neck, careful of his claws, and finding a knot, gently kneaded the muscle. She stiffened, so much so that he nearly pulled back, but it was a large knot and bound to hurt at first touch. He did lean forward then, placed his other hand opposite, and rubbed, keeping her in place until the knot smoothed and she relaxed.

"You think you lost your head?" Shemara pressed.

Torek leaned back but continued rubbing Reshna's shoulder one-handed. "I lost consciousness. What would you call it?"

"Ah." Shemara jotted a note.

Torek's hackles rose again. "'Ah,' what?"

"What about during the attack? Do you think you lost your head then?"

Torek shuffed. "They think I did. And they're worried that if a similar situation occurs, I'll lose my head again."

Reshna's eyes were closed. Her head had lolled to the side, and her entire weight lounged on his calf. He could still do *something* right.

"Does that bother you? That they think that of you?"

Torek shook his head. "They're right about one thing. If another person attacks my estate with lethal force, I'll meet that person with lethal force. I *will* react the same way because I *didn't* lose my head." He cleared his throat. "It's only now, afterward, that I may be losing it."

"You're not losing anything," Shemara reasoned. "We've talked about this. The nightmares, the flashbacks, the depression. They're all natural side effects of—"

"I've killed before. How is experiencing side effects normal? I've never experienced them after my other kills."

"You've never killed a lorok before. And not just any lorok—a civilian. The wife of a fellow Federation service member." She gave him a look. "That's a far cry from your usual kills."

"What I did was terrible, but it was necessary. It's my job—my honor—to protect Onik."

Shemara nodded. "I know that. Your country knows that. But do you know it? Do you really believe it, in your heart, that such a terrible thing was—could ever be—right?"

"I just said I'd do it again, that I *hadn't* lost my head, didn't I?"

Shemara pursed her lips in thought. "Then maybe that's the problem. You feel that what you did was terrible but necessary, and you know that, if necessary, you'd do that terrible thing again."

Torek's hand on Reshna's shoulder stilled. "Is that how I feel?"

"You tell me."

Reshna turned her head to him and whimpered.

He released her shoulder before he broke it and squeezed his mouth instead. He hadn't felt anything in a very long time, but looking into those huge gray eyes, he felt shame, like a swelling tide, rise above his head and choke him.

"Say it."

He released his mouth and stared at Shemara, his mask firmly in place, holding much more than just his face together.

"Verbalize how you feel, and we can end this session. I know it's difficult for you to appear weak or uncertain, but that's okay here. It's just you and me. And Reshna now."

Reshna turned her head to him, as if waiting for his answer.

Torek clasped his hands on his lap, lacing his fingers tight enough to hide their shaking. "I'm sure your spies informed you that I skipped my surgical follow-up this morning. Want to drill me about that next?"

SEVEN

As LUCK—OR, MORE LIKELY, VERY PRECISE PLANNING—WOULD have it, her owner did have his surgical follow-up. He'd rescheduled it directly following his session with Shemara Kore'Onik. At the top of the hour, and not a second too soon, it seemed, he bit off a courteous if curt farewell to his psychologist—what else could a medical specialist of "mind and behavior" be?—and led Delaney down the hall and up two floors. According to the hologram floating outside the door, they'd arrived at the office of Loganak Kore'Onik Renaar, *orboas*: medical specialist of the eyes.

Considering that Lorien wasn't even in the same galaxy as Earth, one would think that human and lor cultures would be entirely different. In many ways, they were, but health care wasn't one of them. Torek greeted a receptionist, pressed his thumb pad to a digital screen in lieu of signing in, and sat in a large communal waiting room. Eventually, the receptionist called his absurdly long, prestigious name and led them back to wait another half hour in a smaller, private exam room.

Torek sat on a chair against the wall instead of on the examination table, which, Delaney noted, did not have restraints. She turned away and sat next to Torek.

He startled, whipping his head at her with a sharp laugh.

Damn, it probably would have been more animallike to sit on the floor again, despite the chapter in her manual that justified the use of chairs for joint health. But maybe he hadn't read that chapter yet. Having sat uncomfortably through his previous appointment, the last thing Delaney wanted was to spend another hour cross-legged on the floor. Well, almost the last thing: she didn't want to be discovered for a fraud and executed either.

She tensed to move to the floor just as Torek lifted his hand and slipped his fingers through her hair.

She hesitated, but his attention wandered, his hand massaging her scalp absentmindedly. She settled back into the chair and tried not to feel grateful.

Some several minutes later—surprise, surprise, there was no mechanism to measure time in this room—a lor, presumably Loganak Kore'Onik Renaar, entered and saluted Torek like everyone else did, by touching his fingertips to his heart. Torek nodded, and Loganak pulled up a chair. He didn't ask Torek to sit on the table or examine Torek's eyes or begin an assessment of any kind. Instead, Loganak asked about Torek's day.

Then he patted Delaney's head and asked after her health, her name, her breed, her age, her behavior, her eating habits—her bowel movements, even. He gave his regards to Torek's men, and asked after Torek's family—a social blunder, somehow, because Torek stiffened and gave a one-word answer so growly as to be nearly indecipherable. But within the next few moments, as the conversation continued, Torek inquired about Loganak's family without inciting a visceral response. Delaney added "family" next to "her diet" and "killing his coworker's wife" on the growing list of subjects that Torek was apparently sensitive to discussing.

This visit seemed friendlier than Torek's visit with Shemara Kore'Onik. The fact that they shared a last name might account for

MELODY JOHNSON

their rapport. Loganak and Torek weren't necessarily related; the last name on Lorien wasn't a family name but rather the place a person was born. Or maybe the place where the oldest living male relative had been born. Something about the place of parentage and birth.

Delaney tried to keep her expression neutral as she cringed inwardly. She'd been without Keil and his classes for so long that she was losing the very skills he'd tried to ingrain in her, everything she needed to survive. He'd warned her that the mind as well as the body withered in captivity, and he was right: it was difficult to care about the finer points of lorienok culture while languishing in a cage.

She did, however, clearly recall the naming convention for military ranks, which Keil had relentlessly drilled her on. According to the rest of Torek's name—Lore'Onik Weidnar Kenzo Lesh'Aerai—he was the military commander of three cities and the estate owner—or, for lack of a better word, the laird—of a fourth. And here she was, a former fry cook turned animal companion to such an important man. Nice to know she'd done Bubba Burger proud.

"Its color hasn't returned," Loganak commented.

Delaney refocused on their conversation, wondering if she'd misheard or misunderstood. A *color* hadn't returned?

Torek pushed a burst of air through his muzzle. "I'm not worried about its color."

"But it should have returned by now." Loganak stood and retrieved a medical device on the rack behind him. "I prefer when things happen as they should."

"I never expected to regain my sight, let alone my eye's original color. Given the choice between the two, I'll take the sight."

"It wasn't an either/or *nusarai*." Loganak gestured toward the examination table.

Torek shuffed again but stood. He turned toward Delaney, his hand raised as he walked to the table. "Stay." And then he sat. "Good girl."

Loganak blinked at her. "You said this is only your second day with her?"

"First full day, really."

"And she already knows and listens to your commands?"

Delaney tried not to cringe. Maybe she should practice disobedience.

"She's highly intelligent. And observant. Do you know any other animal companion that could master the use of door levers, locks, and proximity sensors simply by watching their use? And without reward training?"

Loganak shook his head. "She's remarkable."

"She's something," Torek grumbled. "Can I be honest with you about her for a moment?"

Loganak dropped the device to his side. "Of course."

"If Shemara Kore'Onik caught wind of this, I'd lose my command for certain."

Delaney tensed. She eyed the walls, the exam table, the longer tuft of hair at Torek's elbow, anything to appear as if she wasn't hanging on their every word. *Breathe,* she reminded herself.

"You're not losing anything," Loganak said. "And besides, Shemara has your back."

The nostril tips on either side of Torek's muzzle flared as he shuffed. "That lorok wastes an hour of my life every week, torturing me for her own pleasure."

"Torture?"

"Until my sessions with her, I'd never known a question could be twisted so many ways. They sound like different questions, but really, it's just an hour answering the same question over and over again. Torture."

"She suggested your need for an animal companion to save your command, not ruin it."

"I know. That's the problem. Reshna's my last chance to prove I'm well—or can get well—but within the first twenty-four hours in my care, she sprained her ankle, injured her neck, and cut her arm on my claw." He shook his head, looking bewildered at said claw.

Loganak scanned her over. "She seems fine now."

"The responsibility is more like caring for a child than an animal."

"The more exotic breeds are like that. Lorien knows, even zepraks can be a handful sometimes."

"I should have chosen a zeprak," Torek muttered.

"You could have." Loganak shuffed. "You still can. Exchange her."

A chilling numbness swept through Delaney's body. Exchange her, like she was a pair of shoes that didn't fit or a piece of furniture that was too complicated to assemble.

Like she was fifteen again, and back in the system.

Torek shifted his eyes to look at her.

She met his gaze. What would a real pet do? If she loved him on sight and wanted his attention and affection, what would she do?

She stood, walked to his side, and dipped her forehead into his shoulder.

He lifted his hand and rubbed a curl between his finger pads. "Have you ever heard of an animal companion being on sale for more than a few days?"

Loganak shook his head.

"Reshna was there for the majority of Rorak."

"Is that right?"

Torek tweaked the curl so it bounced and quivered. "No one could afford her care. Or at least no one was willing to invest in it."

"You're not the only wealthy lor on this planet. I even know a few who would *enjoy* owning exotic animal companions."

"None were there that I saw."

A slow grin blossomed across Loganak's face. "You think you saved her."

"I know I did."

Loganak cocked his head skeptically. "You said you bought her from Salvarok?"

"You didn't see her. I saved her."

"The broken commander saved an animal companion, and in

doing so, saved himself. You *should* tell all this to Shemara. She'd gorge herself on it."

"If this first day is anything to go by, saving Reshna is not going to save me. She's going to kill me." His fingers' gentle stroking was near hypnotizing on her scalp.

"Hmmm," Loganak murmured noncommittally. He lifted the device in his hand toward Torek's face. "Look up."

"There's nothing wrong with my eye anymore. I was half blind, and now I can see. You're a miracle worker, as far as I'm concerned."

"Lucky for you, I'm still concerned."

Torek shuffed.

"Here in this office, I'm the commander, and you must obey my orders or people die."

"My eye is not a life-or-death situation."

"Should you lose half your sight again, you most assuredly *would* lose your command, with or without Reshna having saved you. Come Genai, how many more people may die without you in command?"

Torek removed his hand from Delaney's hair and looked up.

TOREK'S SCHEDULE, ALREADY IN DISARRAY FROM THE ADDITION of Reshna's appointment, was entirely shot by the time they returned to the Onik estate. Everything—cooking, eating, bathing—took a little longer with Reshna in tow, so he decided to just give it up to Lorien for the night. He would need to incorporate Reshna into his schedule instead of fighting to remain on schedule, but that was a challenge for another day.

Stomach full and body clean—this time without Torek having to resort to brute force—Reshna bedded down in her cot, under the fur covers, still draped in the fur blankets she'd worn all day.

He sighed warily. He still needed to prepare a private room for her with better heating. He still needed to have fur-lined coverings fitted for her, so she didn't need to wear blankets around her shivering body when they left the estate. He still needed to do a lot of things, but he laid himself down instead, ordered the lights off, and closed his eyes, willing his mind to just let it go.

Torek watched Daerana Weidnar exit the lift. In reality, he hadn't known her name. He'd only noted her presence and the fact that a lorok he didn't know had just entered the estate proper. He knew everyone in his command and nearly everyone who lived in Onik. Although visitor approvals didn't go through him personally, he made it his business to know who'd been approved: one, it was rude not to welcome guests, and two, he preferred to know with whom he was sharing a roof. The fact that he hadn't known her—that she wasn't an approved guest—had been the forewarning that had saved Onik's guard. His dream self saw her and knew her name, but still reacted the same as his real self.

He stepped off the dais, circled around the back hallway, and unstrapped his Federation-issued RG-800.

It was certainly possible that a visitor had accidentally arrived a day early. Dorai Nikiok may have made special provisions for a guest without consulting him or his administration. It was also certainly possible that this someone was unexpected.

Onik's estate didn't do unexpected.

He quickened his steps around the perimeter, looping back to the surveillance hall, and looked out the wall of windows to the courtyard below. The same in his dream as in reality, red streaks stained the snow. He couldn't be sure what they were from this distance, but as he eased around the corner of the hallway to spy on the monitoring stations, he was more than close enough to recognize the red spattered on Daerana Weidnar's fur as blood. She lifted her weapon and aimed between Dorai Nikiok's wide, stricken eyes.

Torek aimed his own weapon and squeezed the trigger.

Tonight, like every night, his dream deviated from reality. His weapon locked. His dream self squeezed the trigger again and again, and as his weapon failed to fire, Daerana Weidnar slaughtered every-one, painting the surveillance hall a bright, shining red.

Torek tore his gaze from the carnage to glare down at his weapon.

His hands were matted with blood.

TOREK'S EYES WRENCHED OPEN TO PITCH BLACKNESS.

"Lights on," he croaked.

The beams clicked and then brightened, illuminating the room in a sudden wash of light.

He wasn't blind anymore. He wasn't dreaming anymore. He wasn't killing anyone anymore.

Torek closed his eyes, then opened them and closed them again, just to prove that he could exist inside himself and still breathe. He lay on his back, stared at the vaulted ceiling overhead, and focused on that breath—in and out, rapid and harsh and grating on his raw throat. Rak, he must have been screaming again.

In and out, he focused on the air passing through his lungs, inhaling and holding it, expelling it and inhaling again over and over, slower and more controlled with each repetition until it didn't feel like every stone of Onik's estate was crushing his chest.

Something shifted in the room to his left.

He clenched his fist, cocked his arm, and turned toward the movement.

Reshna's head, visible only from the nose up, was peeking over the bedcover.

Torek let his fist relax. The remaining pressure constricting his chest eased.

She blinked.

He hesitated, but those eyes—so large and gray and seeming to see so much more than his physical self, seeming to pierce the weary tatters of his soul—stared at him. He was overcome. He patted the bedcover.

She hesitated. Her fear was almost a tangible thing, thick and cloying.

"Did I scare you, little one? I'm so sorry. I was scared too." He patted the bed again. "Up. Up. I won't tell if you won't."

Her head lifted, revealing her mouth, chin, and neck. She placed one small, bare hand on the bedding.

"Yes, come up," he encouraged, still patting.

She crept to her feet and then onto the bed. She lay next to him, her eyes darting around the room several times but refocusing back to him between each uncertain glance. She reminded him of a pinned insect on display. Something unwillingly being examined.

Maybe the lights were too bright.

Torek snorted to himself. Obviously, the lights were too bright—she'd been wakened from a dead sleep in the middle of the night by one of his fits.

"Lights dim."

The light receded to a low glow. Torek reached between them with a slow, unsteady hand and stroked the tender underside of her forearm.

She relaxed in increments. The tension around her pinched lips eased. Her strained shoulders melted into the cushions. Her arms became pliant, her head rested more deeply into the pillow, and her eyes drooped and eventually drifted shut.

"Good girl, Reshna." He slid his fingers down to rest against the smooth curve of her stomach. "Maybe miracles can happen. Maybe we can find courage together."

EIGHT

Torek didn't know why Neyra Aerai was putting him on edge. The tailor came highly recommended by his mother-in-law. She was gushing over Reshna affectionately—her hair, her eyes, her little mouth, her pert little nose, her skinny little fingers, her little everything—and she deferred to Torek with what should have been a pleasing amount of respect while still giving professional and helpful recommendations. Nothing about her attitude should set his teeth to grinding or his hackles to rising. But it was, and he couldn't seem to shake it.

Maybe this was residual restlessness from last night's episode. He'd suffered that same nightmare every night for nearly half of Rorak, but for the first time, he hadn't been alone. And how had he repaid Reshna's offer of comfort? He'd been moments away from punching her before his thoughts had cleared. Torek closed his eyes and rubbed the bridge of his muzzle.

He hadn't punched her. He'd kept his head. He wasn't losing it.

"No more blankets for you, Reshna. You'll have clothes of your own soon. How do you feel about that, hmmm?" Neyra adjusted the tape and measured her from inner thigh to heel. "She'll need boots too?"

No, I intend to give her mine. Torek opened his eyes and forced a smile. "Yes, thank you."

Maybe it was the shop. If the lorok was as proficient in her trade as Mairok claimed, shouldn't she have sufficient funds to rent a larger space for her establishment?

Torek swiped a hand down his face. He was being uncharitable. He turned at the end of the room—when had he begun pacing?—and his shoulders were just wide enough to jam between the narrow row of sample fabrics. The stack wobbled precariously.

Neyra paused in her measuring to glance up.

Torek's face heated behind his fur. "My apologies."

She smiled and returned to her tape. How many measurements did one need to create protective coverings for one animal companion? Reshna only had four limbs, a neck, a chest, a waist, and hips: eight measurements. That couldn't possibly take more than five minutes. But here they were a half hour later, having discussed styles and quantities, and Lorien knew what he'd agreed to in an attempt to speed this meeting.

His *daami* buzzed again, vibrating his wrist for the third time in as many minutes.

Rak, they were running late.

Five strides, and he reached the other end of the shop. When he turned back, Neyra was measuring Reshna's foot.

Next, she'd be measuring each toe. Torek rubbed the bridge of his muzzle again, but not fast enough this time. The vein in his temple throbbed viciously.

Someone laughed, sharp and guttural, almost pained.

Torek snapped his eyes open.

Neyra was tickling the bottom of Reshna's left foot.

He blinked. Reshna could laugh.

Of course, the reaction was probably just an involuntary response to physical stimuli, but still. Torek was transfixed for a moment.

68

Reshna was so often cold and shivering and shy. But she could laugh. She just hadn't much in his care.

He sighed. If it meant that Reshna laughed, maybe upending his schedule wasn't quite the catastrophe it felt like.

He supposed he could add tickling to his to-dos for her, between tonight's training and washing. And he still needed to hire someone to build an addition onto his living quarters for her private chamber. He swiped a hand down his face, stretching the skin taut. His skull was splitting apart at the seams. Even the best contractor couldn't build something from nothing, and finding an entire room within the current footprint of his apartment would be impossible. Then he'd need to heat it.

He pressed his finger pads over his eyelids until stars burst across his vision. Just thinking about living in such heat was making his fur damp.

Maybe he could requisition his neighbor's living quarters and insulate that apartment for her. But evicting a fellow officer seemed excessive for one animal companion. He'd own two entire living quarters for his private use, one exclusively for Reshna. As if he wasn't infamous enough. Then again, he had four titles to his name. He was already known for property excess. What was one extra apartment, really?

Maybe he could expand his walk-in closet for her. He'd need to buy a new bureau to store his clothes and reread her manual's chapter on living quarters to ensure that she could get by in such a small space. It wasn't *that* small. Surely, she could make do. But he didn't want her to just get by or make do. He wanted her to thrive.

Maybe he could—

Reshna's squeals cut short.

Torek glanced up, and his RG-800 was aimed between Neyra's eyes before he'd even realized it was cradled in his hand.

Neyra had a knife poised against Reshna's throat.

She cut a flapping care tag from the blanket around Reshna's neck. "That'll be more comfortable now, won't it? Yes, it will, baby."

Neyra pitched the excised tag, set down the knife, and ruffled Reshna's head hair with both hands.

Torek holstered his weapon, shaking. He'd nearly murdered a tailor for trimming a care tag. By Lorien's horn, he was a public safety hazard.

His throat tightened. His breath shortened. His chest ached, and suddenly, he was seeing Daerana Weidnar's face instead of the cramped rows of fabric racks. Her beautiful face: she'd had one, and then he'd pulled the trigger. The same trigger he'd nearly just pulled on Neyra.

His heart seized. His vision darkened.

Not now. Not in public. Not again.

A FABRIC RACK CRASHED TO THE FLOOR, PHYSICALLY SHAKING the entire shop. Delaney and Neyra flinched in simultaneous surprise—who knew that fabric samples were so heavy?—and then gasped together as if choreographed. The fabric might be heavy, but by far, Torek's limp body was heavier.

He'd collapsed and must have attempted to steady himself on the fabric rack, because half the rack was crushed under his body. The other half buried him beneath a pile of fabrics and furs. They swelled and fluttered as he panted, like he'd run for miles. Except that Torek could carry 130 pounds on his hip one-handed without coming close to losing his breath.

"Commander?" Neyra squeaked.

His head jerked up and out of the fabric pile. His gaze was wild and darting from fabric rack to ceiling to floor and back to fabric rack. Delaney didn't know what he was seeing, but it wasn't rolls of furs and pattern templates. And by the terrified look widening his eyes, she didn't want to know.

The seed of suspicion that his session with Shemara Kore'Onik had planted sprouted into certainty. Why else would a man like Torek, so young and strong, have so many doctors' appointments?

Why else would he need an animal companion? He certainly didn't seem to *want* one.

Delaney dropped to her hands and knees so she'd be on his level instead of hovering over him when she approached. And despite the nerves screaming at her to do the opposite, she crawled to him.

What am I doing? I'm not really a pet. And if I was, it's not as if I'm a trained companion animal to deal with his issues. I'm an unqualified nobody from the backwoods of nowhere north Georgia.

But she was here now, on Lorien, and no matter what she wasn't, she was his animal companion.

What did an animal companion do when her owner was having a panic attack?

Delaney reached under the fabric and rubbed his back.

Torek whipped his head toward her. The pointed tip of his ram horn sliced the air in front of her face, missing her cheek by inches.

She froze under the steel of his dual-colored gaze, her heart pounding.

He didn't move either, except to suck ragged gasps of air through his bared, clenched teeth.

She exhaled. Slow inhale. Her heart calmed enough that she could feel his beating through his jacket, as frantic as a humming-bird's. Jesus.

She resumed petting him in slow, small circles. A minute ticked by. Incrementally, the tension in his muscles loosened: his braced shoulders sagged, his hands unfisted, his jaw relaxed. He lifted a trembling arm and combed his fingers through her hair. Delaney flinched at the rough contact, but his claws, once against her skull, were gentle. She leaned in closer, and when his body remained relaxed and his touch remained tender, she pressed her cheek to his.

She tried to mimic the comforting, rumbling purr of a viurr, but mostly, she just sounded congested. So she switched to a low hum instead and the first tune that came to mind: *Amazing Grace, how sweet the sound. That saved a wretch like me.*

Delaney had a better chance of carrying Torek's two hundred

plus pounds up a mountain than she did of carrying a tune, but comfort didn't come from perfect pitch. His breathing evened. His heart slowed to a healthy rhythm, and eventually, when she eased back to check his face, his eyes had lost their edge of panic.

His gaze cut away from Delaney to the reality of his surroundings. His mouth pinched grimly.

Delaney glanced over her shoulder. Neyra was still there. Still gaping.

"Good girl, Reshna," he murmured.

He stood, avoiding the fabric racks even though he clearly needed something to steady himself. He swayed dangerously, just once, and then reclenched his fists, steeled his jaw, and cleared his throat. The swaying stilled.

"My apologies."

"Of course, Commander. I'm so sorry." Neyra gushed. "Was it the fabric?"

Delaney stared. Yes, the fabric had obviously jumped from its roll and tackled Torek to the floor.

Torek stared Neyra down with the dual ice and velvet of his unnerving gaze. Not one muscle in his face moved except to blink.

"I'll submit your order immediately and begin work on Reshna's wardrobe. Again, I'm so sorry. I don't know what—"

Torek nodded, the sharp movement cutting Neyra off as effectively as if he'd sliced out her tongue. He pivoted on his heel and hustled Delaney from the shop.

The stoic expression tightening his face was unyielding, but the hand at her back, propelling her from the shop, still trembled.

"Stay. Staaaaay."

Delaney lost the battle against rolling her eyes just as Torek eased away from her, both his palms raised. He'd had a rough night followed by an embarrassing morning, so she'd tolerated his lessons all afternoon in good humor, but she was nearing the limit of her patience. He'd "taught" her *sit* and *come* already, and God help her, if she had to choke down one more treat—

"Good girl!" Torek squeezed his clicker—the trick was complete! —rubbed her head vigorously, and as she was grimacing against his rough handling, popped another treat in her mouth.

The treat was savory and light—her favorite, according to her manual (thank you, Keil)—and the first five had been a tasty lunch. The second set of five had been tolerable, but now, two hours and dozens of treats later, she might very well vomit.

Saliva flooded her mouth. Maybe when he wasn't looking, she could spit and hide it under the bed.

"All right, Reshna. Now, let's put this all together."

Would this training session never end?

"Sit."

She dropped to the floor and crossed her legs.

"Staaay." Torek drew out the word as he backstepped, his stride proud and confident this time. He stopped and stood on the other side of the room. The metallic heels of his boots clinked together. "Come!"

The treat still sitting on her tongue had begun to dissolve. She struggled not to gag.

"Come, Reshna!"

God help her, she couldn't bring herself to move.

"You want the treat, don't you?" He waved said treat tauntingly. "Come!"

She stared at him with sudden, simple realization. No, she didn't want the treat, and she wouldn't get it if she didn't listen.

She was so elated, she nearly broke character and laughed out loud. She'd been ignoring people her entire life: her foster parents, social workers, therapists, teachers—everyone who thought they knew best, having never lived her life. She was an expert at doing the opposite of what she'd been told to do. And now the very stubbornness that had damned her time and time again would save her.

"Come!"

Delaney continued sitting, and, for extra effect, let her gaze wander around the room, as if the blank wall was somehow fascinating.

Torek's hand dropped back to his side. He placed the treat into the pouch at his hip and stroked his long, pointed beard as he considered her. His stare was confused, not angry, so Delaney wasn't prepared for his sudden lunge.

She fell back, inadvertently inhaling the sludgy remains of the treat still on her tongue.

His hand rose and crossed his chest, chin high. It didn't matter that she was on an alien planet, interacting with a fur man who only spoke in growled consonants and guttural vowels. She knew his body language as fluently as she knew English: he was going to backhand the disobedience out of her.

She lifted her forearms up to protect her face and braced herself for the impact of his knuckles. The knuckles were always the worst, but if they struck her shoulder or back, they wouldn't break skin. She would bruise like ripe fruit and be tender for days, but that was better than a bloody nose. She curled in tighter.

The room was silent. Torek's knuckles didn't strike. Her tensed muscles began to shake, and eventually, her lungs heaved. She'd been holding her breath.

She blew out slowly, terrified somehow of breaking the silence. She breathed in, just as slowly. Just as silent.

Still no knuckles.

She shifted her head an inch, just enough so that one eye could see over the shield of her arms.

Torek was staring at her, his hand no longer raised. He was calm, actually, and Delaney realized upon reflection that he had never not been calm. He'd been about to strike her, of that she was certain, but not in anger.

Being the unwavering focus of his regard was unnerving, but Delaney's nerves had been tempered by the knuckles of many men. She slowly uncurled herself, sat upright on the floor, and waited.

The scar that bisected his right brow, eyelid, and upper cheek was thick, pink, and raised. It might have been more prominent on a human face because his fur helped to blend its edges, but the icy blue of his iris, in contrast to his other eye and all that brown fur, was spellbinding—the flame that drew a moth to its unwitting death. Delaney was frightened, but considering the pure terror she'd experienced in other facets of her life, not all of them on Lorien, she wasn't as frightened as she should have been. A sharp look, no matter how penetrating—and Torek's look was soul-deep—was nothing compared to the physical act of actual, unwanted penetration.

She met his gaze, both the doe brown and icy blue equally, and tried not to shiver.

Torek narrowed those eyes and leaned forward slightly. He was back to stroking his long chin hair. A moment later, he broke eye contact. He retreated and waved his hand over the digital edition of her care manual on his bedside table. The device lit up, he pressed his thumb pad to the screen, and the projection of her manual sprang into the air before him. He swiped his hand through the projection, flipping to the back of the book, and ran the pointy claw on the tip of his forefinger down a column in the index.

His finger paused midair.

Delaney tried to read the word he was pointing at, but the projection was reversed for her. Before she could wrestle through the symbols backward, he'd already swiped to a different page. She swallowed her frustration before he noticed, not that he was paying attention to her anymore. His eyes shifted left to right, left to right as he read.

His eyes stilled. The slash of his mouth flattened. He glanced aside to her, then back to the page projection and aside once more to settle on Delaney. He let loose a short puff of air through his muzzle, less grunt than sigh, and swiped a hand straight through the page. The page stopped projecting but remained displayed on screen.

Torek knelt down and retrieved the leash from where he'd stashed it next to her bedding. "Come on, then, if—"

Delaney stood at the word *come* and walked to him.

He stared at her, and his already thin lips compressed into a wrinkled line.

As he fastened the leash to the loop on her collar, Delaney peered askance at the glowing manual.

Halfway down, she read:

Due to their highly sensitive constitutions, corporal punishment is typically ineffective. Obedience can be easily attained and maintained through positive reinforcement, including but not limited to praise, petting, and treats.

Her stomach churned with the soup of his positive reinforcement. She should have insisted on *always* ineffective.

NINE

I N DELANEY'S EXTENSIVE EXPERIENCE OF TERROR, SUCH A HIGH-octane emotion isn't sustainable over prolonged periods. The mind and body become accustomed to the feeling, so that the circumstances that once seemed terrifying are simply the new normal. Even living as an animal companion to King Sasquatch on an alien ice planet. Especially to King Sasquatch. Delaney was alone in Torek's bed, a circumstance that should have reduced her to a quivering, panicking mess, but after four weeks of being his animal companion, of sharing not only his bed but his days as well, she could wake up not just calm, but downright bored.

Torek was the most monotonous person she'd ever lived with, even considering the nightmares and panic attacks. Granted, that wasn't saying much; the colorful characters she'd previously had the misfortune to live with had set a high bar for drama. But even his books were boring. Delaney shook her head at the title she'd stolen from his nightstand while he was still away doing whatever it was he did every morning: *Mineral Properties and Soil* Something: *Let Your Crops Do the Work.*

Dirt. He was reading a book on dirt.

And now, so was she.

But if anything was more mind-numbing than a book on dirt, it was the sameness of their days. Torek's schedule ran like clockwork. Literally, he set his schedule to a timer on his wrist, and for the past four weeks, that schedule never deviated.

He woke two hours before dawn, used the bathroom for ten minutes, left for one hour and twenty minutes, and returned a stinky, sweaty mess. He bathed, and as the first sun crested the horizon, they ate breakfast in his private dining nook overlooking the city. Which, admittedly, was the perfect place to eat breakfast. The view was breathtaking.

Torek ate a thick, soupy gruel every morning—possibly their version of cream of wheat, assuming Lorien's climate could sustain agriculture like grain—and Delaney enjoyed a rotation of three break-fast meals precisely as outlined in her owner's manual: one egg (*yark*, in Lori) and a piece of toast (*faenil*, whether it was toasted or not) or a bowl of cereal (*gigok*) with chilled milk (*paellek*, pronounced with that hard, growly *k* at the end that Delaney couldn't mimic with her human vocal cords to save her life) or a thicker slice of faenil with what in all honesty she couldn't even pretend was jelly (*por-atter*) smeared on it.

Yarks weren't native to Lorien. They weren't laid by chickens either, but Keil had insisted that they originated from a bird—not say, an elephant—despite their massive size. And the gigok wasn't really cold cereal any more than the faenil was actually bread—definitely produced from some form of meal or corn, though. As much as Delaney tried to pretend that what she was eating was familiar, she was afraid that she'd forgotten what real food tasted like long before ever arriving on Lorien.

She still daydreamed about coffee and cigarettes and Mr. Todd's baked pasta, the only good he'd ever contributed to humanity, even if she couldn't remember its exact taste. She'd loved those things even when she'd hated her life, so they must have been fantastic. Torek treated her better than Mr. Todd, but if only she could go back, she'd take the pasta and run.

Following her manual-approved breakfast, Torek took Delaney on what she'd dubbed his rounds—where he checked in on, spoke to, nodded his approval at, and guided everyone. His on-duty military staff in the circular computer room was the first group honored with his presence. He greeted them, evaluated their needs, listened to their questions, and steered them toward the answers. He stopped to chat with the off-duty military personnel as he passed them as well, never mind that he was supposed to be off duty too, or so she'd assumed from his sessions with Shemara Kore'Onik.

Then on to his kitchen and cleaning staff for an hour, reviewing the week's menu and their supplies, listing any corrective actions, and giving terse but genuine words of appreciation. After their first two visits, Delaney learned to gird her loins at those meetings: one of the assistant chefs took pride in sneaking her food, which would have been welcome if she then didn't have a mouthful of treats when the head chef decided to vigorously rub her belly in a manner that couldn't technically be deemed petting. More a seismic encounter. He'd decidedly not read the "How to Best Pet" chapter of her manual.

Next, a meeting with department leads. Since Torek had already spoken to their staff, he often knew their department better than they did, which would have been embarrassing except that he seemed to know everything.

They ate lunch in his nook, and then Torek dedicated time to her training. Their sessions never lasted as long as that first day—she stopped taking commands long before her gag reflex kicked in—but he was diligent. He was effusive in his praise when she performed well and equally frustrated and baffled when she stopped taking his commands, but he never moved to strike her again. He couldn't seem to reconcile why she regressed toward the end of every session, but it wasn't as if she could enlighten him. So she performed like a well-trained golden retriever until she'd had enough, and then she ignored him. She must have been making some semblance of progress in his estimation, however, because on the third week of rounds, he trusted her enough to forego leashing her. She came, sat, and stayed on command, and, according to Torek and everyone in his castle, she was brilliant.

Following their training session, he'd bundle Delaney in too many and yet not nearly enough blankets, stuff her like a sausage into a waterproof jumpsuit, and off they'd go outside to round on the common folk for the remainder of the afternoon.

How old was Yolanai now? Two kair certainly did go by in a blink. Jornek still hasn't fixed the piping on your plasma heater? Please pass along my condolences to Coralai. Yes, Reshna is a very good girl, aren't you, little one? Say hello to Koreel.

Koreel was another animal companion, a furry rodent the size of a toaster with the intellect and loyalty of a Labrador. She promptly gave Delaney her back and swatted her long, beautiful tail across Delaney's face. Delaney swatted back, dodging the tail, and everyone laughed, proclaiming what good friends they were. This was followed by head pats and more treats, sans the seismic belly rub.

For hours.

His people talked much more than he did. Encouraged by his terse but interested prompts and avid attention, they gushed—in explicit, fascinating detail—every personal problem in their lives. And it was no wonder; by the following week, their problems had either been resolved or would be addressed in a formal hearing Torek referred to as a *bandwey*. Her definition was based solely on the context of their conversations, so a bandwey could be an execution, for all she knew. But considering the townsfolk's excitement upon hearing that they'd been given one, she rather doubted it.

They ate dinner in his nook, watched programs on his teleprojector for an hour before going to bed, and woke two hours later to him growling and thrashing the bedcovers to ribbons. Even his nightmares occurred on schedule! He'd stare at the ceiling, rub her head, her neck, her back, and cuddle until morning. By the second week, she didn't even bother starting on her cot, and sometimes after the cuddling, he'd fall back to sleep too. But not usually.

And they'd repeat that clockwork schedule for eight days.

On the ninth day, instead of doing rounds, Torek took Delaney back to visit their respective doctors—the vet for her and the surgeon and psychologist for him. His appointments seemed nearly as terrible for him as her appointment was for her. Oddly, hers was more tolerable knowing that he was suffering too, and twice as much with his two appointments to her one. Lorienok culture was obsessed with well visits; the same people shared their waiting room week after week. Keil had warned her that newly harvested animal companions and their health were vigilantly monitored for at least two kair, but being told something and actually living it were entirely different concepts. Two kair on Lorien were the equivalent of two and a half years on Earth. A hundred and some more appointments loomed in her future.

Delaney let the boring dirt book fall over her face and groaned.

On appointment days, instead of traveling back to the Onik estate for lunch in his nook, they ate at Grattao between his doctor appointments. Despite there being dozens of other restaurants in Onik, Torek chose Grattao every time. And despite there being a wide variety of food on Grattao's menu, Torek ordered *rainol e lokks*, essentially rice and red beans with sausage, but without technically the rice or the beans. It had that look, if not the flavor. And it didn't actually have the sausage either, but that cylindrical meat did have a kick to it.

Rainol e lokks was the same meal he ate at home the other eight days of the week. And, just like at home, he split everything unevenly and gave Delaney a third of his plate, which was still too much. Considering the unfathomable amount of calories that Torek consumed, it was no wonder he seemed unable to believe the portion sizes outlined in her care manual. She'd already gained five pounds, which Torek seemed to take great pride in.

And then, following their especially eventful day nine, their schedule circled back to day one.

Oh, she missed talking. She missed understanding language so fluently, it didn't need to be translated. She missed driving and doing things on her own without following in someone's shadow. She missed cooking, even if she didn't miss the cleanup, and choosing her own food at restaurants. Choosing to have an evening out instead of staying in: seeing a movie, visiting the beach, shopping. Making her own schedule. Not having a schedule!

The uniformity of their days made reading the book seem less risky than it really was. Had she not been distracted, appeasing her boredom, she wouldn't have lost track of time. She would have visited the bathroom, realized that she had her period, and at least attempted to hide it. Lorok didn't have periods. Their uteri conveniently absorbed their egg and excess lining, keeping everything nice and tidy and concealed on the inside, just like their male counterparts. But instead of taking preventative measures, Delaney was still lounging on his bed, reading, when Torek entered the room.

She froze, her eyes firmly rooted in the page as he stood in the doorway, staring at her.

Fuck.

Golden retrievers didn't know how to read. They didn't want to read because they weren't bored to death by the prospect of living the same life nine days a week every week for the rest of their lives.

What might a golden retriever do with a book?

She tore out a page and popped it into her mouth.

Torek lunged forward and squeezed her chin, forcing her mouth open.

"No, Reshna! Bad girl! Spit that out before you choke!"

He forced a salty, furry finger between her teeth before she could spit and removed the crumpled page from her mouth himself. She gagged.

"Oh no. Not here, you don't." He flung the fur blankets off her, both the bedding and her makeshift clothing, and gripped her bicep. "You've been a—" He stared, his mouth hanging open midsentence.

Delaney looked down at the focus of his shocked gaze and stared herself. She'd forgotten. After the equal parts relief and terror of leaving that cage four weeks ago, the trauma of that first doctor's appointment, and then the distraction of her utter boredom—the silent, stupid abyss of her dismal future—she'd forgotten the relevance of the passing days and finally consuming a nutritious diet: her resulting period.

"It's all right, little one." Torek's tone, clipped and frustrated just a moment before, was now sickly sweet.

He released her arm and gripped her thighs under the knees, one in each hand, to lift and spread her legs wide.

She squeaked, an animal reaction as much as a human one, thank God—and struggled. She slapped at his head and hands and kicked his back with her heels, but she may as well have been struggling against a solid-stone statue for all that he moved.

His eyes scanned each leg from knee to ass, stuttering on the rows of thin, parallel scars high on her inner right thigh. He hesitated even longer on the mess of crisscrossing scars on her left thigh, but eventually, inevitably, his gaze strayed from the scars to focus on the source of her bleeding. He gripped both ankles behind his head with his left hand, kept her knees spread wide with both elbows, and reached to touch her with his right hand.

She bucked, the words she was desperate to scream—*no, stop, please, don't*—trapped behind her clenched teeth. She whined high and loud, struggling with herself as ardently as she struggled against him.

Torek viurred. "Please, little Reshna. Be still. My claws are sharp."

She froze. Sweet Jesus, she hadn't even thought of his claws.

His finger dipped inside her.

She bit her lip. *Not again.*

But it wasn't, not quite. The sick beating of her heart hurt more than the pressure between her thighs. Nothing stabbed or bled. Nothing tore. The pointed tip of his claw grazed as lightly as his finger, just one, probing slowly, carefully, and not deeply.

He is not Kane Todd. He is not Kane Todd. Not everyone is Kane Todd, she reminded herself with every scraping, frantic breath.

His finger withdrew. He froze, staring for several moments at the clotted blood matting his fur.

He released her suddenly, stood, and stumbled from the room.

She gasped in a deep breath. Held it. Exhaled and inhaled again, over and over until she could breathe without sobbing. Rolling onto quaking knees, she stretched across the bedding toward his bedside table to reach for the thin tablet where the hologram version of her manual was stored. He didn't understand what was happening, and since she couldn't tell him herself, her manual would have to speak for her.

She pressed the code she'd watched him use a dozen times every day to access files.

"Access denied."

Shit. She tossed aside the tablet and jammed her fingers through her knotted hair.

Footsteps pounded toward the room from the hallway.

She lunged for the bookshelf, skimming the titles. He hardly ever read from the print edition. Its size wasn't practical, but maybe—ah ha! She snatched the manual from the shelf and paged through it— past the chapters on temperature tolerance, on the necessity of heating and proper protective coverings, on her diet and warnings about her peanut allergy. There! She splayed it open to chapter six, section four on the human reproductive system, and laid it open on his bedside table. Not subtle, but she didn't need subtle at the moment. She needed effective.

She threw herself back onto the bed just as Torek barged into the room, his arms laden with gauze, a bowl, and bottled water. He locked eyes with her, took a deep breath, then shut the door with his elbow. The latch snicked quietly shut behind him.

Delaney flinched, wondering if a real animal companion would be frightened by his erratic behavior. As if she'd be able to hide her fear.

Torek inched forward, slowly now that he was about to pounce again, and Delaney retreated in a cautious crab-walk until her back hit the headboard. He set his supplies on the bedside table next to her manual and crouched beside her.

Look at the book, she willed.

His movements were slow and measured. Instead of lunging to pin her down again, he poured water into the bowl, soaked the gauze, and slowly, so very slowly, reached out with his other hand to pet her hip.

Delaney shuddered as his thumb stroked softly across her side, even though his touch, as always, was gentle and loving. He cared for her, like the owner of a golden retriever would, and if she'd learned anything from watching his daily rounds, besides the dismal abyss of her future boredom, it was that Torek cared a great deal about other people. He made their concerns his concerns, went out of his way to help them and find justice for them. Although he didn't see Delaney as a person, she suspected his care extended to everything under his protection, even his animal companion.

He reached out with the gauze, and she didn't struggle this time when he touched her. The water-soaked gauze was warm and soft. She clenched her teeth and locked her muscles tight, forcing herself to remain motionless. He wedged the gauze between her legs, cleaning the blood from her thighs. He squeezed the excess water and blood into the bowl and wiped again, closer this time. Delaney watched his movements, his careful consideration and gentle touch, and tried to remain in the present, but the past always had a way of being present.

The pain had been horrible, but Kane's hand on the back of her head, forcing her face into the comforter and suffocating her on her own screams, was what she remembered most. That and the pure shock. *This is not happening,* she'd thought over and over again, even as it continued happening. If she could have seen him, maybe she could have braced herself for the stab and slow slice of his knife—a different pain than she'd expected but terrible all the same.

But Torek didn't push. There was no pain, and he didn't force anything. His movements were slow and sure, even if his expression was grim—granted, that was his usual expression—as he dipped, wiped, and squeezed. Dipped, wiped, and squeezed.

Eventually, Torek released the gauze into the bowl, activated his tablet with a wave of his hand, entered the combination, pressed his thumb to the screen—ah-ha!—and opened the digital version of her manual without a passing glance at the open print edition only inches away.

She collapsed back onto the bedding, defeated.

"I know, Reshna. I know," he murmured, stroking her calf.

Delaney rolled her eyes.

Several minutes passed in silence as he read. His hand continued stroking. Delaney continued breathing, and just as she thought her heart wouldn't pound out of her chest and choke her anymore, Torek released her calf. He turned his wrist to face the flat digital screen of his watch, tapped several times, and said, "Clear calendar and schedule an appointment with Brinon Kore'Onik for this morning, four after first sunrise."

Delaney tried not to react. She shouldn't know exactly what he'd just said, but she did. And she couldn't hold it in.

She covered her face with her hands and groaned.

TEN

"The bleeding is normal, and Reshna is perfectly healthy," Brinon Kore'Onik assured Torek. If Brinon resented the early morning addition to his regularly scheduled appointments, he didn't mention it. He'd met them at his office, performed an evaluation, and returned to the waiting room with Reshna in tow without protest, uttered or otherwise.

An advantage, perhaps, of being captain of the guard, but Torek was okay with that.

Brinon handed off her tether. Reshna minced past and tucked herself slightly behind Torek.

"At her age, assuming she isn't breeding, a lack of regular bleeding would be a cause for concern," Brinon added.

Torek frowned. "What's regular? Should she have been bleeding more?"

Reshna made a choked noise in the back of her throat.

Brinon reached to pat her head, and Reshna flinched.

Torek narrowed his eyes on Brinon's hand.

"Read chapter six of her manual. Her breeding cycle is actually quite similar to the lorok menstrual cycle." Brinon straightened, and

Reshna relaxed into Torek's side. "Not surprising, considering we're of the same mukar. But the lorok uterine lining is absorbed back into her body. Reshna's sheds. And her cycle is much faster. You can expect her to bleed several times every season, every twenty-eight days or so for five to seven days."

Torek's gaze startled up to meet Brinon's eyes. "She's fertile every twenty-eight days? Even during Rorak?"

Brinon nodded and reached down for another head rub, but Reshna dodged his touch. Maybe he should research a new physician for her. Even after several visits, the affection was still one-sided.

"She's hale and healthy. Simply change the gauze four times a day. And read chapter six." Brinon got in a couple of pats on her hip. "And maybe feed her less? She's gained a little weight."

Reshna, who was still cringing away from Brinon's touch, actually swiped out at him and made a loud hacking noise.

"If I didn't know better, I'd say I offended her!" Brinon laughed.

"Well, I agree with her, don't I, Reshna?" Torek tousled her long head hair, and she settled under his touch. "You look much better now, round with health."

She made another hacking noise.

Brinon shook his head. "Still, a little exercise might be warranted. To build her strength now that her diet has, eh, improved?"

"Well, I've never been one to shirk exercise, have I, Reshna?"

She glanced up at him with those gray eyes, and something warm spread outward from the center of Torek's chest.

He straightened away from her and cleared his throat. "Thank you, Kore'Onik. As always, your expertise is much appreciated."

An hour later, after picking up Reshna's new, fitted fur-lined coverings from Neyra Aerai and enduring a disappointing lunch at the Grattao, as usual—at last, *something* as usual—Torek decided to take Brinon Kore'Onik's advice, to a point, and visit his forefathers at Graevlai with Reshna. The day was already wasted. He might as well make the most of it, and as much as he loved the memorials, he hadn't actually stopped to appreciate them in...by Lorien's horn, he couldn't even remember how long.

Torek's father, his grandfather, and his father before him for a dozen generations had served as captain of the guard to one or several of the Federation's estates. In honor of their lifelong service, they were all buried at Graevlai, a vast public memorial park composed of walkways, bridges, hiking trails, gazebos, and fountains. Throughout were ice sculptures depicting the many lor and lorok who had died in service to Lorien. Torek would one day join their ranks, and as perverse as it seemed to look forward to inhabiting one's final resting place, he was proud of his family. In his blackest moments directly following Daerana Weidnar's death, when he was alone in the dark with his nightmares, the threat of not being buried alongside his fore-fathers in Graevlai had kept the last thread of his sanity from snapping.

He led Reshna through one of the winding trails—more vigorous walking than actual hiking—but after only two hours, she began to wheeze. Her cheeks reddened, her stride limped, and her pace lagged.

Lorien, imbue him with strength and patience if she was still cold while wearing her new coverings and boots.

He eyed her critically and sighed. She wasn't shivering. Perhaps she *could* use a bit more exercise than he'd been giving her. He'd have to consult her manual to determine her physical limitations, but having her along for his morning runs could be fun. They could make a game of it; judging by her wheezing gasps, he'd have to find some way to make it more enjoyable for both of them.

Taking pity on her, he stopped at the next memorial they passed. Reshna collapsed onto a bench, reclined against the backrest with her hands locked behind her head, and continued wheezing.

Torek sat beside her and tousled her curls.

The ice sculpture at this particular memorial was one of his favorites. It depicted Deraenik Lore'Onik Weidnar Renaar, his great-great-great-great-grandfather, charging into the fray atop his *banchai* during the first battle of Genai. The sculpted banchai's wingspan was massive, a to-scale representation of the actual creature, and the artist who had created the memorial deliberately chiseled a prism within the layered feathers of its wings. The first sun winked off the prism and fractured into a dozen rainbows, haloing his forefather's shaggy head and illuminating his fierce features.

Torek wondered, as he always did when gazing upon the oldest of his ancestors, how it must have been before the invention of hover and laser technology, when they actually utilized animals as conveyances and not just as household companions. What would it have been like to have felt the power of such a beast as an extension of himself? To have a relationship with it, to trust it to carry him not just high over the city, but into battle. And, in the case of the late Deraenik Lore'Onik Renaar, into death?

"Torek Lore'Onik Weidnar Kenzo Lesh'Aerai Renaar."

Torek turned at the call of his name. Dorai Nikiok Lore'Lorien was rounding a bend in the trail, jogging at a brisk clip, but slowed as she approached him.

Torek stood and strode forward to meet her. Reshna didn't immediately follow. Her tether pulled taut.

"Reshna, come." He tugged on her collar to give her the hint.

She didn't budge, the lazy diva.

Nikiok bridged the distance between them.

Torek touched his fingertips to his heart. "Dorai Nikiok Lore'Lorien."

She nodded. "Commander. So good to see you outside the estate. You don't leave often."

"My duties at the estate keep me well occupied, as you know."

"As I don't know," she chided. "I believe I mandated your leave until the first of Genai or until Shemara Kore'Onik clears you for duty. Has either of those scenarios come to pass?"

"No, they haven't." Torek spread his arms wide. "And so you find me here."

"Hmmm." Nikiok eyed him critically, but he could tell that her rebuke was half in jest—her gaze was sharp, but the left corner of her mouth twitched.

Nikiok wasn't beautiful in the traditional sense. Her forehead was a bit too pronounced, and her hair was styled unfashionably short—not that his long hair was particularly fashionable—but nevertheless, she was quite striking. She was uncommonly tall for a lorok, slightly taller even than Torek. She was uncommonly muscular. Her eyes were uncommonly pale, and she was uncommonly brash, but then, ruling Lorien was an uncommon task. Was it any wonder an uncommon lorok would take on such responsibility?

"Graevlai is one of my favorite places on Lorien," she commented.

"It's one of my favorites as well. I—" Torek attempted to step forward and was stopped by the pull of Reshna's tether. She still hadn't left the bench.

Torek whipped back to face her. "Reshna! Come!" Torek commanded with another firm tug. "Greet Dorai Nikiok Lore'Lorien."

And there went her eyes again, rolling up to study the sky. At first, he'd thought her not as well behaved as her manual indicated, but after their training sessions, he was starting to think her contrariness more a matter of mood.

Like now. Her eyes looped around to refocus on him. She stared as if considering his command, and then she turned away, deliberately disobeying him.

"I'm not sure that you have the same control of your animal companion that you do of your guard, Commander." Nikiok mused. "I'd love to see her, however. She's the first of a new companion species, isn't she?"

"She is."

Torek turned away from Nikiok and approached Reshna. Since, left to her own devices, she was content to become permanently affixed to the bench, he'd have to carry her. He massaged her scalp to reassure and distract, but, smart little thing that she was, she regarded him warily, not reassured or distracted in the slightest. Bully for her. But when he gathered her in his arms, propping her on his hip to carry her to the Dorai, he realized that she was trembling.

His frustration melted.

"I know you're shy and cold, but we can manage a brief hello, can't we, little one?"

Torek offered her up. Reshna fisted her fingers in his fur and clung to him as she hadn't done since that first bath. Her eyes, so wide that their whites showed all around their beautiful gray irises, stared unblinking directly at Nikiok.

And then her gaze slid past, as if she didn't even see her. Or didn't care to. Her little fingers stayed fisted tight.

Nikiok let loose a soft, soothing viurr, the most gentle thing Torek had ever witnessed from her in all his many seasons of service under her command. He tried to reel in his discomfort and settled for averting his gaze.

"She is a beauty. I can see why you chose her over some of the more common animal companions. Well done, you." She pulled one of Reshna's curls, and the lock bounced and quivered when she released it.

Reshna flinched, nearly ripping free a fistful of his fur.

"She's not very friendly," Nikiok mused.

"As I said, she's shy. But she *is* quite the beauty." Torek leaned in and nuzzled Reshna's cheek, trying to simultaneously warm and comfort her as well as turn her face toward Nikiok. He failed on all fronts. "Aren't you, little one?"

Reshna's trembling increased to near-seizure proportions. She buried her face under Torek's chin.

"She certainly is. And if I may, these fitted coverings are adorable." Nikiok stroked a hand down the back of Reshna's neck.

Something wet soaked across Torek's chest.

"I hope to see more of you outside the estate. Take advantage of your leave, Commander. You've earned it," Nikiok encouraged.

"Yes, Dorai."

"Take care, Commander."

"And you, Dorai."

He waited until she disappeared around the bend in the trail and was out of earshot before prying Reshna from around him. "What is wrong with you? One second you're fine, and the next—"

Her eyes were leaking again. They had completely soaked the fur covering his chest.

Torek shuffed. "Enough adventure for one day, Reshna?"

She blinked those damn eyes at him, once and then a second time, her lashes spiked in the chill afternoon air.

He nodded knowingly. "Enough adventure for a lifetime, I know."

DELANEY COLLAPSED INTO A SNOWBANK, PROTECTED FROM THE cold by her custom-fit, fur-lined, hooded onesie and protected from the hard ground by the snow. She tried to catch her breath. Her lungs were burning. Her legs were jelly. Her sides were cramping. From her cocoon of fur and snow, she watched the first sun rise, its muted glow backlighting a blanket of clouds, and seriously considered the chances—and merits—of death by exercise. Of all the ways to die on an alien ice planet, exercise hadn't been her largest concern. Hypothermia, possibly. Infection from a bacteria her body couldn't defend against, certainly. Murder at the hands of the bitch who had shot Keil, most definitely, especially after yesterday's close encounter. But not exercise. Granted, she'd never been particularly athletic, but she'd never considered running a lethal pastime until now.

This wasn't her first collapse. She'd dropped exhausted into three different snowbanks this morning, so she knew that Torek would circle back when he realized she'd fallen behind. He'd yell. He'd cajole. He'd tell her that she was a sweet, beautiful little diva, prop her back on her blistered feet, and take off again, commanding her to *come*. And she would, because where else did she have to go?

The torture had begun nearly three hours ago. Torek had risen two hours before dawn, as usual, but instead of disappearing for an hour and twenty minutes, he'd dressed her in one of her new fur-lined snowsuits, complete with a *fitted* sheet now—ha!—and dragged her along on what was apparently his early morning routine. He ran.

Mystery solved. No wonder he returned a stinky, sweaty mess every morning. No wonder he was so strong and muscular, his thighs the size of big tree trunks. The true wonder was that he expected her to keep up. The top of her head just reached his chin, she took two strides for each one of his, and he outweighed her by at least 80 pounds, but no, she was a diva for collapsing in a snowbank after two hours of keeping pace with him in an arctic tundra.

As she caught her breath, Delaney's thoughts drifted back to yesterday's hike. She'd thought *that* outing exhausting at the time. Granted, worse than Torek's proclivity toward exercise had been the unexpected company.

Torek knew the woman who had murdered Keil. More than that, he was friendly with her. He'd saluted her. He *served* her. And Delaney had lost her cool. Luckily, Torek just thought her shy, but the woman, Dorai Nikiok Lore'Lorien—commander of the entire planet, if she'd translated her military rank correctly—was more perceptive.

Delaney shuddered.

Several minutes later, Torek still hadn't circled back. Delaney sat up and stood of her own volition. Her thighs were shaking. She locked her knees to remain upright and finally took real stock of her surroundings. The first sun had fully risen. If today had been a normal morning, she'd be enjoying a nice bowl of gigok in the comfort of Torek's dining nook. Maybe pretending to eat another page out of his book on dirt and dressing for rounds.

Instead, she was—well, she didn't know where the hell she was, but she was cold and surrounded by ice and snow and spiny thorn bushes, the closest thing this planet seemed to come to vegetation. Presumably, she was somewhere on the Onik estate, but that was about as helpful as knowing she was somewhere on the planet

Lorien. Her knowledge of local geography was too limited; she had no way of finding Torek or, preferably, escaping back to the castle.

Or just escaping.

Nostalgia choked her as sharp and radiating as a bee sting, and as potentially deadly. Delaney tipped her head back and breathed into the falling snow. The flakes were so thick that the white blanket of fluff high overhead might not even be clouds but the dense blur of cascading snowflakes. They melted on her face at first, then started to chill her cheeks and stick. If she ignored the tundra surrounding her —the ice sculptures and jagged landscape and spiny bushes attempting to pass as plants—and if she kept her gaze filled with snow and sky, she could almost pretend she was back in north Georgia, high up on the Appalachian Trail just outside Hiawassee in deep winter. There was even a section of trail that resembled this one, kind of, with its briars and the serene silence that snow and solitude gives any place.

She'd hiked that trail dozens of times, content in its silent solitude, until that one January morning she'd been alone in the wrong place at the wrong time. Now she was here on Lorien, once again surrounded by snow and silence, but not content at all.

She could escape the remainder of the run if she found her way back to the castle, but there was no permanent solution to her overall captivity. There was no more Hiawassee, no more Appalachian Trail, no more north Georgia in her world. There was no more Earth. She brushed off the snow and slush that had accumulated on her face and took in the tundra surrounding her.

Granted, there were no more burgers to flip, and there was no rent to hustle for either. She snorted to herself. The positives didn't outweigh the negatives, not by a long shot, but this was it. This planet and its furry inhabitants, Torek and his regimented schedule and doting baby coos, and the hovering guillotine of keeping her silence: this was her life. Dwelling on the past merely poisoned the future. No matter how impossible her present circumstances seemed, nothing was more impossible than returning to Earth.

She'd thought she'd come to grips with her circumstances during the five-year space journey to Lorien and that her acceptance had been solidified by witnessing Keil's murder. Funny how quickly a little fresh air and a brief, false taste of freedom could make her long for so much more. She'd been dealt a shit hand, no question, but crying about it didn't change it. She'd have to play it through to the end.

She had three choices: she could try to avoid more running by backtracking to the castle; she could attempt to catch up to Torek by following his trail; or she could stay put in the hope that Torek returned for her again.

Delaney trudged forward in the wake of Torek's footprints. The trail wound up a rocky incline, down into a spiny-bush-filled ravine, and meandered through another grove of ice sculptures. She paused to read one of the plaques—maybe they were directional signs—but they were just names and numbers. A field of statuary with plaques listing names with numbers.

They weren't plaques. They were grave markers.

She was in a cemetery.

Delaney accelerated her pace into a steady jog. Her thighs, screaming and rigidly stiff, were going to kill tomorrow morning. She focused on that pain and found a rhythm in her breathing to push back the panic. The grave markers and ice sculptures eventually transitioned back to wilderness. The air changed slightly, becoming not just cold but damp, and a dull rushing noise swelled in what was once silence. But she ignored her surroundings, keeping her eyes and mind tunneled forward as her aching legs carried her onward.

An indeterminate amount of time passed, long enough that other lorienok were strolling the trail now, flying and walking—not running —their animal companions. They eyed her with surprise and concern, glancing about for her owner. Finding her alone, they proceeded to coax her to approach them. Delaney ignored their calls. She ducked her head, avoided eye contact, and trudged onward until she reached the mouth of a five-way crossroad.

The snow had nearly completely leveled Torek's tracks, so his weren't the only ones anymore. All five trails had tracks now, some fresh, some filled in by the falling snow, but none of them obviously produced by Torek.

Damn it, she should have stayed put.

Her muscles were shaking, not just with overuse, but with cold now too. She was lost. On an alien ice planet. Strangers were staring, and now that she'd stopped, they were starting to converge on her from all sides. She couldn't ask for help because she wasn't supposed to have the intelligence to speak. She didn't want to be a pet. She didn't want to be on this planet. She didn't want this life!

Someone touched her shoulder. The hand was gentle and warm. She looked up, nearly limp with relief. Torek had doubled back. Of course he had, why wouldn't—

The fur, arched ram horns, and muscled build were right, but the face and eyes were all wrong. The face was gentle and concerned, but it wasn't scarred. His hair was cropped short on his head and chin. Both his eyes were brown. His muzzle was more pronounced. He was murmuring something about *poor* and *dear* and *scared*, but his lips were fuller, his voice smoother, and Delaney couldn't help it: her heart rate spiked, and her body recoiled. She spun away and slammed back into someone else.

At least five lorienok had surrounded her. As that first lor murmured sweet nothings to her, another lor reached for her collar. Delaney willed her heart to slow and tried to calm the adrenaline urging her to run. She didn't particularly like how they had bullied around her, but they meant well. They were here to help. Considering Torek's status in Onik, they must know she was his animal companion, and they'd return her to him.

Despite her very logical reasoning, she couldn't quite bring herself to allow them to take hold of her collar. She ducked their grabby hands, and as she spun out of reach, she noticed something metallic glint in the morning sun. A lor was approaching who wasn't murmuring sweet nothings. His expression was intense instead of soothing. His gaze darted from her to the surrounding crowd and back to her, a little panicky himself.

He shouldered through to the front of the crowd and approached her, but something was wrong with his arm. He was holding it immobile at his side and had angled his wrist to tuck whatever he was holding out of sight.

She feigned left and lunged right, avoiding another pair of grasping hands, and spied what that lor was hiding.

A knife.

Delaney lost her battle against panicking. She let loose an ear-splitting scream, and as the surrounding lorienok recoiled in surprise, she leapt from the crowd and tore down one of the paths in a blind sprint.

Her heart beat through her entire body, as if even her fingertips, ears, and scalp were contracting in rhythm. The panic drowned everything: the muscle fatigue, the sharp pain of the icy air in her throat, all thought and reason. Suddenly, none of it existed except for the honed singularity that she needed to escape.

Footsteps pounded behind her. She risked a glance over her shoulder. Shit. The lor holding the knife wasn't chasing her, but three others were, one of them only a few strides away. And behind him, the crowd was staring and pointing. Encouraging.

It wouldn't be enough. Even with the extra speed and strength that panic had lent her, she was still only a small human attempting to outrun a massive Sasquatch. She sensed more than felt him reaching for her—all of them reaching for her—and she lunged into the foliage.

The spines on the bushes were needle sharp. Her onesie protected her arms and legs, but the fabric caught on the thorns, slowing her pace. She twisted and screamed, tearing and raging against the spines. She had to yank free of their grasping hands. She had to escape. Where was Torek? Where was she? *Where the fuck was she?*

Something ripped. The resistance holding her back gave as she threw herself forward. The ground disappeared from beneath her feet, and she pitched ass over head down a ravine.

The sky swapped with the snowy slope in a whirl of soft white, spine bushes, and jagged boulders. Her shoulder cracked on something hard. Her hip hit the ground with a jarring thud that stung both her side and her tongue as her teeth clacked together. Her momentum upended her forward into another somersault, and something stabbed into her rib. She rolled, ricocheted off a boulder, and pain exploded through her knee. Spiny bushes and more boulders blurred past. She clawed at them, trying to slow her fall, but the ground's frozen slick beneath its serene, snowy surface shredded her palms without giving them purchase.

She was midair, falling instead of sliding. Her vision became a kaleidoscope of a thousand magnified glimpses: the edge of a cliff, her trail down the ravine, the lorienok still watching, still chasing, the white slope blending into the white of the sky blurred with the white snowfall.

She landed flat on something level but unforgiving. Her head whipped back. A *crack* split her skull, and all that white winked out into blackness.

ELEVEN

TOREK WAS FINALLY RUNNING. REALLY RUNNING. HIS LEGS ATE the ground beneath him, pounding in rhythm with his breath and racing heart. The straining burn in his muscles was delicious, and he fed off that pain, gorged on it, pushing himself to the edge of exhaustion, driving his legs to move faster, stride longer, lunge harder. He delved deep into that pain, pinched it wide until it bled, and turned it into fuel, rocketing past all walls, all sanity and reason until he was nothing but his heart and legs and pumping arms. Finally!

He slowed when he neared the path's end, chest heaving, but his energy nowhere near depleted. The exhilaration of intense exercise was the only perk to staying in shape for combat and the sole reason he forced himself from bed horrendously early every morning. He glared at the height of the sun and shuffed through his flared nostrils.

It was no longer early morning.

A wave of frustration drowned his endorphin-induced high. He was grossly behind schedule. He should already have eaten breakfast and conferred with his guard. At this very moment, he should be meeting with the household staff. Considering the scant distance he'd managed to run, he may as well have stayed in bed and slept away the morning. At least if he'd done that, he'd be on schedule.

He combed his fingers through the fur on his forehead, and some of the strands stuck upright, slick from his sweat. He needed to double back for Reshna.

Another tide of frustration swelled, but he tamped it down this time. He should have known, considering her size and disposition, that including her on his morning runs wouldn't work. She simply couldn't keep up, and if the heat in her dagger-eyed expression was any indication, she had no desire to. He'd need to carve an extra hour out of his schedule and dedicate it to an exercise regimen appropriate for her. As if he had another hour of time to spare.

He nearly shuffed again, but caught himself and swallowed it this time. She needed to build up her strength and stamina, same as any creature—just not exactly the same as him.

Torek about-faced and doubled back over the path he'd just run, quickly reestablishing a vigorous pace. The entire morning was shot, anyway; he might as well enjoy the tail end of his run, since the beginning had been such a complete waste.

He approached the waterfall, hiked its slope, and had reached the second ridge when he noticed the shape of another lor approaching. The lor—a boy, Torek realized as he drew closer—was sprinting, but where Torek was regimented and focused in his pounding strides, the boy looked desperate. His eyes were wide, his breaths were ragged and gasping. When recognition dawned on his face at the sight of Torek, the boy's body nearly overran his legs. He was obviously shaken.

The boy stumbled to a halt and immediately doubled over. He removed a hand from his knee in an attempt to genuflect and almost collapsed.

Torek took him by the shoulders. "Steady."

"Torek Lore'Onik—" The boy inhaled in a long wheeze. "Weidnar Kenzo Lesh'—" He gasped noisily. "Aerai Renaar."

Torek reeled in his impatience. This was simply not his morning. "Yes?"

"You have a new animal companion." He straightened, still panting. "The newest, yes? Long, bare limbs, wearing custom fur coverings? About shoulder high and hair like an ice drill?"

He tensed his grip on the boy's shoulders. "Yes."

"She looked lost and scared. My father tried to catch her for you, to bring her back to the estate proper, but she ran away. She—" The boy's ears, still too big for his adult body, lowered in distress.

"Is she all right? She listens to commands. She can—"

The boy shook his head. "She took off and fell down the ravine into the Zorelok River."

Torek leaned down into the boy's face. "Into? Did she actually break through the ice and into—"

The boy's ears completely flattened against his head. "I don't know! I didn't see! Everyone said she fell, and then Father was running for her and telling me to run for you and—"

"It's all right. You've done well. You—"

The boy was shaking his head, his eyes wide and frantic as they avoided Torek's face.

Torek shook him. "Look at me!"

He did, his ears quivering against his skull.

Torek reined in his emotions and forced a quiet calm into his voice when he spoke. "I need you to be strong just a little longer. You found me, like you told your father you would. Now, I need you to continue on to find someone else, yes?"

The boy hesitated, his ears still flat, but his eyes were sharp and focused now. He nodded.

"Do you have a daami?"

"Not with me. We were visiting my forefather."

Torek unfastened the strap and buckled his daami to the boy's wrist. "You'll take mine. Run until you're out of Graevlai and have clearance to use it. You don't have far to go. Just down that last ridge and past the waterfall."

The boy stared at his wrist, his ears slowly perking.

"Once you have clearance, contact Brinon Kore'Onik. Tell him what's happened and help him however he requires."

The boy was still staring. The daami chirped a reminder, and the boy blinked.

"That's an order," Torek said, but the boy still didn't look up. Torek shook him by the shoulders again. "Repeat my order. What are you going to do?"

"I—I'm to run out of Graevlai, where I'll have clearance to call Brinon Kore'Onik," he said, whispering Brinon's name with a reverence usually reserved for the Lore'Lorien herself.

Torek swallowed back the urge to growl, but even so, he could still feel his hackles rising. He hoped the boy was so distracted by his task that he didn't notice. "Yes. Now, before you go, where is your father?"

"Up the third ridge then across Viprok d'Orell. That's where she slipped down—"

"Viprok d'Orell?" Torek thundered. "Why would she—"

"She ran! We tried to catch her, but—"

"All right. You did well. Now go!" Torek squeezed his shoulder—in thanks and comfort, but the boy winced—and took off in the opposite direction.

Viprok d'Orell. Had it been too much to expect Reshna to stay put after throwing herself into that fourth snowbank? As if her tantrums weren't enough, delaying his schedule for hours, now she'd taken a stroll down the most dangerous, treacherous terrain in Onik.

She looked lost and scared ... tried to catch her ... but she ran away.

The boy's words echoed in Torek's mind, and his frustration soured in his gut. He sprinted up the second and third ridges, pounding over the terrain as hard and fast as his body could possibly be pushed. But each stride stabbed through his heart: Reshna lost. Reshna running scared. Reshna falling. Reshna broken. Reshna dying.

He'd known this would happen. He'd known the moment the

court had mandated that he obtain an animal companion that both he and the poor animal would be doomed. And he'd been reminded of it again when he'd first glimpsed Reshna and her too-long, high-maintenance hair. And again when he'd begun reading her massive tome of a manual. He'd been consumed with keeping her clean and warm, avoiding all foods seasoned with ukok—which didn't leave much variety in their diet—and attending to her well-being, which always seemed to be on the brink of being unwell. It was only recently, after having integrated Reshna into his schedule and achieved some success with her training, that he'd forgotten the inevitable: that he would kill her. The act of killing was inadvertent, but she would be just as dead—and he just as devastated—all the same.

Any deep emotion is fuel, and Torek used the terror stealing over his mind to drive his body. He finished his sprint over the third ridge, made the sharp turn into Viprok d'Orell, and immediately halted to assess the scene before him.

A line of several dozen lorienok were braced on the near-vertical slope, holding hands in a chain down the ravine. Several more lorienok were using the chain of bodies to painstakingly descend toward the frozen Zorelok River. They were a few people short of the river's edge. Several yards downstream and adjacent to that last lor was a fifteen-foot drop, below which lay the object they were trying so diligently to reach: Reshna.

She was lying on her back atop the ice in the middle of the river. Unmoving. From this distance, he couldn't see much detail. She was shadowed by a mountainous overhang covering half the river, but he recognized her by her new fur-lined coverings and wild hair. Something was different about it, though. Darker. It was wet, and inky tendrils of something red expanded like a halo around her head.

Blood.

The realization was like a focusing lens to his perception. Everything was red: the soaked *tuanok* bush thorns, the spattered snow, a glistening branch, a dripping smear along the side of a boulder, twin tracks leading to the edge of the cliff. At the end of that gory path was

Reshna, soaking in the expanding puddle of her own blood on the splintered ice.

The ice must have fractured from the force of her fall, and the blood, still pouring from her wounds—being pumped by her beating heart, Torek hoped—was dripping into and seeping through those spiderweb cracks. It was possible that they were only surface fractures, that her blood would remain on the ice and not drip into the Zorelok River itself. Even if drops of her blood did seep through to the river below, the zorels might not be sufficiently awake from their hibernation to notice or care.

It was also possible that, even if they weren't awake now, the scent of her blood would bring them out of hibernation.

The waterfall at the mouth of the Zorelok River had been gushing this morning and every morning for the past couple weeks, indicating the end of Rorak. The ice was already melting, enough so that the river was raging beneath it, feeding the falls. It would continue to thin, then completely melt, and Genai would be upon them along with another zorel season.

Torek suppressed the spike in his heart at the thought. As the world turned, there would always be a Genai following the Rorak and another zorel season. Whether it came early or late, it would still come. Minimizing mass casualties when it came, not saving individuals, was his sole concern.

But Genai hadn't quite come yet.

Torek rushed forward to the ladder of lorienok and began the descent down the ravine.

"Commander."

"Commander."

"Commander."

Torek nodded acknowledgment to each one, but not slipping took most of his concentration. He couldn't think of the worst, of someone breaking their hold, of the entire chain of lorienok from that person on—twenty-five, maybe thirty lor and lorok—falling down the slope and pounding into the ice. Reshna and her meager weight had cracked it. They would shatter completely through it. He couldn't think of the loss of not just Reshna but the strangers who had banded together to help her. To help him. They were the civilians he'd risked life and limb to protect for ten Genai, but unlike his guard, they were under no oath to serve him or their country. But here they were, risking life and limb for him in return.

Torek's right boot found a particularly slick patch, already bare from someone else's footfall. His right leg shot out from beneath him, and his left leg, bearing all his weight, followed. He lost his grip on the waist of the lor anchoring him, fell on his side, and started to slide down the ravine. He flung out an arm and hooked his elbow around someone's ankle. The lor gave a pained groan as he strained to keep hold of his neighbor's hand. A chain reaction triggered up the line, groan after groan, each straining to hold the additional weight.

But they were two dozen holding one. They held strong.

Torek glanced down the steep, jagged terrain of the ravine and blew out a shaky breath. Reshna had scraped and lashed and bled her way down the entire treacherous slope. He stared at her for a moment—still on her back, the puddle of blood around her either growing or simply appearing larger the closer he got—and took strength. He had to reach her. These people, Lorien bless them, had given him the means unasked, and he *could* reach her. The boy would contact Brinon Kore'Onik, and Reshna, no matter how broken she was now, would be alive for Brinon to heal her because they'd all acted swiftly. He'd get to her in time, and she'd be fine.

Torek found purchase in a patch of rocky terrain beneath the snow. He climbed carefully up a leg, then gripped a hip and finally a pair of shoulders to pull himself to his feet.

The strain on the chain of lorienok eased as Torek once again supported his own weight.

"Are you all right, Torek Lore'Onik Weidnar Kenzo Lesh—"

"Yes, yes. Just *Commander*, please," Torek interrupted gruffly. "Are you all right?"

"Yes, Commander. It's my honor."

The lorok next to him was gaping. "You just saved Torek Lore'Onik Weidnar Kenzo Lesh'Aerai Renaar's life!"

The lor beamed.

Torek squeezed his shoulder. "And I thank you." He cleared his throat and raised his voice slightly. "I thank all of you."

He continued down the ravine, slower and more cautious of his footing, testing his next step before transferring his weight. The pace was agonizing but steady. Eventually, he reached the river's edge.

The last link in their lorienok chain was a young lor who hadn't grown into his ears yet but was past adolescence, sporting a fully curved set of horns. His eyes widened, revealing the whites all around his brown irises as he took in the fact that Commander Torek himself was before him, and not just before him, but gripping his shoulder.

The young lor glanced at Torek's hand and seemed to puff up, only an inch or two shy of Torek's height. He looked up and met his gaze directly.

"What are your orders, Commander?"

His orders. Had he been with his guard, he'd have ordered a two-kair cadet onto the ice to rescue her. A two-kair had enough experience to pull it off and wasn't so experienced that the Federation would lose an essential leader if he didn't. To a teenage civilian, what were his orders?

"Stay here and be ready." With any luck, readiness wouldn't be needed.

"Stay. Here?" The young lor blinked at him. "You can't be serious."

Torek crouched down on all fours.

The lor grabbed Torek's shoulder. His grip was surprisingly strong. "Commander, no! You can't! To risk losing you when I could—"

Torek glared at the lor and then at his staying hand.

The lorok next to him leaned in. "You dare give Torek Lore'Onik

Weidnar Kenzo Lesh'Aerai Renaar a command? Petreok, you shame me."

The young lor—Petreok, apparently—immediately released his hold, stung. "My apologies, Commander. I meant no disrespect. I didn't think. But you can't—"

Petreok pursed his lips and turned to the lorok. "He can't go on the ice."

The lorok glanced sternly at her son, then at Torek, and opened her mouth. But she froze, the words unspoken. No one here had the power or rank to argue against him, and more importantly, no one would.

Torek flattened himself on his stomach. The ground was hard and cold, but not as cold as the ice was sure to be. He spread his arms and legs as wide as possible to distribute his weight—usually an unneeded precaution in Rorak, but the spiderweb cracks beneath Reshna's body indicated otherwise. And there was no gauging their depth. He pushed off the edge of the ground with the toes of his boots and slid over the ice on his belly to Reshna.

The tension that descended over the ravine could have cut glass.

The shadow of the mountain's overhang shrouded him as he reached her. The ice didn't break. The fractures didn't splinter further. Her blood did seem to have dripped rather deep, but there was no telling if it had reached the running river beneath the solid ice.

By Lorien's horn, could a body lose this much blood and still live? She'd fallen with her entire weight on her back and over her leg, so her knee was angled unnaturally beneath her. Her coverings were wet from the inside out, stained at her knees and punctured at the abdomen, but his greatest concern, the one injury that would supersede the rest if it couldn't be healed, was to her head—the epicenter of all that blood.

Her face was pale, as if all the life had already seeped from her. Her lips were nearly blue, and the skin under her eyes was smudged a dark gray. Torek glanced over her uninjured nose, chin, cheeks parted lips, and forehead, taking in the sight of her smooth, baby-soft skin like a balm, but nothing could ease the ache constricting his chest.

Torek reached out to grip her hand, knowing he couldn't pet her head without hurting her, and stopped short. Her palms were scraped raw. Three of her blunt little claws at the tips of her fingers had ripped off, exposing the torn skin beneath.

He touched the soft curve of her cheek instead, the only place he could see that wasn't bleeding or broken.

She didn't move.

The pressure in his chest crushed the fragile sprouts of hope before they could take root. He balled his fingers into a fist, and the fist trembled.

No. This is not happening, not to me and not to Reshna. Not today.

Torek unbound her coverings and placed his palm on the center of her bare chest. For as pale as she appeared and as chilled as her cheek was, her body was warm. He took a deep breath, trying to calm the frantic thunder of his heart so he could feel hers beating. And he would. It would be strong and steady, and no matter her current injuries—Brinon Kore'Onik could heal nearly anything—she would live. She just needed to be alive now and stay alive until he came.

His heart wouldn't slow. Even the silence of the ravine had a deafening quality, as if everyone's collectively held breath had consumed sound. But as he watched her, he realized something about her face that he'd been too distracted by the sight of her injuries to notice. A small cloud of warm air puffed from her mouth. And then another puff several seconds later. And then another, several seconds after that.

Torek rested his forehead against his extended forearm in weak relief. Reshna was breathing. She was alive. For now, in this moment, Reshna was alive.

Thump.

Torek jerked up sharply. The entire frozen Zorelok River quaked.

He waited, holding his breath, but the spiderweb fractures in the ice didn't crack. Nothing and no one had moved, not on the ravine's slope and not on the ice, but he knew what he'd heard. He recognized what he'd felt. The noise wasn't coming from the ravine or above the ice.

Her blood must have seeped through to the river *beneath* the ice.

Thump.

The ice twitched under his body again. On the ravine, snow jumped up from tuanok bush limbs and fell to the ground. A line of gasps and guttural groans echoed down to him as half the lorienok lost their footing. The chain swayed like a wriggling snake as everyone scrambled for purchase. If the tremors didn't cause an avalanche, the lorienok would.

"Commander?" Petreok asked. "Was that—"

"We're going to keep steady and calm. And move swiftly," Torek interrupted before the young lor could incite panic. Positioned within the valley of the ravine and under the concave curve of the slope overhead, his words reverberated in a slow echo. "Once I'm ashore with Reshna, we climb back up the ravine one at a time from the bottom up, the reverse of how we—"

Thump.

Crack.

Torek whipped his head up, surprised by the height of that second noise. The ice wasn't fracturing under him. He wasn't at risk of falling through, but—he squinted at the mountainous overhang shadowing half the river—Rak! A thick fall of snow was about to crush him.

He found some traction with the toes of his boots, gripped Reshna's arm, and slung her body in an arc over the ice. She slid across the river to shore at Petreok's feet. Torek's right boot slipped as he released her, and he slid in the opposite direction, completely beneath the overhang.

"Commander-der-der!"

BEYOND THE NEXT STAR

"Take Reshna. Lead everyone off the ravine. That's a command. Go! Now!"

A solid wall of snow pummeled him flat, smashing his face into the ice and crushing the breath from his lungs as it buried him. Its weight was incredible. He tried to breathe, but the air was thick and spiked. He waited for the ice to finally give, for his body to plunge into the river and come face-to-face with the zorel in its natural habitat for once. The zorel would have to race the cold and current to take credit for his death.

He waited, but the ice didn't give. He tried to inhale air where there was only snow. The silence was more than just the absence of noise. It was the devouring of noise. The devouring of light, scent, and warmth. And the taste of blood.

TWELVE

Delaney jolted awake to the horrible, consuming sensation of being burned. Her left knee, the right side of her stomach, the palms of her hands, and several of her fingertips were on fire. She tried to remember where she was, why she was burning, how she had slept through whatever was happening, but her mind was sluggish. The fragments of memory that she did have were of being cold and slipping down a slope of ice and snow. Which only made the fire more confusing.

She tried to jerk away from the heat and couldn't, not because she was restrained—although she was fairly certain that the pressure around her ankles and wrists *was* restraints—but rather because no matter how hard her mind strained to control her body, she couldn't move.

"Her heart rate is climbing." A high feminine voice growled and hacked in a stilted, harsh language that wasn't English. Delaney recognized both the language and the voice, but she couldn't quite place how she knew either.

The apprehension constricting her throat didn't make any sense. She hadn't experienced such a terrible soul-crushing weight in years, not since living in the Todd household. Had she?

"Should we give her something more for the pain? A nerve blocker?" That same girl. That same language.

"What do you think, Joennel? What is your recommended course of treatment?"

Joennel. The name was vaguely familiar, and that new voice even more so. Its cadence somehow made her feel both at ease and wary. How could she experience such opposite feelings in reaction to the same person?

She tried to struggle against the restraints. She tried to scream and thrash against the flames. She tried to curse them, whoever they were, and fate and God, but she should have known better. He'd turned a blind eye to her pain years ago.

A weak, nearly imperceptible moan emerged from her throat, the only outward evidence of her inner battle.

"She needs the nerve blocker now." The girl's voice was certain this time.

"You don't know that!" A third voice. Its timbre had a man's depth and gravel, but his tone was panicked, giving his words a whiney quality that sounded distinctly immature.

"I do too!" The girl.

"Just because she moaned doesn't mean—"

"Actually, it does. She's finally cognizant enough to not only feel pain but express it. Her brain function is completely restored. See? So, she is probably experiencing the full agony of healing without being able to express it."

"Very good. You're correct, Joennel. Please prepare a dose."

"Of course, she's correct," the boy—he was definitely a boy— muttered. And then more clearly, "Can I administer it?"

A pause. "Where would you administer it?"

Silence.

Jesus Christ, give me the nerve blocker already!

"No, Joennel, give Roerik a chance."

Someone was tapping something, thinking, as Delaney bore her agony.

"Her neck?"

A sigh. "Joennel?"

"The inside of her elbow."

"Correct."

"As if that's a surprise."

Something stung the inside of her right elbow, and nearly immediately, her heart tripped on itself and then slowed. Her lips started to tingle. Her body somersaulted, and her head floated away from it all. She could technically still feel the pain of her burning hands and knee and wherever else, but she simply didn't care. How could she when her head wasn't even attached to her body anymore? Like a released helium balloon, her mind drifted high and away, leaving the people still growling and hacking through their stilted conversation over her body, where they belonged.

Delaney drifted back to herself some time later. The room smelled different now, or rather, she actually noticed its scent, since she wasn't being consumed by flames anymore: sandalwood and spiced vanilla.

She inhaled the scent on a deep sigh and snuggled deeper into the fur blankets around her. She could move. She wasn't restrained. She wasn't burning. She wasn't freezing.

A good day.

"Go. Now!"

Delaney's eyes sprang open. She was nestled in the furs of her pallet beside Torek's bed, which was strange enough considering she hadn't slept through the night in her own bed since that first night. What was even stranger was that full-on midday light was pouring through the window. Had Torek added "nap time" to their schedule? Unlikely.

Strangest of all was the man standing at the foot of Torek's bed. He was staring and blinking at the bed with a pained expression. If

Delaney didn't know better, she'd think he was about to burst into tears.

"Commander, please. See reason. You weren't this sick last night. You had a simple *fepherok,* and now—" He shook his head, perplexed. "Geraevon Kore'Onik charged me with your care. I beg you. Let me care for you."

"Keep calm."

Lying prone on the floor, Delaney couldn't see over the sideboard to the raised mattress. Torek was just a disembodied voice. He must be on the bed.

Torek still in bed. At midday.

"I'll calm when you take some broth," the man pleaded. "You're not well, Commander. You must—"

"Move swiftly! Take Reshna and go!" Torek thundered.

The man cringed. "She shouldn't be moved either. Please, you both need rest, and above all else, you need to eat."

"That's a command."

The man's expression crumpled. "Yes, Commander."

He stepped toward Delaney.

"Go! Now!"

The tears did fall then. Big drops the size of quarters rolled from his eyes and soaked into the fur of his cheeks. He placed the broth on the bedside table, touched his hand to his heart, and left the room.

Delaney turned to stare at the bed, but it was useless. She didn't have X-ray vision. She'd need to stand to see him.

"Take Reshna. Lead everyone off the ravine. That's a command. Go! Now!"

She glanced at the door, then back to the bed, confused. What did he mean, lead everyone off the ravine? And besides which, who was he talking to? The man was still gone.

Her stomach clenched tight with dread as memories began to filter fuzzily through her mind. The morning of the endless run. Falling in snowbank after snowbank and lagging behind. Getting lost.

Running from the lor with the knife, and the lorienok chasing her. And finally, tumbling headfirst down a mountain.

She shuddered. Everything else from that moment forward was just impressions: being cold, shouting, a softness against her cheek. And then being burned by Joennel and Roerik.

She frowned, struggling to make sense of everything. Joennel and Roerik wouldn't burn her, not intentionally, and as much as she disliked Brinon, he wouldn't let them.

Delaney lifted her hands from under the covers and stared at her palms. They weren't burned. They were healed.

"Go! Take Reshna and leave!"

She attempted to stand, but her legs refused to support her weight. They shook, threatening to give out. She fisted her hand in the fur comforter draped over his bed and clawed to her knees. Even then she needed the support to stay upright, and when her eyes locked on Torek lying in bed, she nearly fell over anyway.

Torek's fur was dark, matted, and slick with moisture. She'd have thought him newly showered, he was that drenched, except that the little parts of him where his fur thinned to show skin—his upper lip, his nostrils, his eyelids, inside his ears, even—were beaded with sweat. His lips were dry, split, and peeling. His eyes were opening and closing sporadically, as if he was fighting to stay conscious, and when they were open, they were wide with fear and unfocused. They scanned the room, unseeing, or maybe seeing something other than the reality of the room around him.

"Take Reshna and go. Now!"

Saying that Torek wasn't well had been a gross understatement. Having a head cold was unwell. Having a churning stomach from eating too much fried food was unwell. Having a raging fever and shouting to imaginary people in your delirium? That was a whole new level of unwell. He was sick. Very sick.

Why hadn't that man *forced* the broth down Torek's throat?

"That's a command! Hurry!"

His voice cracked on *command* so that *hurry* was nothing but a weak echo. Below the rage and fear holding the last threads of his consciousness together, he was fading fast. Torek wouldn't last much longer in this state before taking a turn for the worse—assuming that turn hadn't already happened.

"Go! All of you. Don't. Wait. Me." He croaked, gasping between words.

Delaney climbed up onto the mattress, clinging to the fur comforter in fistfuls to hoist herself up. It shouldn't have been this difficult to crawl into his bed. She'd hopped up on the mattress every night for weeks without collapsing from the effort, but she did now, dizzy and spent from the simple task. Maybe the man had been sugarcoating the state of her health too.

Where the hell was *her* broth?

"Take Reshna, and—"

She touched the back of her hand to the sweat-slicked fur of his forehead and cursed sharply. He was radiating heat. He needed more than just broth. He needed a cold compress, water, and ibuprofen for the fever. He needed—

He grabbed her wrist in his meaty hand and squeezed. He wasn't even looking at her. His gaze was focused on a corner near the ceiling, his eyes wide and terrified by whatever he thought he was seeing. If he squeezed any harder, he was going to snap a bone.

Desperate, Delaney did the one thing she hadn't done in months, breaking the most important rule that Keil had ingrained in her. The only one she wholeheartedly agreed with. She spoke.

"Torek, no. Please," she pleaded.

Her Lori pronunciation was atrocious. Her voice was rough and cracked, and besides which, she didn't have the right anatomy to produce the proper growls and deep inflections required for speaking his language. But she had to try.

Torek heard her. He didn't seem to see her, and he didn't release her. But he stopped squeezing.

His head whipped to her a moment later, a delayed reaction to hearing her voice. He looked right into her eyes. His were sunken and bloodshot. His grip, so strong, was trembling. The scar across his face, always a stark slash against the dark fur, seemed more prominent, and Delaney's breath caught in the back of her throat. Maybe he wasn't as delirious as he seemed. God, how would he react to his golden retriever *speaking* to him?

"Take Reshna. Go! Save—"

"Reshna is fine," Delaney said, her words exhaled on a rush of relief. "Everyone is fine."

"Reshna is fine? They made it"—he coughed, a wet, racking sound—"off Viprok d'Orell? Everyone?"

"Yes. Everyone is fine."

Delaney tried to viurr, but as usual, she just sounded congested. Nonetheless, Torek closed his eyes. His body eased back into the comforter. The grip on her wrist loosened, and his head drooped to the side.

"Good," he murmured. "That's good."

"You know what's better?" Delaney reached for the bowl of broth and nearly dropped it. Christ, it was heavy. Was she really so weak that her biceps quivered from holding a bowl? It was a big bowl, but still.

She replayed Torek's rant in her mind. He'd been commanding someone to take her and go. To save everyone and what, leave him to die?

Maybe they'd listened to him.

What had happened out there?

She spooned up some broth and forced it between his lips. He choked at first, having allowed the broth to drop down his throat without swallowing. But then he swallowed. Delaney spooned up another helping. He swallowed a second time with less choking, then a third and fourth and fifth time until he settled back into the bed, completely unconscious. Half the bowl was still full.

It wasn't *that* big a bowl.

Delaney sighed, staring at the line of Torek's stubborn jaw, relaxed in unconsciousness. His breathing was deep and steady, even if his chest rattled with each inhale. A few drops of broth had dripped into the longer fur of his chin—his beard, she supposed. Delaney reached out to wipe it from his mouth.

His lips were softer than they looked. Relaxed instead of sternly compressed, they were more full than usual. Her gaze wandered across his face, along the close-cropped fur along the side of his jaw, and down the sharp curve of his corded neck to his firm, well-defined pecs.

The lorienok were a large, muscle-heavy species to begin with, but thanks to his ritualistic workouts and regimented lifestyle, Torek's muscles were developed for real work. He could run the miles of that mountainous ice trail for hours without stopping. He could carry Delaney on his hip like she weighed no more than a toddler and probably still run. He could hold her immobile, pinned to the floor with a hip and one hand, controlling her more easily than Delaney had ever been able to control Mrs. Todd's damn Pomeranian.

But he could still die from a fever.

Delaney placed her hand on Torek's chest. The rapid but strong double thump of his heart squeezed something inside her own chest. The ache spread outward with each beat—constricting her breath, accelerating her heart, heightening her awareness—and then the ache dropped lower, between her legs in a deep throb.

She pulled her hand back sharply, nearly spilling the remaining broth on the comforter.

The broth. Couldn't waste perfectly good broth. Delaney took up the spoon with her shaking hand—anything to distract herself from her own feelings—and helped herself. The broth was still warm. It wasn't particularly flavorful, but the moment she swallowed, her stomach seemed to wake from a long slumber. It released a long, deep growl, suddenly ravenous.

Less than thirty seconds and half as many swallows later, the spoon clattered into an empty bowl. She blinked, stunned. She'd completely polished it off.

She glanced at Torek, still unconscious, and then at the door behind her, still closed. Should she attempt to find more broth? What would they think if someone caught her carrying a bowl back to the room? Dogs carried bones. Maybe they'd think she was just scavenging. Maybe—

She yawned. Before she could make up her mind, exhaustion took her. She stretched out to place the bowl on the bedside table and almost collapsed from the effort. The bowl was empty. Why was it still so heavy?

She dropped onto her side, facing Torek and his unscarred cheek. In profile, his muzzle had a hump on its bridge and pointed down at its tip. His ears were small in comparison, tucked neatly against his head. Delaney wondered idly about Torek's age. Considering his position in society and mature disposition, she'd guess late forties, but if she remembered her lessons correctly, lorienok aged more slowly than humans. But Torek was battle hardened; his scars indicated that maybe he'd been forced to grow up fast. He didn't have a wife or children, but that could be a lifestyle choice rather than an indication of age. Or maybe he simply hadn't found love.

Delaney rolled her eyes at herself and turned over. However old he was, he was fit and formerly a hulking health advertisement. He would beat this fever. He'd need more liquids, and so would she, but until she figured out a plan to find more food, they also needed rest.

She wriggled under the comforter and closed her eyes. Just as she began to drift, the weight of a furry hand slid over her hip. On a normal night, Torek would just grab and drag her into his embrace, and honestly, he was so warm and soft, like an extra blanket, that she usually didn't mind. But this wasn't a normal night. Her stomach under his palm warmed, but she remained stiff and kept the distance between them even though the rest of her was cold. Nothing was more chilling than that lingering throb.

THIRTEEN

SOMEONE WAS IN THE BEDROOM.

The door had opened a moment ago, and the squeak of its hinge jarred Delaney fully awake. She'd been toying with the idea of leaving the bed, but what was the point of subjecting her body to the nip in the air that her nose was enduring without a solid plan for what to do afterward? The light slanting through the narrow window was dim and golden. Several hours must have passed since she'd fallen asleep. Midday had fallen to dusk, and the temperature had fallen with it. On a normal day, Torek's watch would be chirping, reminding him to finish his final bout of rounds to make dinner.

This was anything but a normal day. Torek wasn't even wearing his watch, and judging by the heavy weight of his arm still draped over her hip, he wouldn't be making dinner anytime soon.

But someone had to.

Footsteps creaked toward the bed.

Delaney held her breath against the stab of fear jump-starting her heart. She opened her eyes.

A young lor stood beside the bed, having moved faster and more quietly than she'd expected. His profile was at eye level as he bent to retrieve the bowl from the bedside table. He froze midreach, and, as Delaney watched, his lips lifted into a fierce, astonished smile.

His head whipped to face her.

"Commander?" he whispered. He was the same man who had brought the bowl and left in tears.

Torek, still obviously unconscious, didn't respond.

The lor's face was only a few inches from hers. This close, she realized that although his horns protruded from his head in a thick, intimidating curve, his ears were overly large in proportion. Instead of remaining immobile and tucked against his head, they poked out on either side of his face and seemed to move independently from each other, almost like a horse's ears, but not quite *that* large. He was a young man on the cusp of true manhood, but young nonetheless.

Some of her earlier hostility toward him dissipated—but only some. Torek was intimidating, there was no doubt about that, but he was sick. The young man shouldn't have walked away. He needed to do something more than just shed a few tears and give up. *Someone* needed to do *something*, damn it.

Delaney took a deep breath. The man had returned. Maybe he hadn't quite given up yet.

He leaned over Delaney, presumably to get a better look at Torek. Delaney rolled her eyes. Was he blind? What was there to see that couldn't be discerned from a healthy five-foot distance? Torek was unconscious, feverish, and dehydrated. He needed liquids and a cold compress. Was that so difficult? And why the man didn't just circle around to Torek's side of the bed was a mystery.

He leaned closer.

Christ, his chest was inches from Delaney's face. He was wearing something musky—maybe they did have cologne on Lorien, but Keil had never mentioned it—and it made her nose tickle.

"Commander," the man repeated. "Do you want more broth?"

Delaney sneezed.

The man straightened as if she'd electrocuted him.

Torek stirred, rubbing her hip with his palm beneath the comforter.

The man's ears pricked forward. "Commander?"

Torek fell back into unconsciousness.

"Whatever you need. Please," the young man begged. "I'm yours to command. More broth? Water, perhaps?" He gnawed his lip. "Geraevon Kore'Onik said your command is final, and I know you commanded me to leave. And I know you only have a fepherok." He wrung his hands. "But it didn't feel right not to check on you. Tell me what you need, Commander."

Nothing.

The man's ears drooped. He glanced down at Delaney with such sad, soulful eyes that when he reached for her with his big hand, she didn't even tense. He stroked his fingers through her hair, leaned forward, and touched his forehead to hers.

Then he backed out of the room, taking the empty bowl with him.

Idiot! Delaney covered her head under the fur comforter and screamed on the inside. Why wasn't Torek in a hospital, being treated by a medical professional with a degree and experience and a spine?

If the young man wasn't going help, Delaney would need to obtain the supplies they needed herself and risk being caught. She could sneak to the bathroom for water and washcloths easily enough, but more broth would require reheating at best, actual cooking at worst. Maybe they had premade broth, like soup cans. Would they notice if some went missing? Did they have can openers?

Why hadn't Torek allowed her in the kitchen pantry?

She moved to whip off the comforter and froze as something occurred to her. Maybe he hadn't allowed her in the pantry because of something in her manual. She racked her brain for something, anything that might have given him the impression that the pantry was dangerous.

But even if she was found in the pantry, it wasn't as if she was supposed to know that she wasn't allowed in the pantry.

Christ, being a pet was complicated.

She glanced at Torek. He was still out.

She turned toward the nightstand and waved her hand over the digital edition of her manual. The device lit up. She picked it up and brought it with her under the comforter. Torek's palm was still cupping her hip. She grabbed his hand and pressed his thumb pad to the screen.

The darkness under the comforter exploded with light as the device projected. She flinched, the harsh rays of the screen blasting her retinas. Torek didn't so much as twitch. She set the device back on the bedside table, blinking to readjust her vision, but when the screen came into focus, she continued to blink, staring.

This wasn't just her manual. Icons were everywhere, swirling colors and flashing reminders. She reached out to one labeled *Owner's Manual: Human* and hesitated. Next to her manual was an icon she recognized, a program she'd used with Keil to write her manual.

A sly smile curved her lips. The man wasn't going to help them without orders? She'd give him some orders.

She selected the icon next to her manual, and the program sprang open to a page with dozens of files.

"Open existing or start new," the device intoned.

Delaney froze. She stared at the door, but following the booming growl of the audio command request, the room and the hallway outside the door remained silent.

"Open exist—"

"Start new," Delaney whispered, but one can't properly pronounce Lori words in a whisper, not with all those growls and hacks and hard consonants.

"Answer undetected. Please repeat. Open—"

"Start new!"

The screen flashed a bright white. The squiggly serpent of a cursor faded in and out, waiting on her command.

Hmmmm.

She considered the title, "Torek's Commands." To the point, but probably too much.

If she were Queen Sasquatch of the ice planet and unconscious with fever, how would she phrase her commands?

She thought of how Torek spoke to his people: with confidence and kindness. He listened more than he spoke, and when he did speak, he didn't mince words. Torek was direct, efficient, and effective.

She bypassed a title. Simple was better. "Broth. Cup of water. Bowl of water. Towels. Soap. Brush. Toothbrush. Toothpaste."

She bit her lip, trying to think of the Lori word for their version of ibuprofen.

She settled for "Medicine," and then as an afterthought, "Thank you."

She left the screen on to project at the door and huddled down under the comforter to wait. Of course, this plan heavily relied on the assumption that the young lor charged with Torek's care would return. If he thought Torek had eaten that bowl by himself, surely he'd return with more. Even without a command.

Surely.

The light of the projected list was nearly the only light remaining in the room, and Delaney had nibbled her remaining fingernails to their beds when the young lor finally returned.

He halted at the door, startled by the projection. He blinked. His eyes scanned left to right, left to right, and a smile burst like a firecracker across his face.

"Yes, Commander! Right away, Commander!" He ran back down the hall.

Delaney settled under the comforter on a self-satisfied sigh.

A few minutes later, the young man returned with everything on the list, including the ibuprofen. He set it all within easy reach on the bedside table, even going so far as to pivot the table so its long edge was flush against the bed. He nodded at his handiwork and beamed at Torek, his chest puffed.

His smile faltered and then leaked away as he gazed upon Torek, but the pride remained.

"Feel better, Commander. You're on the mend now. I'll look forward to your morning commands."

The man touched his heart, about-faced, and shut the door on his way out.

Delaney blinked at the door and then at the bedside table, stunned by how efficiently her plan had worked.

She picked up a clean towel, soaked it in water, and placed it on Torek's forehead. He didn't react. He didn't release a small sigh. His lips didn't curve into a soft smile, and he didn't open his eyes, suddenly cured from his fever. What was a worse indication of health: delusions or deep unconsciousness? She draped a few more soaked towels under his arms and between his legs. Whether he was delusional or unconscious, her efforts would be the same—she needed to lower his fever. At least unconscious, he wasn't fighting her.

If Torek died, Delaney would be thrown back in the system, caged for another six months or longer before someone else decided he needed an animal companion. Maybe someone less kind, less caring, less, less—less Torek.

While Torek was cooling, Delaney soaked another towel, added a little soap, and started cleaning herself. She needed to focus on the mundane tasks of the present before the uncertainty of the future choked her. Neither of them smelled like a field of roses, and while the cool water might or might not eventually ease Torek's fever, it certainly eased the edge from Delaney's mood. She scrubbed her face a little harder than necessary, but the abrasion of towel on skin was grounding. The cool water was heaven, and the soap was comfortingly familiar.

When she finished washing herself—one problem of a hundred solved—she soaked and squeezed the cloth and started on Torek. She wiped down his face, behind his ears and around his neck. She cleaned the bends of his elbows and behind his knees. She rewet the towel, added more soap, and scrubbed his underarms, gave a quick swipe to other unmentionables, and then set down the towel in favor of the hairbrush.

His fur had been sticky with dried sweat before the sponge bath. Even clean—as clean as one could get during a sponge bath—his fur was still snarled from the melted ice, so matted in places that she suspected he'd have to cut it. Some of his longer hair had curled into thick dreadlocks. She thought of the care he took to groom himself every morning and night following his twice-daily showers, and the prick of her temper returned.

He commanded what seemed like the entire planet's military force, but not one of his guard could be spared to clean and feed him while he lay ill?

She stroked the brush through the longer fur at his elbow, starting at the roots. Her movement was slow and tentative, but even so, the brush snagged on a knot within the first inch.

Torek groaned.

She took in the entirety of his body with a critical eye, from his shoulder-length head hair to the snarled fur across his entire belly and every gnarled knot in between—and groaned. It was going to be a long grooming.

She gripped the tuft of hair at the base of his elbow to prevent it from snagging his skin this time, and teased the knots from its tip. As the hair unknotted, she elongated her strokes, teasing inch after inch of the long tuft of hair. A minute later, she could stroke down his arm in one uninterrupted stroke.

One arm down, another arm, two legs, a belly, a back, a beard, and a head of hair to go. Assuming she managed to lift him enough to brush his back. She rolled her eyes. She still had to *clean* his back.

An hour later, Torek's fur was smooth and gleaming, except for a particularly stubborn patch alongside the keloid scar down the side of his abdomen. No amount of brushing or washing could unsnarl it, and Delaney had a knot in her shoulder to show for her failed attempts. But they were both clean, the room smelled noticeably less pungent, and Torek was no longer radiating heat like the faces of both

Lorien suns. He was semiconscious, able to swallow when offered water, and moan his displeasure at being brushed.

Delaney glared at the brush with a wary sort of concern.

She'd never taken particular notice of how much fur Torek shed while brushing himself, and it wasn't as if he had an owner's manual that she could consult to confirm whether intense shedding was normal, a natural byproduct of fever, or an indication of imminent death. He hadn't lost so much fur that his coat was thin or patchy, but the brush was filled to its bristled tips with his tangled sheddings.

She set aside the brush—if only she could set aside her concern as easily—and reached for the broth. He ate another half bowl. Delaney polished off the rest, then stared at the mess she'd made of the young lor's neat supply rows.

Luckily, she was a golden retriever and didn't have the mental capacity to clean up.

Grinning, Delaney programmed another list for fresh supplies and bedded down under the comforter.

Torek's hand slid up her hip, his touch heavy but his palm soft. She snuggled in, forgetting to not enjoy the smooth, clean tickle of fur against her side. She finger-combed the back of his hand, and a strange swell of pride filled her. Not one tangle on that hand.

She closed her eyes, letting the soft fur under her fingers soothe her as much as the petting probably soothed him.

FOURTEEN

"CLEAN TOWELS. FRESH WATER. MORE BROTH." A PAUSE. "Rainol e lokks. Thank you."

"Voice undetected. Please repeat."

"Ohjeezuskryst." A deep sigh.

Torek opened his eyes and squinted through the harsh light blinding his vision. Was his *daarok* turned on? The second sun had already set, and if the shadows dancing across the room were any indication, the damn thing was on the fritz.

"Clean towels! Fresh water! More broth! Rainol e lokks!"

Or a child had activated it. What would a child be doing inside the estate proper? And even more baffling, what would a child be doing inside his room? Her voice was strange, as if her vocal cords had been severely damaged. Perhaps a birth defect.

He tried to speak, but all that emerged from his dry throat was a harsh, growling moan. He reached out blindly. His arm was bound by the weight of the bedcover. Rak, he was shaking from the effort of lifting his hand. His entire body ached. His head was throbbing. He tried to swallow and nearly choked on the dryness of his tongue. If he succumbed to the scratch in his throat and actually coughed, surely his head would explode and end this misery.

"Shhh, before you hurt yourself. Here." The child made a terrible noise, a cross between a cough and a groan. It sounded painful.

Something cool and smooth touched his chin, and liquid moistened his lips. Torek drank gratefully. A child angel, then.

After a few swallows, the scratch in his throat and the pounding in his head eased somewhat. She removed the glass from his lips, and his eyes finally began to adjust to the light.

Reshna was holding the glass, staring at him.

Torek gaped. He blinked, wondering if the daarok's light and dusk's shadows were creating an illusion.

She blinked back at him. As he continued to stare, her eyes widened. The water inside the glass she was holding began to ripple, and he realized she was trembling.

"Reshna?"

The glass slipped from her hand. Water spilled and soaked into the bedcover. It must have, but he didn't feel its wet chill. His body was numb. The air was static. All he could see in the tunnel that had become his vision was Reshna. Her rioting hair. Her pert nose. Her smooth skin. She was just as she should be, except her intelligent, all-too-seeing eyes widened with mirroring shock. And on her part, fear, as the color drained from her cheeks.

Someone knocked.

The door burst open before he could answer.

"Commander!" A deep chuckle. "You're awake and listing my commands, I see."

Torek tore his gaze from Reshna's death-pale face. A young lor had just barged into his living quarters. Would surprises never cease?

But the lor was familiar. Torek frowned. His name was Petreok. How did he know that? How did he know him?

A sudden vision came to him. His room was replaced by the icy slope of the Viprok d'Orell, and in his mind's eye, Petreok's face was scared and questioning but determined—a far cry from his pleased, eager expression now.

"Petreok," Torek whispered.

The young lor stepped forward, filled to brimming with self-importance. "Yes, Commander?"

The memories rushed forward, pummeling him with nearly as much force as that wall of snow. He'd been buried in an avalanche trying to save Reshna.

Torek moved to cover his eyes with his hands and was thwarted a second time by the weight of his bedcover.

He bit back a growl of frustration. "Did you get everyone off the mountain? Was anyone else caught in the snowfall?"

Petreok shook his head. "You were the only one directly beneath the overhang, Commander. No one else was injured, and by the time Reshna was carried out of the ravine, Brinon Kore'Onik had already arrived to tend her injuries."

Relief as potent as a narcotic swept over him. "Thank Lorien," he breathed. "And who do I have to thank for digging me free of the snowfall and carrying me out of the ravine?"

Petreok's expressive ears pivoted forward. He grinned, tried to cover it with a cough, then grinned anyway. "It was a group effort, Commander."

"Is that right?" Torek studied him for a moment, noting for the first time that he was wearing a crisp Federation uniform. "Perhaps some people helped more than others and were rewarded for their actions?"

Petreok's smile widened. "Perhaps."

"Tell me."

"I, well—" Petreok shifted his weight from foot to foot. "I would not brag, Commander."

"It's not bragging if it's truth," Torek fibbed. "Simply inform me of what happened. Consider it your first report to your commander."

Petreok puffed up at that. The foot shifting ceased. "Yes, Commander. Well, I joined you on the ice, mimicking your technique by sliding across on my stomach. Two others joined me, and together, we found you beneath the snow.

Torek blinked. "You dug me out by hand?"

He nodded. "I didn't want to wait, and I'm glad we didn't. By the time Brinon Kore'Onik sent word to Geraevon Kore'Onik, and he finally arrived with the excavation team, they didn't have to waste time clearing the area. We'd already freed you from the snow."

"Four lor plus the weight of the snow on cracked ice above a blood-lusting zorel." Torek blew out a heavy breath. "Quite the risk."

"For you, Commander, we'd risk anything. As you have risked for Onik," he murmured. A moment later, Petreok cleared his throat. "Well, I'll, er, just complete your orders, then, Commander?"

Torek opened his eyes, unsure when he'd closed them. "My what?"

Petreok pointed. "Your orders."

Torek followed his finger and blinked at the list being projected from the daarok.

Clean towels. Fresh water. More broth. Rainol e lokks.

Torek's gaze dropped back to Reshna, but she had burrowed beneath the covers while he wasn't looking. "*My* orders?"

"Yes, Commander."

Torek inhaled deeply. Lorien lend him strength. "Carry on."

"Right away, Commander," Petreok said, sounding relieved. He slammed the door shut behind him, rattling the hinges with the force of his enthusiasm.

Uncertainty cinched his chest and tightened with each breath. He'd never been one to turn a blind eye, but in this one moment, he was sorely tempted. He could rationalize away some of Reshna's behavior, like helping him drink. She could have mastered the use and purpose of drinking glasses as she'd mastered door levers and locks. But the bright, projected characters of "his" orders mocked any further rationale he might wield to explain away all her behavior.

Torek attempted to uncover her, and although his arms shook from the effort, the bedcover was still too heavy to budge.

"Reshna," he barked. "Come out from under there. Now."

Something of hers began to shiver against his thigh.

He swallowed a curse and opened his mouth, intending to repeat the command in a gentler tone. It wasn't her he was frustrated with. Not really.

Not mostly.

The door burst open without any preliminary knocks, and Torek actually startled upright.

Petreok strode inside, laden with supplies.

By Lorien's horn, the avalanche hadn't killed him, but Petreok and Reshna might.

"Here you are, Commander!" Petreok cleared the bedside table, which had been refashioned as a hospital tray, and laid out a stack of towels, a bowl of water, a cup of broth, and a plate of rainol e lokks.

"Just as ordered," Torek murmured.

"Well, of course." Petreok blinked. "Are you feeling all right, Commander? You *look* much improved, but—"

"Yes, yes. I appreciate your efforts."

Petreok beamed. "Serving you these many days..." He shook his head, clearly overcome. "I couldn't have asked for a higher honor."

Torek took a moment to allow that to process. "How many days have I been abed?"

"Six, Commander."

"And you've tended to me this entire time?"

Petreok gave him a strange look. His beaming dimmed slightly. "I haven't tended to you. You wouldn't allow it, but I have obeyed all your commands. It's the least I could do after all you've sacrificed for Onik."

"Yes, of course." Torek licked his lips. "And how long have I been giving you commands?"

"I, well..." Petreok glanced at the list still being project by the daarok and then refocused on Torek. "Are you sure you're well? Should I fetch Geraevon Kore'Onik? He—"

"Not quite yet. So just to confirm—it's been quite an ordeal, you know—I have been abed, writing my commands to you on the daarok for the last six days?"

"No."

Torek sighed. The pressure around his chest eased slightly.

"You've been giving me commands on the daarok for the last *five* days. You didn't have any commands on that first day." Petreok's ears perked forward tentatively. "You've washed and brushed and eaten yourself back from the brink of death, Commander. All of Lorien is talking about it. Only you could have done it. People were saying it *couldn't* be done, but I didn't say that. I *knew* you would pull through."

Torek stared at Petreok, the pressure around his chest contracting in a swift, deadly second strike.

Maybe the avalanche had killed him, and this was all that existed after death.

"No one tended to me. Not even Geraevon Kore'Onik?"

"Well, Geraevon Kore'Onik did upon your arrival. I inquired about your care, and they said that he anticipated a swift recovery. So they granted my request, in honor of my, well..." His ears tucked bashfully. "They allowed me to care for you since you were already on the mend. It seemed only a mild case of fepherok, which was expected considering how much snow had soaked into your fur. Until it wasn't mild." Petreok swallowed. "But you commanded me to leave you to care for yourself, and Dorai Nikiok insisted that commands were given to be obeyed. Even Geraevon Kore'Onik had his doubts, but here you are, healed, and by your own hand!" Petreok ended that final sentence on a rushed shout, clearly jubilant over the prospect of Torek's near resurrection.

A long moment of silence passed, and Petreok's beaming became noticeably strained. He cleared his throat. "Do you need anything else, Commander?"

"No. Thank you. You're dismissed."

Petreok genuflected, closing the door behind him.

The lump that was Reshna shifted under the bedcover, still trembling. Probably suffocating on her own hot breath.

He should just turn a blind eye.

"Come out, little one," he coaxed with reluctant resignation. "Let me see you."

Her shifting stopped, as did the warm breaths against his hip. The trembling increased.

He moved a finger and found a smooth part of her—a shoulder, maybe, or her cheek. So many parts of her were soft and smooth, he couldn't really tell. "Reshna. I haven't seen you since that moment on the ice. Your body bloody. Your leg twisted." He cleared his throat and covered it with a soft viurr before he embarrassed himself. "Let me see your face and know you're well."

Nothing.

For the love of—

Frustration surged through his veins, feeding muscles that, according to Petreok, hadn't been used in six days. He gritted his teeth, and, with a mighty shove that flooded his vision with starbursts, he tossed the cover from the bed. Reshna shot upright. Gasping from the effort, he didn't notice her expression until he'd caught his wind, but once he did, seeing her was equal parts relief and added ache to the pressure squeezing his chest.

She was perfect and healed and beautiful, the little diva. Her curls sprouted like a golden halo around her head. Her skin was clean and soft, and if her cheeks were slightly more hollow than he preferred, well, he could fix that easily enough. But her pink, pinched lips were shaking, and the skin rimming her wide gray eyes was rubbed raw.

She leaned forward incrementally and nudged her head against Torek's shoulder, a shoulder that, by the looks of it, had been cleaned and brushed.

He needed to find the words, but his thoughts were still catching up with the facts in front of him.

One of her curls had sprung in the wrong direction and was tickling his muzzle. He blew at it, but the movement only caused it to tickle more. She nuzzled deeper. The tickling became torture, so his voice was more harsh than necessary when he growled out, "Reshna, stop."

She froze, leaned back slightly, and shifted her gaze to meet his. Her lips stretched into a hideous mockery of a smile.

"You're not in trouble. I don't know what you're thinking or why you're suddenly so terrified. But it's okay. It's just you and me here, and you know how much I love you."

Her trembling eased somewhat.

"There's my good girl." Torek stroked his pointer finger against her skin—the back of her hand, as it turned out—and viurred. "Now, how long have you been able to speak?"

She froze, then cocked her head and blinked.

She was good.

"It's no use. You see?" Torek flicked his eyes pointedly to the evidence of her speech glowing on the projected words behind her. "For six days—no, five—I've lain unconscious with no one else in this room to give Petreok those commands. I know *I* didn't give those commands. Who else does that leave?"

The bed started to vibrate from the force of her renewed shivering, and damn it all, her eyes began to leak.

"What is all this? What has you so inconsolable?" He reached out a shaking arm to stroke her cheek. "Are you that relieved to see me well? Is that it? The worst is behind us now. I'm—"

She grabbed his wrist with a swift snatch, turned her face into his palm, and sank her teeth into his thumb.

He jerked back, and she released him nearly as quickly as she'd turned on him. He stared, stunned. Her teeth were blunt and couldn't break the skin, but her jaw was stronger than he would have predicted. He squeezed his hand into a fist to ease the sting. She'd bitten him.

She'd actually *bitten* him.

He raised his hand to hit her—no matter her fear or relief or whatever all this was about, he couldn't let that go unaddressed—and she stopped trembling. Her eyes closed. Her whole body stilled, and her lips curled up at the edges.

Torek blinked. She was smiling. She was relieved and unafraid now that he was about to beat her.

She was *very* good.

Torek lowered his hand, shaken.

After a moment, Reshna opened her eyes. Her gaze darted between his lowered hand and his face. A wrinkle creased the skin between her brows.

"I risked my life for you, little one." Torek tried to moderate his voice into gentle, encouraging tones, but he was frustrated and shocked and exhausted. No matter his effort, the words still emerged as a growl, but they needed to be said. "You were unconscious. Your head was cracked open. Your leg was fractured. Your hands were scraped raw. And you were lying on the frozen Zorelok River. I didn't just risk my life by stepping out onto that ice for you. I risked the lives of everyone in that ravine. For you. Do you understand the significance of that?"

Her frown deepened.

"Even without the avalanche, we risked a great deal for you: our lives for yours. The least you owe in return is a little honesty." Torek reached out, and this time when he nudged her chin with a brush of his finger, she didn't bite him. Her lips quivered, and her eyes resumed their leaking. But she met his gaze, resigned.

She opened her mouth, her throat strained, and for a moment, Torek doubted his sanity. What was he expecting? Even with the evidence before him, was this really the most likely explanation? How could she possibly—

"I am sorry," Reshna whispered.

Torek gaped, her words like a punch to the gut.

Reshna could speak.

"I not meaning to bite you. I just thought—" Her lips suddenly snapped shut into a thin line. She swallowed and tried again. "I-I not meaning to. I am sorry."

Reshna couldn't just speak. She could speak in full sentences. Kind of. Her words were soft, carefully spoken, and oddly formal. Her voice was childlike and her pronunciation strange, but even without the proper inflections, her words were understandable.

"I accept your apology," Torek murmured, still reeling. He knew several lorienok who couldn't manage to feel remorse and admit their guilt, but his animal companion could do both.

He needed to push past the shock and remain calm if he wanted answers. She was skittish enough for both of them. Her eyes were back to darting around the room, from the door to him, to the window, to the door, back to him. She was still terrified, despite their being alone.

For the first time, Torek considered the possibility that he wasn't the source of her terror.

"Reshna, look at me. It's just us. Just you and me."

She looked. She didn't want to. She actually kept her face turned toward the door, but she flicked her eyes sideways and met his gaze.

"How long have you been able to speak?"

She looked down for a moment, breaking eye contact again.

Torek strained to keep the frayed ends of his patience from unraveling as he waited her out.

"I learn Lori during the, the"—she hesitated, thinking— "during the ride from Earth to Lorien."

"You know more than just calls and commands. You understand full sentences. You can *speak full sentences*. You, you're..." Torek shook his head in disbelief, and for the life of him, he couldn't stop staring at her lips and blinking. "Are you fluent in Lori?"

Her leaky eyes just stared back at him.

"But you don't listen to my calls and commands half the time," he argued, as if any argument could refute the evidence of her actually speaking in full sentences. "If you've known what I'm saying this whole time, why don't you *listen*?"

Her face flushed a bright, patchy red. "I get full."

His nostrils flared. "You *get full*? What's that mean?"

Her eyes rolled into the back of her head. "You can only feed me so many treats before my stomach fills." She patted her belly. "Then I stop listening."

"You ignore my commands on purpose because you don't want any more treats?"

She crossed her arms over her chest. "Yes."

He frowned. "Then why didn't you listen to me on our run through Graevlai? I wasn't overfeeding you then."

"When I not listen to you?"

"I commanded you to run, and you refused to keep up."

She barked out a laugh. "I never run a day in my life, except in *jimklas*," she added on a snort. "You know, drill—but that not count. Without practice, you want me to run forever at your pace, in the cold, with heavy boots, over a mountain?" She shook her head.

Her pronunciation was truly atrocious. Understanding her accent at the tripping cadence in which she delivered her sentences was a challenge. Some of what she said didn't even make sense, but even so, he could decipher her meaning. "When did you have drill?"

Reshna snapped her mouth shut with an audible *clack*.

"You called it *jimklas*." That pressure around his chest, which had just begun to ease squeezed again. He rubbed the skin over his heart as if he could force it to pump at a regular, steady rate. "Did you —" He swallowed and tried again. "Did you have drill on Earth?"

FIFTEEN

Delaney tried to knuckle the frustration and fear from her eyes, but the pressure only intensified her headache. She'd already conceded that she could speak Lori. If Torek surmised anything more about her intelligence and her life on Earth—like that she had attended gym class, for instance, implying that Earth wasn't inhabited by animals but educated people—he would undoubtedly begin to question why she had pretended to be his pet. Why would she stand by after being abducted by aliens and allow those aliens to enslave her under the mistaken assumption that she was an animal?

The answer to that question was a death sentence.

She lowered her hands and glanced at the shut door, the slim barrier between them and discovery. If anyone—Petreok, most likely —overheard their conversation, they would face an entirely different challenge. Imagine the publicity: Captain of the Onik Guard Thinks He Can Speak to His Animal Companion! Would she have the courage to remain silent as Torek was accused of insanity, or would she speak up, effectively pulling the trigger on them both?

"Reshna." Torek clipped her name in a warning growl.

Delaney tore her gaze from the door and met his eyes. He looked so much better than just a few days ago. His eyes were direct and intense as they focused on her. His mind sharp and present. His body would eventually regain its strength, just as his mind had. He would recover. He would recover after all.

"Answer me," he demanded.

Fuck, had there been a question in all this?

"Did you have drill on Earth? Is that why you couldn't keep up with me on our run, because I had deprived you of your routine? Did you lead a less lazy life on Earth?"

Delaney was startled out of her confusion at that last question. "No, actually, I led a very lazy life on Earth. I not keep up because you bigger and stronger than me," she said drolly. "And even at my pace, I never want to run that path, let alone that early in the morning in that weather. I not like to run."

"You don't *like* to run?"

"I not *want* to run. I not *enjoy* to run."

Torek snorted. "I don't particularly *want* to run either, but it's good for my health. How else will I keep up with the first-kair cadets?"

"Good for you, but I not needing to keep up with any cadets. You run if you want, but not taking me with you."

"I admit, integrating you into my morning workout might have been a mistake."

"You think?" she muttered in English.

"But we can integrate a different workout into our itinerary, one modified specifically for you."

"Jesus Christ," she snapped. "Just feed me less treats."

"Jeezuskryst?"

Delaney waved away his question. "Forget it. Just forget all of it. I not needing a workout."

"Changing your diet alone isn't enough. Brinon Kore'Onik says you need to build up your strength."

"Well, I say I not needing to build my strength."

"Considering that *he* has several degrees in the caretaking of animal companions, I'm thinking we'll listen to him over you."

"Oh, and you listen to everything *your* doctors say for your health?"

"I certainly do. They—"

"So Shemara Kore'Onik does not, how you say, waste an hour of your life every week to torture you for her own pleasure?"

"She certainly does! But *you're* here per her prescription, aren't you?"

Delaney crossed her arms. "Am I such a...a weight?"

"A weight?"

"When Shemara say your head is healthy, will you leave me for good?"

Torek's frown was fierce. "I won't leave you at all." He shook his head as if to clear it. "Why are we even arguing about this? I'm your owner, and I say we're adding exercise into your daily routine, and that's that."

Something snapped inside Delaney—her sanity, most likely—and suddenly, none of this was about exercise or hiding her intelligence. "But you did leave me. Your *precious little Reshna.* You leave me on the cold mountain with strange people on a strange planet in the middle of *nowhere*, and you wonder why I not keeping up? Why I not listening to your commands?"

Torek blinked at her. "You're angry with me."

"Of course I angry with you!"

"No *of course.* I *saved* you up on that mountain." He shook his head again. "Graevlai isn't a mountain. It's—"

"I save *you*." She poked her finger into Torek's chest. "Do you know how high your fever is? How long before it break, and if it not break, how long before you die? *Do you?*"

Torek opened his mouth and closed it before opening it again to say, "I'm not a doctor."

"*I* not a doctor! For five days, you lay here. I feed you and clean you and brush you and pray to a-a-a Lorien I not believe in to spare you as you lose more and more fur. Your stomach fur is so thin, it can

142

barely be brushing, and you just..." She covered her mouth before she embarrassed herself further and just shook her head.

"Hey there. I'm all right now." Torek viurred. He reached out to cup her shoulders, drew her down to rest against his chest, and wrapped her in his warm embrace.

She breathed in his clean, fresh vanilla scent deep into her lungs and held on tight.

"I'm not losing my fur because of the fever," Torek murmured. "Genai is coming. The weather will be warmer soon, and in preparation for that, lorienok shed their fur."

"Really?" Delaney eased back slightly, just enough to frown up into Torek's face. "Lorienok on the ride from Earth to Lorien not shed."

"They do, just not during space travel. Federation ships are climate controlled to prevent shedding. Could you imagine venting all that fur?" He shuddered.

But Keil had never even *mentioned* shedding. He'd spent nearly five years educating her on lorienok culture. You'd think something that substantial would have warranted a paragraph on anatomy day!

What else had he conveniently forgotten to mention?

"Petreok not appear to shed," Delaney muttered doubtfully.

Torek let loose a mild chuckle. "He's a young, strong, strapping lad. He'll shed soon enough, shortly after me, I'd wager."

"Being young, strong, and strapping affect his shedding?"

Torek nodded. "Everyone sheds in their own time, depending on their age and health. Children and elderly won't shed until mid-Genai, if at all."

Delaney tugged on a lock of fur on his chest. "What happen on the mountain?" she asked. "After I fall, I mean. You come back for me?"

Torek didn't look down at her. The wall had suddenly become fascinating. "Yes."

"And?"

He shook his head. "And what?"

"And what happen after?" she snapped. She knew her Lori was difficult to understand, but it wasn't incomprehensible. "On the mountain after I fall and you return for me. Then what?"

"All right. Just calm down. Let's not start up again." Torek smoothed his hand over her back. "As I said, we weren't on a mountain. We were running in Graevlai, a public, very ordinary place to visit. I only clarify because I didn't abandon you to the wilderness as you seem to think—"

"Strangers chase me. And you not—"

"But I can see how it would seem that way from your perspective, having never walked so deep within Graevlai before."

Delaney bit her lip, remembering the lor with the knife.

"I was frustrated because I thought you were being deliberately disobedient and dramatic, collapsing into every snowbank we passed."

Delaney stiffened and opened her mouth to defend herself.

"Now I know you're just weak and couldn't keep up."

That didn't sound much better, but at least it was the truth. She stroked his chest fur between her thumb and forefinger with gentle pinches.

"When I reached the end of my workout and realized my foolishness, I returned for you, but you'd already fallen down the ravine and onto the ice. Those *strangers* all banded together, linking themselves into a chain down the slope to reach you. If they chased you, it wasn't to harm you. They were trying to help. They *did* help, at great risk, I might add, to themselves."

"They not all help," Delaney murmured. "One holding a knife."

Torek's hand stilled on her back. "What?"

"A lor approach me with a knife while I trying to find you. I see the knife and run."

"Did he attack you?"

"I, well..." She frowned. "No. I run first."

"Because you felt threatened."

Delaney nodded.

Torek remained silent for a long moment, but his hand was warm and gentle as he stroked her back. "There was a large crowd at Graevlai that day."

"Yes."

"People don't normally attack at close range in such a crowd. Too many witnesses."

"You not there. People push and shove, trying to grab me, and as I dodge their hands, it easier to attack without notice than you think."

Another bout of silence.

"I know what I see," she insisted.

He nodded. "A close-range, opportunistic attack on my animal companion would require a powerful motivation. Someone who'd want to hurt me deeply." He made a low, humming noise in the back of his throat. "I don't have any enemies."

Delaney rolled her eyes. "What happen when you return? You find me on the ice?"

Torek heaved a heavy sigh. "Yes. I climbed down to you and pushed you to safety."

She frowned. "Why push me?"

"The zorel, attracted by the scent of your blood, I think, tried to break through the ice to reach us. The vibrations of her persistent ramming caused a *zivook*."

"A what? I not know that word."

"A deadly fall of snow. It would've buried us, but I pushed you to shore."

An avalanche. Delaney stilled. He'd saved her from an avalanche. "What about you?"

Torek's arms tightened around her. "I'm fine now. Thanks to you."

"It bury you?" She leaned back to properly glare at him. "Why you—"

"It bur*ied* me. Past tense. In the present, I'm fine."

Delaney scrunched her nose at him. "Funny."

"How about you try? Bur*ied*."

"I not care about that. I care about you and why you—"

"Buri*ed*."

Oh for the love of— "Bury."

"Deeper. With more grit. Buri*ed*."

"My throat physically cannot growl low enough for Lori past tense."

"Hmmm." His lips twitched.

She swatted his shoulder. "You trying to distract me."

He grinned, completely unabashed. "Is it working?"

She pursed her lips and tried a different tack. "What is the zorel? You say it try breaking through the ice?"

He nodded. "The zorel is an animal. She, her mate, and their litter *roranok* beneath the ice during Rorak."

"They what beneath the ice?"

"Roranok. They sleep all winter."

Ah. "Ramming the ice not sound like hibernation."

Torek huffed. "Genai is nearly here, and with the scent of your blood—" He shrugged. "I'm not surprised she tried to attack us."

"Zorel attacks happen every day, do they?"

"Only during Genai."

Delaney tensed, feeling suddenly disturbed. His position as commander, the castle high on the mountain, his punishing workouts, their military force... Was it all to protect against a hibernating ice fish?

"What happens in Genai?" she asked.

Torek blinked. "The ice melts."

She exhaled, letting it go for now. She didn't understand, not really, but she didn't have to. She had enough problems to deal with at the moment. "And then what? Back on the mountain, you get out from under the snow?"

"I don't remember much of anything after being buried. Just the feeling of suffocation and the taste of blood. Then I woke up here, to you," he squeezed her gently, "playing with my daarok."

"Your what?"

He pointed at his tablet.

A burst of heat rushed to her cheeks. "I not playing. I—"

"I know. You were saving *my* life." Another tight squeeze.

She patted down the fur she'd just stroked into spikes. Torek's broad hand grazed across her back, and they remained like that, breathing in the silence.

"We have food and water, if you want something," she whispered some time later, pointing to the spread Petreok had set out.

"Yes, I see that." Torek murmured, but he didn't move. Neither did she, and they drifted into another lazy silence until the repetitive purr of Torek's deep, healthy snores soothed Delaney into sleep too.

SIXTEEN

"I am not going, and you not make me," Delaney said, gleefully throwing down the gauntlet at last. Torek was probably having a difficult time taking her seriously while she was bundled in an adult, fur-lined onesie, but now that he knew she was capable of speaking, she'd be damned if she didn't advocate for herself regarding Brinon Kore'Onik.

Today was appointment day, the day of doom for both of them, and the first day in the eight since his fever had broken that Torek was feeling well enough to leave his room. He hadn't resumed his regular schedule yet, but at the rate he was pushing himself now that he was conscious, it was only just a matter of days before he was sprinting the mountain every morning. She'd have rejoiced in the rapid return of his health along with the rest of Lorien if only he wasn't using his renewed strength to bully her, another aspect of their lives that was rapidly returning to "normal."

The verbal inquisition he'd deployed during his convalescence had been both relentless and subtle, gleaning the truth of her intelligence oftentimes before she even realized his intentions. Like that first day, when he'd asked her to pass him four of the five books on his nightstand. She'd asked which ones he wanted, and when he'd changed his mind to three—just the blue and green ones, and the one on mineral properties, please—she'd done so without realizing everything she'd reveal: she could count, read, and knew her colors. He'd taken the books without comment, not even to say thank you, and that along with the hand rubbing the frown between his eyes told her everything he wasn't saying. She was passing his tests, which meant she was failing her own.

She'd been more guarded since then, becoming a mastermind at avoidance and defensive deflection.

"What does drill on Earth entail?" he'd asked.

"Why you not attend drill on Lorien anymore?" she'd countered.

"What was your schedule like on Earth?" he'd pressed.

"Why must everything have a schedule?" she'd parried.

He'd asked her to pass him the sequel to dirt, third book on the left, second shelf.

She'd retrieved the fourth book on the right, first shelf. But at that, he'd only pinned her with a peeling glare. Not everything was a test, especially the second time, and some holes could only be made deeper.

But today, the eighth day of his recovery, his bullying progressed from verbal to physical. She'd thrown down her gauntlet, forbidding him from taking her to the doctor, and he intended to pick it up. Literally.

"We're going. We walk where I will, and we *will* be keeping to schedule today." Torek scooped her up, just snatched her right up off the floor, and carried her toward the bedroom door like a sack of grain slumped over his shoulder.

"Put me down! You not understanding. "

"I understand perfectly. I don't enjoy my doctor appointments either. But we suffer them because we must."

"We can make a new schedule without appointments and keep to that," she tried.

He reached for the door.

"I *hate* my appointments with Brinon. Just stop for one second! *Please!*"

Her shrieks must have hit just the right high note, because he paused midstride.

"Please put me down. Let us talk with calm and reason."

He set her on her feet and, when he stood up, dipped his head so his horns swept sideways. And waited.

She took a steadying breath. "I not want to visit Brinon Kore'Onik. Not today. Not ever."

Torek breathed in a long-suffering sigh. His hands remained on her hips, ready to toss her back over his shoulder at any moment, but for this one moment, he resisted.

"I hear what you're saying, but I don't understand. Why don't you want to visit Brinon Kore'Onik?"

"I not like him. I not *enjoy* the visits," she amended. "He has my best interest at heart, but my appointments with him are... They humiliating and scaring."

Torek frowned. "I've noticed that you're quite emotional after your appointments with him, and I understand being frightened, but humiliated? Aren't you being a bit drama—"

"Calling me dramatic is not listening. You are—" Her hand circled the air in thought. "What is the word for to dismiss my feelings? To not take them as serious as you should and to make me feel stupid for feeling them?"

Torek opened his mouth, closed it, and then opened it again. "Insensitive? Dismissive? Trivializing?"

"Yes, you are those things. Not always," she amended quickly. "Just now."

Torek choked back a laugh. "Brinon Kore'Onik is the best in his field. He cares for animal companions the world over. What could possibly be humiliating?"

"He ties my arms and legs to the table. He touches me in places without asking first. He—"

"I'm sure that Brinon Kore'Onik won't restrain you if you ask him

BEYOND THE NEXT STAR

not to. Just don't struggle when he examines you," he said offhand-edly. "And of course he must touch you. How can he examine you otherwise?"

This was it, then. The final snowflake that broke the ice from the mountain, beginning the avalanche that killed them all. "I not asking Brinon Kore'Onik to not restrain me."

"Why not? Just—"

"I not asking him anything."

Torek frowned. "What are you talking about? Of course you can—"

"No. My speaking is our secret. Just between you and me, remember?"

His watch—a new one, apparently, because he'd spent nearly all yesterday afternoon programming his entire schedule back into it —chirped.

He glanced at its face and growled. "We don't have time for another argument. We're already behind schedule."

Delaney rolled her eyes. Torek and his damn itinerary. "What about the lor with the knife? You not find him."

Torek sighed. "I've interviewed several people who were present during the incident at Graevlai that day, and no one saw anyone holding a knife. And you didn't recognize any of the faces from the images I showed you. There's not much more I can do."

"Exactly. He still out there. It might not be safe to leave."

Torek shot her an affronted glare. "You'll be with me. There's nowhere safer."

"But—"

He tightened his hold on her hips, about to toss.

"Okay, okay!" Delaney held up her hands in supplication. "I agree to the appointment. I not struggle or make a fuss or argue, *if* you keep your promise. My speaking is a secret between you and me. Agreed?"

Torek released her waist, grabbed her wrist, and reached for the door. "Fine! Agreed! Let's just *go*! We're running late."

"Wait! My—"

"You just agreed not to struggle!"

Delaney dug in her heels. "You forget my leash. My tether, I mean."

"What are you going on about?"

She reached back, searching under the pile of furs and blankets on the floor—used more now as a method of losing things than as a bed—and popped back up, tether in hand. "Here."

Torek stared at the tether, but he didn't reach to take it. "What do we need that for? You're well trained, well—" He shook his head. "You're fluent in Lori."

"After what happen on the mountain, no one thinks me well trained. You let me off the tether, and I nearly die." She grimaced. "They think you have no control of me."

"This isn't a matter of control. It's—"

"Yes, to everyone else it is. If you not know I speaking, what you think of me?"

"I'd think, well..." He sighed. "I'd be worried for you, wondering how you might react in public because of your trauma. Whatever spooked you on the ravine might spook you again, and until I discovered what that was, and help you deal with it, I'd tether you. To ensure your safety," he added. The severity of his frown was two mountains creating a deep ridge in the center of his forehead.

"Here you go, then." Delaney shook the leash at him.

"But I know what spooked you." He argued, ignoring the tether. "You told me, and your reasoning makes sense. Being lost in a strange land with strangers chasing you would be very frightening. You panicked. It's completely understandable and avoidable, because I won't be losing you on our way to visit Brinon Kore'Onik. And even if we become separated, it'll be familiar surroundings."

"I tell *you*, but I not tell everyone. They expect you to tether me for my own safety, and if you not, they think you—" She tapped her temple and made a looping motion beside her head.

He shook his head. "I don't care what everyone thinks," he said, but his eyes slid to the side, breaking their locked gaze.

"Of course you do." She snapped the collar around her neck, clipped herself into the tether, and shook the leash at him a second time.

He stared at the handle but didn't move to grab it. "No matter my temporary leave of absence, I'm still Torek Lore'Onik Weidnar Kenzo Lesh'Aerai Renaar. They'll listen to my commands."

"Even you not command what people think," Delaney said, exasperated.

Torek put his hands on his hips, reminding Delaney of a superhero. Chewbacca playing Superman. "They don't question my commands, and they won't question my actions."

"That not always good! You nearly die because they not question your commands."

His arms dropped back to his sides, and he had the good grace to look at least a little shamefaced. "In that one instance, I'll admit, their unquestioning loyalty was to my detriment. But fepherok is rarely fatal except to children and the elderly. I should've been able to rest a few days in bed, as Geraevon Kore'Onik had intended, and recover without any ill effects. The thought of me dying from fepherok, at my age and in my current health is, well—" He shook his head, his curved horns sweeping the air.

"All too possible."

"—laughable."

"I not laughing."

"I know."

"So. Not questioning you is not always good."

"*I know.* But for the purposes of public opinion, their loyalty is to our advantage. How I decide to train and discipline my animal companion is my business, and they will respect my decision."

Delaney shook her head. "They not voice concern, but they still think it. And even not said, thoughts have power."

"Not as powerful as me."

Delaney rolled her eyes and snorted.

The heat of Torek's glare could have incinerated a fly.

"Sorry, but you are wrong. What happen on the mountain might happen again. The next time you leave me on the mountain—"

"It's not a mountain. And I didn't—"

"—I want the lorienok to think me a good animal companion who listening. Not speaking," she said hastily. "Just listening. And they find that hard to think if they not see me wearing the tether now." She forced the handle into his hand and curled his fingers around it.

He continued to glare at her.

She glared back.

His watch chirped.

"We are late," she goaded.

He growled. "Fine. But we're not done here. We'll finish this conversation tonight."

"Sir, yes, sir."

"What?"

"Never mind. Just lead the way, Commander. The sooner we start, the sooner it ends."

THE DISTANCE THROUGH THE ESTATE PROPER TO HIS HOVER vehicle was only a short walk, but everyone they passed—guards, civilians, friends, strangers, *everyone*—stopped them to ask after their health, pat Reshna's head, and wish them well. They didn't have time for such sentiments, but no matter what he denied, Torek knew the importance of public opinion. Besides, at this point, did it even matter if they were two hours late rather than one for their appointments? So he let his people chat and pat to their hearts' content, and when they were finally finished, deleted his remaining reminders for the day before the incessant chirping of his new daami drove him to smash it.

Brinon Kore'Onik's receptionist was indulgent, expressing her joy at seeing them as well, despite their egregious tardiness. They didn't even have to wait for their appointment. He glanced at all the

other lorienok sitting in the waiting room with their animal companions. They had arrived on time and would now be behind in their
schedule because of him.

And despite that, every single one of them fawned over him and
Reshna and their health. One enthusiastic young lorok went so far as
to claim that she might have died herself had they died that day.

Reshna, sitting in the chair next to Torek, locked eyes with him.
Her face was so expressive, he could nearly hear the drip of sarcasm
leaking from her thoughts.

He grinned. *I told you I was powerful.*

Her eyes rolled back into her head. Torek smothered a brewing
laugh.

"Are you ready for your appointment, Reshna?" the receptionist
gushed, reaching to take the tether from Torek's hands.

On impulse, Torek stood. "I'd like to join her in the room for her
exam, if you don't think Brinon Kore'Onik will mind?"

The receptionist straightened, the tether forgotten. "This way
please, Commander."

Torek stepped forward but came up short when the tether pulled
taut. He glanced over his shoulder. Reshna's white-knuckled grip on
the chair was so tight, her arms visibly shook.

He tugged on the tether lightly, hoping she wouldn't make a
scene. "Come, Reshna."

Had he miscalculated? Would she not appreciate his presence in
the exam room? Or was this just the nerves she had talked about?

Torek glanced at the other animal companions in the waiting
room. Most were probably here for their weekly well visit. Many of
them were happily chirping, begging for treats, or trying to encourage
neighboring owners to give them attention and pets. A few were
visibly unwell, their limbs wrapped with bandages, calmly if sadly
waiting their turn to be healed.

None were afraid, let alone displaying such a visceral, fearful
response to being here.

Just as Torek was about to step toward her, Reshna sighed and stood of her own volition. She walked with him to the exam room willingly, if obviously reluctant.

Torek's hackles threatened to rise, and he didn't even know quite why.

Brinon Kore'Onik was already there, surrounded by a group of student assistants. The students stared in awe at his approach, then gathered themselves and scrambled to genuflect.

Brinon nodded warmly. "Torek Lore'Onik Weidnar Kenzo Lesh'Aerai Renaar. To what do we owe this honor?"

"Brinon Kore'Onik." Torek nodded in return. "Reshna is still skittish from her accident. I'd like to remain during her exam to soothe her, if you don't mind."

"Anything for the hero of the hour." Brinon gestured to one of the students. "Roerik, if you will?"

A young lor, presumably Roerik, stepped forward. He looked strong and confident, yet his horns had yet to curl. He squatted in front of Reshna, grabbed her beneath the arms—without asking for permission, Torek's conscience nagged—and lifted her onto the exam table. She could easily have hopped onto it herself with a step stool, had there been one and had she been asked.

Although she remained calm, collected, and completely pliant as he positioned her onto her hands and knees, Roerik fastened a restraint around Reshna's left ankle.

Reshna locked eyes with Torek.

Torek turned to Brinon. "Are restraints necessary? She's perfectly calm."

Roerik paused midreach for the right ankle restraint.

Brinon smiled an indulgent smile that Torek instantly disliked, which shocked him. He'd never before—not during his many seasons in the academy, throughout drill, nor professionally—ever disliked anything about Brinon. "I'm making an exception to protocol, allowing you to remain for her examination. So I beg your leave to conduct this appointment in the manner I see fit."

"Of course, but—"

"I would never dream to question your commands to the guard. That is your military specialty. Caring for animal companions is mine. Please extend me the same courtesy."

Torek bit back his gut response. "Of course."

Reshna looked away, her already pinched expression becoming increasingly grim.

Brinon flicked his eyes to Roerik.

Roerik blinked back, unsure. He glanced askance at his classmates.

One of the young lorok nodded subtly, and Roerik fastened the restraint and then paused, glancing at Brinon as if bracing for a reprimand.

Brinon nodded, and Roerik refocused on Reshna. He unfastened her clothes. She allowed him to pull each arm through its sleeve and push her coverings down her back to pool at her knees. Her skin instantly puckered. She began to tremble, but she didn't fight him. She didn't complain or argue or struggle in any way. After arguing with her incessantly about practically everything for the past eight days, her silence was discomfiting. Sickening, actually, as her tremors increased.

Roerik moved to step back in line. Reshna raised and jiggled her wrist, reminding Roerik that he'd forgotten to restrain her arms. He jumped forward to finish his duty, and a moment later, the third and then fourth restraint locked into place with a final *click*.

Torek glanced around at the crowd of students and then at Brinon himself, but if anyone else thought Reshna's active participation strange, no one spoke up about it. Was no one even remotely intrigued that she'd recalled Roerik's duties better than Roerik himself?

Brinon slipped on a pair of surgical gloves and approached Reshna. "Have you noticed any change in her behavior now compared to before her accident?"

She has conversations with me in Lori now. "She's more skittish, but in private, her behavior has returned to normal."

Brinon pinched her eyes open and shone a light into them, watching her pupils react. "And in public?"

"So far, so good."

Brinon pressed his hands to either side of her throat. "How about her eating habits and bowel movements?"

Reshna heaved a sigh.

"Both back to normal," Torek reported, curtailing his grin.

Brinon shifted one hand from her neck to her back, and the other began to palpate her stomach. "Has she displayed any pain or discomfort?"

"No. She seems quite recovered. Back to her shy self. For the most part," Torek added, so no one could accuse him of being a complete liar. "In your experience, Brinon Kore'Onik, have you ever come across an animal companion that developed the ability to speak?"

The students ducked their heads and glanced at one another, giggling behind their daaroks.

"Now, now, Torek Lore'Onik Weidnar Kenzo Lesh'Aerai Renaar's question, although curious, is quite relevant to our study of animal companions," Brinon said.

At the recitation of his full name, the students bolted upright and into silence.

"Many animal companions have their own modes of communication. Zepraks bark, for example. *Atters* purr. Lombowatts release a hormone, or scent, to signal to other lombowatts when there's danger approaching or if they're in heat. The various means of communication between animal companions, breed to breed, is truly extraordinary."

One of the students, the girl who had nodded to Roerik, raised her hand.

"Yes, Joennel?"

"Have animal companions ever been known to communicate with animal companions of a different breed?" she asked.

Brinon finished palpitating Reshna's stomach and patted her flank. Her cheeks flushed.

Torek glanced between Brinon's hand placement and Reshna's expression, feeling concern and trepidation, like the slow melt of ice, creep through his veins.

"There have been instances of lombowatts seeming to get along and communicate with pourpites," Brinon said, answering Joennel's question, "but atters can't bark and zepraks don't have the scent glands necessary to communicate with lombowatts and pourpites. When they do find a means to communicate, body language is typically the common language."

"And if an animal companion did learn another language?" Torek asked. "Lori, for example?"

Reshna looked up at that.

Brinon glanced at Torek, amused. "Assuming an animal had the vocal cord capacity to produce the varied vowels and consonants that compose our native tongue?"

"Yes, assuming that."

"A big assumption." Brinon picked up a thermometer from the instrument tray and adjusted his position behind Reshna. "If we ever came across such an animal companion, we would likely declassify them as an animal. A being capable of learning a foreign spoken language would likely have the same intellectual capacity as lorienok, and therefore be classified as a person."

Reshna stretched to look over her shoulder as Brinon disappeared behind her.

"A person," Torek said numbly.

Brinon inserted the thermometer into Reshna's anus.

She looked away. The veins in her neck swelled from the strain of biting back a scream. Three, then four tears dripped from her jaw and hit the paper sheet over the table with a soft patter. Her knuckles turned bone white as she gripped the table's edge, and Torek was reminded of her gripping the chair in the waiting room in the same manner, just minutes ago. And him, hoping that she wouldn't make a scene.

Torek felt sick.

Insensitive. Dismissive. Trivializing. His own words returned to haunt him. He was all those things and worse. She was suffering, and by enabling it to happen, he himself was the cause of it.

Brinon removed the thermometer and smiled. He patted her flank and didn't seem to notice her flinch. "Very good, Reshna. You're such a good girl." He looked up at his students. "You may proceed."

The students lurched forward in one excited wave, cooing and fawning over her. Roerik examined her gums and tongue. Torek held his breath, willing Reshna to keep a level head, and she did. She didn't growl, jerk away, or bite as Roerik practically climbed inside her mouth in his enthusiasm to count her molars. Another student flashed a light in her eyes, again, and had to wipe her cheeks several times so his grip wouldn't slip as he held her eyes open. Joennel picked up a measuring rod and was recording the length of Reshna's limbs, then the length of her hair, the circumference of her neck, the length of her arms, the swell of her breasts, her waist, and lower still to the folds of her privates.

Reshna's skin, from the top of her hairline to the tips of her toes, flushed a bright red.

Torek recalled his own exploration when he'd thought her bleeding internally, and the skin under his fur flushed hot with shame.

A keening noise slipped passed her compressed lips.

Torek stepped forward, nudging Joennel and her measuring gently aside. He placed his hand on the back of Reshna's head, squeezed the nape of her neck, and viurred softly.

Reshna completely lost what little tenuous control she had on her composure. Her lips broke open on a wail. She dropped her weight down onto her elbows and muffled her sobs with her hands, but they still racked her small body.

For the first time in all the many times he'd seen Reshna without clothes, Torek realized that she was naked.

All the students froze midtask, uncertain.

"You're finished?" Torek asked, taking advantage of their hesitation.

Brinon stepped forward. "Actually, we—"

"Perfect, because I'm late for my next appointment." Torek snapped open the restraints, pulled Reshna's coverings up and around her cold skin, and gathered her into his arms in one smooth sweep.

She buried her face into his chest, shaking. Torek rubbed her back. His viurrs blended into one constant vibration as he pivoted on his heel and strode from the room, leaving a crowd of gaping students and one protesting teacher behind. But by Lorien's horn, if his fever-delirium-issued commands had the weight to sentence him to death, his actual commands certainly had the weight to spare Reshna this humiliation.

He was Torek Lore'Onik Weidnar Kenzo Lesh'Aerai Renaar. He walked where he willed.

SEVENTEEN

Reshna was shaky and listless, the same as always following her appointments with Brinon Kore'Onik. She was sitting cross-legged on the floor next to Torek's chair in Shemara Kore'Onik's office. Her eyes tracking their conversation were the only part of her that moved. The rest of her was slumped against his chair. He'd always suspected that she didn't particularly enjoy her appointments with Brinon and had considered finding a new specialist for her, but now he wasn't sure what to do. A new specialist would treat her in just the same casual manner as Brinon. Had he witnessed the appointment two weeks ago, before their accident, he wouldn't have thought anything of it. She was a diva. She was sensitive and shy. She'd get over it.

Except, she was a person.

"Torek?"

Shemara's voice cut through the whirl of his thoughts, and Torek startled.

Shemara worried a claw across her lower lip. "I was asking about your recovery, but I'm wondering if we should close our session early so you may schedule an appointment with Geraevon Kore'Onik."

"No, no. I apologize. I'm distracted this morning."

She grinned. "It's afternoon. You were two hours late for your appointment."

Torek swallowed his groan. "Of course. Again, my apologies."

She waved that away. "I heard it was quite the parade getting here."

"Everyone was eager to hail our well-being. More Reshna's well-being than mine, I think."

"What makes you say that?"

"I've been injured many times in the line of duty, but I've never been two hours late for an appointment after emerging from my sickbed."

Shemara double-tapped a claw against the daarok in her lap. Her gaze delved into his to dissect his brain, considering who knew what —his mental instability, most likely. "Is that what had you so preoccupied just now? Thoughts of Reshna's overshadowing fame and popularity?"

That startled a laugh from him. "I was thinking about Reshna's last appointment with Brinon Kore'Onik."

"When he healed her following her accident?"

He shook his head. "The one we just came from."

Shemara glanced at Reshna and then met Torek's eyes, looking troubled. "Did it not go well?"

"No, it did not."

"You can always request to accompany her into her appointments. That typically isn't allowed, but for you, I'm sure he'd make an exception."

Torek dragged a hand down his face. "I did, and he did."

"And?" she encouraged. "What about him distresses her?"

"Everything, I think." Torek leaned down, reaching for the comfort and familiarity of smoothing Reshna's curls between his fingers.

He hesitated. Petting her was an unthinking habit ingrained from their many weeks together, but suddenly, every touch, every interaction, burned through him. He couldn't ask for her permission to touch her, not in front of Shemara. She already thought he was teetering on the brink of a mental breakdown. He clenched his hand into a fist and withdrew.

Reshna turned her head to face him. Her wide, red-rimmed gray eyes locked with his gaze, and for the first time since he'd met her with her spirit deteriorating in that cage, he couldn't interpret her expression. He hadn't wanted an animal companion, and never one as complicated as Reshna. Now here he was, how many weeks later, his life infinitely more complicated than he ever could have imagined, yet that same uneasy burden, the certainty of inevitable failure, crushed his heart at the look in her eyes.

Tak. Tak.

Torek glanced up from Reshna at that double tap. Hot blood rushed to his cheeks. He was still in Shemara Kore'Onik's office, and she was still dissecting him.

Torturing him for her own pleasure.

Torek cleared his throat, hoping his voice didn't sound as strained as it felt. "The entire encounter was distressing for her, but Brinon didn't do anything during her exam that any other animal companion specialist wouldn't do."

Shemara's mouth pulled taut and to the left in thought. "You said that her injuries were healed from the accident."

Torek nodded.

"It's likely she suffered emotional trauma as well. Her accident was severe, painful, and frightening, and the healing process even more so. Brinon could be a trigger for her fears."

"She was distressed by her visits with Brinon even before her accident."

Tak. Tak. "Does her care manual detail her medical history?"

Reshna's head snapped up at that. The bones in her neck actually cracked from the suddenness of her movement.

"She might have endured a trauma before you purchased her that could explain her reaction toward Brinon," Shemara continued. "Or perhaps it's simply a bad fit. That happens too."

"Hmmm." Torek nodded, but her suggestions only reminded him that, should Reshna have a medical history, it had been written in her manual by a Federation domestication specialist who hadn't discovered that Reshna could speak during their four-kair journey from Earth to Lorien. In all that time her trainer had spent exploring both her physical and mental capabilities, he or she had never discovered her capacity for speech?

What else about her had been overlooked?

Tak. Tak.

Torek looked up.

Shemara's lips twitched.

"I apologize." Torek frowned. "Again."

Shemara glanced at her daarok. "How about we call it a day? We're nearly done anyway." She stopped trying to hold back her grin and flashed a row of neat white fangs. "Reshna's a lucky gal with you by her side."

Torek's gaze drifted back to Reshna. If the sick knot in his stomach was right—and he'd always been able to rely on its accuracy—Reshna was actually the most *un*lucky gal this side of the galaxy.

A person, he thought, and shuddered.

After a blessedly uneventful surgical follow-up, Torek was seated in uncomfortable silence with Reshna at Grattao. Mairok had commented on their tardiness, but she could stuff her disapproval down the same hole she'd buried all his failings. She was lucky they were even here. He desperately wanted to return to the estate. He wanted to lock Reshna in his room, the one place no one would dare enter without permission— save for Petreok, apparently—and have it out and done with her. The *last* thing he wanted to do at the end of this miserable waste of a day was to sit and waste more time choking down a plateful of runny, over-cooked rainol e lokks, but Mairok would be severely disappointed if he skipped a week. Technically, he'd already skipped last week's visit, but even she couldn't blame him for that. He'd already disappointed his mother-in-law more than any one person should ever be disappointed in their lifetime, so Torek sat. He'd swallow her rainol e lokks even though he could make better at home, and *then* he'd interrogate Reshna.

He'd made the promise to remain silent in frustration, without truly weighing the consequences, and he'd endured those consequences time and again throughout the entire day. The knowledge that Reshna could speak was like an open wound—the longer he let the matter linger between them, the more it festered, poisoning his mood, his judgment, everything. He couldn't live like this, knowing what he thought he knew and allow Reshna to continue to endure everything she'd obviously been enduring. The wrongness of what was being inflicted upon her was appalling, and he wouldn't be an accomplice to it. He couldn't.

And that was the fatal ingredient of the wound's poison: he'd thought her happy. Yes, she was shy and skittish and constantly shivering with cold and concern, but she'd often calmed at the pressure of his hand on her neck. She'd seemed to enjoy the stroke of his claws over her scalp. She'd curled into his embrace at night, and he was both touched and impressed by her uncanny ability to interpret when he needed to embrace her most. Not so uncanny after all. And that entire time, while he'd been taking comfort from her, being healed by her, she'd just been enduring.

And another thought had occurred to him, worse even than the last: people don't live in the wild, ripe for the taking. People have homes and families and careers. They have their own language.

They have their own names.

Again, he thought of the many nights they'd lain beside one another, the many meals they'd shared—gah, he felt nauseous—the many training sessions, the baths, the groomings, the love and care he'd poured on her. The love he'd assumed was being automatically returned.

It couldn't all have been lies. He recalled her trembling body as she'd braced herself against Brinon Kore'Onik's exam table: she didn't hide her suffering. He'd even noticed it before she'd spoken of it. He'd just never given her feelings on the matter the consideration they'd deserved. The consideration *she'd* deserved. It stood to reason that if she didn't much hide her suffering, then perhaps she didn't much hide her affection either. The bond he'd created with her couldn't all be lies, but neither was it all truth. Not even close.

The wound's poison spread faster with his racing thoughts.

The food would come, Mairok would fawn, and then he and Reshna could return to the estate and have it out and done soon.

Just not soon enough.

Torek sipped on a glass of saufre. Shemara Kore'Onik always gave sound advice, and for once, Torek was excited to follow it. With the prolonged silence between him and Reshna thinning his already frayed patience, Torek activated his daarok, opened Reshna's manual, and found the chapter on her medical history.

The chapter was quite extensive, detailing a variety of scans, findings, and the specialist's interpretations of those findings organized by injury type: bones that had previously been fractured and broken, joints that had previously been strained or sprained, skin that had previously been cut, etc.

Torek skimmed the findings, his eyes catching on one item in particular: the row of thin, parallel scars on her right thigh and the patch of crisscrossing scars on her left. According to the author, the scars' straight, evenly spaced positioning on her right thigh indicated the swipe of claws, but the location of the scars—her upper inner thigh—was curious. And the author was baffled by the scars on her left thigh. Her blood was healthy. Her muscles were underdeveloped but also healthy. Torek heartily disagreed with her "optimum weight" based on her height and body mass, but otherwise, beyond the perplexing presence of those strange scars on her inner thighs, Reshna was in decent health.

Her medical history, however, didn't include an examination of her mental health. The author wasn't completely remiss in his work. He included a chapter on personality and mental well-being in the

Human Nature chapter, but he hadn't expanded on his findings. And why should he? Reshna was only an animal companion, after all. Nevertheless, the presence of those scars bothered him. They should have bothered her domestication specialist too.

And then there was the little matter of her learning Lori during her four kair with him.

Hadn't he noticed? Surely, having learned the language, Reshna had realized she was being groomed for domestic ownership. And even more surely—having realized this, found the proper words, and strung them in the correct order—she would have shouted, *I am not an animal! Release me at once, and return me home!*

What was she frightened of? During her first days of being taken —the word "kidnapped" came to mind, and he shuddered—he could imagine that fear had overtaken all reasoning, but she'd learned Lori well enough to communicate her needs and wants.

She certainly wasn't incapable of shouting her needs and wants to Torek, in private, at least. She was hungry. She was thirsty. She was full. She wanted to know about how he'd saved her. She wanted to know the details. Rak, now that she'd revealed herself capable of communicating in Lori, she seemed incapable of stopping. She was more persistent than a law enforcer hunting a nugget of guilt! Except in one regard: her silence in public.

The waitress delivered their food and an extra plate for Reshna, interrupting his spiraling thoughts. He divided a portion of his meal onto her plate and handed it down to her, feeling a twinge of unease. She didn't sit on the floor at home. Sitting on chairs was better for her joints, after all, but what had once seemed strange—having her join him to dine at the table—now seemed cruel to avoid. If what he suspected was true, it was certainly cruel, if not criminal.

Torek scooped up a helping of rainol e lokks, took a bite, and before he'd even swallowed, reached down and smacked the plate from Reshna's hands. It flew across the room and upended, spattering rainol e lokks everywhere.

Reshna stared up at him, taken aback.

He fell to his knees before her. "Did you eat any of it?" He took hold of her shoulders and shook her. "Did you?"

Her eyes darted beyond him, undoubtedly at the dozens of staring diners, but he didn't care about their audience. He slipped his fingers between her lips to pry her mouth open.

She bit him—not hard, not like before—but with enough intent for him to pull back and shake out the sting.

He cupped her jaw and forced her gaze to meet his. "Reshna, you must answer me." He breathed through the words, striving for calm. "Our food had ukok in it."

Her face blanched, and for a horrible, chilling moment, he expected her to drop dead right there. But she shook her head.

By Lorien's horn, even now, her lips having been inches from tasting death, she kept her silence!

Torek stood and fell heavily back into his seat, deeply shaken. Mairok rushed over, beside herself with apologies. She promised another plate, a proper meal that wouldn't kill his animal companion. She was appalled by the mistake and practically prostrate with remorse, but Torek didn't hear a word. It didn't matter. They were leaving. He preferred his own cooking anyway.

Had he said that aloud?

Torek inhaled a deep breath and focused. He flipped to the back of Delaney's care manual, an idea blossoming from near disaster. Pulling rank was one of the few perks of Torek's position, and, knowing the domestication specialist's name, Torek had no doubt he could obtain his contact information. Maybe a conversation with her specialist could illuminate whatever wasn't written in her manual. Maybe some evidence in Reshna's history or an interaction with her during their training had been deliberately omitted. The list of "maybes" was endless and useless, but maybe whatever it was could be interrogated out of him.

He'd relish a good interrogation at the moment.

The author's signature page projected in front of him, and Torek stared at the name, dumbstruck. That creeping poison from the wound of her silence spread through the rest of his body, infecting his heart: Keil Kore'Weidnar. Reshna's domestication specialist was the husband of Daerana Weidnar, the lorok who had broken into the Onik estate with her husband's RG-800. The lorok Torek had murdered to prevent the mass murder of his entire guard following her husband's suicide, a ruling that Daerana had insisted was false. She'd believed that her husband, Keil Kore'Weidnar, had been murdered.

Torek looked down into Reshna's sad, silent gray eyes and thought about what he might do in the attempt to escape his kidnappers.

Maybe Daerana Weidnar had been right.

EIGHTEEN

S OMETHING WAS TERRIBLY WRONG. WELL, *MORE* TERRIBLY wrong. The entire day had been a nightmare even before someone had tried to poison her, but she of all people knew that no matter the nightmare, it could always take a turn for the worse. Just as suddenly as Torek had saved her, his expression deadened. He stood, calm as could be, and tugged on her tether.

"Come."

That one word had more bite than the nip in the air, and Delaney froze. Their replacement food hadn't been served yet. Their second waitress hadn't chatted with Torek for half an hour, and they hadn't eaten or paid. And they were leaving?

The tether pulled taut as Torek left the restaurant, and Delaney rushed to catch up before he choked her.

He didn't speak to her on the ride home, which was just as well because he knew that she wouldn't speak back, but he didn't look at her either. He didn't touch her or pet her or help her down from the hover vehicle. She'd come three inches from anaphylactic shock, for heaven's sake, but he didn't steady her when she inevitably slipped on the snow in the courtyard, and he didn't pick her up after she cracked a puddle of ice with her ass. He just tugged on her tether, and she trudged along in his wake, knowing that something was very, terribly wrong.

They rode the elevator up the mountain into the castle, stomped past a line of saluting guards, turned down the back hallway with its floor-to-ceiling windows, and, once they were alone in the privacy of his room, the door firmly shut—and locked—behind them, Torek turned to her, finally meeting her gaze.

His eyes pinned her in place. The anguish in them took her aback. He didn't move to unbuckle her collar. He didn't move at all, and neither could she under the weight of that stare.

She tried to speak, but between fear and an entire day of disuse, her voice croaked. She cleared her throat and tried again.

"Torek?"

He continued to stare at her, his gaze becoming more focused and resolved with each passing second. Resolved to do what, Delaney couldn't begin to hazard a guess, but the force and intensity of his regard was unnerving.

"I tell you it not safe," she murmured.

"I told you I'd protect you." His lips compressed to a thin, disapproving line. The tips of both fangs peeked out. "Did I not?"

"You did." Delaney took a deep breath. Maybe anger was easier for him to process than fear, something she understood intimately. She reached out and caressed his forearm. "You save me."

He recoiled from her touch. "This isn't about that."

"No?" She let her hand fall back to her side, stung. "I not imagine what more pressing than the second attempt on my life," Delaney said drolly.

Torek pointed his finger at her. "Don't start in about the knife. You can't distract me, not from this."

"What 'this'?"

Another few seconds ticked by in silence. Torek's expression was naturally disapproving, but he was being especially enigmatic this afternoon. Delaney reached up to unfasten the collar from around her neck, preparing to get comfortable. This argument would obviously be taking a while.

Torek strode forward and past her, tugging her after him before her fingers could release the restraints.

"Wait! Let me—"

Torek jerked the leash, tightening the collar and cutting off her words. She stumbled toward him, yanked off balance by his strength. He caught her under the arms before she fell and plopped her into one of the chairs in his private dining nook overlooking the city. He kept hold of her leash, one hand gripping the table's edge and the other gripping the kitchen counter. Between the bars of his arms, the bulk of his body, and the wall behind her, she was trapped in her chair.

She lifted her hand and rubbed the chafed skin under the abrasive collar.

Torek's eyes melted, then suddenly hardened. He swatted her hand away.

Delaney blinked at him, baffled. "What is your problem?"

"You, Reshna. You're my problem," Torek growled.

"Just realizing that now?" She reached up to undo her collar again.

Torek swatted her hand again, a little harder.

He was not Kane Todd, she reminded herself, but she couldn't slow the sick, pounding racing of her heart. She held her hand to her chest, her breathing ragged.

Torek's breaths were heavy too, but measured.

"Something is wrong," Delaney whispered.

Torek nodded curtly.

She took a deep breath, trying to calm. "What happen?"

"I don't know. But you, little Reshna, *you* are going to enlighten me."

Delaney blinked. "Me?"

"I want to hear it from your lips." Torek thrust his face into hers.

Delaney shrank away from him—his rage, directed at her for

once, was terrifying—but she could only lean back so far without tipping the chair. Torek grabbed the back of it and scooted her forward, so his lips, his fangs, his breath were hot on her cheek as he spoke.

"Before I launch my own investigation and discover the truth for myself, before I begin a hunt to solve questions better left unanswered, you're going to tell me the truth."

Delaney shook her head. "The truth about what?"

He eased back and met her eyes with a probing look. "Why is your ability to speak a secret?"

Delaney pursed her lips.

"Don't give me that look, you stubborn—" Torek cut himself off midsentence. He closed his eyes and seemed to struggle with something, but whether he was struggling to remain calm and speak rationally or whether he was reining in the urge to slap her silly wasn't clear.

"Reshna, please." He opened his eyes, and this time, they pierced her with his desperation. He wasn't angry. Well, he was, but his anger was a byproduct of fear. Deep, panic-driven fear.

Delaney's heart skipped a beat. "Does it matter? I am yours. I—I am h-happy with you. That is enough."

He barked out a mirthless laugh. "Oh, it's enough, is it? This life here with me as my animal companion is enough?"

"Yes," she snapped. "Let it be."

He pounded the side of his clenched fist into the table. "I can't," he bit out. "What do you think will happen if everyone knows you're more than just an animal?"

Delaney sealed her lips shut, but the silence somehow spoke for her.

"Because you're not just an animal who speaks Lori, are you? You're not just mimicking speech. You're creating it. You're expressing yourself in our language. *You're a person.*"

Delaney glanced at the door. "Someone might overhear you."

"Good! They should overhear! Then maybe they won't strip you naked, ravish your body, and rape you with a thermometer!"

Delaney flinched. "Stop. Just stop!"

"Explain to me why I should. Confide in me!" Torek thundered.

Delaney shook her head.

Torek searched her eyes for a long moment, flicking back and forth, hunting for the truth. And then he slumped. "Oh, Reshna." He shook his downturned head on his limp neck. "I already know."

Delaney froze, but her heart slammed against her ribs. "No one know," she insisted.

He looked up, his eyes anguished. "But I can't protect you if I don't know the details."

"If they know, I am dead."

Torek raised his hand. Delaney braced herself for another slap, but his soft thumb pad smoothed across her cheekbone. "They won't kill you. Our people don't give death sentences for self-defense, and once they realize that you're a person and not an animal, they'll have no choice but to pardon you for Keil's murder."

Delaney bolted upright. "What?"

"Shhh," Torek viurred. "It's all right. Once you're pardoned, you'll be sent home. I'll make sure of it. I'll—"

"I not murder Keil!" Delaney shrieked, then slapped her hands over her mouth. Christ, she was shouting at the top of her lungs!

Torek's thumb stilled. "It'll be all right, little one. I won't leave you, and you *will* be pardoned. I can only imagine what you've experienced, being kidnapped and dragged from your home, separated from your family, relocated to a whole different planet." Torek shook his head, his eyes gleaming dangerously. The rage from before returned, but on her behalf this time. "What my people did to you is unforgivable."

Delaney opened her mouth and closed it, dumbfounded. Keil had prepared her for almost everything she'd need to survive on Lorien— he'd taught her their language, their customs, he'd attempted to teach her their geography—but he'd never prepared her for this: a loving owner who wanted to expose her secret for her benefit. Granted, he wanted to expose the wrong secret, but still, if she didn't tell Torek the truth, he'd expose her and get them both killed. But if she confessed, and it got out that he knew, she'd still get them both killed.

Get them killed now or later? What kind of choice was that?

"How did it even happen?"

Delaney blinked herself back to the present. "What?"

"We have technology in place to prevent this very thing, so we only harvest animal companions from uncivilized planets. It's supposedly ninety-seven percent effective!"

"Meaning it three percent not effective."

His eyes blazed. "We'll return to Brinon Kore'Onik, and you'll speak to him. He'll revise your classification, like he said. That'll be the first step. Then—"

"No."

Torek made a hacking noise in the back of his throat. "You don't understand. I'll protect you. I—"

"No, *you* not understand. I not murder Keil. I love Keil. He like the father I never have." Delaney took a deep breath and met Torek's gaze squarely. "I witness his murder."

Torek stared at her. His entire body had stilled. His fist wasn't clenching. His jaw wasn't flexing. He was barely even breathing.

"Keil make the same promise you make. He try to revise my—my—"

"Classification?"

She nodded. "But he—" She groaned as language failed her. "I not know the words."

"Describe them," Torek said, his gaze unflinching.

"He meet to present my care manual to the lorienok who finding and stealing animals from their home planets."

Torek's frown deepened, but he nodded. "Keil presented you to the Animal Companion Committee."

Delaney shook her head. "He not present me. Just my manual."

"It was directly following that meeting that he supposedly killed himself." Torek's grip on the chairback tightened. His forearm flexed against her neck, hard as granite. "What happened when he presented your manual?"

"I not know," Delaney whispered. "But he know they not like"—she groaned, struggling for the correct inflection in Lori —"enjoy, no, accept, allow..."

"Approve?" Torek suggested.

Delaney nodded. "They not approve his chapter on mental acuity without proof. So he perform many trials to demonstrate my correct class—classification. Before the meeting, he is confident with enough proof to send me home."

"And after the committee meeting?"

"After the meeting, she murder him." Delaney gave him a look. "What is the word for something that is clearly the result. Not a surprise. Not hidden. In clear sight."

Torek's expression flattened. "Keil's murder is not an *obvious* result of his committee meeting."

"No, but here I am, not home, so *obvious* his meeting not go well."

"Did you see who murdered him?"

Delaney compressed her lips into a grim line and shook her head.

Torek narrowed his eyes, dissecting her with a look. "You said 'she' murdered him. So you saw enough to know his murderer was a lorok."

Delaney stared back, trying to think how she could rewind her words. She could feign a language barrier, but she'd never confused her genders before. Would he notice? He noticed everything! Something began to rattle. Her trembling had increased enough to vibrate the chair leg against the table.

"All right. Shhh," Torek soothed. He released his grip on the chairback and cupped her shoulder, his touch gentler but somehow more dangerous than his slaps. The pads of his fingers grazed her collarbone. Goose bumps spread across her neck and down her chest. Her nipples puckered.

She shifted, suddenly uncomfortably aware of her body and his proximity.

"Look at me, Reshna."

She gathered the tatters of her resolve as best she could and met his gaze.

He was magnificent. Even now with all that righteous pursuit aimed at her—the hot gleam in his eyes, the grim set of his mouth, the restrained force of his muscles, his stiletto-sharp mind—his presence made her shiver, and from more than just fear. Much more. His palm cradling her jaw. His breath hot on her cheek. His eyes seeming to see through her lies to her very soul. It should have been terrifying, and it was, but more than that, she desperately wanted to melt against him, into his warmth and strength, to make them her own. That aching heat flared and throbbed between her legs again, as unexpected and unwanted as it had been the first time, but no less devastating.

"Tell me what happened after Keil returned from the committee meeting."

She stiffened her spine and turned away. "I did."

The hand gripping her shoulder tightened, not painfully, but his grip was unbreakable all the same. "Where were you at the time?"

"In my cage."

Torek's eyes narrowed. "He kept you caged? But his manual states that you don't thrive in captivity. You need your own bed in your own room with climate control and..." Torek's voice faded. His eyes widened. His mouth opened, but for a moment, no words emerged. And then, "Keil Kore'Weidnar wrote your care manual knowing that you were a person, so your owner would give you privacy and as much freedom as possible."

"That work well," Delaney grumped, glaring around the room they still shared.

Torek shook his head. "He wrote the manual anticipating that you might still be classified as an animal companion despite his evidence to the contrary."

"Just in cases the worst happen." Delaney sighed and rubbed her eyes. "Same reason we agree to keep my secret from the crew during the ride from Earth to Lorien. Same reason we practice ways to make me seem more like an animal: peeing the floor, nuzzling your hand, biting you."

Torek scraped a hand down his face.

"Same reason he teach me all he can about Lorien while in deep space. Because he knowing they send more ships to Earth before his communications reconnect, and he fear the consequences of misclassifying me." Delaney squinted at him through the bars of her fingers, wrung out. "He was right to fear."

"He should have told everyone! An entire ship is harder to murder than one person. He should have—"

She threw her hands up. "And then what happen to me? When I arrive misclassified, you think they just turn back around and send me home?"

"Yes!"

"No! I think they murder me instead and make it look like an accident. Or a suicide," Delaney added pointedly. "To protect me, we plan for the worst and hope for the best. But of course, the worst happen."

Torek shook his head. "Keil wasn't protecting you. He was saving his own skin, embarrassed at having misclassified you. Maybe he never had the committee meeting but presented his findings to one person instead, the Animal Companion Committee commander, perhaps. Or maybe our intergalactic flight commander! Knowing how much Javaek invests in companion trade—ha! Knowing Javaek—I could see him turning on Keil after seeing such findings," Torek mused. "And Javaek is one of only three commanders with the sanction to authorize a private intergalactic mission. Maybe Keil had hoped to send you home quietly, without ruining his reputation publicly. He—"

"Keil not like that. He never—"

"He kept you *caged*."

Delaney sighed. "He only cage me sometimes. To follow the rules while in deep space."

"Procedure."

Delaney raised her eyebrows.

"It's procedure to keep animals caged while in deep space."

"Procedure."

Torek nodded. "Close enough."

"Procedure," Delaney repeated. The Lori word for it sounded like "rakek" but each consonant, like all their damn consonants, was growling Rs and hacking Ks. Her throat was already aching from the pronunciation. And she probably sounded like a snob, using the formal address for most of their words, but their informal accents, like their past tense, required deeper growls than her human throat could produce and not bleed.

Torek grinned. "Like I said, close enough."

"You try speaking English," Delaney muttered.

Torek's gaze sliced to her face. "Is that your native language? In-klish?"

Delaney froze in her seat, her chest vibrating from the force of her pounding heart. How was everything coming so unraveled so quickly?

She nodded slowly, not sure how this was going to bite her in the ass—of all her confessions, it seemed the least likely—but sure it would somehow.

"How do you say 'Reshna' in In-klish?"

"Corkscrew, but Reshna is not my—" Delaney snapped her mouth shut with an audible *clack* of her teeth.

Torek cocked his head, so his horns swept sideways. "Not your what?"

She hadn't thought it would bite back so soon, but there it was, her ass on the hot seat two seconds later. Complete confirmation that she was the person he thought she was.

She wrapped her hands around her stomach and glared at him. "You never give up, do you?"

"Give up what?"

"Pursuit."

Torek's mouth stretched wide enough to reveal a mouthful of fangs. "No, I don't."

Oh, just give it up, Delaney chided herself. He'd known she was a person the moment he'd caught her holding that glass of water in bed and talking to his tablet. His daarok. There was never any coming back from that horror-struck moment, and any attempt to do so was just delaying the inevitable.

She cleared her throat and spoke through the sudden constriction clogging her words. "But the English translation of Reshna is not my real name."

Torek nodded as if this wasn't a revelation. As if she wasn't blowing up his entire world.

Guess she was just blowing up hers.

"What's your real name?"

She squeezed her sides, hunching slightly.

Torek reached out, brushing his soft, furry knuckles down her arm.

"Delaney," she said on a burning exhale. "Delaney Rose McCormick."

"Del-haney Rose Mic-or-mick."

She smiled slightly, despite herself. "Close enough."

He tried again, actually emphasizing the middle syllable in both Delaney and McCormick correctly. She sighed. He *would* be better at English than she was at Lori. Did he have to be master of everything?

He frowned. "Was that not correct?"

"No, it was."

"You sighed, as if disappointed."

"Yes."

His frown deepened, but then he shook it away. "What does it mean?"

"What does what mean?"

"What is Delaney translated into Lori?"

She blinked. "Oh. I not know."

"Describe the words."

She shrugged. "I—I not have the words, not even in English."

Torek tapped his claw rhythmically against the chairback. "Do names on your world not have origins or deeper meaning?"

"They do. My middle name is a type of plant. A romantic plant that people give to show their love."

"And your first name?"

"I not know the meaning of my first name."

Torek seemed taken aback. His claws ceased their tapping, and he blinked several times, trying to come to terms with the underlying implication of someone not knowing the meaning of her name. She supposed it was a difficult concept to accept for a man with six names who knew the intricacies of each one.

"All right. Delaney Rose McCormick. We digress. You were caged. Keil returned from his committee meeting. And then what happened?"

"Just Delaney."

Torek stared.

"Between friends, I mean. Like, er, similar to how you are just Torek to me. Because we are casual between each other."

"Informal." Something passed over his face, a strain to his expression that she couldn't quite read. Not pain, precisely, but nearly. "Because we're friends."

Delaney nodded.

"Understood. But don't try to distract me, Delaney. Keil Kore'Weidnar entered the room following his committee meeting." He stood up to his full height and crossed his arms. The mighty, powerful Torek wanted answers. "What happened next?"

NINETEEN

Delaney's face shuttered closed. Her eyes deadened in wary, stubborn resignation, and her lush, expressive lips compressed themselves into a thin, wrinkled line. Her expression reminded him of a young child refusing her medicine, and he had to compose himself against the sudden unwise urge to laugh. She might take offense, and that would only impede his progress.

Intimidating her into submission hadn't worked. Coaxing her with reason and assurances had only worked marginally better. Tricking the truth from her was more difficult and time-consuming, but effective, and he intended to draw out every drop of truth from her if it took all night.

Delaney Rose McCormick.

Just Delaney, he reminded himself. His heart throbbed. He actually lifted his hand and rubbed his chest, as if Zana's death was a physical pain he could massage away. He hadn't been "just Torek" to a civilian in six kair, and he hadn't even noticed the lack until now, until this very moment.

Rak, his only friend was his animal companion. It would be

laughable if it wasn't so depressing. What was worse, that he hadn't had a friend in six kair or that he hadn't noticed the lack?

Zana's absence was usually more serrated at night when he was alone. Lately, his grief for her had been overshadowed by nightmares, and then, more recently, with concern for Reshna.

Delaney.

Like a wound he'd sustained and allowed to fester over time, his heart ached anew at Delaney's familiarity. The grief was old, but the hope was new. What exactly that feeling of hope meant, he couldn't begin to fathom.

Delaney squirmed under the pressure of his stare. Good. Let her squirm. Staring took little effort, and if she thought a little squirm would discourage his pursuit, she was sorely mis—

She growled.

Torek shot upright, shocked. Her lips hadn't moved. Her teeth weren't bared. Her hackles didn't appear raised, but they were so baby fine and hidden beneath her fall of head hair that he couldn't truly tell.

She looked down at her lap.

He leaned forward cautiously, wondering if his ears had deceived him.

Grrrrubrrrr.

Torek recoiled.

She'd growled again! Without moving her lips. Without even looking at him!

He opened his mouth to reprimand her, but she glanced up, a wary grin spreading across her face.

He hesitated, unsure what was happening.

"Sorry if my stomach scares you," she said dryly, obviously not sorry in the least.

"Your stomach? Your stomach speaks too?" Torek had only just come to terms with a speaking animal companion. He was *not* ready to accept her speaking stomach.

She dropped a hand to pat the offending organ. To placate it?

"When hungry, it does. Not a problem I usually have with you, but we skip dinner, remember?"

Torek peered at her stomach, feeling a strange, inappropriate urge to poke it. Would it protest?

Now that her stomach had mentioned it, however, he realized that he was hungry too. And Delaney, being the delicate diva that she was, probably felt the complaints more deeply. Or just verbalized them more loudly.

Well, it wasn't as if food would hurt his objective. If anything, it could only help.

Torek stepped away from the chair, opened the pantry, and reached for the bag of rainol.

Something clanked behind him.

He paused midreach, glanced back, and suppressed a shuff. In the two seconds he'd turned away, Delaney had unbuckled her tether and discarded it on the floor, and suddenly, he was suppressing a grin. He should have known that intimidation tactics wouldn't work on her. She wasn't one of his cadets to quake under his regard. In fact, the deeper he delved, trying to bare Delaney's secrets, the more exposed *he* felt.

"Can we eat something besides rainol e lokks tonight?" she asked, jarring him from the conundrum of his thoughts.

"Why?" he asked.

She shrugged. "Why not?"

He narrowed his eyes on her. "You can't tell me you don't like it. You eat your entire portion every night."

"I like it, but something different would be nice considering I nearly die from it today."

"I don't like different," he muttered, but let his hand drop to his side. He stared into his pantry, willing something else to present itself.

Delaney snorted. "I notice. The same meal every day. The same schedule every day." She tapped a tiny finger against her pointy chin. "Other restaurants are in town."

"Yes, but we won't be eating at any of them," he said.

"Why not?"

Scanning his pantry was depressing. Most of his reserves were expired, and having been ill, he hadn't bought fresh produce. "I prefer to cook my own food."

Delaney crossed her arms. "We eat at Grattao all the time."

"We don't eat at Grattao for the food."

"Really? Because food is what we get there."

His eyes settled on the yarks, *haekak*, and the few unspoiled vegetables still thriving in the chiller. So decided, he grabbed a pan, flicked on the burner, and tossed on a fat cube to melt. "We also get conversation with Mairok."

Her nose scrunched. "The waitress?"

"The owner. My mother-in-law."

"I not know that word."

Torek slid a knife from its wall sheath and began chopping vegetables. "The mother of my wife."

The harsh crack and pop of splitting *keylak* filled the silence.

Torek looked up from his chopping and over his shoulder at Delaney.

She shook herself free from the freeze that had overtaken her body. "You have a wife." She looked around and then settled, for whatever reason, on the closet, as if Zana would jump out from within.

He chuckled at the thought. Zana could barely stand for most of their marriage, but even after losing her health, she'd never completely lost her sense of humor.

"You not allow her here?"

He returned to his chopping. "When she was alive, we preferred to live in Aerai, our childhood town."

Her mouth opened in an O of understanding. She waited a moment, and when she finally spoke, her voice was overly hushed. "I am sorry for your loss."

He moved on to the *jok*. "She died six kair ago."

A frown puckered her brow. "That is...a long time."

"Yes." He considered the jok with an intensity that chopping it didn't require. "Somehow, though, the pain of her passing feels like she died just yesterday."

She nodded knowingly. "Grief is strange like that."

He glanced up and studied her a moment, mulling over that telling pause as she'd determined that six kair was a long time. "How long is six kair on Earth?"

She shook her head, and her hair danced, each coil springing with a life all its own. "We count time in years on Earth. Six kair is equal to seven and a half years."

"What is the measurement of *years*?" Torek attempted to pronounce the In-klish word, but the enunciation tripped from the back of his tongue to the front of his lip without any hard consonant for grounding.

Delaney grinned. His pronunciation undoubtedly needed practice.

"A year is one circle of Earth around our sun. Our seasons are much shorter than yours; we have four in the time that you have a full Rorak and half a Genai."

Torek turned toward Delaney, his chopping forgotten. "Where do the extra seasons come from?"

"From the tilt of the Earth. It rotate on an angle, but unlike Lorien, it only rotate on one angle." She held up a fist and drew a line over her knuckles to demonstrate the rotation. "As the Earth circle our sun, different parts of the Earth receive the sun's full light. If the sun is here"—she held up her left pointer finger apart from her right fist—"the part of Earth facing the sun receives more heat and light, causing a hot season." She tapped her upturned fingers. "And the part of Earth that is tilted away from the sun receives less heat and light, causing a cold season." She tapped the downturned back of her hand. "When the Earth is on the other side of the sun"—she swung her Earth fist around her sun finger until her arms crossed—"the seasons switch. And then we count the time between, when the ice thaws before it gets hot and the leaves fall before the cold, as separate seasons."

Torek waved his knife left to right. "But when your Earth is between suns, how do the seasons switch? At that point, even if spinning on a single axis, the entire Earth would be in its hot season."

She wiggled her sun finger. "Earth only has one sun."

"Ah." His curiosity about her Earth nearly made him miss the implications of all her knowledge, but as he considered the differences between their two worlds, it struck him. "How do you know about Lorien's many rotating axes? Or how she rotates around our two suns to create seasons?"

Her hands dropped back to her lap, the astronomy lesson abandoned. "I, I telling you about *Earth's* seasons," Delaney hedged.

"No. You know the differences between Earth and Lorien, which means you know about Lorien's seasons and how they're produced as well."

Her shoulders lifted and relaxed. "Maybe I overhear a conversation or—"

"Lots of astronomy classes for you to overhear in deep space, were there?"

Delaney's entire face bloomed bright red, and although he'd been trying to tease the answer from her, he'd accidentally struck a nerve. There *had* been astronomy classes in deep space.

Torek stepped toward her. "Someone taught you about Lorien. Was it Keil? Did he—"

"Your pan is smoking. It catch fire soon."

"Don't try to distract me. I—"

Delaney's eyes bugged. She pointed. "Fire!"

Torek glanced back and cursed. His fat cube had indeed caught fire.

He swung around, slammed the lid on its pan, and let oxygen deprivation kill the flames.

"Does this mean we eat out now?" She asked, obviously hopeful.

He glowered at Delaney over his shoulder. "Eat out?"

BEYOND THE NEXT STAR

"Yes, *out*." Her pointer and middle fingers walked toward the door. "To a restaurant instead of eat *in* here."

She was nothing if not persistent. He shook his head. "No, that is not what this means."

She released such a long-suffering sigh in combination with her diva eye roll that Torek couldn't help but grin.

"For as much as you not want to eat out," she said, settling her eyes back on him, "you must really love your mother-in-law."

"Not particularly. She's a shrew who can't cook." Torek crossed his arms. "Why pay for food you can prepare better yourself?"

Delaney glanced pointedly at the inedible char in his pan, returned her gaze to him, and raised the winged tuffs above her eyes.

"You, little Delaney," he chucked her under the chin, "are a distraction."

She wrinkled her nose at him, and a warmth spread across his chest. His heart throbbed, but not with the bruised ache of deep grief. It throbbed like it thought it could take flight.

"If she a shrew who not cook, why eat there?"

"She's my last living link to Zana, and I'm reluctant to let go. No matter her runny *lokks*." He gave a mock shudder.

Delaney chuckled, but as her laugh faded, so did her mood. Her voice was subdued when she asked, "Tell me about her?"

"Mairok?" he asked, grimacing.

She shook her head. "Your wife. Zana?"

Torek nodded then turned away, rummaging in the cabinet for another pan.

"You have love at first sight?"

"Not quite." Torek found a pan, placed it on the hot burner, and added another cube of fat. He watched the fat melt, determined not to let it burn this time. "We grew up on adjacent estates. My first memories of life are with Zana, playing throughout our childhood, competing with one another in class, being reprimanded for the mischief we found together, and eventually, our relationship blossomed from friends to lovers. Our mothers were best friends. Our fathers were Federation officers. It was a celebrated match for both our families and the community, but for us, it was just the next, natural phase of our lives. I didn't know what life was without Zana." The fat finally melted. Torek slid the keylak and jok into the pan, and they sizzled on contact.

Delaney bit her lip. "What happen?"

He covered the pan and watched the vegetables fry through the clear lid. "Zana was often ill. Rorak was difficult on her lungs—like when you run, actually." He glanced back at Delaney, frowning, and then refocused on his cooking. "But she struggled to breathe under even normal, daily strain, like walking. As she aged, her condition worsened. I often cared for her through Rorak, but one season, her sickness lingered into Genai. I needed to return to my post and protect Onik against the zorel. I didn't want to leave her bedside, but Zana insisted. She was at the end of her sickness. Onik's people needed me more than she did. And Mairok was there, anyway. It's not as if I was leaving her completely alone. Her own mother was there, and she'd cared for Zana throughout her childhood, seasons before me."

The counter cracked, and Torek realized he was crushing it in his grip. He forced his hands to relax and smoothed his palms over the ruined countertop.

"Onik was in mortal danger, and I thought Zana was not. So I left to protect Onik."

A hand touched his back. Delaney had left her chair and was standing right beside him. He relaxed under the gentle pressure of her hand, and with that reassurance, she wrapped her arms around his hips.

"No need to explain your actions. I know you," she murmured. Her hold tightened. "Her death not your fault."

"She died. While I was away, she died." Torek confessed. He knew Delaney had already jumped to that inevitable conclusion, but he had to say it. "It took many, many seasons for me to understand that distinction. She died *while* I was away, not *because* I was away. It's a distinction that Mairok still doesn't grasp."

Torek turned away from Delaney's hold and lifted the lid under the pretense of checking the vegetables, wiping the moisture that had soaked into the fur on his cheeks. "And you, my little one? Are you married?"

She shook her head, releasing him along with a pent-up sigh as she sat back down. He could practically see the questions on her tongue, pressing for release. But with her large, keen eyes, she could see his pain. She was far too sensitive to ask more of him, and Torek was oddly touched by her restraint and compassion.

"A lover, then? Someone you've left behind on your Earth?"

"No. No husband, no lover, no family." She shrugged. "I not stay in one place long enough to make friends."

Torek couldn't have heard her correctly. The tone of her voice, so nonchalant, could not have said what she'd just said. He covered the pan and turned to her. "No family?"

"You keep this up, your food will burn again," she remarked.

She was deliberately changing the subject, but she was also right. He cracked several yarks into a bowl, set the oven to heat, and began whisking. "Your parents are dead? No siblings or cousins? No aunts or uncles or forefathers?"

Delaney crossed her arms. Her upper lip sneered. Had she been a lorok, a single fang would have peeked out. "Family not needed. They are expectations and rules and... and a cage. I make my own path in life, and I better for it."

Torek heard the bitterness beneath her bravado and reeled. No. The answer to every one of his questions was no. "Were you a lone survivor of some accident or disaster that wiped out your entire family?"

"No. They alive for all I know. I just not know."

"How is that possible?" He pulled the haekak from the chiller and spread it out on the counter, pressing it flat with long rolls. "Who raised you?"

"I raise myself."

Still that bravado. Still that bitterness. "Young humans are self-sufficient upon birth?"

"No, of course not."

Torek considered his haekak. It was rolled thin, but could use a little evening. Too thin and the crust would rip while baking. Too thick, and it would not bake through. "So. Who cared for you until you were self-sufficient?"

Her face burned red. "I not know the Lori word."

"When has that ever stopped you?"

She blew out a hard breath. "People the government pay to keep children with no family."

Torek frowned. "We don't have a word for that. All children have family."

A little of that bravado cracked into anger. "All children on Lorien have family?"

"Yes."

She gave him an unfathomable look. "What about the children no one want?"

Torek stopped rolling his haekak. "Children no one want?"

"The ones born from rape. The ones whose parents die young." She crossed her arms. "All children not have a family."

"They do. Even if a child is born in difficult circumstances—by rape or in poverty or by dying parents—extended family will raise the child to maturity."

"What if the child is left for dead in a, a trash heap, for example, and no one know the family she belong to?"

"Are you asking what would happen to a child thrown in the garbage?" Torek blinked. "Why would that ever happen?"

"Why do a million things happen?" Delaney suddenly shouted, her hands chopping the air. "Maybe the mother is young and feeling shame for having a child with no husband. Maybe she on drugs and not handle the weight. Maybe someone attack her, take the baby from her stomach, and toss it aside. Maybe the father is abusive and force

192

her to do it. Maybe the mother die, and the father is too young or too stupid or too selfish to care for me on his own. In those circumstances, what happen to the child here on Lorien?"

It didn't escape Torek's notice that "the child" had turned to "me" in the middle of her rant. *Lorien, lend me your steady breath.* He draped the haekak gently over a shallow pan. If he focused all his concentration on cooking, maybe the horror he felt at her words wouldn't materialize in his expression.

"I don't know," he said, his voice overly calm even to his own ears. "Many of those scenarios are unfathomable. What does bearing a child while young and unwed have anything to do with feeling shame? Why would a child be tossed aside even after a gruesome attack? Why would a father not raise his child, and if he was mentally ill or physically unable to do so, why was he without family to raise the child on his behalf? You're speaking as if the child is a burden."

Delaney stared at him a long moment. Her hands had locked into a white-knuckled fist on the table. "Children are a burden."

Torek pursed his lips. "We don't see children that way. They're a rare gift. A blessing." He strained to keep his voice casual as he continued, but he feared that not all his shock could be contained. "Children aren't cherished on Earth?"

Delaney chewed on her lip, but he didn't think the movement had anything to do with hunger. "They are, by many humans. But children are not rare on Earth. Millions of babies are born every year. Every—" Her eyes rolled up in calculation. "Every Rorak and half of Genai."

Torek jerked back, astounded. "Millions?" There weren't even one million lorienok on Lorien. A few thousand babies were born every Genai, and barely half ever survived their first zorel season.

She nodded. "Children are expensive, and sometimes mothers feel shame in having them, and many of the circumstances I describe happen on Earth all the time."

Torek poured the whisked yarks and fried keylak and jok over the haekak. The yarks pooled in the pan, connecting everything into one mass. He couldn't imagine. So many children, so many blessings, so many resources needed for their survival. He could imagine their burden in such circumstances, but gazing upon Delaney—upon her beauty and temerity, her frailty and stubborn strength—it both grieved and angered him that she would be considered such a burden.

He slid the pan of yark e haekak in to bake and set his daami to chime in thirty minutes, ignoring the itching reminder that he'd considered her a burden when purchasing her as his animal companion.

"So these circumstances happen often enough that your government has a process for giving children a new family?" Torek washed his hands and sat at the table next to Delaney.

"Yes and no," she said. "Sometimes a child gets a new family. But sometimes a temporary family is paid to raise the child until a permanent family is found. I live with several temporary families from when I was born until I was sixteen years, um"—she looked up at the ceiling for a moment—"almost thirteen kair."

"Several families?"

"Yes. One no longer want me in their home. Another is found unacceptable to host children. And I run away from the last."

Torek willed his hackles not to rise. "A home was found unacceptable to host children *after* you were hosted by them?"

Delaney's jaw flexed. She was grinding her teeth. "Yes."

"What happened?"

Delaney slouched in her chair. Her hands dropped to her lap and wedged between her thighs, and Torek realized that he was prying. His questions had crossed the boundary from inquisitive to hurtful, and unlike Delaney and her sensitive retreat when she'd approached that line, Torek was barreling headlong into unwanted territory.

"A permanent family was never found, then?" he asked instead.

She shook her head, gazing away and out the skinny sliver of window to the snowy world outside the estate's stone walls. "I am better off. Imagine if I have family? Of all the humans to abduct from Earth, I am the best choice."

Torek quivered with the strain of keeping his anger in check. "How is that?"

"I am the one missing person who is not missed."

She couldn't hide the bitterness anymore. It bled into every word, and Torek's heart was poisoned by it. He reached out, smoothing his finger pads over her wrists.

She jumped at the contact. Her gaze whipped to his hands.

He pulled her hands from between her thighs and squeezed her fingers gently but firmly. "I disagree. You deserved a permanent family, and you never should've been harvested. But I'm selfishly glad you were."

"Why?" she whispered.

"Because..." Gah, Shemara would gorge herself on this. "Because knowing you has healed parts of me."

She slipped her hands from his. "You not know me. Not really. Not as a person."

Torek squeezed his fists on empty air. "I want to know you as a person."

"Why?" she snapped.

His hackles rose, beyond the ability to hide his anger anymore. "You're part of my family now."

She laughed, but the sound was laced with the same bitterness as her words. Where had he misstepped? "Another temporary family. Joy!"

"Not temporary. I love you, my Resh—" He coughed. "My Delaney. Your home with me is permanent."

"Yes, your *Reshna*. You want to ship me back to Earth, remember?"

Torek considered his possible responses, but she'd cornered him. If he planned to return her to Earth, he was throwing her away, but if he kept her, he was enslaving her.

In the wake of his telling silence, Delaney nodded.

He couldn't help the growl that ripped from his throat. "What would you have me do?" he snarled. "As Reshna, you're my family, for me to care for and indulge and love. As Delaney, you're my prisoner. I can't abide that."

Her eyes rolled. "Now who is the diva?"

"You're not imprisoned?" Rak, when had he begun shouting?

"No, I am not."

He pointed accusingly at her tether lying discarded on the floor. "Yes, you are!"

She grabbed his hand and held it. "You protect me, not imprison me."

"Why do you need protecting? Who are you scared of?"

"Keil and I plan for the worst for five years. The worst happen. I think our plan, five years in making, is better than your plan, five minutes in making!"

"The worst happened." Torek's eyes narrowed. "Who murdered Keil?"

Delaney released his hand and wrapped her arms around herself. Her lips clamped shut.

He cupped her shoulders and shook her gently. "The worst happened, Delaney, but I can make it right if you'll let me!"

"You not make it right! No one can!"

"I can do anything. I'm Torek Lore'Onik Weidnar Kenzo Lesh'Aerai Renaar. Do you know what my many names mean?"

"Onik, Weidnar, and Kenzo are the three major cities on Lorien," she said, ticking off his names on her fingers. "And you are captain of the guard of all three. And the estate owner of a fourth town."

"Yes, and do you know what *that* means?"

"It means you think you command the world!" She was so exasperated, her chest actually heaved with the strain of breathing and shouting.

Torek did not grin. She would think she'd won if he grinned. "I command, and the people of Lorien obey."

"Not all of Lorien! Not everyone!"

"Yes, everyone!"

Delaney shook her head, stubbornly refusing to accept that he was right, to see that he'd just won their argument. He could make anything right against any enemy. He had full reign over every city, over every lor and lorok in all of Lorien.

Well, all save one. He didn't have reign over Dorai Nikiok Lore'Lorien.

His daami chimed. Their yark e haekak was ready.

The zorel alarm drowned the chiming of his daami and all contemplations of matching wills and winning against Delaney. His stomach hitched into the throat.

Genai had come.

PART TWO

Genai (noun): The slightly less bitterly cold season on the planet Lorien, lasting approximately six Earth months.

TWENTY

Talk about being saved by the bell. Torek's infernal gut logic had launched a full missile attack on the truth, blowing past every barrier she'd attempted to erect against a direct hit. He'd been getting there too, right before the power had cut, replaced by dim emergency lights, and the fierce, ear-stabbing wail of a fire truck's siren pierced the room.

Delaney slapped both hands over her ears, attempting to muffle the sound. "What is that?" She screamed, then froze, realizing she'd spoken in English.

The siren cut midwail and was replaced by a monotone voice over an intercom.

"Third quadrant. Zone forty. Point three, two, seven, nine, four, two, two..."

As the voice droned, Delaney realized that Torek hadn't heard her anyway or wasn't paying her any mind. He'd retreated to his bedroom and was getting dressed. She blinked. Fully dressed. Not just in his usual waterproof workout jumpsuit and weapons holster, but in head-to-toe uniform. He pounded his claw-tipped toes into spike-soled boots, smoothed his long hair into a bun at the back of his head, and faced her as he tugged the bottom of his jacket to lie flat against his broad chest.

Her breath caught. She'd joked with him about his commanding the entire world because he seemed so arrogant and the deference people gave him seemed ridiculous, but now, faced with his solemn, confident, powerful presence, she realized that she'd misjudged. He was a commander.

The commander.

"Take dinner out of the oven." He strode toward the door. "Stay here. Don't leave this room. I'll return before you even finish eating."

Delaney jumped up from her chair and blocked his path. "Wait! What happen?" She waved her hand at the flashing lights.

"It's our first zorel breach. Early this season, but considering your accident on the Zorelok, I'm not surprised." He gripped her shoulders and moved her bodily aside. "The yark e haekak. Take it out before it burns."

"The what?" She clung to his biceps. "Stop! Where are you—"

The siren wailed again, drowning out her voice.

"This sounds serious!" she shouted. "Should we leave the building?"

Torek picked her up and settled her on his hip. Cupping his mouth, he spoke directly into her ear. "No. People will evacuate their homes and come here if necessary, but it won't come to that. Not yet. This early, we can probably reinforce the ice before she escapes. You're safest here."

She grabbed his head and turned his face aside to speak into his ear. "But you leave?"

He glanced askance at her and grinned. "I must reinforce the ice."

He strode to the dining nook with her still on his hip, opened the oven door, covered his hand with an oven mitt—he smelled like vanilla and used oven mitts—and took out the omelet pie. It looked absolutely delicious, like a well-baked quiche. Her stomach rolled, but not with hunger. She'd be eating alone.

He set the quiche on the table, plopped her down on a chair, and extracted himself from her grip. He pointed at the pie, then leaned down to shout in her ear. "Eat. I'll return."

The siren cut.

"Third quadrant. Zone forty. Point three, two, seven..."

Torek stepped back, but Delaney lunged out and grabbed his hand. "You return before I finish dinner?"

He blinked once, then tightened his hold on her fingers. "Eat slowly."

Torek released her hand, about-faced, and strode from the room, shutting the door behind him.

At least he didn't bother trying to lock her inside.

Delaney puffed her cheeks and sighed her frustration, staring at the quiche. It really did look absolutely delicious even if World War III was being waged outside their bedroom door. Better than rainol e lokks any day.

But she'd eaten rainol e lokks every day for a month straight, so maybe she was biased.

She tried to stay calm despite the sirens, emergency lights, and droning intercom, and took Torek's advice—she refused to think she was following his orders. She sliced into the pie, taking care to carve and remove a neat wedge from the whole. She found his obsidian tableware—technically not *silver*ware—and scooped up her first bite.

The crust was flaky, and the egg was soft, and the chopped plants were both sweet and mouthwateringly savory. After the day she'd endured, it took some restraint not to inhale the entire pie. She forcibly enjoyed each bite—slowly, as he'd *recommended*—but when she finished fifteen minutes later, he hadn't returned. She had another slice, and another, until she finally gagged and had to give up.

A disaster that warranted sirens, power containment, and official government prerecorded messages wouldn't be averted in fifteen minutes. She washed the dishes as she waited. She dried and returned them to the cabinet, then crawled into bed. She was not going to stare at the tablet's digital clock display. She stared at the ceiling instead. She scratched an itch on her arm and another on the back of her leg. The ceiling remained unmoved.

Her resolve buckled.

Only one symbol had changed on the clock. Less than a minute.

She contorted her arm to scratch at the small of her back and groaned.

What was going on out there? How could a hibernating ice fish warrant this kind of protocol? And how did one "reinforce ice"?

And why the hell was the bed so itchy?

She peeked under the comforter and sighed. Torek's shedding was out of control.

She glanced at the tablet again. A second symbol hadn't changed yet.

Staring at the time wouldn't make it pass any faster. Her hand curled into a fist. She refused to scratch. She refused to clock watch. She—

The sirens pierced her ears a third time, completely obliterating her frayed nerves. Before she even realized what she was doing, she had opened the door and was poking her head outside.

Considering the urgency of the sirens, she'd half expected the hallway to be under siege, but it was completely deserted. The emergency lights were flashing outside the bedroom in pulsing rhythm with the swell and ebb of the blaring siren.

Delaney stepped out, closed the door behind her, and crept down the back hall. She was distinctly aware of the fact that she was directly disobeying Torek's explicit orders, but the sirens spurred her forward. Step after hesitant, halting step, their blaring call stole her breath and reason until an ignorance-induced panic completely overshadowed any sense of self-preservation. Delaney reached the end of the hallway just as the siren cut back to droning coordinates. She steeled herself against whatever was around the corner and peeked into the large round room where Torek's guard typically sat, presumably guarding.

She blinked. They were watching a movie.

Their individual hologram computer stations were feeding a giant 3D projection in the center of the arena. It was a sci-fi flick, complete with a hover vehicle and ray guns. The hover vehicle was zapping a giant creature that had busted through the icy surface of a frozen river. Only half the creature had emerged, but judging from the half she could see, she most assuredly did not want to see more.

The creature was enormous, easily the size of a blue whale, with the head of an anglerfish, one of those alien-looking deep-sea creatures with dead eyes and millions of needle teeth. Its giant, unhinged jaw was larger than the hover vehicle. Behind its jaws where its neck should have been, or gills, considering its fishy nature, it had a flapping, rattling mane, similar to the poisonous dinosaur that had killed Ned in Jurassic Park. Its burnt-orange-and-brown-striped body was slick like sealskin, and it had arms like the rigid, boney claws of a vulture instead of fins. Those talon-tipped, skeletal appendages were reaching out between ray gun blasts to swat at the attacking vehicle.

"Talk to me, Commander," Dorai Nikiok Lore'Lorien intoned. She was watching the movie and presiding over everyone from the vantage of the dais. Shemara Kore'Onik stood next to her, tight-lipped and wringing her hands.

The projection split into two images, the aerial battle on the left and a close-up of Torek's face on the right.

"She's out for blood, literally, I think," Torek's projection said. "Rak." He pulled back on a steering column.

The vehicle on the left somersaulted around a swatting claw.

"My reinforcement team is on the ground on standby," he said.

"Your team cannot reinforce the ice until she is beneath it," Nikiok said. Her voice was calm, as if she was expressing her opinion on bagels vs. donuts for breakfast and not the best technique to ice a giant Anglervulturasaurus.

"Yes, Dorai. I'm aware."

Shemara leaned into Nikiok's side. "He shouldn't be in combat. I haven't cleared him yet."

Nikiok waved her claws dismissively.

205

"How did he gain access to the flight hangar?" Shemara pressed. "He can't—"

"He can and he is," Nikiok hissed. "I cleared him."

Shemara blinked. A lifetime of restraint poured into that one blink. "You?"

Nikiok faced forward, returning her attention to the movie.

Shemara shook her head. "He's not ready," she insisted. "We've made progress, but you can't just—"

Nikiok cut her off with a glance.

Shemara bowed her head. "Dorai. Respectfully. Torek Lore'Onik Weidnar Kenzo Lesh'Aerai Renaar should not be leading this combat mission."

"Thanks for the vote of confidence," Torek said dryly.

Shemara glanced up at the hologram. "It's not my confidence you need, but my clearance."

The guard shifted uncomfortably. They glanced at each other, at Shemara, and back at each other, uneasy.

"Filuk Renaar is ready," Shemara persisted, oblivious. "Torek's second is well chosen and well trained, and I—"

"You never finished your thought from earlier." Nikiok didn't look away from the hologram. "What can't I do, Shemara Kore'Onik?"

Shemara bowed her head again. "Nothing, Dorai."

Nikiok leaned into Shemara's face, her gaze never leaving the hologram, and hissed. "He's already in flight. Whether or not you approve, *I* approve, and he *will have our support.*"

Shemara's bow deepened. "Yes, Dorai."

Delaney glanced from the movie and Torek's likeness to gaze out the window. She wasn't sure what made her look. A movement in the corner of her eye, maybe, but that seemed unlikely considering how small and distant the movement was. Instinct, more likely. No matter its size and proximity, or what had made her look, there it was. A hover vehicle was maneuvering in crazy acrobatics midair, blasting rays of light into the dark valley of a snowy ravine.

This far away, the hover vehicle was no bigger than a gnat, but its sweeping movements as it dipped and flipped and charged were identical to the vehicle on screen. Its little spits of light and the explosive blasts detonating in great holographic detail mirrored real life.

This was no movie.

Jesus Christ, this was happening. That was Torek. And the, the *thing* he was battling was the hibernating ice fish this world was fortified against. The zorel.

That wasn't a fucking fish. That was a nightmare creature from frozen hell!

She recognized the ravine with sudden startling clarity as the same ravine that she'd fallen down. The ice, now blasted through by the zorel, was still stained with her blood.

Out for blood, Torek had said, and Delaney covered her mouth at the quelling thought that crept into her mind: this was her fault.

He'd told her to eat slowly. That he'd be back before she finished dinner.

All the many helpings of omelet pie that she'd devoured curdled in her stomach.

He might not be back at all.

"Commander?" Nikiok intoned.

"Just one moment. She's locked in on me now. I just..."

The hover vehicle swirled into a nosedive, its trajectory plummeting directly into the creature's unhinged mouth.

The horror, the guilt, the insensible denial: it all slammed together in a triple-decker pileup inside Delaney's throat. She covered her mouth before it released a scream.

The zorel ticked its mouth open another notch, if that was possible, so its jaws were practically bent back 180 degrees, forcing a protective layer of its slick skin to seal over its eyes.

Torek jerked the hover vehicle up and out of its nosedive moments before he would have plummeted straight down the creature's esophagus. He was reversing out of the jaws surrounding him but hadn't quite cleared them yet when he blasted a volley of fire down its throat.

"Got it!" Torek confirmed.

The creature shrieked. Its trilling cry reverberated from the many speakers inside the arena in harmony with its real scream echoing across the countryside. It tossed its head, snapped its jaws closed, and swiped out in blind panic and outrage.

Had Torek reversed out of its jaws in time? Was he trapped inside the hover vehicle, inside the mouth of that *monster*?

The projection speckled with dancing white flecks as the creature collapsed in on itself, still shrieking. Delaney squinted, but the static was so thick, she couldn't discern what was happening. Had it plunged back under the ice? Were they losing signal? Was someone going to fix it?

Where the fuck is Torek?

A low rumble backdropped the creature's incessant shrieks, and a disorienting sensation tickled the back of Delaney's mind. She glanced out the window again and noticed that the shadow of the ravine was blurred by a white cloud. She blinked. Not a cloud, a poof of snow. Blowback from an avalanche.

A streak of snow punched through the blowback, and the gnat-sized hover vehicle soared across the sky like a comet.

Torek.

Delaney's lungs heaved.

"Mission complete. The zorel is neutralized, and our reinforcement team is well underway."

The room erupted in cheers. Lorienok jumped up from their desks and punched the air. They lifted both hands high overhead, turned to their neighbors, and bumped the sides of their fists together. They whooped with joy and relief and victory.

Delaney doubled over and retched. Just air at first, and then the second and third heaves were all half-digested egg, crust, and vegetable slop.

She wiped her mouth with the back of her hand and froze,

glancing up at the celebrating guard, but the sick lay there, as unnoticed as the animal who'd produced it. She crept back a step, tensing to leave.

Again, she didn't know what made her look; she couldn't blame movement this time. Perhaps the complete lack of movement had caught her attention. As everyone else was celebrating, Dorai Nikiok Lore'Lorien remained completely still, her laser-precise gaze homed in on Delaney.

Delaney let her gaze wander smoothly past Nikiok without blinking, without pause or hesitation. She was a golden retriever, and she didn't recognize or fear the suspicion and calculation in Nikiok's gaze. Shit, she was trembling. Delaney left the congealing slop of her dinner on the floor and wandered back down the hall to her room, where she should have damn well stayed until Torek's return.

TWENTY-ONE

TOREK CAUGHT HIMSELF ABOUT TO KNOCK ON HIS OWN DOOR. Anger, resentment, frustration, and, above it all, concern flooded over the exhaustion that his adrenaline high had left behind, and in that void of quaking vulnerability, he couldn't ignore the telling scent of antiseptic.

Delaney had left the room while he'd been away, as he'd expected she would. But she'd been sick in his absence, which he hadn't expected. Petreok had eagerly informed Torek upon his return that he'd cleaned the hallway himself. He'd beamed with pride, as if the thought of Torek's ill animal companion was something to beam over.

Torek should count his blessings. He'd returned whole and hale from the season's first zorel breach, not something that could be said of every Genai. He'd been greeted with praise and adoration upon his return, something that *could* be said of every zorel victory, the support of which had prolonged the heady rush that battle always stoked in him. The danger, the flight, the fear, and resulting praise was like a drug he couldn't quit, and no matter how many seasons passed, no matter how wrong a zorel containment could go, the many times it had gone right was enough motivation that the horror of coming face-to-face with death was always tinged with a strange, indescribable feeling of homecoming.

Zana had never understood. She'd never doubted or questioned him, but she'd never really understood. Some of his fellow guard didn't either, but a select few—usually the ones who died young or who made a lifetime career of it, like him—shared his sentiments. Same as his forefathers, the fight was in his blood, and with his blood surging in that moment of attack, he reached a higher plane of clarity.

His thoughts were blades. He could see the zorel's muscles bunching and tensing, and he'd know her next move before she did. How did he flip the hovercraft mid nosedive? How had he known the killing hand of the zorel was swatting his right blind spot? How did he escape her jaws when his monitors were iced by snowfall?

He didn't know. He just did.

He'd tempted death and evaded its clutches for so many seasons, innumerable times, that he lived on it. The danger nourished him. The adrenaline strengthened him. The perfect synchrony of mind and beast made him bigger than his mortal body. He stared down the yawning maw of that mighty creature, down into death itself, and was mightier.

But the high didn't last. Fear and doubt and self-chastisement at the risks he'd so readily taken depressed him long before the cheers of his people faded. They were still celebrating his victory and would for days, maybe weeks, to come. Until the next zorel attack, most likely, and he'd face her and the yawning snap of her jaws again gladly.

Yet the thought of confronting Delaney made him hesitate entering his own living quarters.

Steeling his resolve, he dropped his fist and opened the door.

His room was empty.

"Delaney?" His eyes scanned the room and narrowed. The window was open.

He strode to the window, equal parts uneasy and feeling ridiculous for that unease. Becoming ill with fright after seeing the zorel was one thing. Throwing herself off the ramparts of the estate from that same fear was quite another. Still, his heart was racing as swiftly as his stride as he lunged forward, ducked, and angled his horns through the window, craning his head outside.

Delaney was sitting on the ramparts, huddled with her knees to her chest.

"Delaney," he whispered carefully, loath to startle her from her perch. "What are you doing?"

She glanced over her shoulder at him, then away. "I need to think."

"Think inside, where it's warm."

"I like the balcony, where it's private." She turned a glare on him. "You reinforce the ice?"

"Yes." He glanced down at the courtyard far below. At this height, he could cover the fountain with his thumb. "Come inside."

"No, thank you."

"That wasn't a request. Come inside, now. You're freezing."

"I am fine." She huddled into her fur coverings so only her eyes were exposed. "I finish dinner long ago."

He tamped down the spark of frustration that tried to light. She needed compassion right now, not admonitions. "I'm sorry I'm late."

"Late," she said, her voice muffled by the fur. "You leave me then go die in battle but sorry for being late."

He sighed. "Come inside, and we'll have this conversation in the warmth of my living quarters."

She twisted to face him, and he breathed a sigh of relief. He held out his hand to steady her.

But she didn't take it. "You lie."

"I never lie." He growled. Rak, patience.

"You say you return."

He spread his arms. "And here I am!"

"*How you return if you die?*" she burst.

Ah. "I wasn't in danger of dying. Well, there's always *some* danger, but—"

"I see you in battle! I watch as you fly that hover vehicle into—into—" She slapped her wrists together, her curled fingers chomping the air.

"The zorel."

"—that giant mouth with teeth, and you say you not in danger of dying? You lie!"

"I was closer to death during my fever than I was battling the zorel."

Her pale face turned bright red. "And I battle for you against that fever. I risk everything—"

"*You* risked everything?"

"—just for you to fly into that monster's mouth and die."

"I don't need your permission to protect my people and my estate," Torek snapped. "I'm captain of the guard. It's my job to—"

"You still on medical leave."

Torek barked out a laugh. "Is that the excuse you'll give the people of Onik when the zorel storms the estate on a path of blood and death? Parents will be comforted when their children and spouses are slaughtered knowing that I'm completing my therapy. Oh, that's right, no one will hear your excuses because they'll all be dead!"

"I not give excuses. I not *speaking*!" She shook with the force of her shout. "When you die, they sell me to someone else. Maybe that someone will care for me like you, and maybe that someone not care. But that someone not you." Her glare and her sneer and her words were fierce, but her voice suddenly cut short on a trembling whisper. Her hand lifted to cover her mouth. "That someone not *you*."

Torek's anger deflated. She'd been terrified. He could see it in the shudder of her body as she endured the punishing cold. He could hear it in the wet cotton of her words, and he could smell it like the copper tang of spilled blood. He couldn't begrudge her that. In fact, as he witnessed her distress, the opposite occurred. His chest swelled with answering affection, and his voice, so harsh just a moment ago, was soft and coaxing when he murmured, "Come here, little one."

"No."

Oh, his little diva. He eyed the window warily. He wasn't even sure he'd fit through the narrow panel, but there was no help for it. Grasping the windowpane, he hoisted himself up and jammed his upper half through the opening.

Delaney's hand jumped off her face. "What are you doing?"

"You won't come to me? I'll come to you."

"Stop. You get stuck." She eyed the rampart's edge. "Or pop through. The momentum carry you over the railing."

He wedged the breadth of his chest through the window and promptly got stuck.

"See?" She pushed at his shoulders, but he still strained forward. "Stop! You pop through and fall!"

He paused his efforts and lifted his hand to her.

She sighed. "*Ofalltheidioticridiculous...*"

She continued muttering insensibly but took his hand. He guided her carefully back to the window. When she was within reach, he wrapped his hands around her waist, pulled her to him, and embraced her shivering body tight to his chest.

She wasn't an animal companion, but his heart didn't understand that. She was still his, somehow—to hold, to protect, to love. The relief and warmth that overtook him nearly made his knees buckle.

"What am I to do with you?" he murmured against her hair.

"Tell me the truth from now forward," she muttered. "Would be a good start."

He released a barking burst of laughter. "Considering the lies of omission you've dealt me over the past several weeks, how about we call it even?"

"Agreed." She pushed her small palms flat against his chest and leaned back to meet his eyes "Torek?"

"Mmmm?" My Lorien, but her eyes were wide, their gray depths fathomless. His heart flip-flopped.

He'd need to leave Delaney home one day and discuss these inappropriate feelings with Shemara.

"Is it my fault?"

"That I'm irrationally stressed? Yes."

She punched his chest lightly. "The zorel attack. You say it hunt for blood. My blood?"

He tightened his hold on her. "Your accident was just that. An accident. The zorel breach was no one's fault."

"But my blood cause it." She bit her lip.

"Genai comes, following Rorak like it comes every kair, with or without your blood. The ice keeps the zorel contained and in hibernation, but once the ice melts, there's no stopping it from hunting."

"Once the ice melts. But it hunt now before it melts."

"Technically, but—"

"It taste my blood, so it hunt early." Her forehead fell against his chest in defeat. "My fault."

Torek rubbed the top of her head with his chin. She was too perceptive for her own good. "Come. Let's get you warmed up."

He nudged her toward the door, and she actually followed his guidance for the first few steps without resisting. But once his hand gripped the door lever, she balked.

"Where we going? I change into dry clothes here."

"You're chilled to the bone, Delaney. A hot bath will warm you faster and more effectively. Your manual says—"

"I know what my manual says," she muttered. "I help write it."

He blinked back his shock. Keil's murder, Daerana's attack on Onik, Delaney's manual: it all pieced together. For both their sakes, he needed to discover how and complete the picture if he ever wanted to understand Delaney and the nightmare she'd witnessed. But he could only solve one problem at a time. "Then I shouldn't have to tell you that in addition to providing warmth, a bath will relax your stressed muscles. Despite original evidence to the contrary, you like taking baths." He gave her a look. "Or so you wrote in your manual."

Her eyes rolled. "Fine."

Her put-upon expression would've been more convincing had her jaw not been chattering.

He hustled her through the hallway, into the washroom, and locked the door behind them. When he turned back to face her, she'd already crossed the room to the tub and started the hot water. She leaned over the tub's edge, hand extended, testing its temperature.

Torek stared, feeling suddenly like he was intruding. All the times he'd bathed her, cleaned her, touched her, and all without asking permission. Shame burned beneath the fur on his face. Delaney didn't need him, not for this anyway. More importantly, she probably didn't want him.

Torek cleared his throat. "I'll return soon."

She glanced over her shoulder and met his gaze, both her brows raised. "Animal companions not bathe themselves."

Torek glanced at the closed door and then back at her. "What would you have me do?"

"We bathe as we always bathe. Together."

"We can't." His voice was more guttural than he intended, but bathing her now was unthinkable. Just remembering how they'd always shared a bath, how blithely he'd changed in front of her, changed her—defecated next to her!—it was mortifying. Lorien skewer him, what she must think of him.

"To them, I am an animal. We must keep up appearances."

"You're not an animal to me."

Her cheeks flushed a becoming shade of red. "We bathe together before."

"Don't." He lifted a hand. "Just...don't."

She threw her hands up in the air. "Then I bathe alone. But stay, and let them think we bathe together."

"If we tell everyone the truth, then this charade won't be necessary," he argued, but ruined his resolve by giving her his back.

She made a sick, sad attempt at shuffling. "Yes, no need to share a bath when we both dead."

The splash of her testing the water again.

"And I am not dramatic," she continued. "You not there. You not see Keil and how he—" Her voice became thick and wet. She cleared her throat. "You not see."

The wet plop of her clothes dropping to the tile.

Torek stared studiously at the door rivets. "It's possible you're mistaken in what you think you saw."

"No."

He tamped down his frustration with her flat, automatic answer, but not before a low growl slipped passed his lips. Rak, she made him lose control with a single word. "You couldn't identify the lor with the knife who chased you off Graevlai."

"Fukyoo," she snapped.

"In traumatic situations, sometimes witnesses aren't certain—"

"I am certain. I know what I saw. I know what is at risk, and that is that."

"That is what?"

"That ends this topic."

"I disagree. I have plenty more to say on this topic."

"Then talk. But I not listen."

He choked back the urge to whip around and shake her. He breathed. He fisted and flexed his hands. He counted door rivets.

When the flash of his temper had cooled, he finally spoke. "How is it that with your freedom at stake, I'm the only one willing to fight for it?"

"Keil already die for me. I not let you die for me too."

"Your concern is admirable but misplaced. I won't die, and I won't let anything happen to you either."

"Things already happen. The knife attack—"

"You said yourself, he didn't attack you."

"—the ukok poisoning—"

"Was an accident." His palms ached from the force of his

squeezed fists. "A potentially fatal accident, but an accident all the same." Mairok didn't resent him that much, surely.

"Because the cooks at Grattao not know my allergy? They not make my lunch every week since I arrive?" she scoffed. "Revealing what I am will make the attacks worse."

"We'll speak to Brinon Kore'Onik together. He'll—"

"Jeesuskrystnotthatbullshitagen." A heavy sigh. "Please, Torek, I beg you. Just stop."

"And once he realizes that you're a person," Torek persisted, "not an animal companion, he'll begin the process of reclassifying you. Then we can—"

"You say the point of this bath is to relax!"

He shuffed. "And to warm yourself."

"And relax," she insisted.

"Fine, but when you're warmed and relaxed, we—"

"Ohfuk!" A crack, a splash, and a shallow swell of water bathed his feet.

"Resh—" He shook his head. Damn it. "Delaney?"

Silence.

He peeked over his shoulder. She was under the water. He stared. Three heartbeats passed, and she didn't emerge.

He lunged into the bath, gripped her under the arms, and raised her above the water. "Delaney!"

She burst from the water, sputtering. "Now you want to bathe?"

"I'm not bathing you. I'm saving you."

"I not need your saving," she denied, coughing.

"I've never known you to bathe without needing my saving."

Her glare was fierce and adorable, with the mop of her hair covering half her face.

He smoothed back her hair and grinned.

Her eyes narrowed with focus and evil intent, which should have been warning enough, but it never was with her, not when she'd been Reshna and certainly not now that she was Delaney.

She splashed him in the face, blinding him with soapy water. He released her, but as he reared back, his feet slid out from under him. She tried to steady him, and damn him, he grasped the nearest thing, her reaching hands. But her sharp tug overcorrected his weight on the slick tile, and he fell into the tub fully dressed, flight jacket, trousers, and all.

TWENTY-TWO

THE FACT THAT ANY WATER WAS LEFT IN THE MASSIVE MINIPOOL of a tub following the tidal splash from Torek's nosedive was a miracle. As it was, the water hovered just below Delaney's breasts. They bobbed at the surface even as she slouched as low as possible with Torek hogging the majority of their cramped space. He reemerged with a mighty roar, sluicing more water over the tub's rim in a second, less impressive wave following the first.

"Are you certain you saving and not bathing?" she asked, managing to keep a straight face.

Torek shook the water from his eyes and fixed her with a menacing glare that might have been quite fierce had his long hair not dripped water into his face. A particularly well-aimed sudsy drop assaulted his eyeball, and he winced.

Delaney covered her mouth, but her laugh still escaped in a smothered snort. "The great Torek Lore'Onik Weidnar Kenzo Lesh'Aerai Renaar, defeat by soapsuds."

"Don't. Just, ack." He swiped at his hair as another foaming drop stung his eyes.

She chortled. "You not worry. I keep silent."

"Of course you'll keep silent. You don't speak to anyone but me. You—" And then he got a good look at her through squinting, bloodshot eyes and realized she was joking. He grunted.

"If you not laugh at yourself, who you laugh at?"

"Easy for you to say. You're laughing at me."

"I am laughing *with* you if you laughing too."

He shrugged out of his jacket, peeled the bedsheet-like undershirt from his body, maneuvered out of his pants, and dropped everything on the tile floor in a sopping heap. But it wasn't until he lifted his boots from the bath and upended the water out of them that Delaney gave up on subtlety and let herself crack up.

A wall of water smacked her in the face. She choked midlaugh, coughed, and then splashed him back, laughing harder.

He roared, his menace interrupted by the spurts and hiccups of his own laughter. The force of his return fire left the remaining water level dangerously low.

"Oh, God," she groaned, clutching her stomach.

Torek was recovering from their bout of insanity too, but at her words, he glanced at her inquisitively.

"Sorry," she said, realizing she'd spoken in English. "I not laughing like that in a long time."

He sobered slightly. "Since leaving Earth?"

"Yes, but before leaving Earth too." She pulled herself together on a deep sigh.

"I don't laugh often either, but my place and position isn't prone to laughter. But with you..." He paused, considering. "With you, my place and position fades, so I'm just Torek."

Something sparked inside her, so the hot water wasn't the only source of heat warming her body. She eased herself more fully into the bath and splashed up more suds, suddenly sharply aware of her nakedness.

"I know your feelings," she murmured.

Torek turned on the faucet to refill the tub, then lounged back, relaxing rather than hiding in the water. "Was your position and place on Earth not prone to laughter?"

"My position and place on Earth very different, but yes, not prone to laughter."

"Different in what way?"

Delaney bit her lip. *In every way imaginable,* she thought. "You serious because you the Commander of Onik. You must be an example to your guard."

"Your career didn't dictate your seriousness?" he guessed.

"No. I take food orders in a restaurant. Many other people with my career not serious."

"Then what caused your seriousness?"

"Just me, I guess. My unhappiness. My stress and worries."

He raised a doubtful eyebrow. "You have stress and worries here too."

"But here I not worry about my next meal or if I can afford the payment for my, my living quarters. I not share living quarters with people who take pleasure in hurting me." Delaney blinked with sudden clarity. "In many ways, living with you, even as your animal companion, is a better life than my freedom on Earth." She shook her head. "How sad."

Torek's eyes dropped to the water covering her breasts, and Delaney wondered if he could see through the suds to her body below. That throb pulsed between her legs.

Did she want him to see her body below?

They were classified as being in the same mukar, after all, like dogs that could interbreed. She winced on that wayward thought; just because a Chihuahua could technically mate with a Great Dane didn't mean she should.

But what if she actually wanted to?

"You lived with someone who hurt you? Who took *pleasure* in hurting you?" Torek asked.

She cleared her throat. What did it say about her that talking about the Todd family was actually sturdier ground than examining her feelings for Torek? "Yes. The family who is unacceptable to host children."

Torek stared at her, his expression inscrutable.

She shrugged. "It happens."

When he finally spoke, his voice was impossibly deep, and the words as much as their tone scraped something raw inside her. "It doesn't happen here on Lorien. I can't imagine that it should, not even on your Earth."

"Yes, well, what should not happen and what happen are often the same thing."

Had he asked her about Kane directly, she would have clammed up. She didn't want to talk about her past any more than she wanted to make snow angels in the courtyard nude—nothing was more point-less and exposing than reopening past wounds—but he didn't ask. He shifted his leg, unseen beneath the water's sudsy surface, and gently rubbed his calf alongside hers.

"The Todd family same as all the other families I live with over the years," she said before she could bite off her words. "At first."

The silence stretched.

Torek's calf continued its comforting, grounding strokes.

"The father is quick to anger. Quick with his fists too, but a good cook," she continued despite herself. "The mother is beautiful. Long, thick blond hair. Big brown eyes. A killer body. She—"

"She killed with her body?"

A laugh startled out of her. "No, just something we say. Her body is so beautiful, someone kill to have it."

"Killer body," Torek said, sounding amused.

Delaney nodded. "She is an addict to pain relief medicine and do anything for more. She steal a, a—" She mimed writing a prescription on her hand. "A thing doctors use to order medicine. I hear her call the drugstore and act like a doctor's assistant." She shook her head. "She do anything."

"What did she do to you?" Torek asked when she lapsed into a second silence.

"Nothing," Delaney whispered. "She do nothing."

Torek stroked his leg against hers again, but she hugged her knees and pulled her legs close to her chest, away from Torek's touch. Nearly eight years, three with therapy, and an alien abduction later, and still, talking about it felt like a cheese grater against the back of her eyes.

"Their son is my age," she continued. "We in the same grade, go to the same school, and ride the same bus. He help me settle into my new home, they say. He help me in my new classes and make new friends. We be such good friends, they say."

"Who is 'they'?"

"The government people who pay the Todd family."

"But you didn't become friends," Torek said, his voice deep and low, nearly a growl.

"No. We not become friends."

"Did you ever speak to someone about the Todd family?" Torek asked. "Like I speak to Shemara Kore'Onik?"

Delaney nodded, staring at the bubbles.

"Do you know *why* I speak to Shemara?"

"Because you have PTSD."

"I have what?"

Light glinted off the bath bubbles, creating a miniature rainbow inside each one. Hundreds of mini rainbows trapped in bubbles of their own making. "Your nightmares and night sweats and panic attacks and—"

"Yes, but *why* do I have those things?"

"Because you risk your life for your country for many seasons, and bad memories haunt you."

He actually grinned. "No."

"Because you love Shemara in secret? She understands you like no one before and no one will."

He stared at her, the dual gaze of his warm brown and ice-blue eyes peeling her apart.

She compressed her lips to forestall a threatening grin, then slowly sobered for the truth of her next guess. "Because your wife die young, and you blame yourself?"

"No."

She returned his look this time.

"Partly, perhaps," he half conceded. "But no."

She rolled her eyes. For a man who claimed to prefer dour stoicism, he certainly had a flair for the dramatic. "Why then?"

"I murdered a lorok."

Her eyes snapped down to meet his. "You not."

Torek cocked his horns sideways. "I'm a liar, then?"

"Maybe you kill a lorok. But you *not* murder her."

"A negligible difference."

"The difference between right and wrong often is," she whispered.

Torek thought about that a moment, then nodded deeply. "She thought that our government had done a grievous wrong to her and her family. She retaliated by breaking into the Onik estate with her husband's RG-800 and attempting to murder my entire guard."

"RG-800?"

"A powerful military weapon. With it in hand and in her mind-set, she possessed the means to wipe us out."

"But you stop her," Delaney said, certain.

"She'd already slaughtered a few dozen lorienok on her way through the courtyard, but yes, I killed her before she murdered anyone else." He took a deep, unsteady breath. "In all my seasons of service to Lorien, in my entire life, I'd never killed a lorok before. And now I've come to learn that she had some right to her anger."

Delaney jerked, taken aback. "A right to kill a few dozen people?"

He swallowed. "Her husband's death was ruled a suicide without a thorough investigation."

Delaney's teeth clacked closed. She knew what he was going to say, but he needed to actually say it for her to believe it.

His lips twisted bitterly. "Her husband was Keil Kore'Weidnar."

She inhaled. Then exhaled. She looked upon Torek—he refused

to meet her gaze directly—and shook her head back and forth in slow denial.

"You not know," she said, her voice guttural and not her own. "And even if you know, you never choose her life over your guard."

"Of course not," he said. "My point is that of all the many wounds I've survived, it's the one that didn't leave a physical scar that actually injured me the most."

His leg stroked hers again. It didn't look like he was stretching, but he must be to reach her while she was curled so far from him.

"There's no shame in surviving," he said. "As much as we might suffer afterward—and there's no shame in that either—life is worth it. We have struggled. We *are* struggling. But we are here."

Delaney lifted her eyes to meet his.

"And I'm here with you," he murmured.

He was. Torek was the highest-ranked military commander on Lorien—as different a person from her as she could possibly imagine —and yet, he really was here with her in this moment. He knew her in ways she wasn't sure she even knew herself.

"They remove me from the Todd house and give me to a different family," she whispered. "A perfect family, but I hate them. I want to light my eyeballs on fire watching them eat dinner and laugh together. Baking cookies, playing games, watching...watching the teleprojector. They try including me, but..." She shook her head, and a laugh scraped up from the back of her throat. "They not even fight right. No yelling or hitting or threats. Their love is like a deep well they all drink from, and they thrive from its nourishment. But for me, seeing their love is poison." She wedged her hands between her thighs, feeling the raised parallel tracks. "They say it about control and pain release. I not know. I just remember their laughing. I cut myself while the sound of their love echo up the stairwell and through my locked door. It stab deeper than any blade."

"Which thigh?"

Her gaze snapped to his. "My right."

"And your left?"

She pursed her lips. "I not self-inflict the cuts on my left thigh."

"You earned those scars while with the Todd family." His naturally deep, guttural voice dropped an octave so the sentence was more thunder than words.

Delaney dropped her gaze to watch the bubbles bob over the water's surface and nodded.

Torek leaned forward this time, abandoning his efforts to reach her unobtrusively beneath the water's surface. His hand found a forearm under the suds, and by feel alone, he stroked down her arm until her clamped thighs blocked his progress. His thumbs drew soft, coaxing circles on her skin as he waited. His gaze drilled through her self-conscious fear and shame to the core of her aching heart.

Like lava inside a volcano, the story churned inside her, but she'd trapped it without an outlet, letting it gain pressure for years. If she released it now, it wouldn't just seep out. It would erupt, and she didn't know what was more painful: the burn of keeping it inside or the devastation of eruption.

Her thighs parted, lured into relaxation from Torek's constant soothing. The space was slight, more just unclamped than actually open, but enough for Torek to pull her hands free and sandwich them with his own. His palms were noticeably warm, even in the warm water, and strong and large—hands accustomed to holding heavy burdens.

"The Todd father abuse his son." The words cut unwillingly from her throat like vomiting razor blades. "After years of punching and slapping and slicing into him since childhood, it no surprise he is what he is. It no surprise he do what he do."

"What did he do, Delaney?" Torek's voice was only a low rumble. A comforting murmur and a growling threat all at once.

She took a deep, shaking breath.

"He come into my room at night. The first time, I not expecting him, and before I even realize, he push me face-first into the pillows to muffle my screams. The four other times, I did scream. As loud and long as I could while I could. But he muffle me with the mattress, the pillow, the sheet, his sock—whatever available. I not know why he bother. His father work nights, and his mother..." Delaney shook her head. "The house catch fire and burn to ash around her, and she not notice."

"She did nothing," he murmured, horrified now.

Delaney swallowed. "He muffle my face into the mattress and cut my thigh. He enjoy it. He...he take pleasure in it."

Delaney tried to slip her hands from his to cover her face. Torek's gaze was relentless, and she couldn't watch him watching her as she remembered the sticky slide of Kane's cum in her hair, on her back, smeared into the blood between her thighs. But Torek tightened his hold.

"His mother never ask about the mess. She just clean the sheets and the next week, when it happen again, she clean the sheets again. Like it normal."

Torek narrowed his eyes. "Like it had happened before?"

She shrugged. "Maybe. I not know. My doctor report the cuts to the government people who pay the Todd family, and they give me to the perfect family."

Torek squeezed her fingers. "At least you can take comfort in knowing the Todd family was fed to the predators of your planet."

Delaney blinked, so thrown that she gaped for a long moment, replaying his words in her mind several times. But no, she hadn't misheard or misinterpreted him. It must be a Lori euphemism. "Fed to the predators of my planet?"

"They were caught. I'm assuming they were punished appropriately."

Delaney blinked again. "Is that what happen on this planet? Literally?"

"If a son were convicted of torturing another person under the eye of his parents? Yes, they would be imprisoned in the deporak, our underwater containment facility, until the coming Genai then released under the ice and fed to the zorel. She may as well become full on our evil people rather than our innocents."

"Jesus Christ."

"I've assumed incorrectly?" Torek asked dryly.

Delaney laughed. She couldn't help it. "Yes, very incorrectly. We do sometimes kill our 'evil people,' as you say, but only for bad crimes."

"The crimes against you were grievous."

"Not grievous enough on my planet." She was still chuckling under her breath.

Torek blinked. Then thundered, *"He's still alive?"*

God, she couldn't believe she was talking about all this and still laughing. "Sorry to disappoint, but we not have a zorel on Earth."

"Blood should be repaid in blood."

Delaney continued grinning even as the scalding pressure behind her eyeballs leaked down her cheeks. "I enjoy the sound of that," she whispered brokenly.

Torek released her hands, raised his arms above the water, and hesitated with his hands hovering over her shoulders. Drops of water from his fur dripped onto her skin and slid over her collarbone. His eyes darted from her face to the water's surface and back to her face. He'd forgotten she was naked. Honestly, so had she.

Her entire body blushed so hot and fast, she actually felt light-headed.

"I would..." He cleared his throat. "May I touch you?"

His hesitation was her undoing. Her face crumpled in on itself, and a sob burst from her throat. She slapped a hand over her mouth to contain it the best she could, but she couldn't contain it alone.

She nodded.

Torek wrapped his broad hands around her shoulders. They were so large, they cupped her from collarbone to shoulder blade, and the certain, calm strength in those hands drew her forward. One hand slid across her back, pressing her to his chest. The other slipped into her hair, cupping the back of her head. He tucked her face into the crook of his neck, and the vibration of his low viurr against her forehead was as soothing as the steady double thump of his heart against her cheek.

She cried and shook and raged against him, and he took it. The pain, the shame, the doubt, the embarrassment and guilt and resentment—they were the blades that had shaped her past and the person she'd become, but they didn't have to shape her future and the person she chose to be. Not if she chose to shape it.

Torek cocooned her with his arms and sheltered her with his chin over her temple. His legs braced on either side of her, and the solid muscle of his abdomen spooned against her flush body. At first, all she felt was the secure pressure of his hold. His arms could protect an entire country from the zorel; they could certainly protect her from herself. As the wracking of her sobs subsided, however, she realized that her hands had left her mouth and were fisted in his fur.

She released her hold. Most of the fur came loose in her hand. She winced, but he didn't seem to notice. The hand stroking her back didn't pause, and the steady hum of his viurr never faltered.

She smoothed her hands flat against his chest and stroked her nails through his fur. His viurr did falter then, just a hiccup-like inhale before he resumed his soothing.

She slowly became aware of his chin abrading her temple, his wet beard dripping tickles of water across her cheek and down the back of her neck. They dribbled between her shoulder blades, and he wiped them with the comforting brush of his stroking hand.

She was safe and understood and wanted—more so than she'd ever been in her entire life—and she wasn't quite sure when it had happened. However unlikely the circumstances, she was happier in this moment with Torek on Lorien than she'd ever been with anyone else on Earth.

Her brain instantly recoiled—he was an alien Sasquatch, for heaven's sake!—but he was, without a doubt, a man in every sense of the word, in gender and deeds. She could have dismissed him had it just been his gender, but everything he'd done for her—his kindness and compassion, the strength he'd lent her—couldn't be ignored. And neither could the warmth and want and hope his hands stoked inside her.

He was about to ease away from her. She could feel his retreat in the minute slowing of his circling hand. Her grief was assuaged, but she didn't want his hands to stop touching her.

She burrowed deeper into his embrace, and he readjusted his grip, holding her without stroking.

She exhaled, content in his embrace.

His nipple tightened from the heat of her breath. His abdominal muscles jumped in reflex, and the arms around her froze. Despite being pressed skin to fur, cheek to chest, an unbridgeable distance suddenly yawned between them. She wasn't sure what had just happened, but something had from one moment to the next, and he was going to push her away.

"What scar your eye?" she asked.

TWENTY-THREE

Torek Lore'Onik Weidnar Kenzo Lesh'Aerai Renaar had never once in his entire twenty-five kair of life released himself without deliberate intent, and he wasn't about to do so now. Especially not after having just consoled a very dear, lovely creature who needed his kindness and comfort, not his cock. But that was the rub, wasn't it? She wasn't a creature. She was a person. And she wasn't just any person. She was clever to have fooled everyone with her charade, courageous to have survived such extraordinary challenges, undeniably intelligent to have learned an alien language and assimilated herself in their culture, and loyal to have cared for him while he was sick. She was tender and soft and beautiful, inside and out, and his cock was a throbbing bruise inside his sac, aching for release.

He was the worst sort of monster.

Two touches—the delicate scratch of her blunt little claws across his chest and her warm breath against his nipple—and he'd nearly lost his self-control entirely.

He froze. He didn't shove her away, which perhaps he should have, but if he moved even one muscle, other muscles would move, and he'd be lost. *Concentrate!* He stared at the ceiling. The vents could use a good scrubbing in preparation for Genai. Who on his staff could he ask for a report on the vent-cleaning schedule? Maybe—

His cock throbbed.

After a moment, he realized that she'd asked him a question. He hadn't heard it through the rushing in his ears. He'd only known she'd spoken at all by the vibration and breath of her voice against his chest.

Rak, his self-control wasn't the only thing he was losing his grip on.

"Torek?"

He took a deep breath and forced himself to relax, first his cock-sac—Lorien skewer him—and then his thighs, biceps, abdomen, and finally, his jaw, so he could actually express himself with words like a lor. Even if he felt like an animal.

"Yes?" The word was barely more than a growl despite his best efforts.

She blew out a soft exhalation that nearly undid him a second time.

Get a grip, Torek!

"I am sorry. I should not ask." She tensed to pull away.

He locked his arms around her. "No, it's my fault," he ground out, and congratulated himself. His voice was only mildly gruff this time, as if he wasn't throbbing in agony. "I was imagining feeding your Todd family to the zorel."

She grinned. "A satisfying thought."

"Extremely." He nuzzled the top of her coil-haired head. "What did you say?"

She hesitated, then relaxed into his embrace. "What scar your eye?"

Maybe words would sufficiently distract him where the vent-cleaning schedule had not. But... "There isn't really a story there."

"I doubt that. A scar like that has a story."

"Not all scars are visible, remember? Not all visible scars are worth a retelling."

Delaney resumed her innocent scratching. His nipple puckered. His breath hitched, and his cock-sac contracted. The warm rush of bathwater caressed its tip.

"I was injured during a training exercise," Torek blurted, desperate for distraction. "Applicants for the Federation are typically taken at a young age, around thirteen kair, but Dorai Nikiok made an exception for me because my father was a war hero. It was generally expected that I would follow in his footsteps, continuing the family tradition of our many forefathers, so who better to train me than my father, the former captain of the guard? But it was just a well-executed excuse so that I could remain at home in Aerai."

Her face shifted against his chest. He glanced down; her brow was pinched into a frown. He stroked his thumb lightly across the back of her arm.

"You not follow in his footsteps?"

"Eventually, yes. But leaving for Federation training would mean leaving Zana."

"Ah." Her face shifted again. He could feel without looking this time that she was smiling. "And you could not leave her?"

"No, I couldn't, and truly, it wasn't much of a hardship. Much to the indulgent chagrin of my family, I had a real talent for horticulture."

"A talent for what? I not know that word."

"I could make plants grow even in the most unlikely circumstances. I'd nurture them and the soil, and the sickliest plant would suddenly take root and thrive when it should have died."

Delaney leaned back slightly, her smile widening. "You, a gardener?"

Torek shuffed. "Gardeners plant flowers for aesthetic beauty. My work could've transformed Lorien's entire agricultural system."

Her smile widened further. "You want to be a farmer."

He thought about that. "I wanted to invent a new way of farming, yes. One in which we could grow crops on Lorien's surface without the wasted energy of plasma heaters."

She glanced over his body with a sweep of her eyes. "I can see that."

He grinned back. "My body is built for battle, and truly, my mind is as well, but having a talent in one field doesn't preclude having a talent in another."

"I not being..." She opened her mouth and closed it, then shuffed in frustration. Almost a real shuff this time. "I not know the word. I being truthful. I *can* see it. I of all people know your ability to nurture and protect. I am that unlikely plant, thriving in the wrong climate."

"Not everyone can see that," he murmured. "Not everyone can see me."

The left corner of her grin tipped down ruefully. "How can they? Do you show anyone else your true self?"

Torek was quiet for a long moment. Honestly, he hadn't thought of his dreams for the future of horticulture since Zana's death. But he couldn't bring himself to say so now. He was already uncomfortable and uncertain of himself with Delaney in his arms; inserting Zana between them would only further complicate his uncertainty.

Delaney continued without his participation anyway. "You wield strength and power to a purpose, and who says that purpose must be battle?" The fingers combing his fur suddenly stilled. "Your father?"

"No, no," he corrected her quickly. "My father was baffled but not unsupportive of my career choice. Horticulture is an honorable industry, just different from his own. And my father never begrudged diversity."

"Dorai Nikiok?" she guessed. Her voice had dipped into something dark and bitter.

Torek cleared his throat. He hesitated to tell her that she was right, but of course, she was. "My father and his father and our forefathers before have all earned the honor of captain of Onik's guard. To not have me in the running for the position was unacceptable. So—"

"So she force you into the Federation against your wish and your father's will."

"No," he said, stifling a laugh. No need to encourage her tenacity.

"Whose story is this?"

She raised the winged tufts above her eyes, her expression offended, but whether he'd truly given offense or she was putting it on, she lifted a hand and zipped her lips closed.

He grinned to himself. "I pursued horticulture, and my father battle-trained me privately until the time came to join the other recruits for our Federation exams."

He waited a moment, but when she remained silent, he nudged her head lightly with his shoulder. "I warned you this story wasn't one worth retelling, but I didn't think you'd fall asleep."

"You reprimand me for interrupting. You reprimand me for quietly listening," she said, mock severity creasing her brow even as her lips widened with repressed amusement. "What do you want?"

He bit back a grin. "There's a balance between interrupting and sleeping through a story that you haven't found yet."

She giggled and settled back into his embrace. "I work on that."

Torek chuckled, but, when his mirth faded, lapsed into silence. He stroked his finger pads up the bumpy column of her spine and across the smooth muscle to the hard cut of her shoulder. Her skin was so delicate and soft, like a flower's petal.

"Well?" She leaned back slightly, peeking up to spy his expression. "What happen? You injure your eye during the exams?"

"No," he said and sighed. "I *lost* my eye during the exams."

"What?" She struggled back, and he let her pull away. She goggled at him. "You lose your eye? But you have it now."

"The miracles of modern medicine," he said dryly.

Her little claws gripped the fur on his chest in twin fists. "What happen?"

He sighed. "It was my own fault. I'd trained with my father my entire life. I was good for my age, better than everyone else, and accustomed to sparring against the former captain of Onik's guard. My father was not known for pulling his punches," he said, and even he could hear the wry humor deep in his voice. "The exams required us to spar with fists as well as with a variety of our traditional and

236

modern weapons. During one of these matches, my less experienced sparring partner became frightened for his life. I attacked him too forcefully, and he fought back with equal force but with less ability and less restraint." He touched the scar that still bisected his blue eye. "In what he perceived as self-defense, he stabbed a knife through my eye."

Delaney sucked in a sharp breath and covered her mouth. "Oh, Torek."

"Loganak Kore'Onik Renaar healed me, and after several surgeries, I regained my eyesight. But I still needed to regain the strength, talent, and vision that I'd lost while convalescing. The Federation doesn't allow one-eyed pilots, you see."

She wrinkled her nose. "Cheap shot."

The phrase was strange, but her meaning clear. He chuckled. "As you've already mentioned, I'm not known for my sense of humor."

Her eyes rolled.

"Eventually, I regained and surpassed the battle skills of my former self. I retook and passed my exams—more cautiously the second time around—and accepted my position in the Onik guard."

"As captain of the guard?"

"A first-kair captain of the guard?" He shook his head. "Horaicek Lore'Onik was captain of the guard at the time. When he died, his second became captain, and I became his second. And when he retired, I was promoted to captain."

"What about farming?"

"Horticulture? I still enjoy it, or I would if I had the time," he added after being pinned by her look. "But following my accident, I became so driven to regain my strength and battle skills, my interest in horticulture sort of, I don't know, faded. I would've chosen horticulture before the accident, but the idea that the choice had been taken from me..." He shook his head. "I had to prove that I was still capable. To myself and to Onik. And I did."

"Hmmm," she murmured.

"I told you it wasn't a story worth the retelling."

"I disagree. It tells the growth of your life and what shape the lor you are today."

So it did. Rak, she was insightful. "Then what is it?"

"Nothing. Just..." She bit her lip. "Nikiok get her way in the end."

"*Dorai* Nikiok. She is Lore'Lorien and has earned the right to its title," he chided. "She was obviously pleased that I joined the Onik guard, but I wouldn't say she *got her way*."

"You not." Delaney tucked her head back into his neck and murmured, "But I do."

Her words were treasonous, and he had to check his natural instinct to vehemently defend the Dorai. Delaney was neither a member of his guard nor a Lorien citizen nor even a lorok. She'd been grievously wronged and was entitled to her opinion in a way that lorienok were not.

"What exactly are you accusing her of?" he asked softly, deliberately modulating his tone and temper.

The heat of his frustration must have sparked through his tone anyway, because Delaney stiffened.

"Nothing."

She was still frightened of him. Or frightened of something that she believed he couldn't protect her from. He tightened his arms around her and wrestled to find the right words. Battle was so much easier: people were in danger, so he fought that danger. But gaining Delaney's trust wasn't a problem so easily solved. It required a level of finesse he didn't think himself capable of. He'd have to rely on honesty and hope that his caring and compassion for her would bridge the gaps in his ability to express himself.

"You know that you're safe here with me, right?"

She nodded, her smooth cheek a warm friction against his chest.

"Our opinions may differ on occasion, and that's okay. You don't feel my devotion and loyalty to Dorai Nikiok, and I don't feel your fear and animosity toward her. But that doesn't mean I don't want to understand your point of view. If I can understand your fear, maybe we can resolve its misunderstanding."

"That is the misunderstanding," she whispered. Her back began to tremble under his palm. "There is no misunderstanding."

He sighed. "Whatever your fear toward the Dorai, misunderstanding or not, you don't need to fear me."

"I not fear you." She swallowed. "I fear *for* you."

"Are we finally circling back to Keil's murder?" Torek asked softly, knowing he was making fragile progress. One misplaced or overly heavy step, and her trust would crack. "Will you tell me what you saw?"

Her trembling increased violently. The silence stretched.

"Fine." He heaved a loud, long sigh. "Then there's no reason not to petition Brinon Kore'Onik for your reclassification and appeal your return to Earth to the Dorai herself."

"No! There is reason not to," she ground out. A fistful of fur fell loose in the pressure of her grip. An early Genai, indeed.

"What reason?"

A terrible noise escaped from her pinched lips, like a suppressed scream was being dragged out of her by fishhooks.

He tightened his hold, nuzzled her forehead, and waited.

"I see it." Another fistful of fur ripped free. "Nikiok murder Keil. She walk in, sh-she point the weapon at Keil's head, and she pull the trigger."

"Keil didn't try to run or fight his attacker?"

"He not see her coming."

"What was he doing when she opened the door?"

"Talking to me."

"So his back was to the door? His body between you and Dorai Nikiok?"

"I know what you not say." She pushed back from him, scowling. "I see her kill him. I see her bend over his dead body and place the weapon in his hand. I see her rise and step up to the cage, and I pretend not to know all I see because if she know *I* know, she murder me next."

Torek considered her, idly stroking her arms with his thumb pads.

"The uniqueness of our features are less pronounced in Rorak because of our fur. Maybe you didn't recognize—"

"I not know her then, but I know her now. The lorok who murder Keil is Nikiok," she insisted.

Delaney's voice was both grim and emphatic. Torek couldn't deny that she was completely certain in her opinion, but he also couldn't fathom that Nikiok would do what Delaney was accusing her of. Keil had been murdered, that much was clear. They'd need to exhume his body and conduct the autopsy that had never been completed, the autopsy that his wife had been willing to kill for—to die for—and still hadn't received.

Something was grievously wrong with all of it: Keil's death, Daerana's attack, Delaney's halted reclassification. The truth had been buried on all three counts, and he couldn't fathom why or how. Or worse, by whom.

"Okay," he said.

Delaney blinked.

"I believe you."

She blinked again, twice more. "You do?"

"I believe you think you saw Dorai Nikiok, and I believe that you witnessed Keil's murder."

She slapped both hands over her face and released a scream.

"Come now." He viurred. "It's all right. I'm on your side. I want to find the truth as much as you do."

"That is not my side! I already know the truth!"

"If that's so, then tell me this: why did Dorai Nikiok murder Keil?"

"Because he pushing for my reclassification!"

"But why is that motive for murder?"

"I...I do not know," she whispered.

Torek rubbed her shivering, puckered arms. "And that's precisely what I need to find out."

TWENTY-FOUR

As usual, interaction with Torek took Delaney two steps forward and three steps backward before blowing up in her face. She saved his life, and he discovered her ability to speak. She convinced him to keep her secret, so he witnessed her doctor shove a probe up her anus. She acquiesced to being comforted after his ill-advised battle against the fish monster, and he jumped headfirst into the bath with her—which, admittedly, had been welcome, but that wasn't the point. The point *was* that after all the contrariness she'd endured from him, she shouldn't be surprised that moments after she'd given him her trust, he declared to break it.

But she was surprised, so much so that she stared, stunned speechless as he set her aside and exited the tub, leaving her in a luke-warm, waist-deep sludge of suds and fur sheddings.

He'd already mopped up the water-slicked tile and was beginning to towel-dry his shoulder-length head hair by the time she'd recovered enough to form a response.

"How will you solve Keil's murder without telling everyone I speaking Lori?" She crossed her arms for the dual benefit of conserving warmth while also covering her naked breasts.

"I'll *nomaikok* his body and request an autopsy." He leaned over and squeezed the excess water from his hair with a furry towel.

"Request an autopsy just like, like—" She snapped her fingers. Or tried to. Her palms were caked with fur. She threw her hands up, beyond exasperated.

He glanced up at her flailing arms, then met her eyes. "Like what?"

"Insufferable man," she groaned in English.

His lips quirked as if he'd understood her.

She swatted away his grin. "So you order another autopsy, but they wonder why. All this time later, why now do you want answers that you not want before?"

"That my animal companion begged me to isn't enough?" he asked, grinning. He tossed the towel to his other hand and shook out the hair on the opposite side of his head.

"I beg you do the opposite! Let it go, Torek. Please! We just continue living like before you know I speaking."

"We can't."

"We can!"

"I can't." He tossed the towel aside and lifted a claw-tipped finger. "I can't keep you like a pet." He lifted a second finger. "I can't maintain such a pretense to my family, the guard, and all of Lorien." He held up a third finger. "I can't allow you to live in constant fear unnecessarily."

"My fear is very necessary!"

He held up a fourth finger. "I can't allow Keil's death to remain a suicide."

She sighed.

He spread all five fingers out wide and opened his mouth.

She lunged up and clapped her hands around his damning fingers. "I understand you have reasons—many reasons—but to protect me, you must protect my secret *despite* your reasons." She tightened her grip, willing him with her entire being to understand and actually *listen*. "I have reasons to break my silence, but the risks are heavier than the benefits. I living. And I want to stay that way."

He squatted next to the tub, his elbows on its rim, and brushed his thumb pad across her cheek with his free hand. "I won't tell anyone that you can speak."

Delaney blew out a long breath.

"But I *will* launch an official investigation into Keil's death."

She jerked away from his touch. "But they wonder *why*? If I not tell you, how—"

"I'll ask Shemara Kore'Onik to claim that closure is essential to my healing process."

She snorted. "Because you so deep in her good graces right now."

He stood, flicked on the air dryer, and cupped his ear as if he hadn't heard her.

She rolled her eyes.

He laughed and stepped into the dryer stall. The wind pressure fluttered his fur, tousling his long hair and beard. He finger-combed through the fur on his face and neck, across his arms, chest, and torso, and down each leg to thoroughly dry himself. A cloud of fur shed-dings began to swirl around him like a tornado.

Delaney blinked, but no, she wasn't mistaken. The fur tornado was thickening. He disappeared behind it. She wondered if that was normal. He'd never shed like this before his fever. Although he didn't seem worried about it, he hadn't seemed terribly worried about battling an ice monster the size of a blue whale either. His measuring rod for worry wasn't the same length as hers.

The dryer stall made a strange noise, and the fur gradually thinned, being suctioned from overhead like a giant vacuum. Eventu-ally, the air cleared, revealing Torek. He was still standing in the dryer, tousling his hair and swiping the remaining sheddings from his body, but that body was bare.

Delaney stared. Her eyes soaked in the sight of him, from the shifting cords of his neck to his flexed runner's calves, and every carved abdominal muscle in between, but even after several blinks, the sight didn't change: Torek's hands were rubbing over pale skin as smooth as marble.

His face, neck, chest, torso, arms, and legs—everything, even the backs of his hands—were fur-free. His head hair, beard, and thick brows were unchanged but devastatingly pronounced against the smoothness of his skin. Longer tufts of hair still covered the back of his arms near his elbows, but otherwise—dear sweet baby Jesus—Delaney struggled not to gape. He was naked and a stunning Adonis of male virility. Not that he hadn't been seven foot three and 210 pounds of beefy, naked muscle all along, but without the fur, she could actually see that muscle in all its intimidating glory.

Heaven help her, that was the same arm that had just been wrapped so securely, so tenderly around her. That was the chest she had just bathed with her tears. Those were the abs that spooned against her every night. Give the man a flannel shirt to hide the excess elbow hair, and holy shit, he was Paul Bunyan. Granted, Paul Bunyan with ram horns, but still, Paul Bunyan all the same.

No woman in her right mind would ever willingly give him a shirt to cover all that beautiful muscle.

He turned to shut off the dryer, and Delaney's eyes dropped and stuck on another hitherto unseen sight. That was his ass. His unexpectedly bare, well-shaped, muscular ass. She couldn't think of any interaction she'd previously had with it while it had been covered with fur, but suddenly, fiercely, she could think of several interactions she wanted to have with it now.

The deep center between her clenched thighs throbbed. She couldn't deny it this time. The feeling was so powerful, and he was so real in a way he'd never been before—yet still Torek—that she didn't just gape. She drooled.

He had the body of a warrior. Which made sense, obviously, because he was a warrior. Judging by looks alone, a war had certainly occurred, and they'd fought it using his body as a shield. The gash across his abdomen was just the worst of his scars, thick enough to show through his fur. His hairlessness revealed a patchwork of scars

BEYOND THE NEXT STAR

across his body, thin and flat and long-ago healed, but everywhere. From neck to ankle, scars of all shapes and sizes sprinkled his entire body, a road map of his career to captain of the guard. There wasn't an appendage that was spared.

Well, perhaps one appendage.

She could kill Keil for never educating her on the finer points of lorienok shedding. If he hadn't already been killed.

Torek faced Delaney, but she couldn't lift her gaze. He had a cock. Of course he had one. He was male, and his thick hardness pressed against her back as they snuggled every night. But she couldn't precisely see it, even without the fur. Something large—her breath hitched, abnormally large—was bulging beneath his skin from groin to navel, and at the base of that bulge was a slit between his legs.

The bulge was swelling.

She jerked her eyes up, then blushed so hard, she nearly passed out. His eyes were narrowed on her, two focused laser targets examining her face while she'd been examining his everything else.

"Are you—"

"I not—"

They spoke over each other, then lapsed into simultaneous silence.

"You were." His gaze was relentless.

Another throb echoed through her womb, but she shook her head.

He stared at her for another hard moment, his eyes seeming to flay open her chest and bare her heart to open air.

A moment later, he nodded, a clipped movement that broke more than just their gaze. Her heart ached more sharply than the ache between her legs, a crushing pressure that she couldn't account for. He was Torek. He owned her. He was an alien. *And he owned her.*

And he'd saved her. From the ice, from loneliness, from herself. He was Torek.

He wrapped a towel around himself, under his armpits, and left the bathroom. He closed the door behind him.

Delaney dropped her forehead to the cold metallic rim of the tub and groaned.

That night after she'd exhausted all forms of procrastination—rinsing her hands, scrubbing out the fur-lined tub, cleaning the toilet and tile floor, and drying her own hair—she crawled into her cot on the floor instead of into his bed. He didn't correct her. She took a deep breath, but she couldn't breathe easy with her confusing and contradictory emotions, like a physical weight, constricting her chest. She hadn't slept in her own cot since waking after the avalanche, and that hadn't been her own doing. Before that, she hadn't slept alone in weeks, but she couldn't bear the thought of sharing a bed now, not with him looking more man than beast and knowing what was growing beneath his skin.

Suspecting, she corrected herself. She didn't know for certain what was growing under his skin, she only suspected, and the shocking desperation with which she longed to confirm her suspicions was enough to make her deliberately and determinedly avoid such feelings. And him.

But that didn't mean that her avoidance, and his acceptance of it, didn't come at a cost.

Minutes that felt like hours passed in heavy, painful silence. Well, silence between *them.* The room swelled with the sounds of their fitful attempts to sleep: the spring and groan of the mattress beneath his tossing and turning, the huffs and puffs of her pillow fluffing, his growls, her sighs.

Delaney stared at the ceiling, the pillow still uncomfortable under her stiff neck, but she refused to fluff it a fourth time. Not that her movement would disturb Torek. He should have been in the unconscious throes of a heart-pounding nightmare by now, but no, there would be no dreams or nightmares or any form of sleep tonight for either of them, apparently.

This was stupid. They'd slept next to one another, spooning in the curve of each other's bodies, for nearly two months without issue. She didn't have to make an issue of it now. Except that the body spooning hers had always felt like another fur blanket around her. A breathing, living, heated fur blanket, yes, but that was all the better because she was always so unbearably cold on this miserable ice planet. Now she'd be able to distinguish his body from the blanket.

If they spooned now, they'd be skin to skin.

Heat blossomed from the inside out, and for once, she found herself shivering from something other than the relentless cold.

She sat up, forgetting her vow not to fluff what was obviously a determinedly flat pillow, and punched the pillow anyway.

Torek groaned. "You're punishing me, aren't you?"

"I not know your meaning." She gave the pillow a final punch and collapsed face-first into it. It flattened instantly.

"'I not know your meaning,'" he mocked in falsetto. "You're punishing me for battling the zorel."

"Why do I do that?" Her voice was muffled with pillow. *Of course, he's still focused on the zorel. I'm combusting on the memory of his naked body, and he's thinking about the giant ice fish.* Delaney turned her head to the side, so he could hear her sarcasm clearly. "You get Dorai Nikiok's permission to battle. What more do you need?"

He growled.

"You need not warn me before leaving to risk your life. You need not wait on Shemara Kore'Onik's permission. Who are we? How you say, lorienok who have no power to give commands or advice and must obey blindly?"

A slapping sound. "I had a great victory today. I don't deserve this."

"What good could come of talking to those with no power?"

"I should have built your own room. Then I'd have peace!"

"Yes, you should build my own room, as required by my manual!"

"Yes, a requirement that claimed you would 'wither and die'

without it. I don't see you withering. If anyone is withering, it's me! Perhaps the separate room was actually for my well-being, not yours."

"I want sleep too, you know," Delaney snapped. "I not *enjoy* being tired and stressed and—"

"The Dorai cleared me for battle!"

"Oh, she a mind and behavior specialist? No, I forget, she a medical doctor. No, I mistaking, she a murderer, but that gives her the right to clear—"

"Shut your mouth. Just shut it!"

His upper body leaned over the side of the bed, his hands grabbed her shoulders, and in one swift, smooth lift, he hoisted her up on top of him. She straddled his waist, trying to steady herself on his chest before she toppled over, but he kept her upright. His finger pads dug painfully into her skin.

"Torek! What—"

He shook her. "You're going to listen to me now and understand this time. I won't say it again."

"You hurting me."

He shook her harder. "I'll investigate Keil's death. I'll determine the truth and keep your secret. I'll do everything in my considerable power to protect you, but I refuse to listen to lies."

"I am not lying," she gritted out. "You say you believe me."

He sighed, relaxing his hold slightly but not letting go. "Poor word choice. I know you're not lying. I refuse to listen to untruths."

She struggled against his hold, falling into English. "Stupid. Arrogant. Pompous. Ass—

He tightened his hold again. "You're not listening! If you'd just —" He grunted, inhaled a sharp, pain-filled gasp and then exhaled on a low growl.

Something that hadn't been there before, something large and hard and physically throbbing, thrust between them.

Delaney froze.

Torek was naked. Delaney was wrapped in a fur blanket, but from the waist down, the intimate parts of her were rubbing against the intimate parts of him. Skin on skin, just as she'd suspected, made her acutely aware of him as a man and her as a woman in a way that she hadn't allowed herself to consider. In a way that could no longer be ignored.

Torek's expression mirrored the agony in his growl. His brow bunched together into a merciless scowl. His lips thinned into a hard line, and his eyes screwed shut. His breathing turned ragged.

"Torek?" Delaney whispered.

He didn't release her. He didn't look at her. He didn't so much as move, except for the appendage which pulsed between them, the obvious source of his pain.

His eyes did open then, and despite the differences in his bicolored gaze, the emotion spilling from them was identical. He wasn't in pain. He was embarrassed. Mortified, even.

She glanced down.

"Delaney, don't—"

She stroked the smooth, tense muscles of his forearms. They flexed at first, but his fingers relaxed slightly under her gentle reassurance—his grip still firm but no longer bruising—and she looked.

His cock was at least twelve inches long, in proportion with the rest of his massive body, she supposed, but unnecessarily aggressive nonetheless. It was pink. Its skin was thick and soft, almost like a tongue with a steel core, and just as slick. She couldn't tell if the slippery substance was secreting from its pores or from within the sheath it had sprung from, but either way, considering its length and girth, having a self-producing lubricant was considerate of it.

Delaney tried to school her expression. What was worse: looking shocked, considering she was an alien; looking interested, considering she was still technically his pet; or looking frightened, considering he knew she was a woman. Considering she was feeling all three things toward it, masking her reaction meant having no expression—which, perhaps, was the worst reaction of all.

His arms flexed, and his grip tightened. "That's enough. This is wrong. I can't—"

She reached forward and, with a tentative touch, brushed a rogue lock from his forehead. His brown hair was straight and soft. She combed her fingers through it, caressing her nails through his scalp, and rubbing his skull at the base of his horns.

His cock swelled and throbbed. Dear God, it had the capability of growing larger?

He let loose a low, vibrating moan. His hands released her shoulders to cover his eyes. "Dear Lorien. Lend me your steady—rak. Just skewer me."

Delaney glanced up from her inspection. His jaw was flexing, nearly in perfect rhythm with the throbbing of his body.

"Are you?" She cleared her throat. "Are you feeling pain?"

A bark of laughter escaped him. He lowered his hands and met her eyes. "Of sorts," he said, but his tone seemed self-deprecating. "It's a physical reaction that I can't..." He groaned again. "And I accuse you of lies," he murmured on a sigh. "I'm sorry."

Delaney bit her lip. "What if I not?"

His head turned toward her at that, so her face was the entire focus of his regard. "What if you're not what?"

"What if I not sorry?"

TWENTY-FIVE

S HE WASN'T SERIOUS. OR SHE DIDN'T KNOW WHAT SHE WAS saying. Or she'd lost her mind. Or he had, because her expression, although tentative, was very serious, and she seemed to know exactly what she'd said. And what that implied. And Lorien skewer him, he couldn't look away. He couldn't respond. His mind had gone blank with confusion and desire and panic, but most of all, he couldn't look away.

Her hair had dried in a wild tangle around her head. She hadn't bothered to brush it after their bath, and now it was a rioting mess, sprouting from root to tip in untamed spirals. Her breath had caught, and her color was high. The patchy red stain brightening her cheeks spread down her neck and across her collarbones, disappearing under the blanket's edge, where it likely warmed the plump mounds of her breasts.

He was deviant and a lecher, two things he'd never associated with himself before. But his life had bifurcated into two simple but profound categories: life before Delaney and life after Delaney. Before, he'd been certain in his resolve. He'd never been dissatisfied by the longing for more, had, in fact, pitied people who constantly searched beyond the next star. Always striving for what they didn't have, they never saw what was within their grasp.

Now, he wasn't certain of his resolve. What he longed for was so unfathomable, he couldn't see the stars, let alone dare to reach for one. Dare he? Rak, he was trembling with indecision. *Trembling.*

He sexually desired his animal companion.

Such an amoral, abhorrent act was beyond comprehension, but she wasn't an animal companion, or rather, she shouldn't be. Her species was an advanced, reasoning, moral people, if Delaney was any representation of the whole. They were of the same mukar, according to her manual. They were of the same relative intelligence, based on his interaction with her. *Fekok*, she possessed a *higher* cunning if her successful deception was any indication. Had she been classified correctly, desiring her wouldn't be any different than desiring a *havenian* or a *frayon*. Uncommon, yes, but not criminal.

But the most elemental and possibly the most undeniable thought that passed through his confused, grasping brain was that she was Delaney. Just Delaney. And he cared for her more than any lor had a respectable right to care for any lorok.

She didn't look shocked by him and the thoughts she could undoubtedly interpret from his expression. As if she needed to interpret his expression to know his thoughts with his cock proudly exposed between them. Her eyes, so fathomless in their gray depths, stared right back. She didn't look disgusted. She didn't even look particularly surprised, which was a little startling. It made him consider whether he'd missed anything else about her—as if he hadn't missed enough! She didn't look nearly as lost and confused as he felt.

Her tentative touch was shy but not uncertain. She caressed his scalp with a tender, caring inquisitiveness that constricted his throat. She didn't mind him wanting her in this way, and if he was so bold as to make a leap of logic based on those wandering fingers through his hair—and the fact that she hadn't bolted when he'd released himself— she wanted him as well.

Or at the very least, she didn't *not* want him.

Her fingers found a particularly sensitive area behind the base of his ears. He closed his eyes and groaned, his already scattered thoughts completely obliterated by her touch. He felt himself swell and couldn't even drum up the shame to care.

"Do you—" Gah, those fingers were magic! "Do you understand what you're saying? What *that* is?" he finished gruffly.

"It not so different from the human male reproductive organ. Just bigger. With more lubricant and inside most of the time." She bit her lip. "Except..."

Torek forced himself to calm, to listen and understand that a "but" was coming, and he needed to brace himself for the possibility that they would be stopping this intimacy in the next few moments. As unforeseen as this moment was, now that it had begun, stopping seemed impossible.

"Except?" he growled.

"Except, I never sleep with someone I care about. Someone I really like." She released that lip and licked it. "Someone I trust with more than my body."

Lorien skewer him, she didn't understand. He was quivering with the effort to sheath himself. It *was* impossible. He was too far gone. "You're mistaken."

She froze. "I am?"

He nodded. "We wouldn't be sleeping. I've been unpardonably rude. I'm sorry. I—"

She placed a finger over his lips.

Torek stared at her, silenced. Her lips *still* were not twisted in horror. They quirked slightly in abashed amusement. She was shaking her head.

"'Sleeping together' is an English phrase that has two meanings. I mean sexual intercourse, but I not want to sound so medical."

Ah! A smile curved his lips, but before he could respond, she plunged ahead.

"On Earth, 'mating' is for animals. We are, for me, anyway..." She cleared her throat. "Making love? Sexual intercourse with caring and respecting and...and warmth?" She glanced away, face flaming. "Jeesuskrystimfukingthisup." She ended on a swift, ranting burst of her In-klish.

Her phrases were unfamiliar, but her meaning was clear. And reciprocated. He raised his hand and caressed her flaming cheek until she met his gaze. "Our hearts would beat as one."

She blinked. Her lips formed the words silently, and then they curved into a soft smile to match his.

He sat up to breathe into her neck.

She placed a staying hand on his chest. "Do you have protection?"

He lay back. "Protection?"

"Maybe you can just pull out? Before ejaculation, I mean."

He blinked. Rapidly. He could *not* have heard her correctly. "Is that wise? We're of the same mukar."

"Yes. Your point?"

"It means we're classified as having similar physical forms. We're treated with the same medicines, eat the same foods..." He circled his hand in the air, then let it drop to his side. "And we have compatible reproductive systems."

"Compatible reproductive systems."

"It means we can reproduce to create children. My cock goes inside your—"

"I know where it goes!" She swatted his chest. "And I know what mukar means. That is why you should pull out."

"Children are always a blessing. Always. But..." He must tread carefully here. "In this one instance, it may be wise to wait. At least until you're no longer classified as an animal companion and more tests can be performed to predict the outcome of such a union. I'd want to know what to expect and prepare a birth plan for those expectations. Even so, there's always some risk, being the first to spark life between two species." He reached up and caressed her arms. "I'm not ashamed of you and would be honored to have you bear my children." He swallowed. "After you're reclassified."

"Right." She stared at him. "So just pull out."

Really, he couldn't stop blinking. "So, you *want* to risk having children? Even before being reclassified?"

Delaney rubbed her frowning brow. "I know we speaking the same language, but it not seem like it. Explain, in very simple words, how we risk having children if you pull out?"

"Pulling out prevents my *genok* from killing my seed, so you could conceive."

Her hand stopped rubbing. "Your genok?"

He nodded, relieved. They were finally getting somewhere.

"What is genok?"

Or not. "When I finish at the end of sex. It's a liquid that releases from my cock and prevents pregnancy."

"So you ejaculate genok at the end of sex, not seed?"

He nodded.

"When is your seed released?"

"It's not released, per se. My cock is slick with seed all the time from being inside its cock-sac."

Her mouth opened in silence for a moment. Her eyes glanced down. "Interesting."

His cock swelled anew at her attention, but Torek waited, hesitant to trust the hope that they might actually be in agreement.

"So to prevent pregnancy, you ejaculate inside me?" she asked.

He nodded.

"Convenient." She grinned, flashing the entire mouthful of her square white teeth. "We do that, then."

Yes! Torek sat up to breathe into her neck. Again. Finally.

She leaned down to breathe into his, or so he thought, until her face veered left and their foreheads collided.

"Oh!" She rubbed her forehead, scowling at him. As if *he* had veered into *her* forehead.

The inappropriate urge to laugh bubbled up, but he had the good sense and experience to suppress it immediately. "Are you all right?" he asked.

"Yes," she hissed, still rubbing her forehead.

"Should we try again, then?" he asked.

She continued glaring but didn't resist when his hands urged her closer. He leaned in again, much slower this time, and Delaney didn't move. She was no longer using her hand to rub her forehead but rather using it to cover the spread of her grin.

Torek burrowed his muzzle in the curve of her neck and breathed her deep into himself. She was clean and fresh, with the scent of his soap still clinging to her skin and hair. Beneath that was a sweetness he couldn't identify, something that would be smooth and soft on the tongue, refreshing and quenching but addicting. Nothing on Lorien smelled like that. Torek wondered if the scent was singular to Earth or singular to Delaney. He breathed out to clear his scent receptors and filled his lungs with her again.

Her skin puckered against his lips. It shriveled into small bumps that he knew meant she was cold. And indeed, she clung to him and shivered, but the low moan that escaped her throat was scorching hot. Her scent in combination with her sudden embrace and that moan went straight to his head and then immediately to his cock, leaving him breathless and dizzy. A surge of heat rushed to his groin. He bucked, rubbing himself shamelessly against her smooth skin, matching her moan with his.

Rak, he could breathe her in all night. He'd suffer for it—his cock could not possibly swell any larger, and they hadn't even properly begun—but it was torture he'd gladly endure for the pleasure of her essence inside himself.

He nuzzled her a final time, wondered distantly why she wasn't nuzzling him back, and eased away to ensure his instincts were right about the source of her trembling.

She leaned in, finally. He stilled in anticipation and then in astonishment as she veered toward his face again instead of nuzzling. Her lips landed with uncanny accuracy over his lips.

He jerked back, trying and likely failing to mask his shock.

Her eyes opened. She was flushed and suddenly confused as she blinked at him. With a leap of insight—two in as many minutes, he was on a roll—he realized that touching mouths must be part of human intimacy. And he'd interrupted her.

He imagined if she'd pulled away as sharply and vehemently as he'd just done while he'd been nuzzling her. No wonder she looked confused and embarrassed.

"I—" she began.

He placed his hands on either side of her face and silenced her with his lips.

Her eyes fluttered closed, and she groaned deep in her throat, affirming his suspicions. Her lips were soft and coaxing as they moved against his, brushing back and forth. Pressing and licking. Nibbling.

For a moment, he forgot that this was her mouth, filled with saliva and bacteria and food particles, and allowed himself to be swept away by her enthusiasm. The spike in her scent was like a physical blow. He staggered from its hit and the answering need it triggered within him.

He applied his own gentle pressure to her lips.

She groaned in immediate response, angled her head, and deepened her movements. Her arms around his shoulders tightened—when had they moved from his scalp?—and she scored his back with her blunt little claws.

He growled into her mouth. Her tongue took advantage of the opening and plunged inside, a mimicking precursor of how he longed to plunge into her. Her hips bucked in rhythm with her tongue's dance, and he lost what little control he'd managed to maintain.

Torek gripped her shoulders, jerked her mouth from his and rolled her beneath him. Careful of his weight and claws and fangs—Lorien help him, her tongue had made him forget about his fangs!—he propped himself on his left elbow and reached between them with his right hand. His knuckles skimmed across her upper thighs, past her patchwork scars—she stiffened on a caught breath—and eased his fingers inside her.

Her canal was slick with juices, slicker than anything he was accustomed to. There wasn't much texture to navigate, nothing to indicate whether he should be caressing one area instead of another. Nothing but a cushion of suction. He envisioned his cock within that greedy pressure—two fingers fit, but barely—and shuddered in anticipation.

He glanced down at her face. Her gaze was heavy lidded. Her breath was ragged, and her cheeks still flushed. She wasn't *not* enjoying it, but... "Am I... Is this right?" he asked, his voice hoarse and breathless.

"Yes, kind of. I enjoy it higher. But okay, we can just—"

He pressed his fingers in deeper. "Like this?"

She winced.

Nope. He eased back. "Where higher?"

"You are not...I can—"

Torek bent down and nuzzled her neck. Intoxicating. "Lorok have a specific place they touch to find pleasure. It's here."

He rubbed his fingers inside the back of her canal and grinned as her skin puckered. The fine hairs along the slope of her neck stiffened as if shocked, and her entire body shuddered beneath him.

"You like this, but if I found the specific place you prefer, I think you'd like it more." He breathed the words against her skin.

She turned her head and sealed her lips over his mouth. He matched her movements—pressure against pressure, bite for bite, tongue to tongue—and when a flood of her juices once again coated his fingers, he pulled away to try again.

"Is it in your canal?"

"My what?" She licked the curve of his throat and blew on it.

He shuddered. "Fekok! Just—"

She blew again, and he fell into her neck, breathing and growling.

"Your place of pleasure!" he gasped out. "Is it in here?" He wiggled his fingers inside her.

"My...oh." She frowned. "So they say."

A thought occurred to him that gave him pause. His logic had never leaped so far or so readily as it had during his time with her. She'd warned him in a way, but maybe he'd misinterpreted her meaning. "Is this your first time? Ever?"

She jerked back, scowling.

Nope. Wrong again.

"What makes you say that?"

"I—" *How to recover?* "You don't seem to know your place of pleasure. But that's okay." He grinned, sure of himself this time. "We'll find it."

Her eyes rolled. "I know my *place of pleasure.* I make sex before. I just..." She sighed. "I never maikluv before."

Torek blinked. "Maikluv?"

"It's two words: make love. My heart never 'beat as one.' I-I never feel much pleasure before." Her cheeks burst into color. "But I want to feel it."

Ah. "Then let me give it. Show me where."

Her color deepened. "Whyisthisohard?" she grumbled nonsensically.

He pressed his lips to hers, and she moaned into his mouth. He led the union of their lips. He set the pace. He licked her tongue, and in his exploration of her, discovered something new—although not entirely surprising—about himself.

He enjoyed conquering her will. Not just being the aggressor or being in control or being the dominant partner. He'd always enjoyed that. For whatever her reasons, Delaney was somehow resistant to pleasure. He assumed by her shy enthusiasm that she wasn't resistant to him—not all of him, anyway. And she wanted their hearts to beat as one. She'd made that clear. But despite everything she said she wanted, she still seemed resistant to the pleasure that he could give her.

Breaking down that resistance and witnessing her unravel was the greatest pleasure *he'd* ever experienced. He was seducing her, right now, this very moment with his tongue and lips and fingers and body and breath, and its success was seducing him.

"Here?" he asked, trying the back of her canal.

She shook her head and nibbled his ear.

He gritted back a gasp, refusing to be distracted. He withdrew and caressed her entrance. "Here?"

She blew on the lobe of his wet ear, and he nearly spent himself.

Lorien save him!

He flicked her earlobe. "Here?"

She paused in her pursuit to drive him to insanity. "You serious?"

"No, but without direction or encouragement, I may as well be."

"I give no encouragement?" She wedged her hand between their bodies and gripped his cock.

His blood surged. "Not. Fair."

She stroked the length of him in her clenched hand, and he saw stars.

Giving up his pursuit in favor of blind, aching lust, he ground himself against her. His cock rubbed between the folds of skin above her canal, and she closed her eyes on a guttural moan.

He stilled—*Ah, ha!*—and then experimentally ground himself against her again.

She arched back, gouging his shoulders in an unseeing, uncaring fever grip and groaned louder.

"It's outside the canal," he said, drunk on his prowess and discovery.

She nodded. "And above the—yes!" Her hips bucked as he replaced his cock with his more dexterous finger pads.

Her eyes rolled back and closed. Her back arched off the bed. Her claws raked across his back. Her mouth opened on an impressive growl, having been produced by her human throat, and she slapped her hands over her mouth to muffle the sound.

Pride swelled through him, as powerful an aphrodisiac as her scent. She was magnificent! So responsive. So genuine. So...

So Delaney.

He eased her hands from her mouth. "Don't cover your pleasure. Let it out. Let me in, and let it out."

Her eyes flicked to the door.

After a week of shouting arguments, now she worried about discretion. Ha! "Our walls are thick. They can't hear us." He nuzzled her neck. "Let me hear you."

The swollen nub and retracted hood beneath his finger pads was precisely what he'd been searching for; hers was just positioned differently: outside instead of within. But now that he'd found it, he plied it with every experience-tested weapon in his arsenal. He circled above it, spread her wide and tapped it, rubbed at its base and over it. He was gentle and quick and mercilessly relentless, and soon, he'd driven her completely mindless. She was bucking off the bed with abandon, gasping and muttering nonsense. His fingers were soaked in her pleasure. His back was scored by it. His ears rang with it. His scent receptors reveled in it.

"Pleezimredypleez!"

He suspected that she didn't even realize she was screaming at him in her native language. And he'd done that. He'd driven her so over the edge of thought and reason that she was confusing her tongues.

He shifted himself over her, aligning the head of his cock over the base of her canal. He could barely grip his own cock, he was so wet. Even combined with her own juices, a novel and intriguing prospect, he wasn't sure of her body's capacity to take him without tearing. She was physically much smaller than him, her skin softer, more pliable— so she might stretch rather than tear—but the possibility was chilling. So he eased in slowly. Progress was minimal. The sensation was torture, but he was a patient lor. He could do this and only produce pleasure for her. He could—

"Jezusfukingkryst, Torek," She groped for an ass cheek in each hand and bucked her hips. "Pleez!"

She wanted this. She really wanted this.

She wanted him.

He eased all the way into her canal until his pelvis touched hers. He was seated to the hilt within her body, her milking, grasping canal as greedy and wet and soft and as perfectly excruciating as he'd hoped it would be.

He withdrew. She arched back on a gasp. He thrust back inside. She scraped her claws down his arms. He withdrew again and gritted his teeth against sensation. He wouldn't be overwhelmed. It had been so many seasons—four long, lonely, brutal kair—but he refused to be overcome by his own pleasure.

He dipped his head down, bending nearly in half to reach her neck. He nuzzled her, breathing her in, and then captured her mouth the way she liked. He thrust inside her, again and again, focusing on her ragged breaths, her nipping teeth, her grasping hands. Anything but the raging fire she'd ignited within him.

TWENTY-SIX

She hadn't known. She was partly to blame because of her bad taste in men, her low self-esteem, and her tendency toward self-punishment, but mostly, she simply hadn't known. And how could someone seek out and strive for something she hadn't known even existed?

But now she knew, and she was ruined. A woman couldn't *un*know something like this. Even as it was happening, she recognized that this was it: this was the experience by which she would judge all future experiences. And she had a sinking suspicion that this wasn't normal. This was something unique to Torek, maybe unique to them, and without Torek, without *this*, what was the point?

He was drinking in her scent in long, savoring draughts—Thank God she'd just bathed!—as he stroked in and out of her. And it was truly stroking more than thrusting or bucking or humping. He entered hard but withdrew in an angled slide that caressed nerve endings she hadn't known existed. Which shouldn't be shocking because she apparently didn't know anything—not about sex, not about herself, nothing—but it was, and every time he hit that magic nerve deep inside, her body sang like a live wire, simultaneously catching fire, melting, and drowning all at once.

He pulled away from her neck, his movements somehow both lazy and fierce, as if he was drugged. Maybe he was: drugged on her. She grinned at the thought, and the movement caught his eye. He grinned back and sealed his mouth over hers in a moving, nipping, licking kiss that blew the top of her head off.

For someone who'd never kissed before, he caught on quick. She should have known he'd be athletic in every way, not just in ways that benefited his military—*the Federation*, she thought in Lori. His stamina, discipline, agility, and adaptivity translated from captain of the guard to lover seamlessly, but she hadn't anticipated other aspects of his personality to translate, adjectives that she'd never associated with sex before: generosity, care, concern.

In her experience—from which she was reasonably knowledge-able—her pleasure had always been a byproduct of the pleasure her partner had sought for himself. She'd enjoyed it at the time, but she'd never had this...this...this—Ah, he nibbled her neck—*tempest* of relentless determination bearing down upon her. Maybe that was the difference between having sex and making love.

Or maybe that was just the difference between everyone else and Torek.

Even now, between strokes and kisses and long drags of her scent, he was attuned to her. When she moaned, he deepened his thrusts. Finding a particularly sensitive spot—her breath caught on its discovery—he drove into it, wringing every morsel of pleasure from it. She didn't like attachments and emotions. She didn't like wanting something enough to worry about losing it, but she'd cared about Torek and been terrified of losing him long before wanting him. Whether she liked it or not, she couldn't deny it: the man in her arms, inside her, pleasuring her with the intensity and single-minded resolve of a zealot was incinerating her preconceived notions about herself and life and what she wanted from it.

She wanted him.

His hips shifted, and suddenly, his rhythm became frenzied. He broke away from her neck on a ragged gasp and growled deep in the center of his chest. His head dropped down to rest on the pillow above her again, his frown a deep chasm between his brows. He was losing control. This man who literally set his life to a timer, who could run relentlessly and without pause for miles in rough terrain, who had risked his life for his country for years, who had nearly died saving her life, and who could do all that without losing his breath was winded inside her.

Delaney's blood surged at the thought, and, combined with the fresh angle of his thrusts, something cataclysmic stirred. His strokes were shorter, but deep and fast and sliding at an upward angle. He hit another something unexpected, something no one else had ever reached.

Something no one else had ever *tried* to reach.

Her nipples tightened to aching points. Her skin was somehow simultaneously burning and shivering. Her toes curled. Her vagina throbbed. Her breath caught.

She needed more. Harder. Longer. Deeper. Faster.

He complied. Had she spoken out loud? Had he read her mind? Maybe he just felt the same, but however he'd known, he acted. He lifted her thighs up over his shoulders, gripped her hands, and used her legs like a spring to slam into her. Hand in hand, he pulled her back for more, his hips ruthless, driving home toward a destination she'd never reached, had in fact always suspected was heavily fictionalized. The sensations ratcheted higher and hotter, pounding relentlessly into a body too small to contain the amount of pleasure he was pouring into it.

Like a pressure cooker with no outlet for release, her body detonated.

Hot, feral, fantastic sensation erupted from her core, finally. *Finally!* Every muscle contracted in quivering ecstasy. A scream tore from her throat. Light bursts speckled her closed eyelids, and everything—her body, her mind, everything she knew about life, herself, men, and sex—exploded apart and was completely obliterated. Blinders were ripped from her eyes, and in their absence, the sight of her own ignorance left her raw and exposed. This was real. She might not have had it before, which was a brutal shame. But then, some people never found it.

Her mind eventually fused back together with her body, but even as she became aware of herself again, she didn't feel like herself. She was lethargic and exhausted and completely spent, lying limply on the pillows. Could a person actually pass out from too much pleasure? Could a body and brain be so completely overcome by another person that it shut down to all sensation?

But no, she could still feel her fingers and thighs and toes bursting in twitching aftershocks. She could still smell his inexplicable sandalwood-and-spiced-vanilla musk. She could still hear. Torek was roaring in her ear.

She turned her head and forced her eyes open. His face was still half buried in the pillow, but his scarred right eye was visible, screwed shut and frowning. His mouth was open, his fangs exposed, as he bellowed. His entire body tensed. The only part of him moving was his cock. It was vibrating inside her. Not pulsing. *Vibrating*. His warm cum—well, genok, she supposed—sprayed a constant stream into the deepest part of her.

She tried to work up an emotion—awe at the amount of genok he'd produced, distaste with its sticky slide as it oozed between them to coat her thighs, niggling doubt regarding its ability to stop conception, *something*—but she trusted Torek with her life. She certainly trusted him with her body, and her body was singing his praises. Her vagina was still throbbing. Her muscles were still quivering. She closed her eyes and sighed, content.

She'd never felt this way, not ever and especially not after sex, and only now that she was experiencing it did she recognize its absence. The fact that she was feeling it now, on Lorien, was perhaps obscene—Stockholm much?—but Torek was the furthest thing from obscene that she knew.

He collapsed beside her on a low, agony-filled moan, smothering himself fully on the pillow. Her arm was trapped under him, so she curled it around his neck and stroked his hair. She twirled a lock around her fingers, massaged her nails through his scalp, and fingered the base of his horns.

He stirred a moment later, just enough to roll his head half toward her. His heavy-lidded, icy-blue electric gaze skimmed over her from head to toe before meeting her eyes, as if double-checking his work. Still attuned to her. Still seeking feedback. Whatever he saw must have been satisfactory because his eye drifted closed, and his cheek lifted in a smug grin.

"Something amuse you?" Was that throaty rasp her voice?

He nodded but didn't elucidate. Speaking would probably waste too much energy, energy he needed to catch his breath.

Delaney grinned a little smugly herself.

"You." He took a deep breath. His eyes were still closed, his face still buried in the pillow. His grin still widening. "You are self-sabotaging."

Delaney glanced at him with a sly side eye. "A few visits with Shemara Kore'Onik, and suddenly, you an expert of mind and behavior?"

"I've seen her weekly for nearly half of Rorak. That's more than just a few visits." He turned his head to face her and shuffed. His grin had spread across his entire face. "I may not be an expert in mind and body, but I'm quickly becoming an expert on *your* mind and body."

Delaney turned away to stare at the ceiling and shuffed right back in mock indignation. Maybe she should feel real indignation, but she simply couldn't work up the energy.

"You take pleasure in sex," he continued.

She scrunched her nose. Was he really going to hash this out *now*?

"I could see and feel your enjoyment. Don't try to deny it. Yet you tried, again and again, to thwart my efforts to pleasure you."

"I not thwart you," she denied.

"But you not help me either. *Supposedly* knowing your place of pleasure, but refusing to tell me," he insisted. He rolled onto his side and brushed the curve of her collarbone with the back of his knuckle. Her breast puckered at his grazing touch, and his grin turned salacious. "Because you are self-sabotaging."

She lifted a brow. "Does that matter? You find it on your own."

His fangs peeked out from between his lips. "I sabotaged your sabotage."

She barked out a surprised laugh. "You want a reward?"

His nostrils flared. "Sure, I'll take a reward." He rolled onto his back, fingers laced behind his head, and waited. His cock was still out. Still hard. Still ready.

She stared at it blatantly. "How is that possible?"

"It can be a reward of your choosing. You may place your mouth on mine again or nuzzle my throat." He glanced down. "Or my—"

"I know how 'giving a reward' is possible. How is *that* possible?" She pointed.

"Biology? The product of my gender? I'm not sure what you—"

"You came! The evidence is dripping out of me." She swept her hand down to wave between her legs in case they were experiencing another language barrier and not a deliberately obtuse one. "How is it possible that your cock is still hard and ready for another round?"

He considered her a moment. "Are human males not always like this?"

She blinked. "Are you?"

He reached down and tucked himself back into the slit between his legs with a quick press and flick of his wrist. His eyes were still intent upon her face, scrutinizing her expression.

His abdomen flexed, and his cock sprang free, jutting out and up into the air.

She jerked back, gaping.

He laughed. "Oh, your face. Anatomy wasn't a part of your space curriculum? Just astronomy?"

"I learn anatomy. It just, I assume—" She shook her head, still staring. "Male humans are hard while feeling desire, and then after sex, they become soft. And stay soft until they feel desire again."

"I'm feeling desire again."

She tried to shuff, but it emerged from her lips as a giggle. "Yes, I see that. But it takes longer for a human male to recover."

His nostrils flared. "Recover? From sex? Desire isn't a disease."

She rolled her eyes. "Recover, like the way you need to recover from running a long distance."

He looked skeptical.

"The way *I* need to recover from running a long distance," she amended.

"You can't run long distances."

She growled in the back of her throat. "The way I need to recover from running a *short* distance, then!"

He threw his head back and laughed.

She shook her head and glared, suppressing her own amusement. "Go reward yourself. I not feeling desire."

"Hmmm." He grazed his knuckle across her collarbone again but continued a direct path to her aching breast. He stroked a thumb over the areola and pinched lightly.

She shuddered.

"Really? You're not feeling desire? Not at all?"

She narrowed her eyes. "No."

He leaned over and licked her nipple.

She bit back a moan.

"Do human females require time to recover?" He swirled his thumb over her saliva-slickened breast, alternating between light teasing and hard pinching.

"Yes," she gasped. Her eyes fluttered closed of their own accord, and she did moan then, a sighing, exhausted, guttural sound. How embarrassing. She moaned again.

Jesus, she was losing her mind along with her heart and body, but she honestly couldn't drum up the energy to care.

He moved on to torture her other breast. "Should we test that theory?"

"It fact, not theory."

"Hmmm," he murmured noncommittally. He rolled away from her.

Her eyes shot open. Wasn't he going to test it?

He stood and walked to the sink, soaked a cloth, and brought it back to the bed.

One look at the intensity in his expression, and another grin tried to take over her face. She strove to remain chiding and aloof.

He smiled, seeing through her facade. Standing over her, he lifted the sopping cloth and wiped her thigh, cleaning his genok from her skin.

She startled. The water was freezing!

He chuckled, a low, deep vibration that turned into a viurr. "Lie back. Considering I'm the cause of your exhaustion, let's see if I can't help you recover."

She eyed his exposed cock dubiously.

He nudged her shoulder. She looked up, meeting his eyes, and the calm, predatory anticipation in his gaze jump-started her pulse. Against her better judgment, but in accordance with her baser instincts, she conceded and lay back.

He swept the cloth up her thigh again, and she shivered from the cold and his touch. The combination of his gaze and the texture of the cloth against her bare skin was erotic—what wasn't erotic lately? —and stole her breath. It was a miracle she was still alive considering the time she'd recently spent breathless.

His strokes were long and luxurious: in the crease of her bottom, down the inside of her thigh, behind her knees, up the outside of her leg to her hip, across her stomach, and down her other leg. He'd produced a shocking amount of cum. The majority of it had dripped down between her thighs, which he'd already cleaned with a few efficient strokes, but she couldn't bring herself to tease him about the mess. A person needed breath to speak, and she'd lost hers hours ago.

He leaned down, buried his muzzle between her thighs, and inhaled deeply. "Mmmm," he murmured in satisfaction. And that was her only warning before he shifted up and claimed her nipple with his mouth.

She arched off the bed, gasping. He flicked her areola with his tongue, laved the nipple in determined, pressured strokes, sucked hard, and bit lightly. The long strands of his coarse beard abraded the hypersensitive skin along her ribs. She gave in to the mounting feelings, gave in to him, and moaned shamelessly. Again.

He leaned back and dipped his head questioningly. "Are you feeling desire now?"

She choked back a laugh. "No," she gasped. "Not yet."

He clucked his tongue. "A long recovery indeed." And attacked her other breast with the same thorough attention as he had the first.

She writhed under his ministration, so focused on the attention he was giving to her breasts that she didn't notice the slow glide of the cloth across her thigh until it reached her clitoris.

"Oh!" Her hips bucked defiantly, resisting the sensation. She was too sensitive. This was too soon, too much, too...

"Do you feel desire now?" he whispered. His lips and breath caressed her ear as he spoke. He licked its shell, nibbled the lobe, and then breathed again.

Something emerged from her throat. It wasn't words, or any type of intelligible response that she was aware of, but then, she wasn't aware of anything beyond his mouth, the vibration of his voice, the swirl of his finger pads—when had they replaced the cloth?—and the shivering inferno that raged through her skin.

"Say it. I want to hear you say it." His lips spoke against her neck now, whispering his way across her collarbone, kissing down her breast, nipping her nipple as he passed it on his way to nibble her stomach, and all the while his fingers—those deft, strong, capable fingers—worked their expertise.

"You desire me," he murmured.

His voice vibrated against her inner thigh, and she jerked taut.

His whiskered cheek nuzzled against her self-inflicted scars. His right hand still swirling her clit. He leaned over and licked the mess of scars on her left thigh, then nibbled his way higher, continuing his path to its ultimate goal, as if the ruined skin on her thigh was just another part of her body ripe to ply with his pleasure. His eyes—both the brown and the scarred blue—focused on her face as he kissed and licked and tortured her until he reached the center of her. His fingers didn't stop, but his face leaned in close. He breathed on her, then breathed her in.

"Admit it," he insisted.

It took her a moment before she could pick up the thread of their game. "What? You not know for yourself? You not see it? Smell it?" She smiled with inspiration. "Maybe tasting it will convince you."

But he didn't smile back. "I desire you, Delaney," he said, his eyes serious, nearly melancholy at the admission.

He wasn't playing anymore.

Her breath caught. "I desire you, Torek. I not want to, and I know you not expect to—"

He shuffed.

"But here it is. And I not take it back."

"Neither do I." He did smile then, flashing all his pointed teeth and fangs, before dropping his gaze, angling his head, and replacing his fingers with his mouth.

Delaney's hips bucked up off the bedcover. Sensation, too sharp and penetrating to be considered pleasure, shot through her body from her core outward. She cried out and fisted Torek's hair for purchase, but he was relentless, gripping her hips with his strong hands to hold her in place and heating her body even against its will. The tide turned in a sudden drop, nearly from one tongue stroke to the next, from aching pain to burning desire, and Torek, feeling her yanks on his hair switch to pushing encouragement, switched from licking to sucking.

"But... I am about...to...oh!"

Torek entered her in one smooth thrust. The combination of her juices, the natural slick of his cock, and his new confidence made it easy this time, but once inside, he stilled. He leaned forward, bathing her cheeks, her eyelids, her temple in tender kisses. His hips pressed forward and then eased out, a languid torture that was both delicious and frustrating. She could feel her pulse slowing, the flames inside still stoked and expanding, but somehow starting anew, and an inhuman growl emerged from her throat.

She bucked against him, attempting to roll him over, but he was too heavy. "Let me up," she gasped. "I want on top."

He leaned back and blinked as if waking from a dream. "You?"

She frowned and then she couldn't help it. She laughed at the dumbstruck expression on his face. "Yes, me. You have a problem with that?"

"No, I just never..." He shook away whatever he'd been about to say with a toss of his head. "Why?"

She narrowed her eyes. "You do everything I want without me asking. Now I asking, and you want to know why?"

He renewed his slow, torturous movements, and Delaney closed her eyes on a pained groan. "Please!"

"Why?"

"You not doing it right!" The words just flew from her mouth, more sensation than thought, and she stilled. Shit. She opened her eyes.

He barked out a laugh. "I hadn't heard any complaints."

She relaxed, suppressing an answering grin. "I complaining now."

"So you are." He gripped her hips and held himself inside her as he rolled. She straddled atop him, all that chiseled muscle between her legs, hers for the taking. "By all means, show me how to do it right."

Both his fangs peeked out from between his lips. He was watching her with a strange expression on his face, both amused and anticipating, and her body flamed with self-consciousness. She should just have let him go at his pace. However slow they'd been traveling, at least they'd been going somewhere. She froze on top of him, surrounded by air instead of his body, unsure of herself, of what she wanted, and too shy to seek it out.

He stroked his hands up her hips to her ribs. She shivered and placed her hands on the rippling cuts of his flexed abdomen. They contracted under her cool touch. His breath caught.

She grinned to herself. Yes, let *him* be breathless for a change. She traced the long, raised scar across his belly with a gentle finger, then scratched her nails lightly down his lower stomach and contracted her inner muscles.

His eyes rolled back and closed on a groan.

Something powerful and addictive coursed through her veins at his reaction. She rocked her hips forward in a smooth thrust.

His groan cut short. His grip on her hips tightened.

She lifted and pressed again, slower and more agonizing than even he'd been moving before, just to see the awe-filled pleasure bloom across Torek's face. His hands on her hips were shaking. She did this to him. This massive, powerful man who commanded an entire army, who protected an entire country, who battled aquatic alien monsters, whose touch could be as gentle as it was strong; this man trembled under her.

She began to move in rhythm over him, still slow and agonizing, but steady. The spark between them was so deep, it felt as if the tip of his cock was caressing the insides of her nipples. But the more she moved, the more they ached. She pinched them with both hands, rolling her areolas between her thumbs and forefingers. Her head fell back in equal parts relief and heat.

Torek growled.

Delaney glanced down. He was watching her, his heavy-lidded gaze drinking in the sight of her hands on her nipples. He bucked up into her, forcing her to a faster pace. She braced herself on the swells of his shoulders, lifted her hips and took back the rhythm, impaling herself on his cock as hard and deep as she could. She withdrew until the wide brim of his tip stretched her opening, then slammed home again and again and again as the heat that they'd stoked suddenly surged between them.

His hands at her hips lost their rhythmic urging and kneaded at her in needy abandon. His face was flushed. His eyes closed again. His brow was furrowed, nearly in pain, except his mouth was lax, his voice a growling moan that grew louder as she moved faster.

She leaned back, seeking a new angle. Just a little more... There! Oh, whatever that was, it was heaven, and Delaney pummeled it with every ounce of strength and finesse she possessed. Her nipples tightened, her vagina throbbed, her abdomen tingled as her fingers and toes caught fire. But it still wasn't quite enough. Maybe her weight alone wasn't enough pressure. Maybe he'd need to be on top after all, and she could—

"Look at you," Torek murmured.

Her gaze shot down to meet his.

"You're incredible."

Delaney watched Torek watching her. The need and want and affection in that one look was more powerful than all his brawn. His need tipped her over the edge where hers couldn't. She climaxed, her entire body seizing in exploding abandon.

His growls turned into a roar. His every muscle clenched—his arms around her, his thighs beneath her, his stomach against her—as his cock vibrated inside her.

She fell onto his chest in a boneless, quivering heap. His heartbeat under her ear was racing, his breaths deep and labored. She grinned to herself, catching her own breath.

His hand flopped up and rested against her lower back, deliciously heavy. The soothing tickle of his wandering fingers caressed along her hip, and she breathed a deep, contented sigh.

Imagine, all the time they'd wasted not doing this. She should have revealed herself eons ago.

"Yes, you should have," he breathed, but his voice didn't sound accusing. His voice didn't sound anything but lazy with exhausted satisfaction.

"I not meaning to say that out loud," she murmured. Heat swept over her skin in a full-body blush. "I not in my right mind."

"Good, then I'm not alone in this insanity."

She huffed out an exhausted laugh. "No, not at all. Have you—" she began, then bit her tongue against the words and what they would reveal about herself and her feelings for him.

He glanced down at her, his brown eye so velvet and kind and his blue eye so sharp and seeing. His upper lip had caught on his fang, exposing its sharp tip. His hair was mussed; a hank of it was flopped in the wrong direction and tangled in his left horn.

She smoothed the lock into place, and Torek closed his eyes on a viurr.

"You ever feel this way before?"

He opened his eyes and met her gaze.

"I mean, I know you love your wife. You feel this with her, but is it this, this..." Her body glowed with embarrassment, and she lost the courage to finish her question.

"This powerful? This moving?" He turned his head and nuzzled into her hair. "I did love Zana. She was my first and best friend. The first lorok who shared my heart. The only lorok who shared my heart until now." Another deep breath and a lick.

Delaney stroked his smooth cheek and focused on breathing through the sudden contraction in her chest.

"But Zana was often ill, weak, or thinking she was about to become ill. She was sweet and wonderful, but she wasn't physically or constitutionally strong. She never would've survived an intergalactic kidnapping."

Delaney let loose a chuckle, the pressure in her chest easing slightly.

"I was always careful with Zana. We were intimate and loving, but very careful. I couldn't lose myself in her for fear of hurting her."

Delaney reached up and combed her fingers over the base of his horn. "You careful with me too, when it unnecessary. Maybe—"

"You communicated my unnecessary caution and your displeasure with it," Torek said ruefully. "Zana communicated the opposite. Her frailty was a concern she shared as well. With good reason." He sighed. "So yes, I loved Zana, but I couldn't be my full self with her. I never felt the lack, until—" He breathed in sharply and buried his face in Delaney's neck.

"Until?"

"Until today." He ducked his head and whispered into the shell of her ear. His beard scratched the side of her neck and puckered her breasts. "Until you."

The pressure around her chest broke, and something wild sprang free and soared.

"I not know it could be this way," she whispered. "I think maybe our caring and respecting—our hearts beating as one—made it different."

"I cared for Zana. More than cared. I cherished her. But I hadn't known it could be like this either."

"Torek, I—"

A siren blared over the intercom, drowning the rest of her sentence. Dread poured ice through her veins.

Not again.

TWENTY-SEVEN

"Third quadrant. Zone forty. Point three, two, seven, nine, four, two, two..."

Torek stiffened. That couldn't be right. They'd just reinforced that quadrant.

Delaney relaxed her hands from over her ears, still cringing. "Again? You say it too early for a zorel attack."

He plucked her up from his body, nuzzled one last breath from her neck, and stood. "It is too early."

"But this the second early breach." She scrambled to the edge of the bed, pulling one of the furs around her body.

He walked into his closet and dug his yenok and fur-lined coverings out of storage. He'd need to find his fur-lined pants too. Rak, if he still had them after last season. He'd never shed this early in Genai in his life. Then again, the zorel had never come out of hibernation this early either. He yanked a yenok over his head, shrugged into his jacket, and emerged from the storage closet only to collide with Delaney.

"Well?" she demanded.

He nearly tripped over her. As it was, he had to steady himself on the closet wall to prevent himself from tipping over and crushing her beneath him. He opened his mouth to berate her—he didn't have time for chitchat and idle questions!— but then he caught the look on her face.

He blew out his anger on a weary sigh. The dim emergency lights shadowed her wide, frightened eyes. Her lips were trembling. Her entire body was trembling. Her knuckles were white as they gripped the furs around her boney, narrow shoulders, and he couldn't remember the last time he'd fed her. He'd known from the start, from that first look at her in that cage, that she was high maintenance, exotic, delicate, and temperamental. Rak, she was a heavy burden, more so now that he knew she was a lorok, not an animal.

More so now that she was his lorok.

He knelt on one knee before her, putting his eyes at chest level. "What would you have of me, Delaney?"

She wrapped her arms around his head and drew him close. He let himself be drawn—let, ha!—and nuzzled the fragrant, plump mounds of her breasts as she massaged his scalp.

"Stay with me," she whispered.

He enveloped her in his embrace and smoothed his hand over her back, trying and failing to soothe her tremors. "I'll be back."

"You have a second-in-command. Filuk Renaar."

"How do you—"

"Let him take lead. He ready."

"*She* probably is, actually." He leaned back slightly to see her face. "What do you know of her?"

"Nothing."

Torek shuffed. "You know her name."

"I know you. You would never choose a second who not ready to lead."

He stood to press his lips against her forehead. "You're amazing."

She stared at him, and the hope in her gaze was crushing.

"But I can't stay. I have a duty to Onik." He stepped back,

retreating into the storage closet for the fur-lined pants that must be there if they were anywhere.

She followed him in. "Please. You can—"

The zorel alarm pierced the room. Delaney's face collapsed into itself, and she slapped both hands over her ears.

By the time the alarm cut to the recitation of coordinates, Torek had found his fur-lined pants, smoothed his hair back into order, and donned his boots. Delaney's concern had escalated from worried to panic.

She grabbed his hand just as he was attempting to clip his weapon's holster, and his RG-800 nearly unbuckled.

"Careful," he chided gently. He didn't dare chide ungently; she looked about ready to lose her mind. And not in a good way.

"Stay," she begged, picking up right where she'd left off as if the alarm hadn't interrupted her a full minute ago.

Before she could drop to her knees, Torek did. One last time, he pulled her close, burying his face deep in her chest. She clung to him. He didn't like the desperation in her hold—the trembling of her breath, her shaking arms, the little half-moons she dug into his neck with her clawlike grip—but he couldn't shirk his duty. Not to his country and certainly not to her.

"Lives are at stake, Delaney," he murmured into the valley of her breasts.

"What about me?" she tried.

"Who do you think I protect when I leave to reinforce the ice, hmmm?"

She fisted her hands in his jacket and shook him. "Nikiok kill Keil. If something happen to you, she kill me next."

"I protect all of Onik: the civilians, my guard"—he stretched up and stroked the side of her cheek with his knuckles—"and you."

"Someone else protect Onik seasons before you, and when you leave, someone else protect Onik seasons after you." Delaney released her grip from his jacket to cup his face. "Let someone else protect Onik now."

"I'm their commander. I must—"

"You not their commander. You still on leave."

Torek pinned her with what should have been a quelling look. "I'm not discussing this again. I was cleared for active duty by the Lore'Lorien herself."

"She not have your best interests in heart! When you dying with fever, she allow you to remain ill with no one to tend you."

"That was a mistake, as you well know. I'd commanded Petreok to—"

"And now she force you into battle. As always, she gets her way, no matter the cost."

"What possible motivation could she have for 'allowing' me to remain ill? Or for 'forcing' me into battle? I am her captain of the guard. Where else would my best interests lie but in her heart?" Torek shrugged from her grip, stood, and took both her hands in his own. "We must agree to disagree on the matter of Dorai Nikiok."

"I not agree. She is wrong. She is selfish. She is a mur—"

Torek tugged her forward and buried his muzzle into the soft, sweet curve of her neck. "Stay in my living quarters this time."

"—derer." Her muffled voice finished into his shoulder.

"Don't overeat, and don't climb out the window."

She wrenched herself out of his arms. "Do not treat me like an animal."

"Then don't act like one."

Her expression crumpled. "Ofukyoo."

He tried to reel her back into his embrace, but she braced her arms against his chest.

"Come now. I know you're upset, but I'm leaving for battle. Give me a proper goodbye."

"Just go. Lives are at stake," she mocked. "Go protect us. Onik needs you."

Torek tamped down his hackles before they could rise. "And I need you."

She crossed her arms. "Obviously not as much as Nikiok need you."

"Delaney, don't—"

The zorel alarm wailed.

Torek growled in frustration.

Delaney pointed at her ear and shrugged. A strange twisted grin slashed across her pale face.

He considered waiting for the alarm to cut back to coordinates, but he'd delayed long enough. He needed to leave now, or he needed to send Filuk in his stead. She was ready—Delaney was correct about that—but she was also correct that this was a second early zorel breach, and on reinforced ice. Something wasn't quite right, and with that uncertainty hanging in the balance, the weight of responsibility tipped solidly onto Torek's shoulders. Delaney would still be here after he returned from battling the zorel. If he stayed, he didn't have the same confidence regarding the citizens of Onik.

Against the ache in his heart, he listened to logic and left.

DELANEY STARED AT THE CLOSED DOOR AND SHOOK HER HEAD. Torek was never going to believe her account of who had murdered Keil. Not so long as it implicated his high-and-mighty Lore'Lorien.

She slapped her hands over her face and groaned. Torek cared for her, as deeply as she was horrified to realize she'd come to care for him, but his loyalty to Nikiok was as much a part of his identity as his rank and many property titles. She'd need proof. Maybe Torek was right: requesting an autopsy and reopening the investigation into Keil's death might provide Torek with the evidence he'd need to finally believe her. But could their investigation be discreet enough to pass beneath Nikiok's notice?

"Are you all right, Reshna?"

Delaney's head snapped up. Dorai Nikiok Lore'Lorien was standing in the doorway as if the ferocity of Delaney's thoughts had summoned her.

Fuck!

Nikiok stepped into the room and shut the door behind her.

Anger froze instantly to quaking terror. Delaney stared a moment, let loose a low whine, then looked away, forcing her attention to wander.

Fuck! Fuck! Fuck! Fuck!

"Oh, poor little Reshna. Are you still frightened of me?" Nikiok reached out a fisted hand toward Delaney's nose.

Delaney leaned in, sniffing obligingly, and, when Nikiok threaded her fingers into Delaney's hair, Delaney forced herself not to cringe.

"Good girl." She massaged Delaney's scalp with her talons, pressing just a little too hard with her too-sharp claws. "Of all the animal companions to choose from, I can see why he purchased you."

Delaney forced out a pathetic-sounding viurr.

Nikiok released a long, weighted sigh. "For all our sakes, I just wish he hadn't, Delaney."

Delaney jerked back at her words, but Nikiok lunged forward, locked her arm around Delaney's head, and jabbed something sharp into her neck.

Delaney attempted to struggle. She cocked her fist back, but it fell limply to her side. She braced to leap away, but her legs wouldn't move. Her neck was on fire, and the burn spread in a heady rush through her chest. In the time it took for her to inhale a scream, her entire body numbed. Her vision blurred. Her heart gave one final lethargic throb, and her head floated off her shoulders, the scream forgotten.

The room flopped sideways. Something heavy clunked against the stone floor, and Nikiok's grim face swam past—Delaney's last image before she succumbed to darkness.

TWENTY-EIGHT

THE INCESSANT JACKHAMMER THROBBING THROUGH DELANEY'S skull woke her from a heavy sleep. She couldn't find the energy to open her eyes, and she suspected she didn't want to. The air was frigid, the floor she was lying on ice. Her body ached, her head was in agony, her mind was sluggish—not that the jackhammer was helping —and the smell...Wherever she was, it wasn't Torek's living quarters anymore.

Delaney opened her eyes. God, she hated being right.

She was confined in one of a long line of glass cages, but the occupants in the adjacent cages weren't animal companions. They were lorienok. And they didn't look particularly well-off. They were scarily emaciated. What little fur some of them still had was matted. Many were missing teeth. All were bruised and bleeding.

The smell was their feces.

Based on that telltale sign alone, it appeared as if the cages hadn't been cleaned in weeks. Considering their gaunt bodies, maybe the cages hadn't been cleaned all Rorak.

Their eyes were dulled by hopeless dejection, but oddly focused.

Delaney turned her attention in the direction of their unified gaze, but she moved too fast. The throbbing jackhammer drilling through her temple hit a nerve, and the room spun out into dark starbursts. Saliva flooded her mouth. Her stomach turned. If she vomited now, her brain would rupture, even without that hitherto prayed-for aneurism.

She closed her eyes, let the jackhammer do its worst, and focused on breathing through the nausea. In and out. After a long moment, the pain eased enough that her vision cleared. Her stomach settled. She reached up to clutch her aching head. Her numb fingertips were heaven against the goose egg swelling on her forehead. A sticky river of blood poured from it and down half her face.

Another few, foggy breaths later, she tried again. She looked up, squinting through her shaking fingers.

More glass lined the far wall, floor to ceiling. She suspected, however, that whatever the material, her prison wasn't actually made of glass. The wall was clear and smooth, but had it been glass, it likely would have shattered from the pressure. This prison, wherever it was, was underground—more precisely, underwater—and circling just inches on the other side of that too-thin not-glass wall, was a zorel.

Her breath caught. The creature was so gigantic that this close, she couldn't see its entire body. She couldn't even see its entire face. The floor-to-ceiling not-glass wall was at least ten feet high, but that only revealed the zorel's massive, jutting teeth protruding from its underbite, part of one scaly mane, and half its shoulder.

Where was she? How had she—

And then the person standing just outside her cage came into focus, the person all the other prisoners had been staring at—not the zorel.

Dorai Nikiok Lore'Lorien.

Her visit to Torek's room. The stabbing pain in Delaney's neck. Her subsequent collapse into unconsciousness. Everything came rushing back with brutal clarity.

Nikiok knew Delaney wasn't an animal companion.

Delaney inhaled sharply at the realization, and Nikiok glanced away from her conversation to look at Delaney. Her expression didn't alter. Her eyes didn't register any emotion except a cold determination that constricted Delaney's throat.

I told you so, Delaney thought to Torek, and then a subsequent realization sank cold and killing deep into her heart. *I might never see him again to tell him so.*

"I'm not accustomed to repeating my orders, Petreok," Nikiok said, still staring at Delaney.

Petreok? Delaney's gaze darted sideways to stare at the lor next to Nikiok. His fur had shed, revealing a deeply cleft chin, wide dimples framing his muzzle, and a mole high on his left cheek. But his other features were just as she remembered: the curled black ram horns of an adult lor, the alert, expressive ears of a boy, and those large, round doe eyes. She wasn't sure she would have recognized him on her own, but now that she knew who he was, the resemblance was startling, like gazing into a mirror and seeing someone else's face staring back.

"Open the release chamber," Nikiok ordered. "Now."

Petreok blushed a bright, painful fuchsia. His ears tucked tight to his head and quivered. "I can't, Dorai. Per judgment law #73625 approved and signed by Dorai Niki—well, *you*—I can't open the release chamber without a writ of release signed by both you and the sentencing judge." His ears sprang out and forward. "Who's the sentencing judge? We could—"

"*I'm* the sentencing judge," she ground out.

"But you're Dorai Nikiok. The Lore'Lorien." He blinked. "Are you a judge now too?" His ears leaned tentatively forward, hopeful again. "Do you have the writ with your signature in both places?"

Nikiok rubbed a hand down her face. "No wonder Torek buried you down here."

His chest puffed. "It's an honor to serve Onik."

Nikiok pulled something from her belt, held it at arm's length, and aimed the cylindrical end of it at Petreok's proud, dimpled face.

His head vaporized into a floating puff of ash. His body jerked back and fell with a hard *thud*, spilling a river of blood from the gaping hole at the top of his singed neck.

Delaney bolted upright. Dizziness smacked her sideways, and she just barely braced her elbows against hitting the stone floor headfirst.

She'd killed him. Dorai Nikiok had murdered Petreok.

Petreok is dead.

Delaney concentrated on the difficult task of not screaming. Those doe-brown eyes. Those expressive ears. Those hidden dimples. She remembered tricking him into thinking that Torek was the one giving him orders. She remembered his caring enthusiasm for Torek's recovery. He'd actually puffed his chest in pride for serving Onik even if it meant serving in this shithole. Even as Dorai Nikiok was disparaging him.

That brave, helpful, trusting young man: gone. Obliterated into ash.

Because of Delaney.

How was this happening *again*? But this time, she didn't have the cushion of pretending stupidity to save her.

Nikiok picked up Petreok's limp arm and dragged his body in a slick red path to a console. She pressed his hand to its screen.

The not-glass wall slid open to reveal a small chamber, tall and wide enough to fit one person. The chamber's floor, ceiling, and three walls were all that same glass-like material, but the far wall wasn't actually a wall. Delaney squinted to make sense of what her battered mind was seeing. The far wall was another sliding door, but the door didn't connect to another hallway. It opened to nothing but water and the circling zorel.

Nikiok strode toward Delaney's cage, painting a blood trail with Petreok's body behind her.

Delaney scrambled to the far corner. "I can h—" Her words dissolved into a coughing fit. Her mouth and throat were cotton.

Nikiok pressed Petreok's thumb pad to a panel beside the cage, and the door slid open.

The coughing produced enough saliva to swallow, and its hot slide eased the scratch in Delaney's raw throat enough to speak. "I can help you," she croaked.

Nikiok dropped Petreok's arm, and it splashed heavily into a puddle of his own blood.

"No one knowing who I am. What I am. People talk in front of me. I am your eyes and ears." Delaney's eyes darted to the not-glass chamber that opened to death. "I report to you, and you are everywhere. Know everything."

"I already know everything. Why do you think you're here?" Nikiok chided. "Torek's about to nomaikok Keil Kore'Weidnar's body and launch an investigation to solve his murder because of you. He wants to waste millions to send you home. Waste *billions* in future revenue from the other humans we're already en route to harvest. Because. Of. You." Each accusation was punctuated by the hard clip of her boots striding forward.

Delaney was already pressed flush against the wall as far back as she could retreat. "You waste billions. The other humans not act like pets."

Her lips twisted ruefully. "They won't need to."

Delaney's breath caught on a spike of cold dread. "What have you done?" she whispered.

"What I've always done." Nikiok reached down, fisted her hand in Delaney's hair, and wrenched her head back. "Whatever necessary."

"You trying to kill me for weeks," Delaney choked out. She glanced down the hall toward the elevator. Only a dozen yards away. Maybe if she kept Nikiok talking, kept her distracted, Delaney could buy herself enough time and opportunity to make a run for it. "The lor who chase me at Graevlai. The ukok in my rainol e lokks. That is all you."

Faces inches apart, the foggy puffs of their labored breaths mingled.

"We had an unspoken agreement, you and I," Nikiok whispered.

Delaney shifted her eyes to meet Nikiok's accusing gaze.

"We did!" Nikiok hissed. She twisted her hand, wrenching Delaney's hair from the roots. "Our eyes met just like this after I'd"— her jaw ticked—"taken care of Keil. And you looked away. You remained silent." She shook her head. "When I saw you and Torek together in Graevlai—your bond, your trust and mutual affection for one another—I knew you'd break that unspoken promise. You should have kept your silence."

"But why kill Keil in the first place?" Delaney rasped through her chattering teeth. "Why not just reclassify me and send me home?"

"Do you know how much it costs the Federation to launch an exploration mission? The backlash that the intergalactic exploration division would receive if the public knew how utterly our technology failed to detect intelligent from animal life?" Nikiok snatched Delaney's wrists in one hand and pinned them behind her back. She stood upright and strode from the cell, dragging Delaney across the floor by her hair and wrists. "People would start asking questions, like whether our technology had ever failed before. And *that* could *not* happen."

Delaney bucked and tried to kick free, but Nikiok dropped her hold on her hair. She twisted Delaney's wrists high and to the side, forcing her to touch Petreok's body. A stabbing pain knifed through both shoulders.

Fuck, Nikiok could pop her joints out of socket as easily as a chicken wing.

Nikiok wrapped Delaney's hands around something grooved and cylindrical, then forced her fingers wide. Whatever it was clattered to the floor in a splash of Petreok's blood.

Nikiok yanked her head back again and dragged Delaney through that puddle, painting her own path across the stone.

"He should have classified you correctly before diving into deep space," Nikiok spat. "By the time I received his reclassification request, I'd already launched another ship and invested in preparations for a new animal companion breed. Humans." She shuffed.

"People make mistakes." Delaney gritted through her clenched jaw. Was her scalp ripping?

"This mistake would cripple Onik's economy, and my duty is to Onik, no matter the cost. The lives of two lorienok and you, *little one*, is nothing compared to the price they must have paid after bringing home the baby zorel and its little mate all those many seasons ago. Not every creature can be domesticated." She huffed out a bitter, self-deprecating laugh. "The biggest mistakes are often the ones you only recognize in hindsight. But the stink of this mistake is right here within my grasp." She shuffed into Delaney's neck, nostrils flared wide. "Besides, I am Lore'Lorien. I walk where I will."

Nikiok released her, and Delaney dropped to the floor, gasping. The clear not-glass floor.

Delaney's head whipped up. She was in the release chamber, but the elevator was right there, only a few yards away now.

Time. She just needed a little more time.

"Why wait?" Delaney asked. "Why not kill me and Keil together? Frame a murder suicide?"

"And let the public question why Keil, who dedicated his entire life to the domestication of foreign animals, would kill one?" Nikiok tutted and exited the release chamber. "You were willing to cooperate at the time, so I waited, letting the news of Keil's death settle. Letting you play your part as I played mine." She retrieved Petreok's body and lifted his hand toward the console.

Delaney edged toward the exit while she wasn't looking, but Nikiok's gaze snapped up. She lifted the weapon that had incinerated Petreok's head and leveled it at Delaney.

Delaney froze, her hands raised. "I can still play along. Please, you don't—"

"You healed Torek, so I'm glad I waited. But now..." Nikiok sighed as if the weight of her own actions, crippling to someone else, was just now becoming a burden for her. "I'm sorry this won't be as painless as simply shooting you. You don't deserve this death."

"I don't!" Delaney tried, grasping at Nikiok's guilt like a sieve does sand. "Please, release me."

"Torek will investigate your death, and when he does, he must find evidence that supports your crimes and just punishment for them." She grinned sadly. "I must do what's necessary."

TWENTY-NINE

Delaney hadn't stayed in his living quarters. She wasn't in the washroom. She wasn't in any of the kitchens or the sitting rooms. She wasn't in the back hallway or the surveillance hall. Torek searched the entire guard tower, sparing a moment to consider and then dismissing the lift. He needed to focus on reality and the many places she could actually be, not worry over the worst place she could possibly be.

Torek fisted both hands in his hair and closed his eyes. His heart was about to erupt from his chest.

Inhale. Exhale. Inhale and hold. Exhale.

Rak! He stumbled back to his living quarters and sat down before he fell down. He could see the headline now: *Torek Lore'Onik Weidnar Kenzo Lesh'Aerai Renaar Returns from Zorel Battle Unscathed Only to Die from Panic Attack over Lost Animal Companion.*

Breathe. He'd find her, but to do that, he needed to remain conscious. And to remain conscious, he needed to breathe!

Perhaps he was expecting too much of her. Was it too much to expect his lover, posing as his animal companion, to remain safely ensconced in the luxury of his private living quarters while he battled the zorel? Was it too much to expect her to leave a message on his daarok, detailing her whereabouts so he didn't panic upon his return? Was it too much to want to bury himself and his exhaustion in her soft body, to hold her in his arms and be reminded of the treasures that made life worth living rather than embarking on a futile hunt that would at any moment result in his heart failure?

Granted, he hadn't actually protected Onik from anything this time. The breach had been a false alarm. He'd need to investigate and reprogram the Zorelok sensors if they were failing. But Delaney didn't know that. For all she knew, he was risking life and limb for her at this very moment, and what was she doing? Who knew, because she wasn't anywhere to be found! By Lorien's horn, he'd skewer her himself when he did. And he would. *He would.*

He was Torek Lore'Onik Weidnar Kenzo Lesh'Aerai Renaar, captain of Onik's Guard as was his father, grandfather, and their many forefathers for generations. He commanded officers into battle. He protected all of Onik from the zorel. He had clearance to every Federation room, sensor, camera, and mission file. He had—

He had the security cameras.

He lunged for the daarok, waved it to life, and keyed through the series of coded passwords to access the security system and, specifically, the hallway camera outside his living quarters. He rewound the footage. A flurry of activity blurred his doorstep after he'd left, and then there he was, leaving the room.

Torek stopped the footage and started it from there. He watched himself leave, and then the hallway was empty. A full minute later, it was still empty. Torek drummed his claws against his jaw. He didn't want to watch this in real time. He didn't want to miss anything either, but it could be hours until Delaney stirred from the room. He didn't have the time or the patience to watch security footage for that long. Rak, maybe he could—

The hallway washroom door was ajar. It had been shut a moment before. He'd blinked, and now, the door was cracked. Not being opened by someone—just open. The movement was minute, a blip, but the sliver of daylight between the door and its frame was unmistakably absent one moment then there the next.

Torek scowled and double-checked the time stamps. They continued ticking as if the door had glitched in real time.

Someone had tampered with the security footage while he'd been called away to battle the zorel. The zorel that hadn't needed to be battled.

Torek took note of the time stamp, then switched views to the adjacent camera at the far hall. He watched and waited.

Nothing.

He cut the feed and tapped into the camera on the opposite side of the hall, then watched and waited some more.

Fekok. This was insane. Who would tamper with the security feed and to what purpose? Was he really suspecting that someone under his command had—

There. A shadow in the corner by the lift was there—barely, but there—then gone.

Torek switched feeds to the cameras in the lift, rewound to the appropriate time stamp, and waited.

Nothing. Nothing. Nothing.

He was insane. Besides himself, no one had access to the security footage except Filuk Renaar and Dorai Nikiok Lore'Lorien.

His stomach soured even as he rolled his eyes at himself. He was a lovesick idiot if he suspected either of them of...of what? Foul play with his animal companion? Who would he suspect of foul play next? Zana, risen from the grave? He trusted Filuk Renaar with his life, and Dorai Nikiok was the Lore'Lorien. She was his commander and leader, and she—

She was the only lorok who could feasibly tamper with the security footage.

On a leap of dread-filled foresight, Torek left the room, ran down the hall, caught the lift just as a pair of guards were exiting, and

BEYOND THE NEXT STAR

jabbed the deporak's combination into the console. The doors closed, and the lift descended.

Torek seethed. His hackles were raised on an ill feeling and a hunch, but his instincts had never failed him before. His fists clenched. He deliberately opened his fingers wide and then clenched them again in torn uncertainty. Had he suspected anyone else of what he suspected from Dorai Nikiok—and what did he really suspect?—he'd be calling on his guard for reinforcements. His hand hovered over his daami. Could he call reinforcements against Dorai Nikiok Lore'Lorien? It was unheard of, completely unprecedented, but then so was the act of robbing his private living quarters of his animal companion. Assuming that was what she'd done. Assuming he wasn't jumping to rash, emotional conclusions based on what? A suspiciously timed skip in their security footage? Maybe their tech was just glitchy today. And maybe Delaney was mistaken about Keil's murderer. Maybe she'd overreacted when the lorienok had chased her in Graevlai. Maybe the ukok in her rainol e lokks had been an accident.

Too many maybes.

Delaney's soft, sweet voice echoed in his mind: *"No one knows the truth. If they did, I'd already be dead."*

Before he could settle on a decision and act, the lift doors slid open, revealing the deporak: a long hallway of one hundred and fifty-seven containment cells, seventy-three of which were occupied, the viewing wall opposite the cells, and the release chamber.

Delaney lay on her side within the release chamber. She was struggling for purchase, trying to crawl toward the exit, but her efforts, though valiant, were in vain. Her limbs were unsteady—sluggish, and uncoordinated—and she kept slipping on the slick of her own blood.

Her forehead was split and swollen to the size of his fist. Tears had cleaned twin tracks down her blood-smeared cheeks. The desperate grunts of her ineffectual escape made him flinch, but that shameful movement finally jarred him enough to notice the room beyond Delaney.

Dorai Nikiok was standing at the release panel, holding the wrist of a headless lor. His mind stuttered on that for a wasted, critical moment—who'd been on duty tonight, Kialok or Petreok?—as Nikiok lifted the dead guard's hand to the console.

She was about the close the release chamber with Delaney inside.

But Nikiok wouldn't. There was another explanation, because Dorai Nikiok was not a murderer.

Nikiok pressed the hand to the console.

The door began to slide closed.

Torek reached for his RG-800, but Delaney was faster. She wiggled her head between the door and the jamb, preventing the chamber from sealing shut.

The alarm buzzed, and the door reversed its slide, reopening.

"Fekok," Nikiok hissed. She dropped the guard's hand. His body slumped to the floor, and Nikiok strode into the release chamber.

"Please!" Delaney begged. Her voice was both hoarse and wet at the same time. "We can—ahhhh!"

Nikiok fisted her hand in Delaney's hair, yanked her head away from the door's sensor, kicked her ribs twice, and slammed her face into the wall.

Delaney's scream cut short. She collapsed, unmoving—horribly, completely unmoving.

Torek unstrapped his RG-800 and leveled his sights. "Dorai Nikiok, stop. Raise your hands where I can see them."

Nikiok froze. She turned her head slowly and locked eyes with Torek. At the sight of his weapon, she raised her hands above her head. "Stand down, Commander. She's been charged and convicted of Keil Weidnar's murder."

Torek exited the elevator, his aim steady. "Step away from her. Now."

Nikiok withdrew slowly from the release chamber but crouched, reaching for the guard's body. Petreok's body, he realized.

"Stop, or I'll shoot," he growled.

Nikiok stood, holding Petreok's wrist at her side. "And I said, stand down. That's an order, Commander."

She raised Petreok's hand toward the console again. Delaney was still curled limply on her side in the release chamber, and Dorai Nikiok was, beyond all doubt, going to kill her.

Lorien, lend me your steady breath. Torek squeezed the trigger, and Dorai Nikiok's right hand burst into ash.

Petreok's body fell to the stone floor.

Nikiok didn't fall. She didn't even scream. She whipped to face Torek, her face blazing. "*Stand down!*"

Delaney still hadn't moved. Was she still breathing?

Nikiok bent and grabbed Petreok's wrist with her left hand.

Torek re-aimed. "Stop. Step back from the console, or I'll shoot your other hand."

Nikiok didn't move.

Neither did Torek. He kept his eyes carefully trained on her, resisting the urge to check on Delaney a second time.

"This is treason," Nikiok hissed. "If one of our guards walked in at this moment, what would they do?"

"Dorai Nikiok." Torek snarled. "Step. Back."

"She's a murderer."

"You can't put down an animal companion without her owner's signature."

"She's not an animal companion. She's a person."

Torek blinked, taken aback for a moment. Nikiok knew, just as Delaney had claimed.

"But you knew that." A strange look came over Nikiok's face. Torek couldn't pick the meaning from it, but something about the set of her jaw soured his gut. "Did you know that she murdered Keil Kore'Weidnar too?"

It took all of Torek's life-long training and considerable iron will not to flinch. He hesitated, just a moment between opening his mouth and speaking, but she noticed.

"She deceived you about being an animal companion. Is it so hard to think that she deceived you about Keil, as well?"

Torek shook his head, his aim unwavering. "You knew Keil hadn't committed suicide, and you didn't launch an investigation?"

There went her jaw again. "I did," she said. "Immediately following his death. She was found guilty of his murder."

"And not pardoned?"

"No."

Torek narrowed his gaze. "Why wasn't I made aware of the investigation or that my animal companion was suspected of murder?"

"You were on medical leave, Commander. You weren't involved in any investigations. Besides, Shemara Kore'Onik reported that your health was greatly improved in Reshna's company. I couldn't interrupt your recovery until we knew for certain who was involved."

Torek shuffed. "If you were investigating Keil's murder, someone should have told his wife."

Nikiok's nostrils flared. When she spoke, her voice was deep and somber. "We can't predict the power of grief."

Torek edged forward. "Where are the papers?"

Nikiok blinked.

"The signed writ of execution. Where is it?"

She laughed. She actually laughed! "You sound like a first-kair cadet. My word is enough."

"It's not, as any first kair would know. As Petreok knew, I'm assuming?" Torek lifted a brow. "Or did Delaney kill him too?"

"Yes, she did."

"With the RG-800 in your holster?"

"With his." She jerked her head to the side, indicating the blood outside an open cell door. Sure enough, an RG-800 lay amidst the spill.

Torek shook his head slowly, finally recognizing the defensive certainty in Nikiok's expression for what it was and why he hadn't liked it.

He'd never liked liars.

"You tampered with our security feeds to cover your tracks, putting our guard at risk," Torek ground out. "But tampering with our Zorelok sensors puts all of Onik at risk!"

Nikiok shuffed. "You're losing your head, Commander."

Torek jerked back. "What did you say?"

"Are you willing to lose your guard, your position, and your forefather's legacy, all for one animal companion?" She tutted. "Come to your senses, and sheath your weapon before I have you court-martialed and convicted of treason."

"Dorai Nikiok. In courtesy of your rank as Lore'Lorien, I'll ask one more time before I shoot again. Step back. Now."

Delaney moaned.

Torek broke his aim in an involuntary reaction to glance at her. His distraction was only a moment, but a moment was all Nikiok needed to slam Petreok's limp hand against the console.

The door slid shut.

RAK! Torek pivoted to aim at the door.

Nikiok dropped Petreok's hand and leveled her RG-800 at Torek's head. "You shoot that door, Commander, and I'll shoot you."

Torek didn't hesitate this time. He dove forward, hopefully out of Nikiok's line of fire, and squeezed off three shots before she could vaporize his head.

The door cracked on the first shot. The laser ricocheted in wild abandon, taking out a chunk of ceiling. The second shot split that crack into three, but the door still remained whole even as the laser recoiled, blasting a crater into the floor.

The third shot struck home. The door shattered into three large slabs and a million shards. The mechanism that opened the release chamber ground to a halt, leaving Delaney safely huddled on the ground where she lay.

Well, safe from the zorel, at least.

But the third laser ricocheted off a holding cell. Its wall cracked, and the laser beam pinged into the viewing wall. That wall cracked, and the laser shot back, splitting the next cell and the next, zigzagging across all one hundred and fifty-seven containment cells before striking the last cell at the far end of the hall in an explosion of stone. But worse than the damage to the containment cells, a web of cracks and fractures weakened the viewing wall in the laser's wake.

Torek hit the ground and rolled, clenching his teeth against the pain suddenly searing his back. Nikiok must have pulled her trigger too.

He re-aimed his RG-800 at her chest and fired.

She lunged away from the console, protecting herself with Petreok's body. His torso took the hit. The laser burned a hole through his uniform, ate his skin to ash, and his stomach belched his innards at her feet.

"Torek?"

He didn't look this time, but his heart clenched along with his nerve. "Delaney. Stay down."

"What shhht—" Her arm slipped on a palmful of shards and blood.

He tried to move in front of her, to shield her with his body, but his back was on fire.

"I'm sorry, Commander. This wasn't what I wanted, but I'd sacrifice anything for Onik." Nikiok wiped her face with a shrug of her shoulder, but tears soaked into fur faster than the fabric of her uniform, staining her blond cheeks a dark brown. "Even you."

Dorai Nikiok aimed her RG-800 between Torek's eyes and fired.

THIRTY

D<small>ELANEY OPENED HER EYES TO THE MOST TERRIFYING SIGHT</small> she'd ever seen. In her twenty-seven years, her eyes had seen quite a lot—more than the average person's, she'd hazard to guess, considering the hovels she'd had the misfortune to live in, the abusive derelicts she'd had the misfortune to live with, and the aliens she'd had the misfortune to be abducted by—but nothing compared to the zorel. The creature had stopped circling. Its overcrowded, jutting bottom jaw and rows of giant, needle-thin, ten-foot-long teeth were inches from Delaney's face on the opposite side of the floor-to-ceiling not-glass wall.

Delaney groaned. She closed her eyes and turned away from the sight. When next she opened her eyes, she realized that she'd been wrong. That hadn't been the most terrifying sight she'd ever seen.

This was.

Nikiok was using Petreok's headless body as a shield. Torek aimed a cylindrical object, and the light beam that sparked from the device hit Petreok's stomach and ate away his skin like acid. His organs spilled across the floor in a putrid splash.

Delaney tried to sit up, but something embedded in her palm.

She slipped on it, shredding her forearm as she collapsed onto her side. The agony encasing her ribs stole her breath and sight.

When she opened her eyes again—who knew how much time she was losing between blinks—she realized that she'd been wrong yet again. Neither the zorel's jaws with only an inch of glass between them nor Petreok's evisceration were the most terrifying sights her eyes had ever seen.

Watching Nikiok level that same cylindrical weapon at Torek's forehead took the cake.

Delaney's heart stopped and then slammed against the fire of her broken ribs. *Oh, Torek.* Nikiok's aim wasn't an idle threat. Torek was already horribly injured. His back was a ruin of raw burns from his right shoulder to the bottom of his left hip. Bloody welts oozed from the blackened skin. He tried to move, and the wound separated, exposing torn, charred muscle.

He staggered, gasping.

Delaney's gut curdled, watching him struggle. This was it—either Torek was family or he wasn't. Either she could let go of the past to reach for the future or she couldn't. She had something all her own now, more than just a name, but like names on Lorien, it had been both earned and given. Damn Kane, Nikiok, Reshna, and the tatters of her self-worth that had ever made her feel undeserving of it.

She would keep it for herself.

Delaney lunged in front of Torek. She snatched up a larger chunk of broken glass amid the shards and lifted it before them like a shield in the same moment that Nikiok squeezed her trigger.

A ray of light zapped from the weapon and hit the makeshift shield. The not-glass exploded in Delaney's hands, slicing her palms to the bone. Nikiok dodged the laser as it ricocheted back at her. It bounced off a cell door, pinged the already cracked glass wall separating them from the zorel—*why was that wall, of all walls, cracked?*—and zigzagged down the entire hallway in a deadly game of Pong.

A high whine split the air.

On the other side of the cracked not-glass, a long, gray, knobby finger rose in front of the zorel's needle-thin teeth. The pointed tip of its sharp claw wedged into the crossroad of all those spiderweb cracks.

A spray of water spurted from the wall.

Oh, Jesus Christ.

Delaney was swept off her feet. A blistering-hot shoulder jammed into the agony of her ribs, strangling her scream. The room spun. At first, she thought the pain was playing havoc with her vision again, but no, Torek had about-faced. The prison cells rushed by in a blur as he ran.

Her cheek bounced limply against his back. Maybe she had passed out again, if only for a moment. She struggled upright, but the pain was too much. She settled for just tipping her head up instead.

God, why couldn't she just stay passed out?

That talon-tipped finger, backdropped by those ten-foot-long needle teeth, wiggled persistently, chipping away at the cracked glass. The spurt of water burst into a spraying shower.

The prisoners had snapped out of their hopeless lethargy and were pounding on their cell doors, shouting. Nikiok chased Torek's heels, several yards behind. The spiderweb cracks in the glass wall stretched outward, expanding in high creaks and whines. Three other places where the cracks converged suddenly sprouted leaks, and the shower flooded into a hemorrhage.

Torek ran into the elevator, punched a code into its panel, and the doors began to close.

The glass wall shattered.

Water flooded through the room in a lethal rush. The prisoners' screams soared to heights Delaney hadn't imagined a voice could hit, then cut to silence.

Nikiok wouldn't make it, not without help and not before the elevator doors sealed. Not without killing them as well.

Torek pressed a button on the elevator panel with one hand and reached between the closing doors with the other. "Jump!"

Nikiok lunged forward. She stretched her lean body as long as she could, extending her right arm to Torek.

Her right arm with no hand.

She stared at that severed wrist, startled. It spattered blood in a wide arc across Torek's uniform, missing his fingertips by inches.

Torek snatched his arm back as the elevator doors closed, sealing them off from the rush of raging water and Nikiok's wide, incredulous brown eyes.

Delaney stared at those closed chrome doors, waiting. Any second now, the zorel would wedge its black claws between the seam and pry the doors open. The water would burst through, and the zorel's many needle teeth would be waiting.

Her stomach bottomed out.

Delaney startled, nearly bucking off Torek's shoulder before she could come to grips with the sensation. It was just the elevator. They were rising, not dying. Just the elevator.

Torek collapsed. Delaney dropped with a pained grunt onto her side, half crushed beneath Torek's chest and half trapped against the side of the elevator. His gasping breaths filled the silence. She'd be gasping too, as soon as she could inhale a full breath.

Her heartbeat was deafening against her eardrums. Her limbs quivered in weak relief and lingering panic. Her head throbbed in time with her pulse, her ribs were a ring of fire around her chest, and her palms stung like they'd been dipped in lye. Or sliced to the bone by shattered glass.

She basked in the pain. She was in the elevator with Torek, with air and both hands, and leaving the zorel far below the surface where it belonged. She was alive.

And Torek, thank the God whom she'd thought had forsaken her long ago, was alive too.

Light shot through the elevator window. They'd exited the prison and were catapulting into the sky. Instantly, the terrible wailing zorel siren assaulted her ears.

Torek and his damn alarms.

Delaney wedged herself a little higher, fighting her ribs and the slick puddle beneath her palms to get a better view of the courtyard: the snow-spouting fountain, the ice sculptures, the benches and running children. In seconds, Delaney and Torek were high overhead among the clouds, leaving the courtyard like a toy set far below.

"Torek," she croaked.

He didn't move. Her heart skipped and sank before her brain registered that he couldn't hear her over the wail of the loudspeaker. She tapped his shoulder to get his attention, harder than probably necessary, because he startled up and whipped around, wincing from the movement.

Recognition sharpened his gaze, and he grimaced.

"Sorry. I didn't realize—" he began. She read his words from the movement of his lips. He strained to lift himself up, his arms trembling. "Are you—"

Delaney caressed her palm along his jaw. She pressed her thumb across his mouth to hush his words and inadvertently smeared a line of blood across his lips.

"I—I—" she stuttered. She would've struggled for those three words even in English, but she couldn't for the life of her remember the words in Lori, if she'd ever known them to begin with. Not that he could hear her anyway. But it wasn't for her life. He'd saved it. He'd saved them both. She had a lifetime to learn the words, which hardly seemed a challenge considering the hurdles she'd survived to find it.

To find him.

He turned his face into her palm, closed his eyes, and viurred. The vibration pierced her injured palm, bone-deep, and a matching, penetrating ache warmed her heart.

EPILOGUE

Ten months later.

They were leaving Lorien. They were going home. They were returning to Earth.

No matter how she phrased it, Delaney's mind still couldn't seem to come to grips with the reality of the situation enough to have a normal, calm conversation about it. What was "normal" anyway? As if being abducted by aliens was anyone's definition of the word. What did Torek expect? Obviously not hysterical laughter, sarcastic zings, and abrupt topic changes. She knew she was acting strange and being difficult and whatever, but she couldn't help it. They were leaving Lorien tomorrow on a five-year intergalactic journey to return to Earth.

If she focused on the "they" portion of that sentence and ignored the "Earth," she could almost say the words without having an inappropriate, emotional reaction. Almost.

Delaney wriggled deeper into the furry comforter. She was going to miss this bed. Yes, they would have a bed during their journey, but it wouldn't be this same bed with this comforter. They would have regular meals, but none of them would be at Grattao. She would have a room, but that room wouldn't have a balcony that overlooked a snow-glittered courtyard. Torek would undoubtedly form a schedule, as was his habit, but it wouldn't be the same schedule they had here on Lorien. No townsfolk to round on. No Graevlai to hike. No ice to slip on.

She'd never even particularly liked their schedule, or having a schedule at all, for that matter, but now that everything was changing, *again*, sameness seemed safer than change, even if that sameness was a cage.

She tried recounting the changes that couldn't twist against her: no collar, no treats, no doctor's appointments.

Well—she sighed—no veterinarian appointments.

At the release of that sigh, Torek rolled from his back to his side, gathered her in his furry arms and held her in a secure, warm embrace.

"I think Keil would have liked his ice sculpture, with all his seventy-three animal companions surrounding him," he murmured.

Delaney discerned Torek's forearm from the comforter and stroked her nails though his fur. "His wife like it too, I think."

"If she could've seen it, yes. I think it's exactly what she would've wanted." Torek nuzzled the back of her neck.

Delaney took comfort from the steady rhythm of Torek's breathing, but her own still hitched. "They do not capture Petreok's ears correctly in his sculpture."

"Petreok's mother seemed content with it." He shuffed. "As content as can be expected."

Delaney rolled and buried her face in Torek's chest fur. "I see where he inherit his courage."

Torek nodded. His chin rubbed against the crown of Delaney's head. "But I don't think that thoughts of this morning's memorials are what keep you up tonight."

Delaney just breathed. Torek's fur tickled her nose. She moved her head, scratching that itch on his chest.

"I'm sorry I failed to close all the investigations before tomorrow's departure," he murmured tightly.

Delaney stiffened. She leaned back to meet Torek's gaze. "What are you talking about?"

"I'll have Filuk continue investigating in my stead. The lor who attacked you in Graevlai *will* be brought to justice."

"And I tell you, many times, to drop that investigation." She pinched a lock of his chest fur into a spike. "Pardon his crime like you did the lorok who try to poison me."

"I can't." He gathered her close and spoke against the top of her head. A few curls caught in his breath and fluttered across her cheek. "The lorok who attempted to poison you stepped forward. She admitted her guilt. She was repentant, and her testimony was key to corroborating Nikiok's crimes against you."

"A proper autopsy was enough to reveal Keil's death as murder," she reminded him.

"Yes, but not enough to determine who murdered him. And proving the circumstances of Nikiok's own death wasn't so straight-forward: no body, no crime scene, no security cameras. Without that testimony and Brinon Kore'Onik reclassifying you, we didn't have much beyond my word and your toxicology report to support our account of events."

She glanced up. "Yes, thank Lorien that Nikiok pump me full of poison."

Torek grinned ruefully.

"The investigations are done. The harm that lor intend for me is past, gone with Nikiok's death. Filuk and the other Federation commanders have a planet to govern and other amends to make that are more pressing. Let them, and let us move on."

Torek rubbed her back. "Filuk is capable of multitasking."

Delaney rolled her eyes on a snort and buried her face back in

Torek's chest. "We will not even be here to see the justice you seek. What is the point?"

Silence. Torek's heartbeat thumped steadily against her cheek.

"We can stay if you want," he murmured. "It's not necessary that we leave with the expedition."

She glanced up at him. "You are leading the expedition," she said dryly.

He tightened his hold and curved himself around her. "Rak the expedition." He whispered the words against her neck.

She shivered, delighted despite herself. "Then who will stop the Federation from harvesting more humans?"

"I'm not the only person capable of leading a Federation mission. Filuk can go in my stead, and I'll remain commander here if you prefer, helping to govern Lorien and rebuild the trust of our people."

"That you launch an expedition with the full support of your people is a miracle. We should not push our luck," Delaney chided. "Dorai Nikiok is right about one thing: going public did nearly cripple the economy."

Torek tapped her nose. "Only until I launched plans for the expedition. Nothing boosts morale and the job market higher than planning a Federation mission. And after the mission commences, we'll have the deporak reconstruction to keep the economy afloat. That will easily take three kair. Whether I make reparations by leaving on the mission or staying to claim my seat on our new ruling council, I have the public's support."

"You think the public continue to support me and the expedition if you are not leading it?"

"Gaining and retaining their support wasn't 'a miracle,' as you say. It has nothing to do with divine intervention. They want justice for you and your people as much as they want justice for ours. More so, in fact, because the injustice done to you and yours is an affront to Lorien. Besides, they walk—"

Delaney rolled her eyes. "They walk where you will, I know."

Torek placed his hand over her heart. "And I walk where *you* will, Delaney Rose Lisha'Aerai. If you want to stay..." He cocked his head, uncertain.

She shook her head and sighed. "I not want to stay."

Torek resumed the soothing, circular motion of rubbing her back. "Grammar."

She pulled back slightly, narrowing her eyes.

"You're doing so well lately! And programming my daami for English translation is easier and faster now that you understand proper verb conjugation. Once you master the past tense—"

"After all this time, you're still in denial. My throat physically cannot growl that low."

"It can with practice."

"Fekok. It cannot!"

He pressed his forehead to hers. "You can do anything."

"Not anything. I cannot even decide what I really want. Leaving does not feel like returning home. It just feels like returning."

"I know one thing you want." He nibbled the side of her neck.

Delaney shivered. "What I want, I so rarely receive."

Torek pulled back at that.

"Until I meet you." Her face flamed. "I still do not know how to trust it."

He cupped both his large palms on either side of her face, and their eyes locked. "You trust me."

Delaney nodded.

"We'll travel to Earth, stop my people from harvesting yours, and prevent whatever atrocities Nikiok had planned for them. That's something you want, isn't it?"

"Of course." She bit her lip. "But then what?"

Torek placed his hand on her belly, and his lips quirked in a toothy, lascivious grin.

She scowled down at his caressing hand. "This is not the time to start that argument."

"Why must we argue? We're talking four kair from now. Five Earth years, yes?"

Delaney sighed. His near-perfect English pronunciation was as infuriating as it was endearing. "Yes."

He nodded. "In either measurement, a long time."

She pursed her lips. "I suppose."

"Then we have a long time to figure it out. Which planet to live on. Whether to have five or seven children—"

"Whether to have one!" Delaney shuffed. "I do not care that our reproductive compatibility tests return positive. There is still a lot to consider!"

"Yes, and five whole years to consider it. Why agonize over such a crossroad until we arrive?" He nuzzled the top of her head. "Shall I describe our intergalactic exploration Federation ship to you again?"

As if she hadn't traveled on one during her five-year journey to Lorien. Of course, this time would be different. She wouldn't be caged. She wouldn't be lost and scared—well, she wouldn't be scared witless, anyway. She wouldn't be trapped, and she would have what was most important.

She tightened her hold around Torek's waist, tracing the long slice of the furless burn scar across his back with her fingertips. He took that as encouragement to continue.

"We'll have our own private living quarters together, same as we do here, but the few times we leave our room"—he nipped at her earlobe, and goose bumps shot down her side straight to her nipples —"we can enjoy the recreation pool, spa, and gym. There's a large cafeteria and a few smaller eating alcoves as well. Most nights, we'll enjoy entertainment, plays and singing, as well as live music and dancing."

"Is this a Federation expedition or a pleasure cruise?"

"A what?"

"A, you know, time off from work to lounge. A vacation?"

"Ah." He smiled. "It's a five-year journey, remember. We must keep our minds sharp and our skills honed."

"With music and dancing and spa treatments."

He nipped at her shoulder. "Among other things."

"And what might those 'other things' entail?" Delaney asked archly.

He nuzzled the sensitive skin between her shoulder and neck and inhaled deeply. "Shall I demonstrate now in preparation for the journey?"

"Hmmm, you better. I hate to embark on an intergalactic vacation without proper preparation."

He exhaled on a low growl. "You are my heart, Delaney."

"As you are mine. Make them beat as one?"

Torek propped himself over her and pressed her down into the bedcover with the delicious weight of his hard body. She gave herself over to him. He was right, even if she was prone to anxiety. They had five years to figure out their future together, and in the meantime, they'd have five years of *this*. Maybe it didn't matter where they eventually settled—Earth or Lorien—because she didn't want to live on either world, or any world, without this man. After a lifetime without a family or security, she'd found both in the least likely place. In the shelter of Torek's arms, she'd found the home of her heart.

LEARNING LORI: INTERGALACTIC POCKET DICTIONARY

TRANSLATIONS BY: DELANEY ROSE LISHA'AERAI

Atter (noun): A small amphibian native to Lorien that hops like a frog and has eight eyes and spindly legs like a spider.

Banchai (noun): An aerial, winged, feathered mammal native to the planet Fray, similar in appearance to an eagle, in temperament and size to a horse, and carnivorous. Historically used as modes of transportation before the invention of hover technology. Presently extinct.

Bandwey (noun): An easily obtained hearing with the local laird/estate owner to settle common disputes.

Daami (noun): A device worn on the wrist that performs a variety of functions, including timekeeping, daarok syncing, and telecommunication.

Daarok (noun): A tablet technology with hologram functions instead of a touchscreen that performs a variety of functions, including timekeeping, security monitoring, file storage, and writing applications.

Deporak (noun): An underwater prison beneath the Onik estate where prisoners on death row are detained until Genai.

Dorai (noun): Madam; a formal, polite address for the Lore'Lorien to show respect.

Faenil (noun): Sliced bread (sort of) manufactured from the nil grain.

Fekok (noun, verb): An expletive used to express that a person, thing, or circumstance is stupid, untrue, misleading, or deceptive.

Fepherok (noun): An illness lorienok are susceptible to if their fur becomes wet for an extended period of time. Supposedly not fatal except to the already ill, children, and elderly.

Fray (noun): The name of the planet inhabited by Frayon.

Frayo (noun): The people inhabiting Fray. Singular: Frayon

Genai (noun): The slightly less bitterly cold season on the planet Lorien, lasting approximately six Earth months.

Genok (noun): A natural spermicide that lor release during ejaculation to conveniently prevent pregnancy.

Gigok (noun): Cold cereal (sort of) typically eaten while soaked in paellek and made from the nil grain.

Graevlai (noun): A public memorial park approximately six hundred acres composed of walkways, bridges, hiking trails, gazebos, fountains, and throughout, ice sculptures depicting the many lor and lorok who died in service to Lorien.

Grambles (noun): A wild mammal native to Lorien, the size of a Chihuahua with puffy fur, whiskers, and a long, fluffy tail; essentially an arctic squirrel.

Haekak (noun): a flattened pastry roll used for baking.

Haven (noun): The name of the planet inhabited by haveni

Haveni (noun): The people inhabiting Haven. Singular: havenian

Jok (noun): A long, crunchy vegetable, similar in appearance and consistency to zucchini after the outer layer of spines and thorns are removed.

Kair (noun): A pair of seasons consisting of a consecutive Rorak and Genai, lasting approximately fifteen Earth months.

Keylak (noun): A fat, round vegetable, similar in appearance and consistency to onion, if an onion's layers were stacked like artichoke and purple.

Kore (noun): Federation rank; doctor.

Lesh (noun): Laird or estate owner.

Lisha (noun): A designation added to one's last name when entering into a family by law.

Litork (noun): Tactile; of or connected with the sense of touch.

Lombowatts (noun): A scaled reptile native to the planet Haven, similar in physical appearance to a snake with the temperament of a cat.

Lor (noun): A singular, male lorienok.

Lore (noun): Federation rank; captain.

Lori (noun): The language spoken by lorienok on the planet Lorien.

Lorien (noun): The name of the planet inhabited by lorienok. Referred to as a spirituality, like Mother Earth, to be praised and respected.

Lorienok (noun): The people inhabiting Lorien.

Lorok (noun): A singular, female lorienok.

Mukar (noun): The highest taxonomic classification on Lorien utilized primarily for breeding on-world animal companions.

Nikarok lukai (noun): An infection of the stomach and small intestine caused by a virus, bacteria, or parasite.

Nirarai (noun): The urinary tract.

Nomaikok (verb): Exhume; to dig out from the ground.

Nulistorak (noun): Physical or mental stimulation.

Nusarai (noun): Scenario; a postulated sequence or development of events.

Onik (noun): Lorien's capital city.

Orboas (noun): Eye; a globular organ through which people and animals see.

Paellek (noun): Manufactured milk.

Por-atter (noun): Creamed atter eggs.

Pourpites (noun): A scaled reptile native to the planet Haven, similar in physical appearance to a snake with the temperament of a dog.

Rainol e lokks (noun): A traditional, spicy lorienok dish similar in appearance to rice and red beans with sausage.

Rak (noun, verb): A Lori expletive, derived from Rorak, their bitterly cold season; an exclamation of the killing temperature and irony that it keeps the zorel at bay.

Rakek (noun): Procedure; the official way of performing a task, especially in reference to military duties.

Rel (noun): An extinct farm mammal historically used to produce milk and butchered for mass consumption. Similar in function to a cow. Lorienok retain no record of its appearance. Presently extinct.

Reshna (noun): Corkscrew; a spiral-shaped, handheld tool used to drill into ice.

RG-800 (noun): Military-issue weapon distributed to Federation officers which uses concentrated light beams to instantly vaporize its target.

Rolorak osir (noun): Neurological disorder; a sickness or abnormality of the brain, nerves, or spinal cord.

Rorak (noun): The bitterly cold season on the planet Lorien, lasting approximately nine Earth months.

Roranok (verb): Hibernate; to spend a season in a dormant state.

Salvarok (noun): Historically the most popular, well-respected animal companion purveyor in Onik. Presently up for sale.

Saufre (noun): A cold, caffeinated drink, similar to iced coffee without the ice.

Shuff (verb): A huffing snort through a lor muzzle. Similar in meaning to a human snort, either in humor or derision. Often combined with flared nostrils when in derision.

Taekok (noun): a large hover freight used to transport goods over long distances.

Tidokai (noun): Auditory; of or connected with the sense of hearing.

Tuanok (noun): A thorn-covered bush native to Lorien. The only vegetation capable of surviving the deep freeze of Rorak.

Ukok (noun): A common seasoning used in most lorienok dishes, which contains the same protein found in peanuts.

Viprok d'Orell (noun): A dangerous path that meanders from Graevlai to the ravine along the Zorelok.

Viurr (noun and verb): A maternal vibrating noise, similar to that of a cat's purr. Used to put one at ease, to soothe and comfort.

Yark (noun): A lombai egg.

Yark e haekak (noun): A traditional lorienok comfort dish consisting of scrambled yark and various vegetables inside a baked haekak. Vegetables typically include keylak and jok.

Yenok (noun): An article of clothing worn during Genai when lorienok shed. Used to absorb sweat from their furless skin and preserve the cleanliness of their fur-lined clothes.

Zeprak (noun): A medium-size, furry, domesticated rodent with the intellect and loyalty of a Labrador.

Zivook (noun): Avalanche; a deadly slide of snow.

Zorel (noun): A giant anglerfish commonly known as being native to Lorien but likely the result of a failed animal companion domestication; the size of a blue whale with arms instead of front fins and ten-foot-long needle teeth. Lives under the Zorelok and hibernates during Rorak. Historically and presently terrorizes Onik during Genai. Not likely to become extinct anytime soon.

Zorelok (noun): Lorien's main body of water inhabited by the Zorel.

ALSO BY MELODY JOHNSON

Love Beyond Series

Beyond the Next Star

Sight Beyond the Sun (coming soon)

Night Blood Series

The City Beneath

Sweet Last Drop

Eternal Reign

Day Reaper

Holiday Anthology

Grave Promises (coming soon)

THE CITY BENEATH

NIGHT BLOOD, BOOK 1

I NEARLY LIMPED RIGHT PAST HIM, CLOUDED BY MY own physical pain and the churning unease in my gut, but the rattling hiss that growled from the alley tripped my interest. I stopped walking.

The night was cool and quiet in the aftermath of sirens and flashing lights. My scalp tingled in response to the noise emanating from the alley, and I thought of all the things I should do: I should return to the main crime scene, I should finish my interviews, I should write my story and submit it to print like a good, reliable, by-the-book reporter. The hiss rattled from the alley again, but as I'd never been one to leave questions unanswered, I slipped a can of pepper spray from my brown leather, cross-body satchel and side-stepped into the alley to find the source of the noise.

What I found was a man, and the rattling hiss was his struggling, gurgling, uneven breathing. His entire body was ravaged by third-degree burns. Tucked into a shadowed alley between two buildings on the corner of Farragut Road and East 40th, he was crouched down as if warding off an attacker—perhaps in his case a flamethrower—and not moving. I cringed, thinking about the injury that was blocking his throat to produce such a horrible rattling. Maybe he was crying. Maybe he was just trying to breathe. I couldn't decipher his expression because his burns were so devastating. His face wasn't really a face anymore beyond the rough distinctions of a lump for a nose and a hole for a mouth. The unease churning in my gut all night bottomed out. I wouldn't have imagined that someone so injured could still breathe.

Trading the pepper spray for my cell phone, I dialed for Detective Greta Wahl.

"Wahl here." She answered on the fifth ring, just before I suspected my call would transfer to voice mail. "I already gave you a statement, DiRocco. Let the other sharks have a bite, will you?"

"I found another victim, G," I said without preamble.

"Alive? Where?" Greta asked, snapping from friend to detective instantly.

"A block up Farragut. He's still breathing, but he's different from the others. No bites." I swallowed the bile that clogged my throat like hot ash. "His entire body is burned to charcoal."

"Is he wearing a necklace, like the ones from last week? They were gold with a wolf pendant."

"I remember," I said. "And no, he's not wearing a necklace. And he's not shot execution-style like those victims, either. He's burned. This is probably a different case altogether."

Greta sighed. "Stay with him. I'll send a paramedic to you ASAP. It might be a few minutes, though. We've still got our seven victims being stabilized here."

"Got it. We'll be waiting." I hesitated a fraction of a second before asking, "Any one of our victims talking yet?"

"The few that still have throats haven't said a word. They're all in shock. It's not pretty down here, DiRocco."

"I know. Keep me posted, and send Nathan to me if you can."

"Will do," Greta said.

I ended the call and sat gingerly on the ground next to the man to offer what comfort I could and to give my arthritic hip the rest it needed. Injuries were supposed to heal with time, but the scar buildup on mine had only increased in the five years since I'd taken a bullet. The first stakeout of my career had set a high standard for my field performance, but it had also left a permanent reminder to listen to my gut. My hip ached on a regular basis, and lately, it would click and grind when put to excess use. After an entire day on my feet, interviewing officers and tracking down witnesses, my activities had apparently escalated way past excess.

Once I settled on the pavement, I held the man's left elbow—one of two visible patches of skin not blackened or blistered—and felt an overwhelming, humbling gratitude, no matter my past injuries or current residual pain, that none of these victims had been me.

According to the brief interview I'd snagged earlier in the night from Detective Wahl, my sometimes informant and longtime friend, seven other victims were still alive at Paerdegat Park out of the twelve or so they'd been able to identify. Most of them were in critical condition. I hoped Greta could send one of the paramedics here soon, and preferably my brother, Nathan, because he wouldn't tip my competition. If the victim's harsh, wheezing gasps were any indication, however, sooner rather than later might not even matter. I'd seen a lot of carnage at varying crime scenes through the years, but I'd never reported a recovery from injuries this severe.

My part-time nemesis and full-time boss, Carter Bellissimo, would chew my ass out for stepping away from the scene to comfort one of the victims. I'd have to race back to the paper, sift through my recorded interviews for quotes, slap the copy together, and make it to press before distribution. We'd be working against the wall, as usual, but I'd always adored the race and the adrenaline of breaking news. Meredith Drake, my photographer and sister (in love if not by blood or in law), thought I was a little sick to enjoy the taste of only just making the wire. She took pleasure in lazily gazing at the world through her viewfinder. Nights like tonight, when the world was writhing and in pieces, I'd rather feel the pressure to write on deadline than capture a close-up of one of those ragged, bloody bite marks.

The victim next to me made another rattling hiss, the same

agonized noise he'd been making with every few breaths. He wasn't visibly bitten like the other victims, but his wounds looked wholly more devastating. The only other body part spared from the burns was the left half of his chin, which, ironically enough, bore an old, healed scar. The scar was thin and pink, and it puckered slightly. It tore through his lower lip in a downward pull, and continued diagonally over his chin where it disappeared into the wreckage of his burned flesh.

A paramedic finally jogged to us from around the block, but I didn't recognize him. He was tall and lanky and very young looking—even younger looking than Nathan, which was hard to accomplish—but thanks to Nathan, I knew all too well that young looking didn't translate to incapable.

As the paramedic approached, he absorbed the scene; his eyes flashed over the victim's body and his surroundings, and eventually, his gaze locked on my hand holding the victim's elbow. I resisted the urge to pull my hand away.

"Detective Wahl said you called in a burn victim." The paramedic snapped on a pair of latex gloves.

I nodded. "Yes, that's what it looks like."

The paramedic knelt next to us, hovered over the victim with his ear over the man's mouth, and trained his eyes on the man's chest. He pressed two fingers on his charred neck. I winced. After about fifteen seconds of concentration, the paramedic straightened and sat back on his haunches.

"What the hell is this?" he asked. He didn't make any moves toward actually opening his equipment case. "We have live victims that need tending at the main crime scene."

I didn't like his tone, and on a normal night, I would react with a blast of attitude. My short-person syndrome wasn't becoming any milder through the years. If anything, turning thirty had completely eliminated my ability to tolerate most people. But this wasn't a normal night, so I played nice and swallowed my temper.

"Yes. Greta did mention that you were busy," I responded civilly.

"I appreciate you coming away from the main crime scene to tend to this victim."

The paramedic shook his head. "This man's dead. You've got to return to the police barrier with the rest of the media."

The anger I'd doused flared in a sunburst. I took a deep breath against the words I wanted to say and spoke through clenched teeth, "This man is still breathing, and I'm farther behind the police barrier than any of the other reporters. I think I'll stay where I am."

"You know the drill, Miss . . ."

The paramedic waited for me to finish his sentence, but I just stared right back. Let him finish his own damn sentences.

He cleared his throat. "Look, I'm needed back at the scene, so if this is all you called me here for, I—"

"Are you going to help this man or not?" I finally snapped.

The paramedic stared at me like I was insane. "I told you; this man is dead."

I blinked at him and then down at the man whose elbow I was still holding. After a moment of silence, I heard it—a faint rattling exhale from a man who didn't have a nose to exhale with anymore. I shook my head. "He's been making noises. He's struggling to breathe."

The paramedic crouched to listen again with his ear over the man's mouth. He placed his index and middle fingers over the man's raw neck for a second time, but after another fifteen seconds of concentration, the paramedic shook his head. "The man is dead. He's probably been dead since before you found him."

"No, I've heard the noises. It's like a strained exhale that—"

The paramedic straightened away from the victim and placed his hand on my shoulder. "They do that sometimes."

I narrowed my eyes on his hand, and he pulled away.

"This man does not have a pulse," he said, sounding defensive. "He's dead."

I shifted my glare to the paramedic's face, but the man didn't so much as squirm. "He's dead," I repeated.

The paramedic nodded.

A rattle hissed from the man's chest again, louder than before. He didn't sound dead. He sounded in pain.

"Listen, I've got to get back to the scene, and I suggest you do the same before the police extend their boundaries and catch you tampering with their evidence."

I pursed my lips. "No problem. Where do we take him?"

"We're saving cleanup for the day shift," he said, already walking away. "We've got to get the wounded to medical as fast as possible, which means leaving the bodies for later, once the police finish processing the scene."

"Wonderful," I muttered, not appeased in the least. My story needed to be submitted by midnight; I had less than two hours until the paper was put to bed. It felt wrong to just leave, but deadlines were deadlines. I squeezed the man's elbow gently before letting go. I hoped the paramedic was right. I hoped the man was dead long before I stumbled upon him, and that he'd found a better place than this.

The man's chest rattled.

I stared at the man, hard. He'd been pronounced dead, and I had a story to write. That alone should have been enough to send me on my way, but staring at the scar on his chin, at the proof of a life lived before this burned hell, I couldn't simply leave him the way I'd found him.

I texted Nathan to bring me a backboard, and he appeared around the corner a few minutes later. His thick black hair was straight and identical to mine except for the cut. Where mine hung past my shoulders and was usually yanked back in a high ponytail, Nathan's was close-cropped at the edges and longer toward the top in a faux hawk. His nose ring glinted in the streetlight as he approached.

"That was fast," I commented.

"You've never texted me at a crime scene before, Cass, and I've never seen you walk away before Meredith was done with her shots.

Today you did both. You're damn right I came fast." Nathan frowned. "Is it your hip again?"

"No," I said, which wasn't a complete lie. I'd left the scene because of my hip and my attitude, but I'd stayed away because of the man. "How is it down there?"

"Not good. Have you spoken to Detective Wahl?"

"Yeah, Greta and I had a little chat. If she thought an animal attack in the middle of Brooklyn was crazy, she won't have a clue what to make of him," I said, pointing to the man between us.

Nathan whistled. "None of the other victims were burned. Does he have any animal bites?"

"Not that I could tell, but I need you to take a look. The other paramedic wouldn't treat him, and he's still breathing, Nathan."

He frowned. "I thought that Donavan pronounced him dead."

"That's Donavan? Your partner?" I asked. At Nathan's nod, I snorted. "Donavan can't hear a pulse, but I—"

"If he doesn't have a pulse, then he's not breathing," Nathan said flatly.

"I can hear him breathing," I insisted stubbornly.

Nathan stared at me, hard. I knew that look. He was checking my pupils and watching my reaction, calculating the possibility that I was high. I hadn't abused painkillers in four years, and had, in fact, gritted through my hip pain during occasions when a Percocet was probably necessary because I never wanted to slip down that steep spiral again.

I gave him the look right back, annoyed that even after all this time, even after everything I'd accomplished, my brother was the one who still couldn't forget.

Nathan shook his head glumly and laid the board next to the man. "You know what's more ridiculous than checking the respiration of a man without a pulse?"

I shook my head, knowing he'd tell me with or without my encouragement.

"A trial for whoever is responsible for tonight."

I rubbed my eyes, beyond caring if my eyeliner was smudged to hell if I had to listen to Nathan's vigilante speech again. "Everyone deserves a defense. Everyone, no matter what they've done, deserves to tell their side of the story."

"You think there's another side to this story besides insane hate and violence?" Nathan asked, incredulous. "Someone should hunt these psychos down and tear off their limbs. Disembowel them like they tortured these victims." He glanced at the man between us. "Light them on fire."

"Murder does not justify murder."

"The hell it doesn't."

"Killing a monster isn't justice, Nathan. It only makes you a monster, too." I sighed. "Will you please check his pulse a second time? If you're killing anyone right now, it's me."

Nathan rolled his eyes.

"I know you don't believe me, which is why you're stalling, but like you said, I've never texted you at a crime scene before. I'm only asking for this one favor." I locked my gaze on his. "Please."

Nathan sighed heavily, but nevertheless, he squatted next to the man and pressed his ear to his chest. "If I had the opportunity to confront the people responsible for crimes like this, I wouldn't wait for them to confess their side of the story. I'd make damn sure they never—"

The man exhaled in a high, rattling hiss.

Nathan met my gaze, his eyes rounded with shock. "Oh my God."

"You heard it?" I asked, astounded.

Nathan bounded to his feet and unbuckled the backboard straps.

"I told you he was breathing. I told you that—"

"Fuck, don't just stand there. Help me board him!"

I ignored my hip and helped Nathan clip the man onto the back-board. "As much as I hate to say it, I can't help you carry him—"

"Hey!"

I looked up from the backboard straps and groaned. Donavan was

jogging toward us, and if the frown creasing his brow was any indication, he had a temper to rival mine.

"What do you think you're doing? The police haven't processed
this scene yet. You can't just—"

Nathan stood to face Donavan, and I finished snapping the
buckles on my own.

"He's still breathing," Nathan whispered hotly.

Donavan paused, mid-rant. "What are you playing at?"

"You take his head. If we can get him back to the ambulance,
maybe—"

"He's dead," Donavan said, shocked. "Why would we—"

"No, he's not." Nathan said. "We've wasted enough time, time we
could've spent treating him. Help me get him back to the
ambulance."

Donavan shook his head. "You're crazy. I checked him myself.
He's been dead for a while, and I—"

Nathan leaned closer, so I had to strain to hear his next words.
"Mistakes happen. Sometimes people notice and sometimes people
don't. Cassidy and I noticed, but if you help me get him back to the
ambulance, no one else has to."

Donavan stared back at Nathan, shock and anger giving way to
fear as he realized that Nathan was serious. He looked down at me. I
stared back at him, trying to convey that my mouth was a steel trap,
but mostly, I felt wary. He looked back at Nathan, and I knew
Nathan's expression as well as my own reflection. Even three years
my junior, our shared grief and bitterness could line Nathan's face
with an identical aged determination.

"He didn't have a pulse," Donavan whispered, but he bent in
front of me and gripped the head of the backboard anyway.

Nathan and Donavan hoisted the man between them, and an
ambulance met them curbside just as they turned the corner. I
watched as the man was packed into its rear, locked in tight, and
transported to the hospital in full lights and sirens. I'd originally
wanted to achieve some distance from the gore and death—reminders

of my parents that seemed everywhere lately—but as I limped back to the main crime scene, both my hip and my spirits only felt more burdened.

MEREDITH AND I MADE PRINT with an entire fifteen minutes to spare. The article flew from my fingers in hyperdrive, as was usual when faced with a perilously approaching deadline. I included a statement from Greta about the animalistic savagery of the attack, and Meredith found a shot of what nearly looked like a human bite had it not been so inhumanly wide or deep. The eyeteeth broke through the victim's skin, and blood pooled in the center of each impression.

I was reviewing my article and Meredith's picture when Nathan called with the bad news. The burn victim I'd found in the alley had died. He'd gone into cardiac arrest en route to the hospital and couldn't be revived. Nathan said that they'd brought him directly to the morgue, and I was sure that's where he'd remain until fingerprint analysis or dental records were completed. A next of kin would be contacted to claim him once he was identified, and then he would be their albatross. I rubbed my eyes, but even after five years, I still remembered every detail of the process.

I hadn't expected the man to live. I told as much to Nathan, and he repeated the same back to me, but I stared at the picture of that bite mark for a long while before I could finish editing my article.

With the paper put to bed, I was ready for bed myself, but I had an interview in four hours. As a favor to Greta—I was all for racking up the favors—I'd pitched a humanitarian piece to Carter about her cousin, the owner of a new bakery on Eighth Avenue. The article would certainly counter all the doom and gloom I'd been reporting lately, and frankly, I needed the pick-me-up. Carter hadn't been particularly impressed with my scoop, but he also knew the merits of a favor for Greta when he saw one and let it ride.

Jolene McCall, baker extraordinaire, was extremely excited about being featured in the paper, and even more excited for her grand opening. Her optimism was exhausting, but her miniature cupcakes were darling. She gave Meredith and me two each, and although one had been intended for the road, the little cakes hadn't survived that long. If our samples were any indication, Jolene's Cake Designs would be a finger-licking success, and if Jolene herself was any indication, she would spread joy along with her icing with every cake.

Back at the office, Meredith prepared a jaunty picture of Jolene in her tall, white baker's hat atop her tinsel-streaked, dirty-blond hair. She wore a pink-trimmed apron while balancing plates of cakes and pastries in various colors and patterns. I fluffed up the content with bakery puns to make the article light and sweet like the cupcakes themselves, so people would want to brave the murderous streets I'd depicted the day before for a taste of heaven at Jolene's Cake Designs.

I smiled as I stared at our edited work. I'd have to snag a few extra copies for Greta when it printed. We submitted our copy by five, and Meredith convinced me that sushi was in order after the night we'd witnessed. I agreed, but that didn't prevent my body from powering down.

Halfway through my second California roll, I tried hiding a yawn behind my palm and nearly poked my eye out with a chopstick.

"Don't you dare cut out early," Meredith warned, waving her own chopsticks at me. "We did great. We deserve this."

"I know. I'm trying to enjoy it," I said, cramming my mouth with another roll before I could yawn again. The roll was tangy and salty from the soy sauce and damn good. Sleep would have been better.

"I *am* enjoying it," Meredith said, stifling her own yawn.

We stared at each other for a long moment, so beat that even sushi couldn't spark our energy. I almost felt like crying, I was so tired. Meredith giggled. I smiled, and she giggled harder, and suddenly we both burst out laughing.

"For the road?" I asked when the heaves had subsided, gesturing to my remaining five rolls.

Meredith nodded, wiping tears from her cheeks. "Jolene really did have the right idea."

"Some girls just know how to do it right," I agreed.

Once our server had boxed the leftovers, Meredith stood, using the table as leverage. "I'll see you bright and early."

"Yeah," I scoffed, ducking under the strap of my shoulder bag so it hung across my body. "I can't wait."

We parted ways outside the Japanese restaurant, still laughing from our moment of sushi insanity. Sunset was creeping later and later as summer approached; eight o'clock and the streets had just plunged into full darkness. The walk to my apartment, however, was only a few blocks and brightly lit from street lamps and storefronts.

I was one block from my apartment, deciding against doing laundry before going to bed but contemplating a glass of cabernet, when a black and glowing blue blur smashed into my ribs and slammed my back into the wall of the alley adjacent to my building. My head snapped back and cracked against the brick exterior. I couldn't move for a moment, dazed from banging my head.

Inexplicably, the first thing I noticed was my take-out box tipped sideways on the sidewalk, my California rolls spewed across the concrete. My awareness slowly pounded into focus like a jack-hammer through my skull, and I realized that the blur that had hit me was a man. He was holding me off the ground against the wall by my arms, so we were eye to eye. A strange, rattling hiss vibrated from his chest. I could feel the purr of it against my body.

I couldn't look away. The man wasn't a man. Well, he was the general shape of a man, complete with a body, two legs, two arms, and a head, but something I couldn't quite account for—something crucial—was missing. He stared at me from inches away with icy white eyes ringed by a dark midnight blue. The pupils reflected a strange green tint from the street-light as he cocked his head, studying me. The motion was almost bird-like.

His skin was flawless, the angles of his cheeks, chin, and jawline sharp, nearly gaunt in their severity. His face was hollow, but his body was unbelievably strong. When he hissed again, the lips sneered away from his teeth. I couldn't look away from the glint of the man's sharp, pointed eyeteeth and the thin, puckered scar pulling at his lower lip. The scar was raised and pink and continued across his jawline, stopping near his jugular.

"That was quite an article you wrote this morning, Cassidy DiRocco, although I was mildly disappointed not to have been mentioned."

He spoke, but my brain couldn't wrap itself around the deep, cultured voice that emanated from the man's fanged mouth.

"The police didn't include you in their statement," I replied shakily. "They considered you a separate scene, so I didn't include you in my article about the animal attacks."

"Fortunate for them," he said.

His nostrils flared on another rattling hiss, the same rattle I'd heard from him in the alley last night, and I thought numbly, *I was right. He was breathing.* I eased my hand along my side slowly, attempting to slide the pepper spray from the outside pocket of my leather shoulder bag. I should have carried it in my hand while I was walking. What good was having pepper spray in my bag if I couldn't reach it when I needed it?

Suddenly, he crushed me deeper against the brick, gripping my upper arms a fraction tighter. Talons protruded from his fingers and pierced my skin.

I screamed.

"I don't like feeling grateful," he said, and the rattling hiss vibrated inside his chest again as he spoke. "But I wouldn't have survived another day if you'd left me at Paerdegat Park."

I shook my head, nearly panting from the sharp pain tearing through each shoulder. "I don't...understand," I said haltingly. I continued shaking my head, staring with numb awe at the scar on his chin. "You're not possible."

He smiled indulgently. "How so?"

I swallowed. "You died before the ambulance even reached the hospital. They brought you to the morgue."

"Yes, and I thank you for that. You had impeccable timing."

"You were burned beyond recognition. They said you weren't breathing, but I could hear it. You were alive, but you didn't have a pulse," I said, starting to feel a little hysterical.

"No, I don't."

I didn't know how to respond to his lack of circulation, so I stared into his unearthly white and midnight blue eyes, feeling helpless. The sound of my own pulse beating through my ears was deafening.

He leaned in suddenly. I hadn't even seen him move. One moment he was staring back at me, and the next, within the span of a thought, his face was buried in my neck. I could feel his swift inhalation. He held his breath a moment, and his chest rattled as he finally exhaled.

"Your fear smells sharp and poignant, like cinnamon." He traced a slow, wet lick from my collarbone to just over my carotid. His tongue lingered over my pulse before pulling back. "Lovely."

I kicked out frantically, trying to land a blow between his legs, but my struggles were useless. He merely bared his teeth at me again in a sick semblance of a smile.

"Please," I asked. "What do you want?"

"I'll get what I want," the man said. "But I also wanted you to know that I *am* grateful. You saved me, so I shall return the favor."

My anger finally flared over the panic and pain. "I've never been saved before, so I could be mistaken, but I'm pretty certain that this doesn't qualify."

He stared at me a moment before grinning widely. Too widely for a human mouth. "Temerity becomes you," he replied. "Killing you, the photographer, the detective, and the two paramedics would be the easiest method of concealing my existence, but I'll take the time to . . . disarm the five of you instead. That is less efficient, more difficult, and time-consuming, but your life, and theirs, in exchange for having saved mine, is my gift to you."

I kicked out again, my knee in search of his groin. I opened my mouth to scream.

The man pulled me away from the wall before slamming me back against the brick—more ruthlessly than the first time, if that was possible. The breath punched out of my lungs along with my scream.

"Cassidy, look into my eyes."

I felt a sudden pull from the core of my being, desperate to look into the man's eyes. In defiance, I worked to fill my deflated lungs so I could prepare another scream.

"Cassidy DiRocco, you will look into my eyes *now.*"

The man's voice soaked through my resolve and drowned my brain. Unwillingly, I looked into his eyes. The moment his blue-and-ice gaze met mine, the pain and panic and fear leaked away. I felt my body suddenly go limp as it forgot to resist. My head lolled to the side, too heavy to support, and my expression sagged with the release of tension and strain. The physical world narrowed to his penetrating gaze on mine and my willingness to act on the breath of his next word, even as my mind shrieked at me to fight.

"You will write a retraction of the article about the deaths at Paerdegat Park," he stated.

Never! my mind screamed. "I will write a retraction," I murmured. My voice was compliant and monotone and not my own.

"The wounds on the victims were clean slices, from knives perhaps. Not animal bites," he continued.

"The wounds on the victims were probably inflicted by knives," I repeated, internally horrified. "Not animal bites."

"You never saw me burned yesterday, and you never saw me here today. If I ever have need to seek you out again, I will kill you."

My anger skyrocketed, breaking his hold on my mind. The pain and fear and adrenaline spiked through the mental fog, and I shouted, "You sick son of a bitch! If *I* ever see *you* again, I'll stab you through your fu—"

His gaze burned into mine again, and I drooped back into limp numbness. "Cassidy DiRocco, you encountered me neither here nor at the park!"

Fuck! "I never encountered you."

"Someone tried to mug you at knifepoint on your way home from dinner with Meredith. He stabbed you in the shoulder. You used your pepper spray, he stabbed you once more, and then he ran off with nothing more than having spilled your sushi. Your shoulders will heal without medical attention."

"I was mugged, but I don't need medical attention." *Dear God,* I thought, *he knows everyone I know and everywhere I've been.*

"There's a good girl," he growled. "Is anyone in your apartment at the moment? I would hate to leave you wandering the streets with armed muggers on the loose."

Yes, I have a six-foot-four, ex-linebacker husband and a trained, attack Rottweiler waiting for me at home. "My apartment is empty," I droned, wanting to tear out my own throat.

He cocked his head slightly, no longer studying me but obviously studying something. He wasn't breathing or moving or even blinking. I realized after a moment that he was listening.

"Most people are eating in," he commented. "Something you should perhaps consider in the future when it's this late. Are you on the first, fourth, or fifth floor?"

"Fifth," I whispered. I couldn't tremble because my body was limp and pliant in his talons, but my heart clenched in a hard, shivering knot of dread. He was going to know where I lived. And I was going to be the one to tell him.

"Does one of your windows face this alley?"

"Yes."

"Perfect," he said, refocusing on me. His eyes bore into mine again when he spoke. "Tell me I may enter your apartment, and you may sleep."

"You may enter my apartment, and I may sleep," I gritted out smartly, and my eyes slammed shut. My body completely sagged, boneless, suspended from the wall only by his talons. My mind, however, remained awake. I felt the man dislodge his fingers from my upper arms and catch me against the front of his body. His claw-like hand pressed firmly at the small of my back, clamping me to him. He crouched forward for a moment. My head lolled back. The rattling hiss in his chest intensified, and I felt his breath move over my throat, the side of my neck, behind my ear. He smelled inexplicably like Christmas, like soft pine next to a hearth. His teeth grazed the slow, calm beat of my pulse. In my mind, I screamed and fought and died with my spirit and dignity intact. In reality, I lay bent back over his arm, immobile and defenseless.

The man suddenly sprang from his crouch. My stomach bottomed out from the movement, and I felt a swift rush of wind against my face as if he'd leapt into the air, but gravity did not pull us back down.

I heard the quick slide of a window opening and smelled the vanilla lime scent of the candles in my fifth-story apartment bedroom. His footsteps tapped on my hardwood floors, and I realized that the man must be wearing dress shoes. How his shoes could ever matter after all this, I didn't know; I just found the thought of him wearing dress shoes, like his voice, at odds with the sheer animal of the man himself.

He laid my body down on the bed. My head dropped at an uncomfortable angle that constricted my breathing. I heard myself wheeze. He cupped the nape of my neck and positioned my head on the pillow at a more natural angle. His fingernail scraped across my hairline to my neck. I felt his thumb caress the skin under my ear as he lingered.

The man's breathing suddenly turned ragged, and his hand disappeared. "Good night, Cassidy DiRocco," he said.

The air whooshed around me as he disappeared. The window snapped shut, and my room was still and silent and peaceful in his absence.

The moment the man was gone, however, my body sprang to life. Everything returned in an overwhelming rush—the fear, pain, panic, adrenaline, and control—and my throat constricted with the aching burn of tears. Trembling and weak, I pulled my leather bag across my chest. I kept my eyes trained on the bedroom window with steady obsession, bracing for his reappearance, but even after what felt like an eternity, he didn't return. I dug the phone from my bag and dialed 911.

The moment that dispatch answered, I whispered shakily, "I need to report an assault. I've just been attacked outside my apartment on 346 East 29th Street. And hurry. He may still be nearby."

CONTINUE READING THE CITY BENEATH AND BE SWEPT AWAY
BY CASSIDY AND DOMINIC'S STORY.
LOVE ISN'T ALWAYS FOUND AT FIRST SIGHT... BUT RATHER, AT
FIRST BITE.

ABOUT THE AUTHOR

MELODY JOHNSON

MELODY JOHNSON IS THE AUTHOR of the "out of this world" Love Beyond series and the Night Blood series published by Kensington Publishing/ Lyrical Press. The City Beneath (Night Blood, book 1) was a finalist in the "Cleveland Rocks" and "Fool for Love" contests.

Melody graduated magna cum laude from Lycoming College with her BA in creative writing and psychology. Throughout college, she wrote contemporary love stories, but having read and adored the action and dark mystery of vampires and aliens her entire life, she decided to add her fingerprint to the paranormal and sci-fi genres.

When she isn't working or writing, Melody can be found swimming at the beach, hiking with her husband, and exploring her new home in southeast Georgia.

Keep in touch with Melody on social media or sign up for her newsletter to receive emails about new releases and book signings. Website: authormelodyjohnson.com

facebook.com/authormelodyjohnson

instagram.com/authormelodyjohnson

goodreads.com/authormelodyjohnson

amazon.com/author/melodymjohnson

CPSIA information can be obtained
at www.ICGtesting.com
Printed in the USA
LVHW111021230620
658782LV00008B/24/J